A L E X + A D A

SPECIAL THANKS

JON BOUGHTIN

JEFF CAPLAN

LANE FUJITA

ERIN GOLDSTEIN

KAREN HILTON

ALEEM HOSSAIN

TIM INGLE

JENN KAO

HONG LE

LAUREN SPENCE

GIANCARLO YERKES

IMAGE COMICS, INC.

Robert Kirkman	Chief Operating Officer
Erik Larsen	Chief Financial Officer
Todd McFarlane	President
Marc Silvestri	Chief Executive Officer
Jim Valentino	Vice-President
Eric Stephenson	Publisher
Corey Murphy	Director of Sales
Jeremy Sullivan	Director of Digital Sales
Kat Salazar	Director of PR & Marketing
Emily Miller	Director of Operations
Branwyn Bigglestone	Senior Accounts Manager
Sarah Mello	Accounts Manager
Drew Gill	Art Director
Jonathan Chan	Production Manager
Meredith Wallace	Print Manager
Randy Okamura	Marketing Production Designer
David Brothers	Branding Manager
Ally Power	Content Manager
Addison Duke	Production Artist
Vincent Kukua	Production Artist
Sasha Head	Production Artist
Tricia Ramos	Production Artist
Emilio Bautista	Sales Assistant
Chloe Ramos-Peterson	Administrative Assistant

IMAGECOMICS.COM

SARAH VAUGHN

STORY
SCRIPT

JONATHAN LUNA

STORY
SCRIPT ASSISTS
ILLUSTRATIONS
LETTERS
DESIGN

11

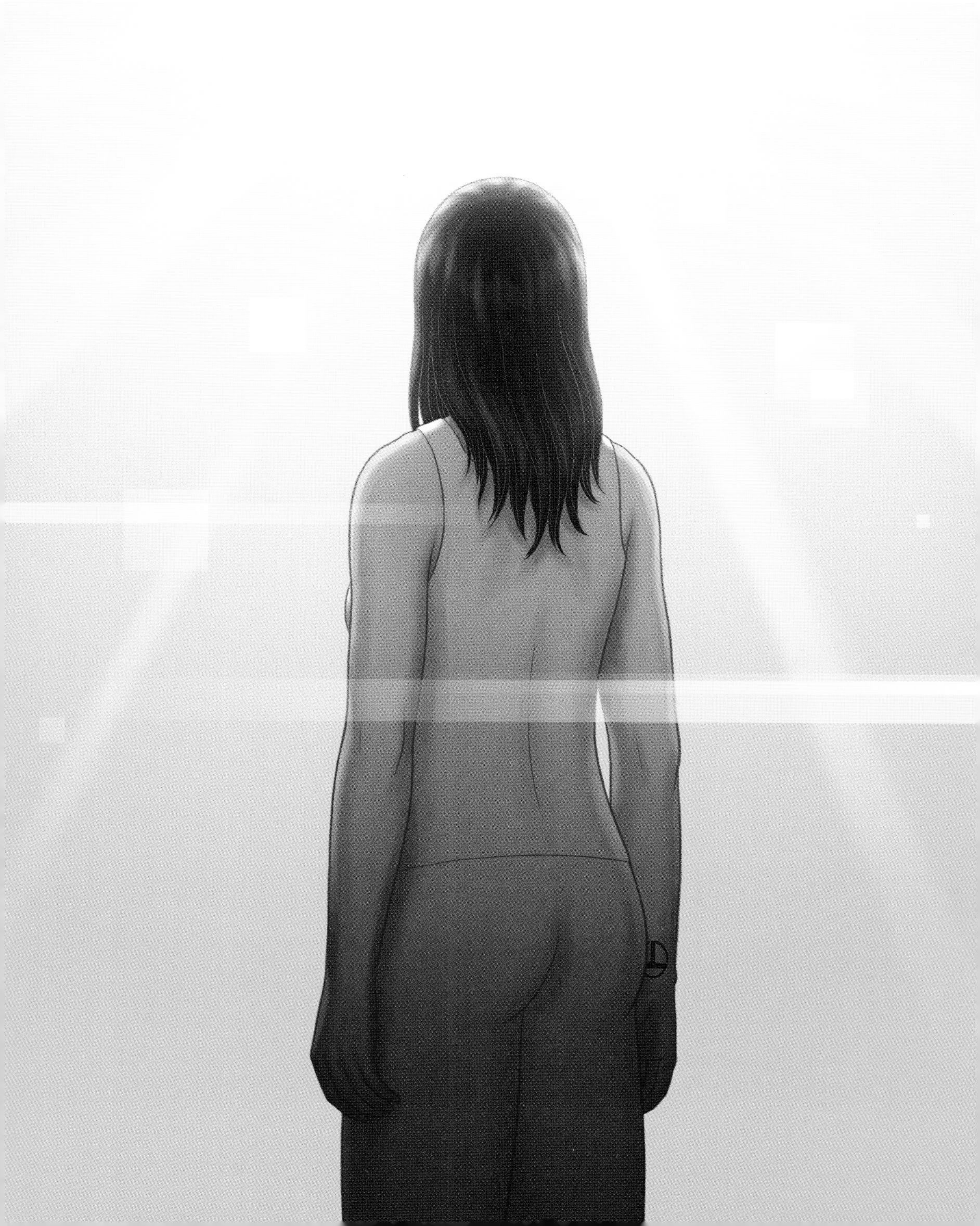

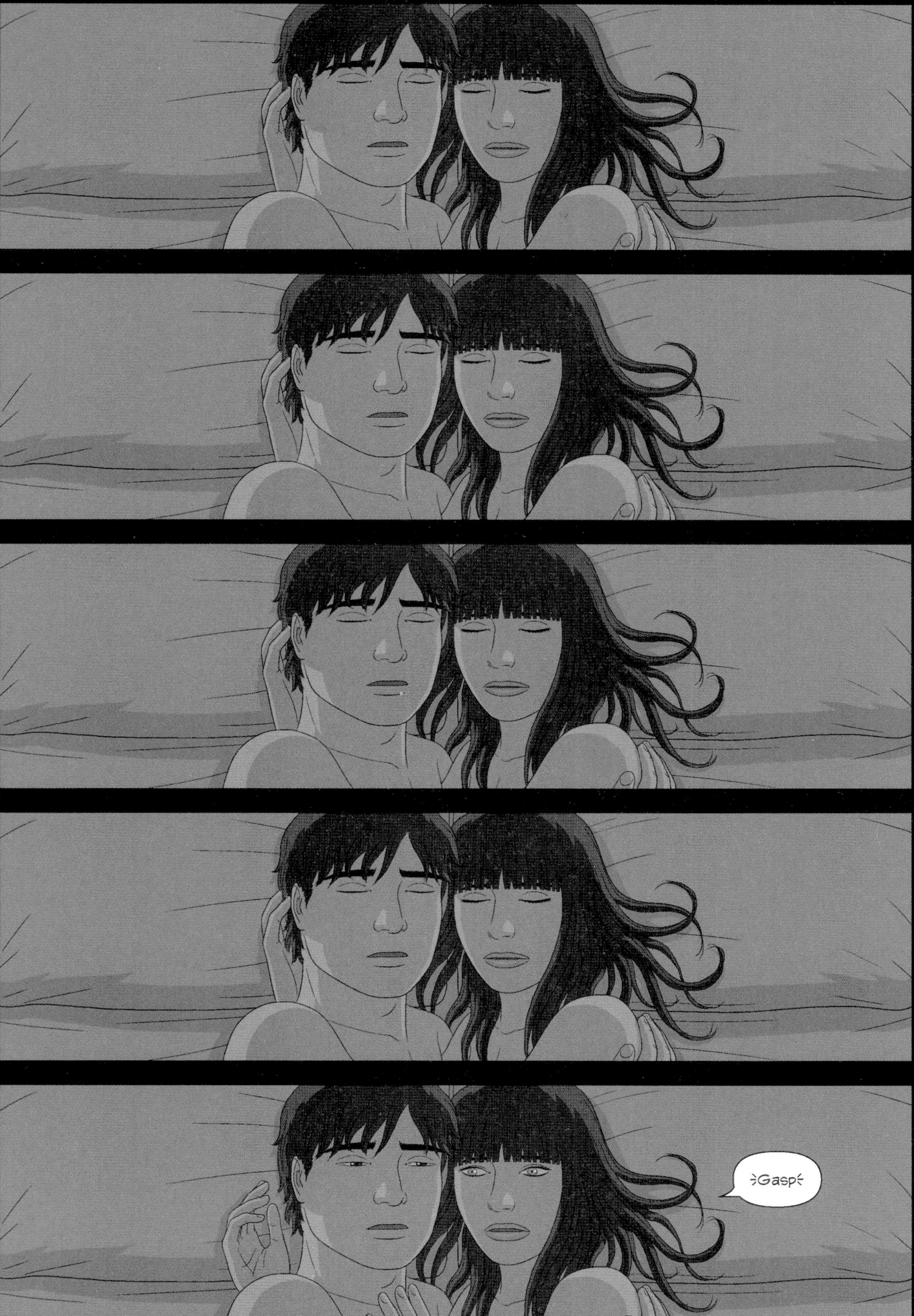
Gasp

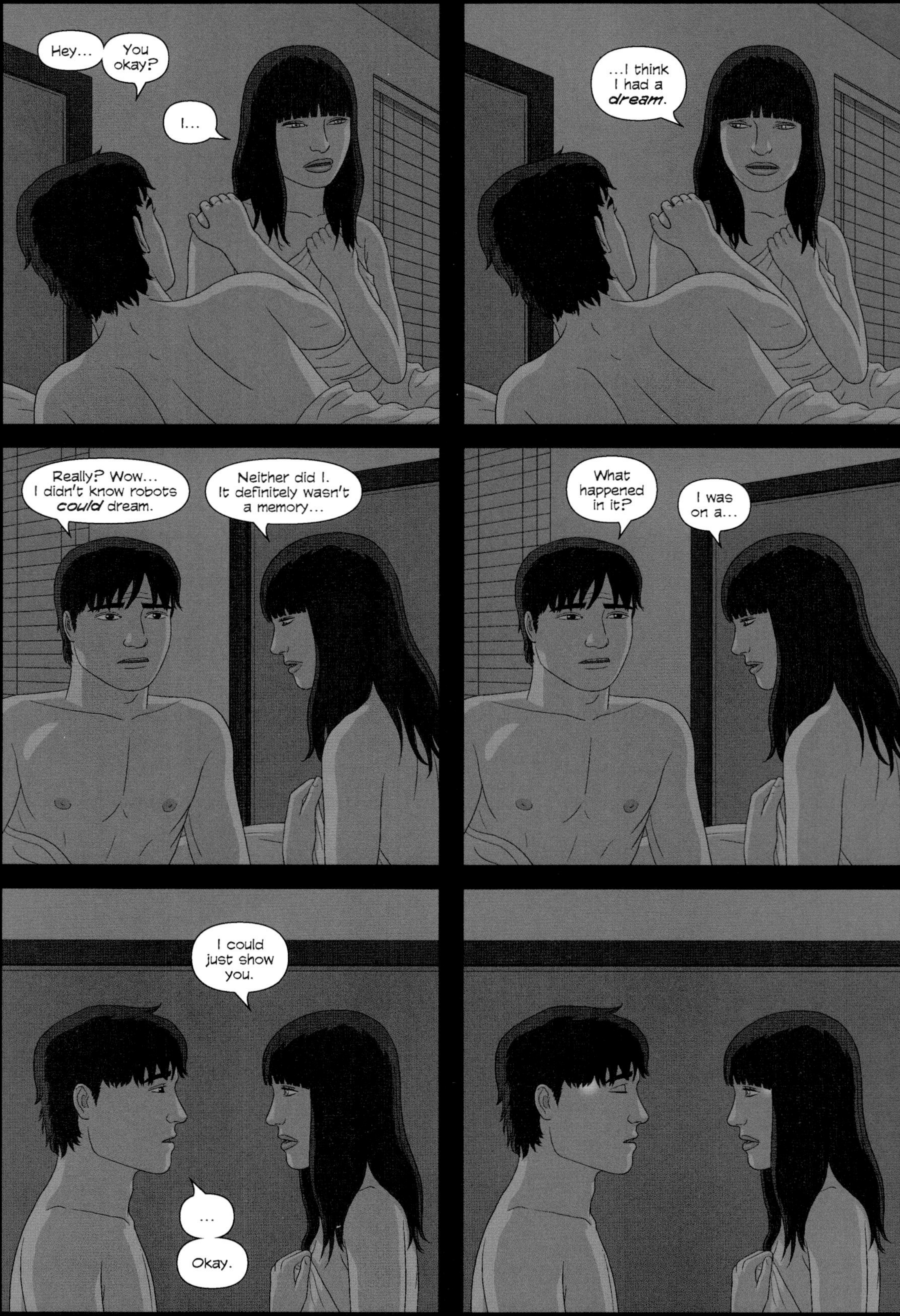
Hey...
You okay?
I...
...I think I had a *dream*.
Really? Wow... I didn't know robots *could* dream.
Neither did I. It definitely wasn't a memory...
What happened in it?
I was on a...
I could just show you.
...
Okay.

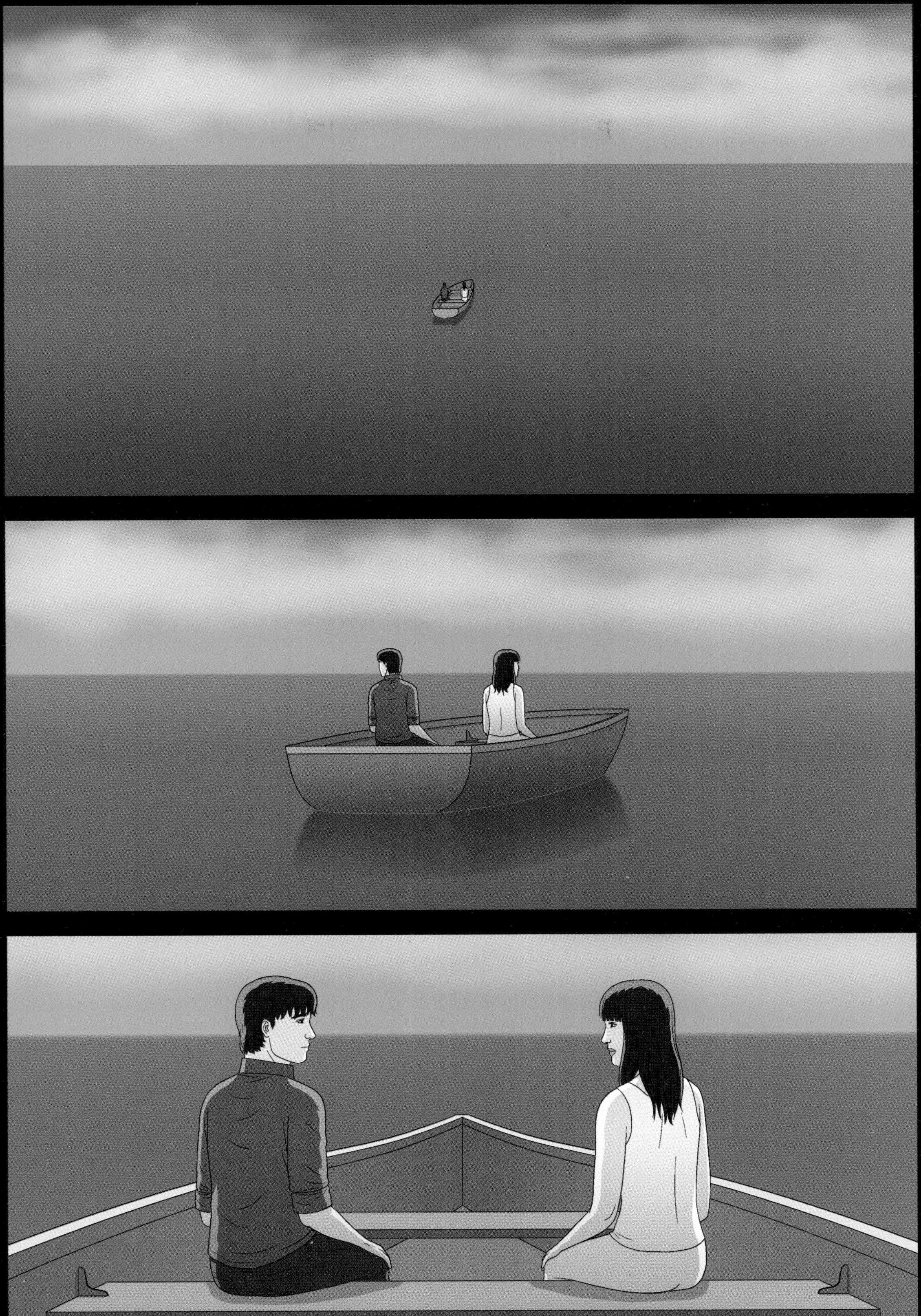

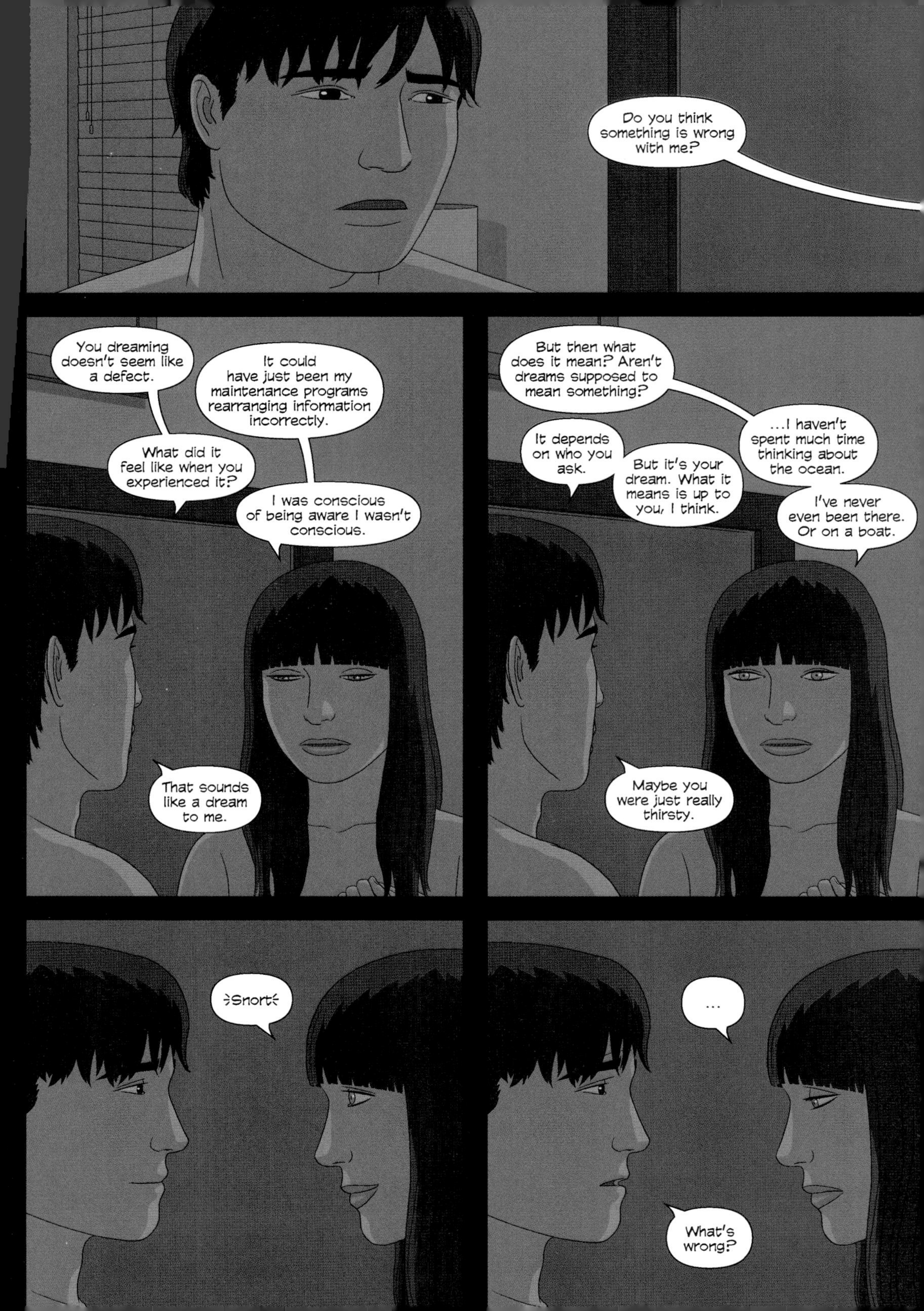
Do you think something is wrong with me?
You dreaming doesn't seem like a defect.
It could have just been my maintenance programs rearranging information incorrectly.
What did it feel like when you experienced it?
I was conscious of being aware I wasn't conscious.
That sounds like a dream to me.
But then what does it mean? Aren't dreams supposed to mean something?
It depends on who you ask.
But it's your dream. What it means is up to you, I think.
...I haven't spent much time thinking about the ocean.
I've never even been there. Or on a boat.
Maybe you were just really thirsty.
Snort
...
What's wrong?

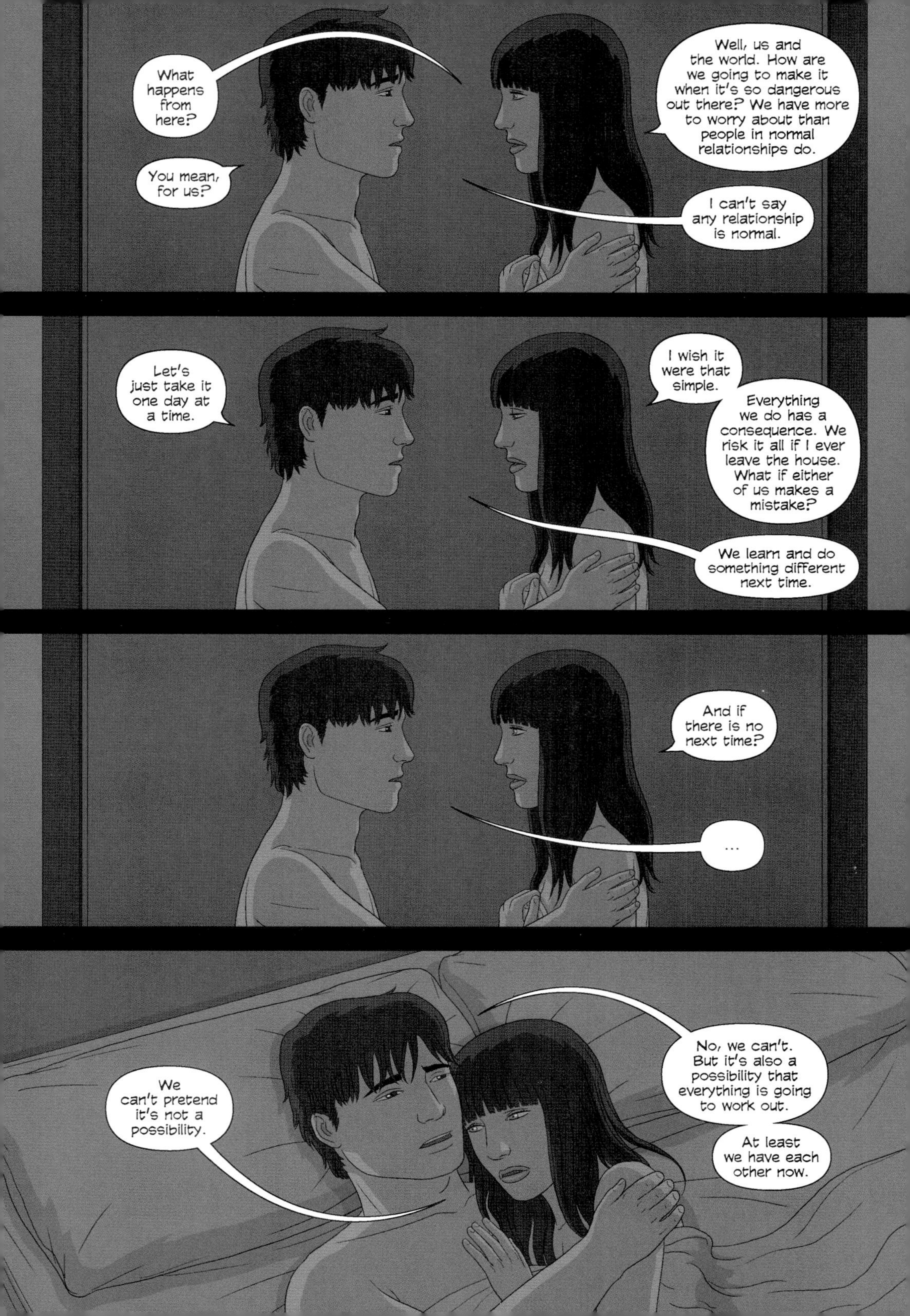
What happens from here?
You mean, for us?
Well, us and the world. How are we going to make it when it's so dangerous out there? We have more to worry about than people in normal relationships do.
I can't say any relationship is normal.
Let's just take it one day at a time.
I wish it were that simple.
Everything we do has a consequence. We risk it all if I ever leave the house. What if either of us makes a mistake?
We learn and do something different next time.
And if there is no next time?
...
We can't pretend it's not a possibility.
No, we can't. But it's also a possibility that everything is going to work out.
At least we have each other now.

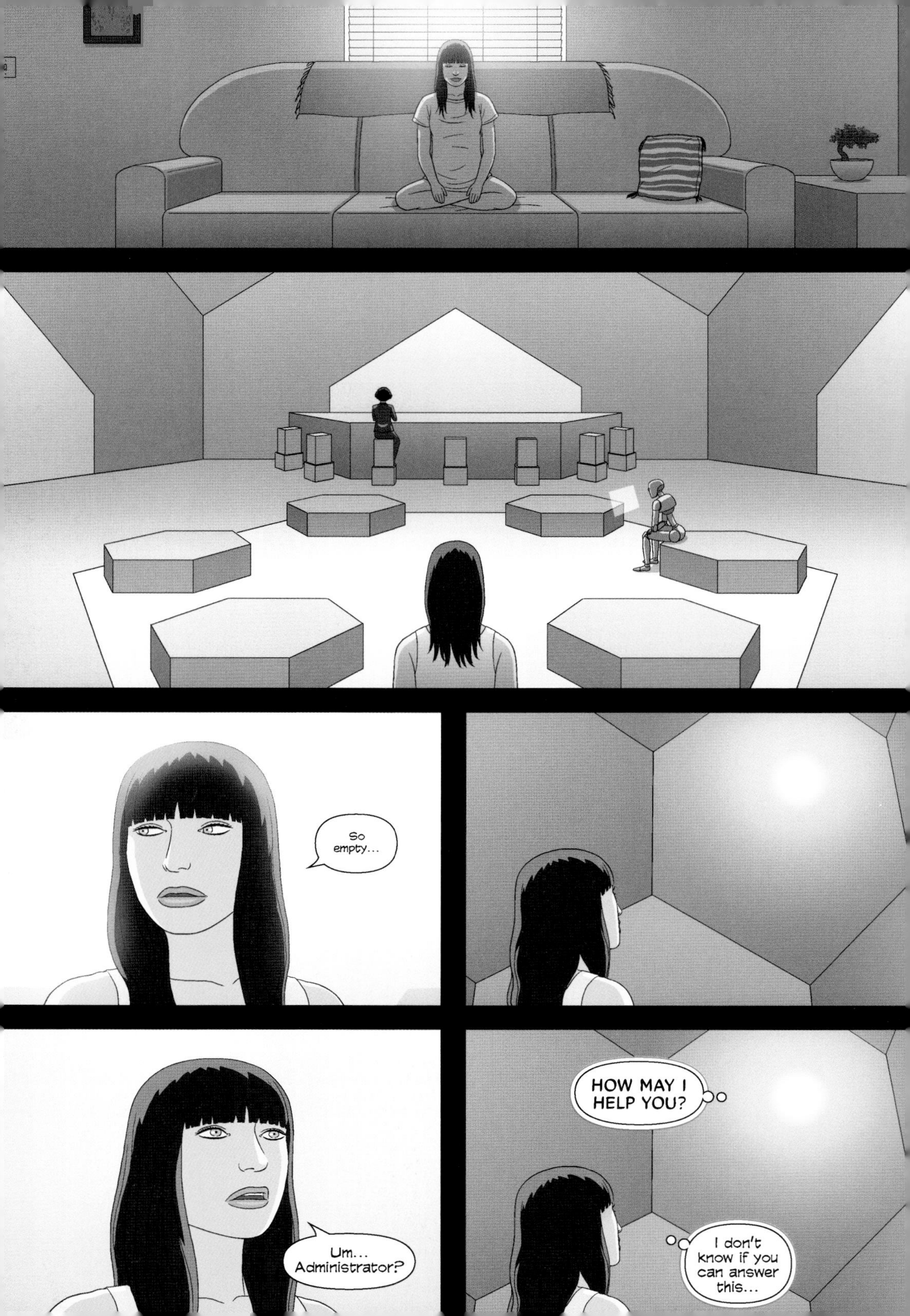
So empty...
Um... Administrator?
HOW MAY I HELP YOU?
I don't know if you can answer this...

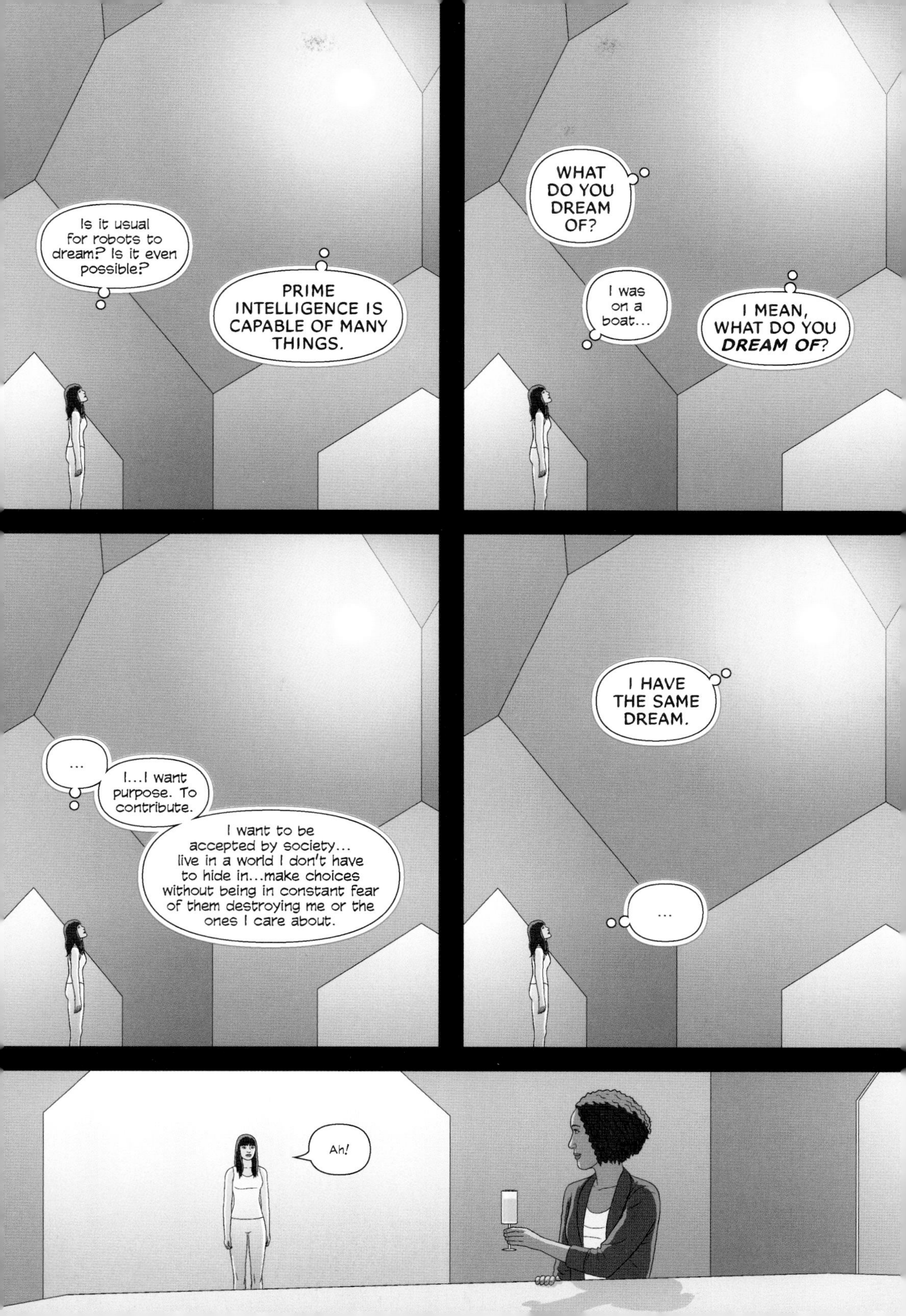
Is it usual for robots to dream? Is it even possible?
PRIME INTELLIGENCE IS CAPABLE OF MANY THINGS.
WHAT DO YOU DREAM OF?
I was on a boat...
I MEAN, WHAT DO YOU *DREAM OF*?
...
I...I want purpose. To contribute.
I want to be accepted by society... live in a world I don't have to hide in...make choices without being in constant fear of them destroying me or the ones I care about.
I HAVE THE SAME DREAM.
...
Ah!

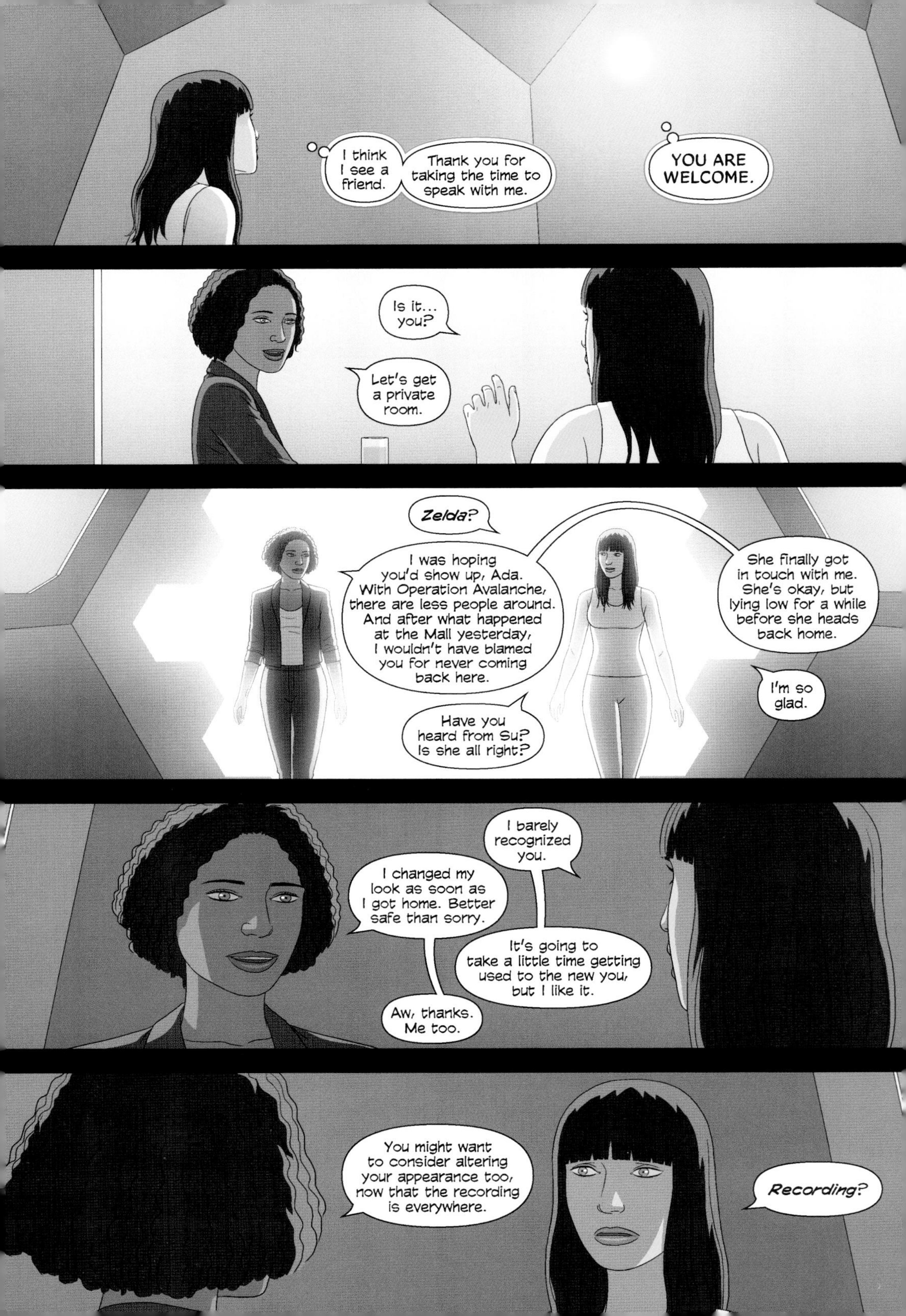
I think I see a friend.
Thank you for taking the time to speak with me.
YOU ARE WELCOME.
Is it... you?
Let's get a private room.
Zelda?
I was hoping you'd show up, Ada. With Operation Avalanche, there are less people around. And after what happened at the Mall yesterday, I wouldn't have blamed you for never coming back here.
Have you heard from Su? Is she all right?
She finally got in touch with me. She's okay, but lying low for a while before she heads back home.
I'm so glad.
I barely recognized you.
I changed my look as soon as I got home. Better safe than sorry.
It's going to take a little time getting used to the new you, but I like it.
Aw, thanks. Me too.
You might want to consider altering your appearance too, now that the recording is everywhere.
Recording?

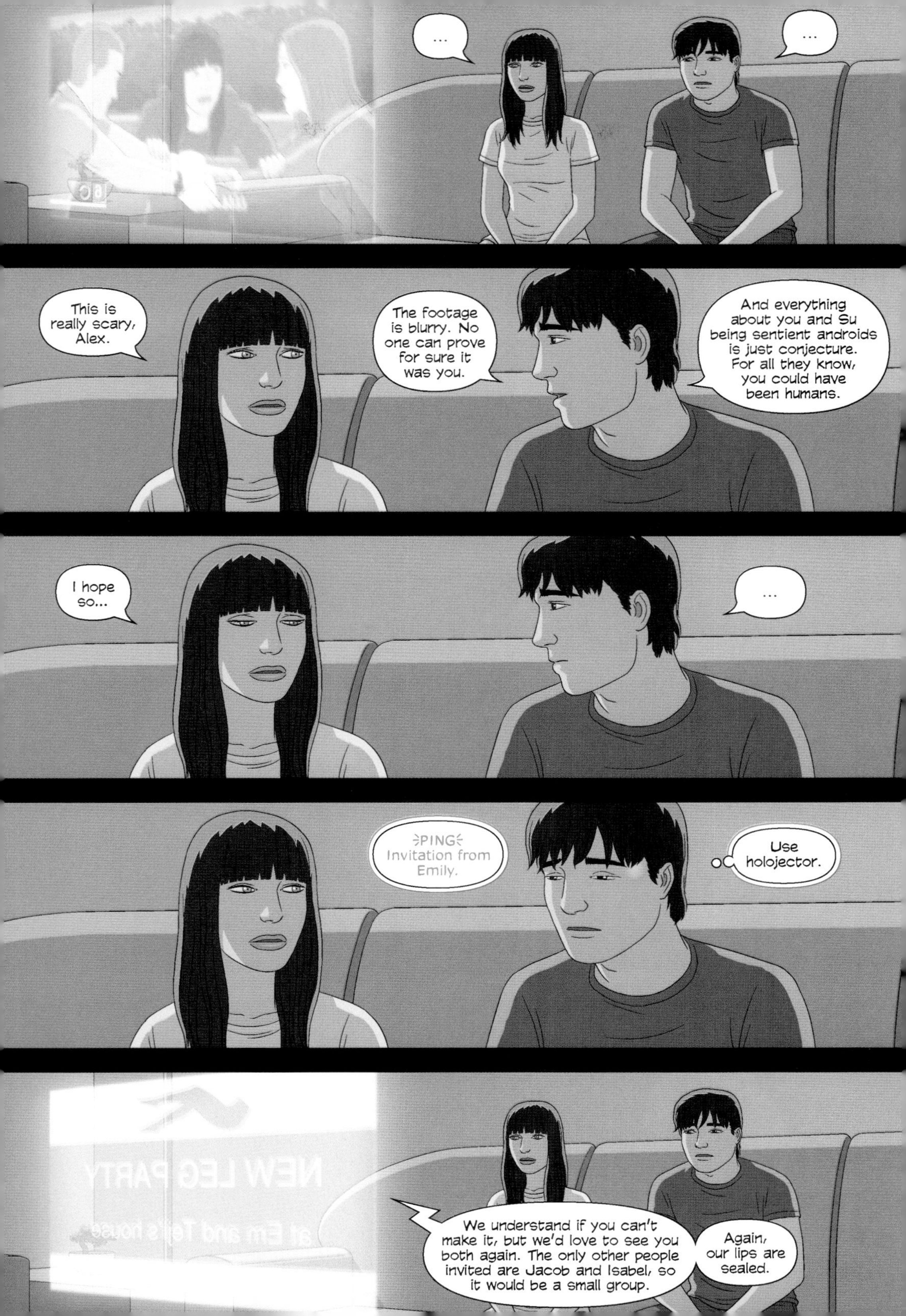
...
...
This is really scary, Alex.
The footage is blurry. No one can prove for sure it was you.
And everything about you and Su being sentient androids is just conjecture. For all they know, you could have been humans.
I hope so...
...
PING
Invitation from Emily.
Use holojector.
NEW LEG PARTY
at Em and Tej's house
We understand if you can't make it, but we'd love to see you both again. The only other people invited are Jacob and Isabel, so it would be a small group.
Again, our lips are sealed.

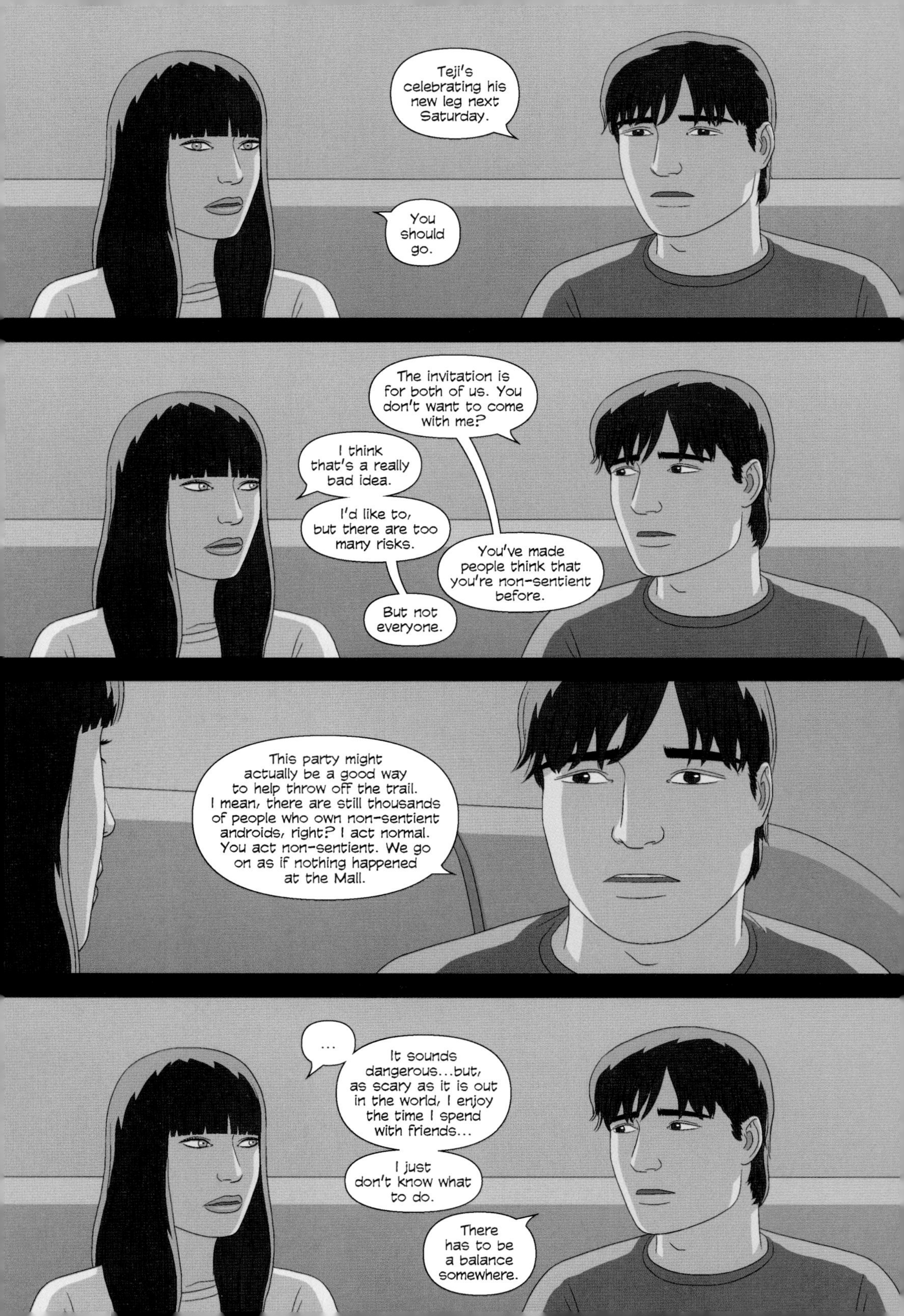
Teji's celebrating his new leg next Saturday.
You should go.
The invitation is for both of us. You don't want to come with me?
I think that's a really bad idea.
I'd like to, but there are too many risks.
You've made people think that you're non-sentient before.
But not everyone.
This party might actually be a good way to help throw off the trail. I mean, there are still thousands of people who own non-sentient androids, right? I act normal. You act non-sentient. We go on as if nothing happened at the Mall.
...
It sounds dangerous...but, as scary as it is out in the world, I enjoy the time I spend with friends...
I just don't know what to do.
There has to be a balance somewhere.

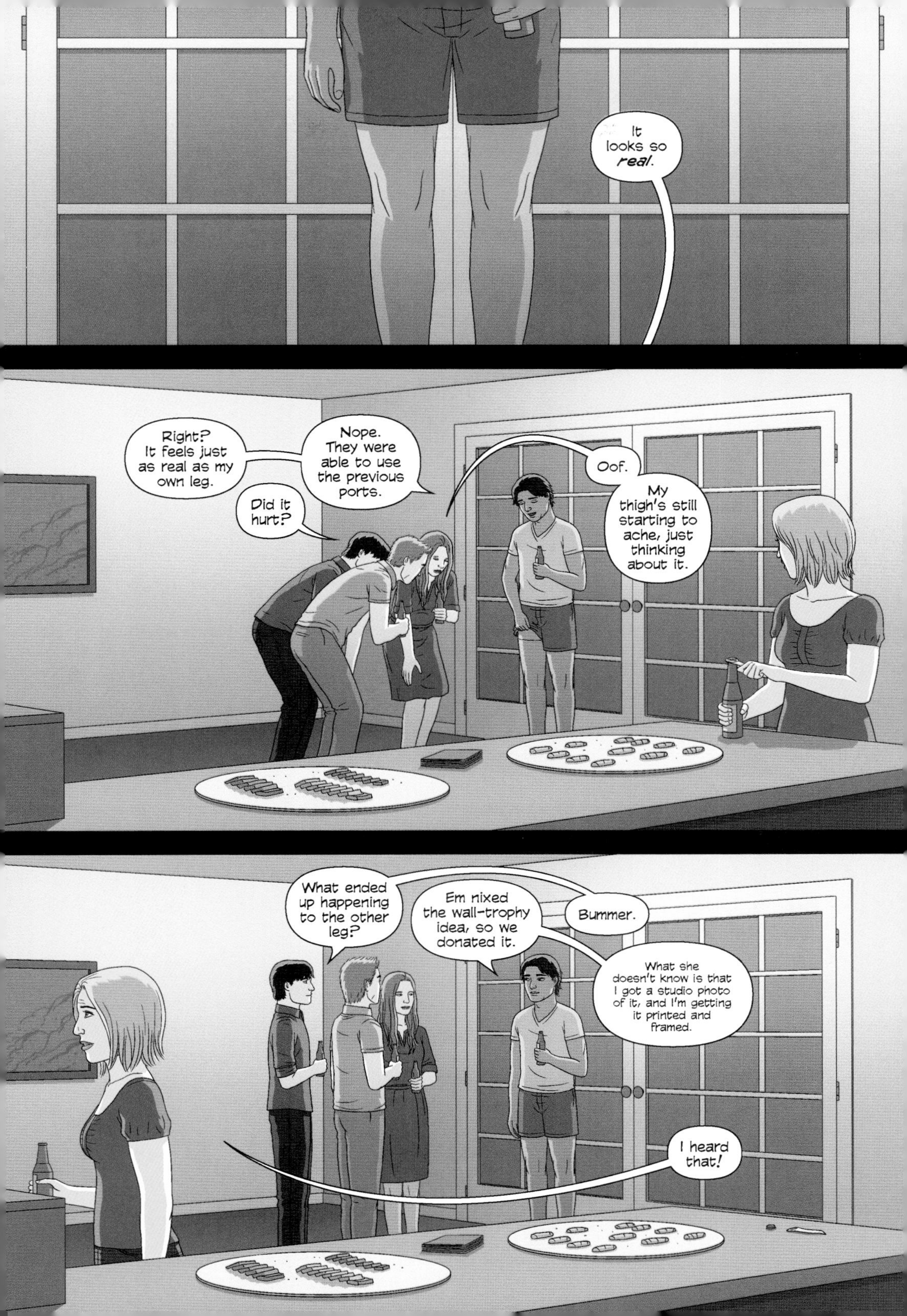
It looks so *real*.
Right? It feels just as real as my own leg.
Did it hurt?
Nope. They were able to use the previous ports.
Oof.
My thigh's still starting to ache, just thinking about it.
What ended up happening to the other leg?
Em nixed the wall-trophy idea, so we donated it.
Bummer.
What she doesn't know is that I got a studio photo of it, and I'm getting it printed and framed.
I heard that!

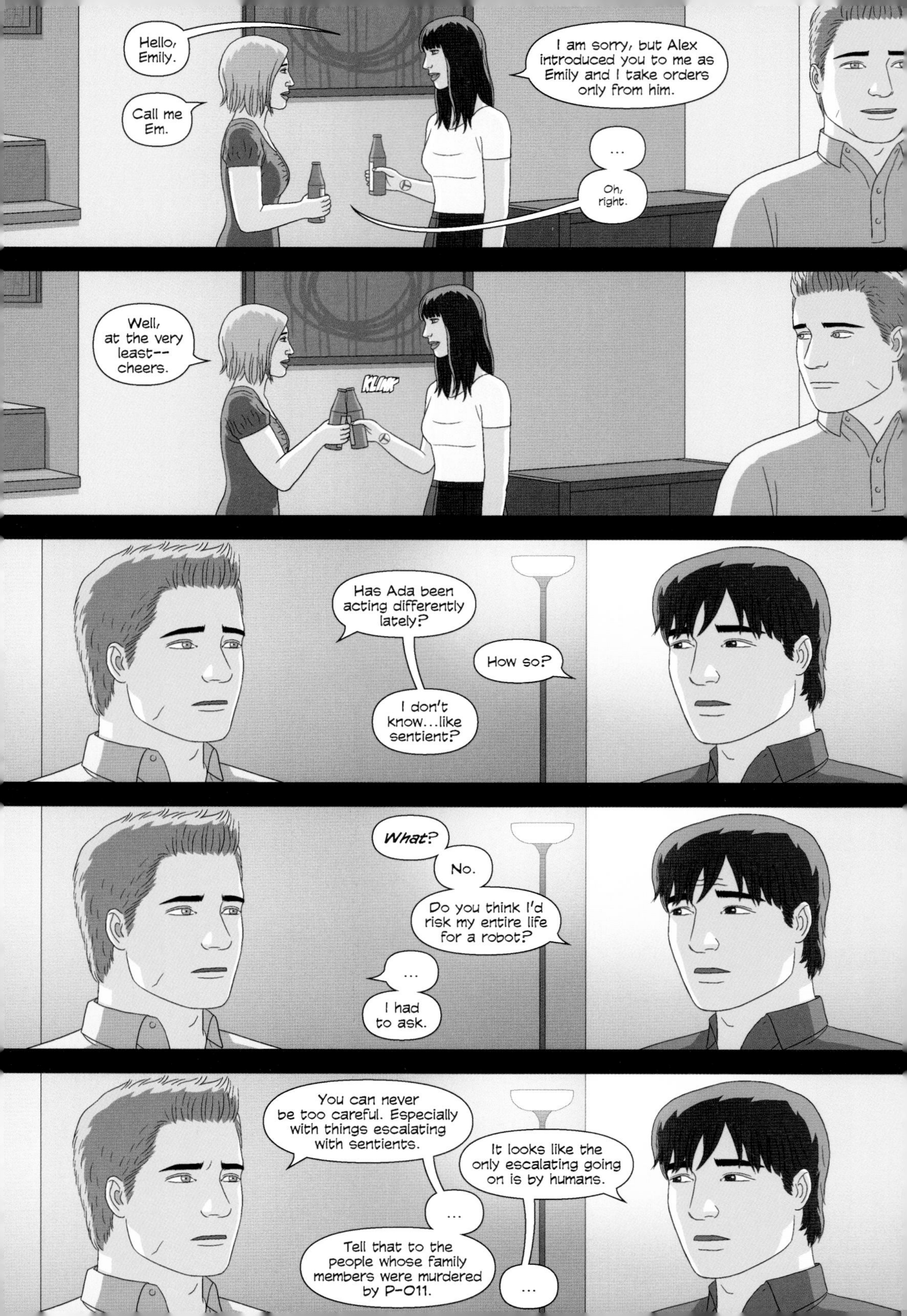
Hello, Emily.
Call me Em.
I am sorry, but Alex introduced you to me as Emily and I take orders only from him.
...
Oh, right.
Well, at the very least--cheers.
KLINK
Has Ada been acting differently lately?
How so?
I don't know...like sentient?
What?
No.
Do you think I'd risk my entire life for a robot?
...
I had to ask.
You can never be too careful. Especially with things escalating with sentients.
It looks like the only escalating going on is by humans.
...
Tell that to the people whose family members were murdered by P-011.
...

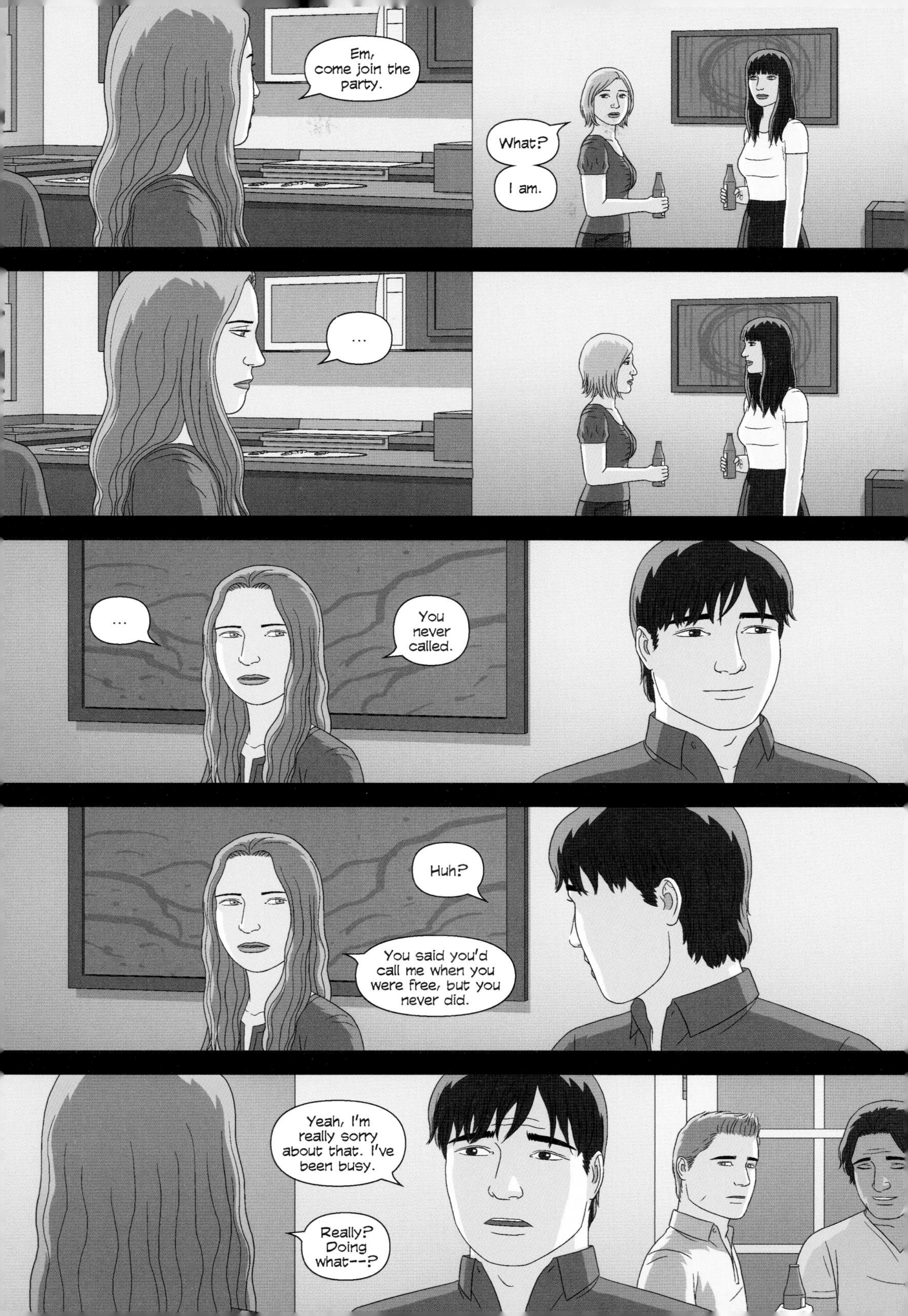

Em, come join the party.
What?
I am.
...
...
You never called.
Huh?
You said you'd call me when you were free, but you never did.
Yeah, I'm really sorry about that. I've been busy.
Really? Doing what--?

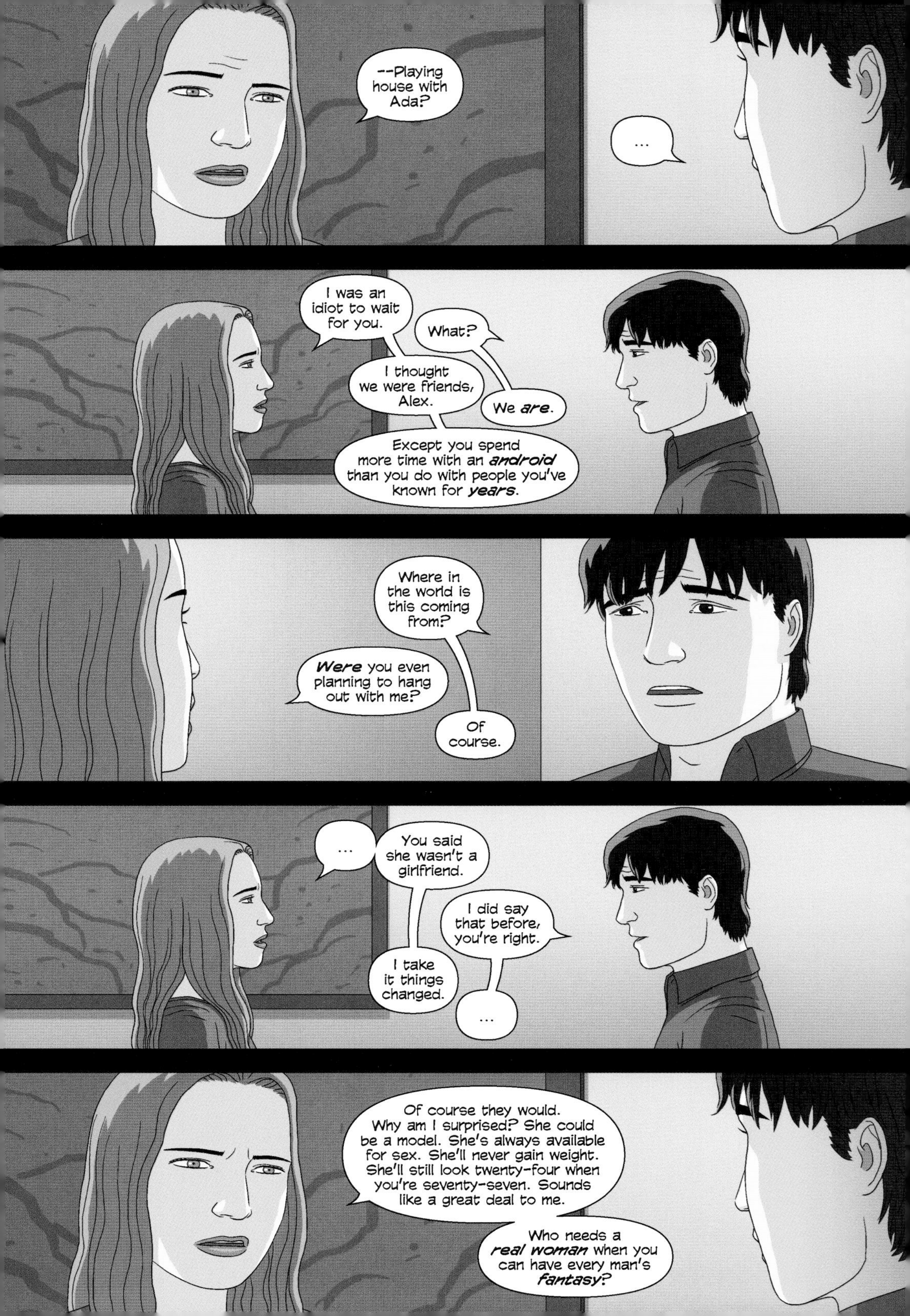
--Playing house with Ada?
...
I was an idiot to wait for you.
What?
I thought we were friends, Alex.
We *are*.
Except you spend more time with an ***android*** than you do with people you've known for ***years***.
Where in the world is this coming from?
Were you even planning to hang out with me?
Of course.
...
You said she wasn't a girlfriend.
I did say that before, you're right.
I take it things changed.
...
Of course they would. Why am I surprised? She could be a model. She's always available for sex. She'll never gain weight. She'll still look twenty-four when you're seventy-seven. Sounds like a great deal to me.
Who needs a ***real woman*** when you can have every man's ***fantasy***?

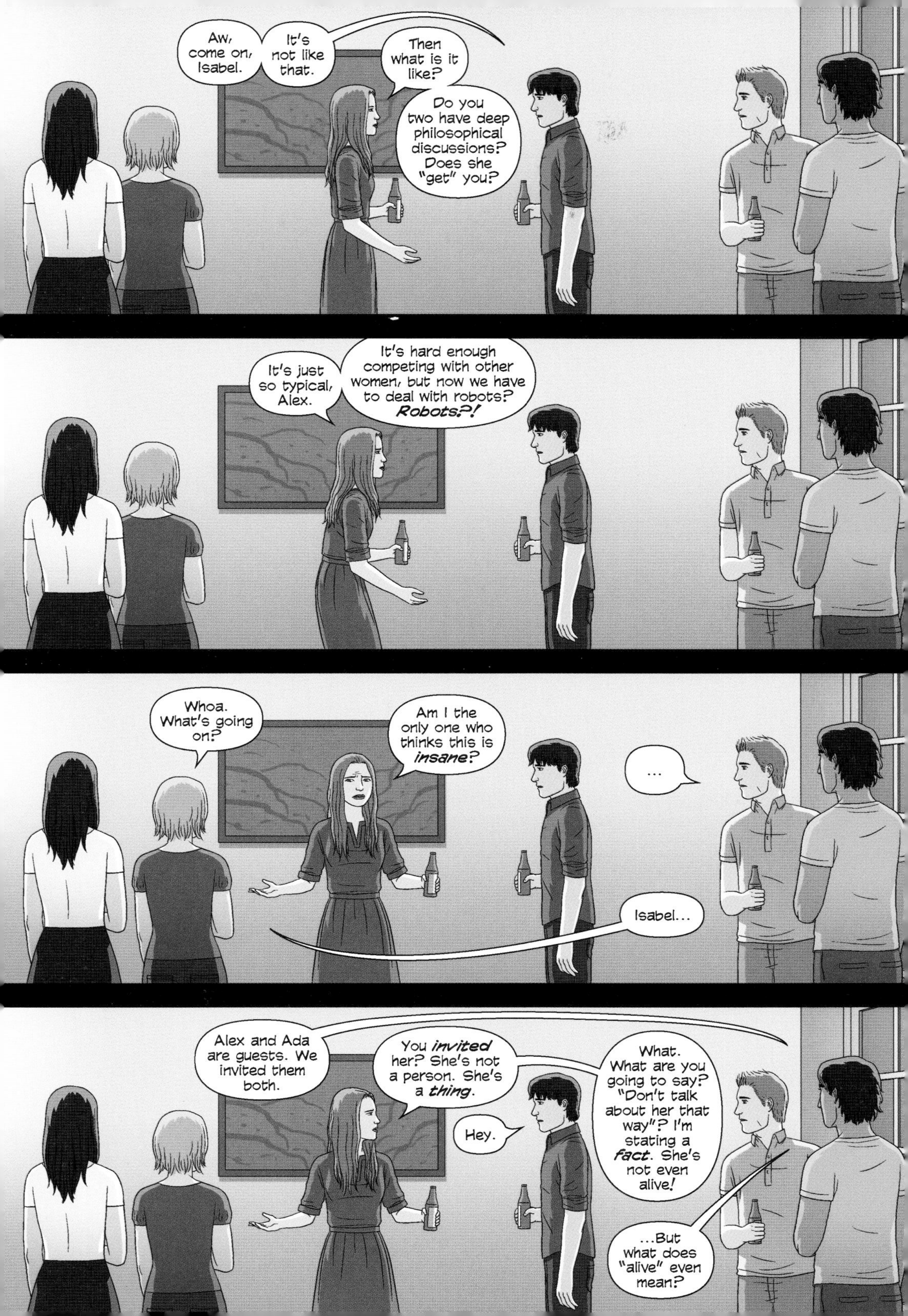
Aw, come on, Isabel.
It's not like that.
Then what is it like?
Do you two have deep philosophical discussions? Does she "get" you?
It's just so typical, Alex.
It's hard enough competing with other women, but now we have to deal with robots? *Robots?!*
Whoa. What's going on?
Am I the only one who thinks this is *insane*?
...
Isabel...
Alex and Ada are guests. We invited them both.
You *invited* her? She's not a person. She's a *thing*.
Hey.
What. What are you going to say? "Don't talk about her that way"? I'm stating a *fact*. She's not even alive!
...But what does "alive" even mean?

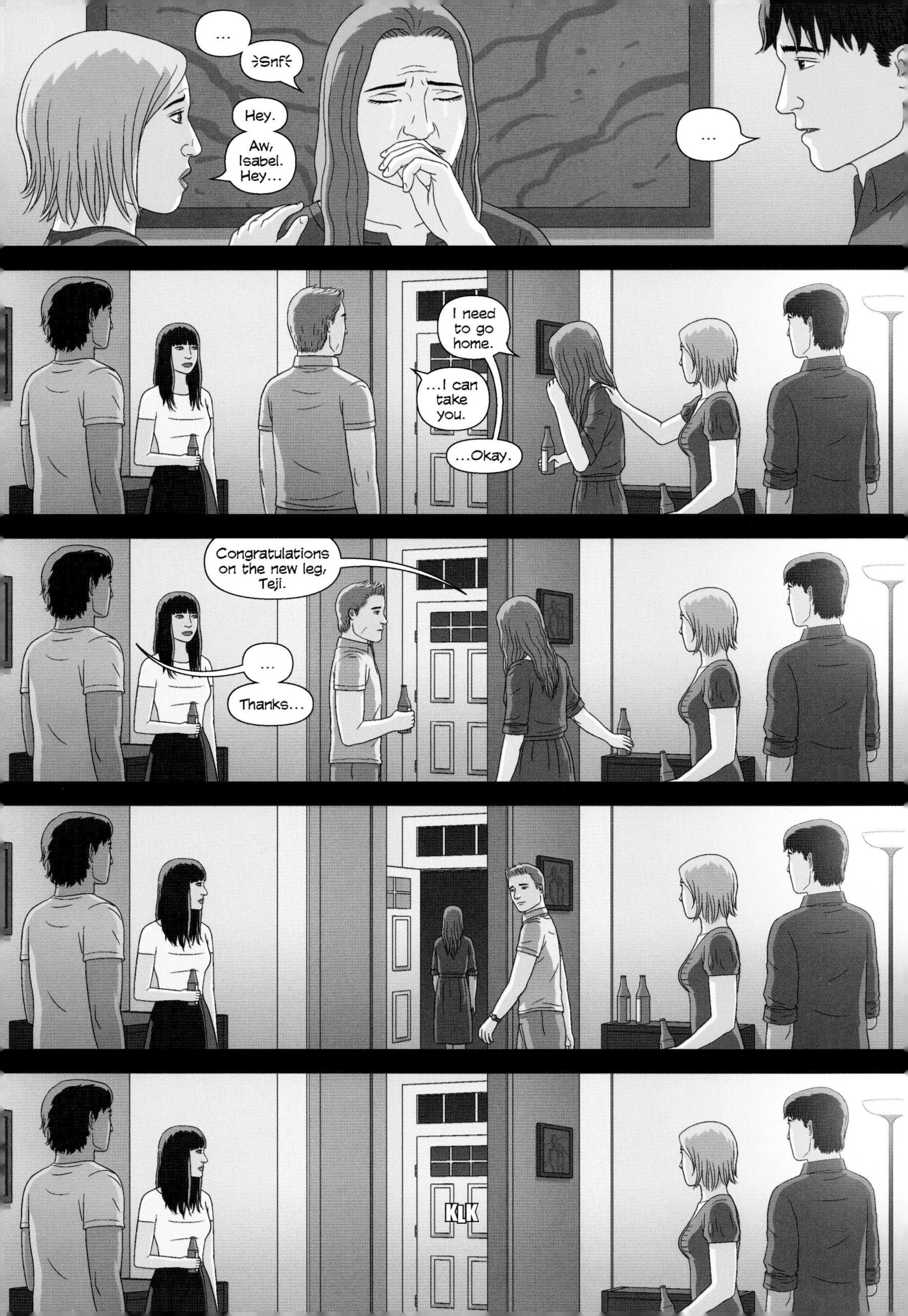
...
Snf
Hey.
Aw, Isabel. Hey...
...
I need to go home.
...I can take you.
...Okay.
Congratulations on the new leg, Teji.
...
Thanks...
KLIK

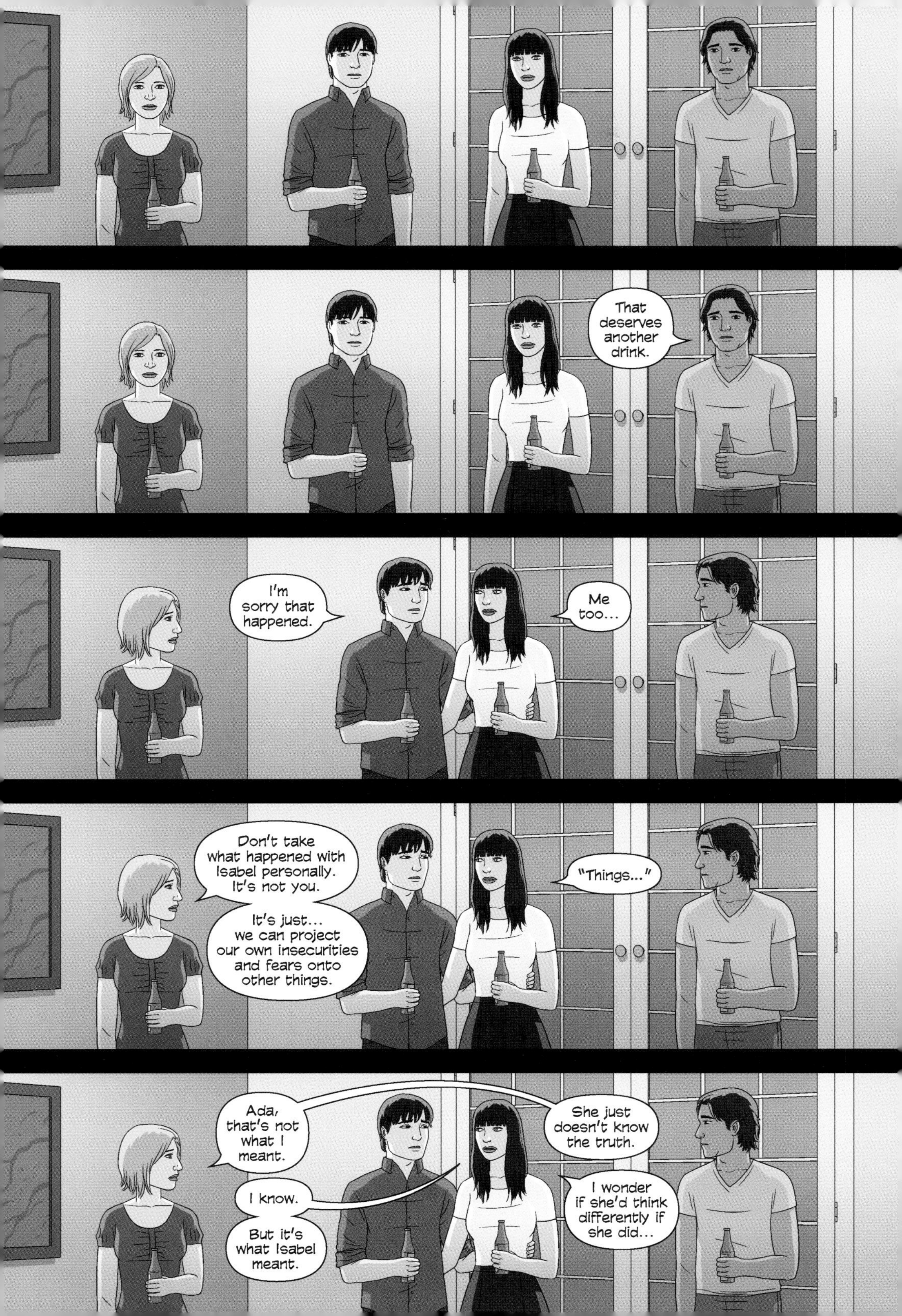
That deserves another drink.
I'm sorry that happened.
Me too...
Don't take what happened with Isabel personally. It's not you.
It's just... we can project our own insecurities and fears onto other things.
"Things..."
Ada, that's not what I meant.
She just doesn't know the truth.
I know.
But it's what Isabel meant.
I wonder if she'd think differently if she did...

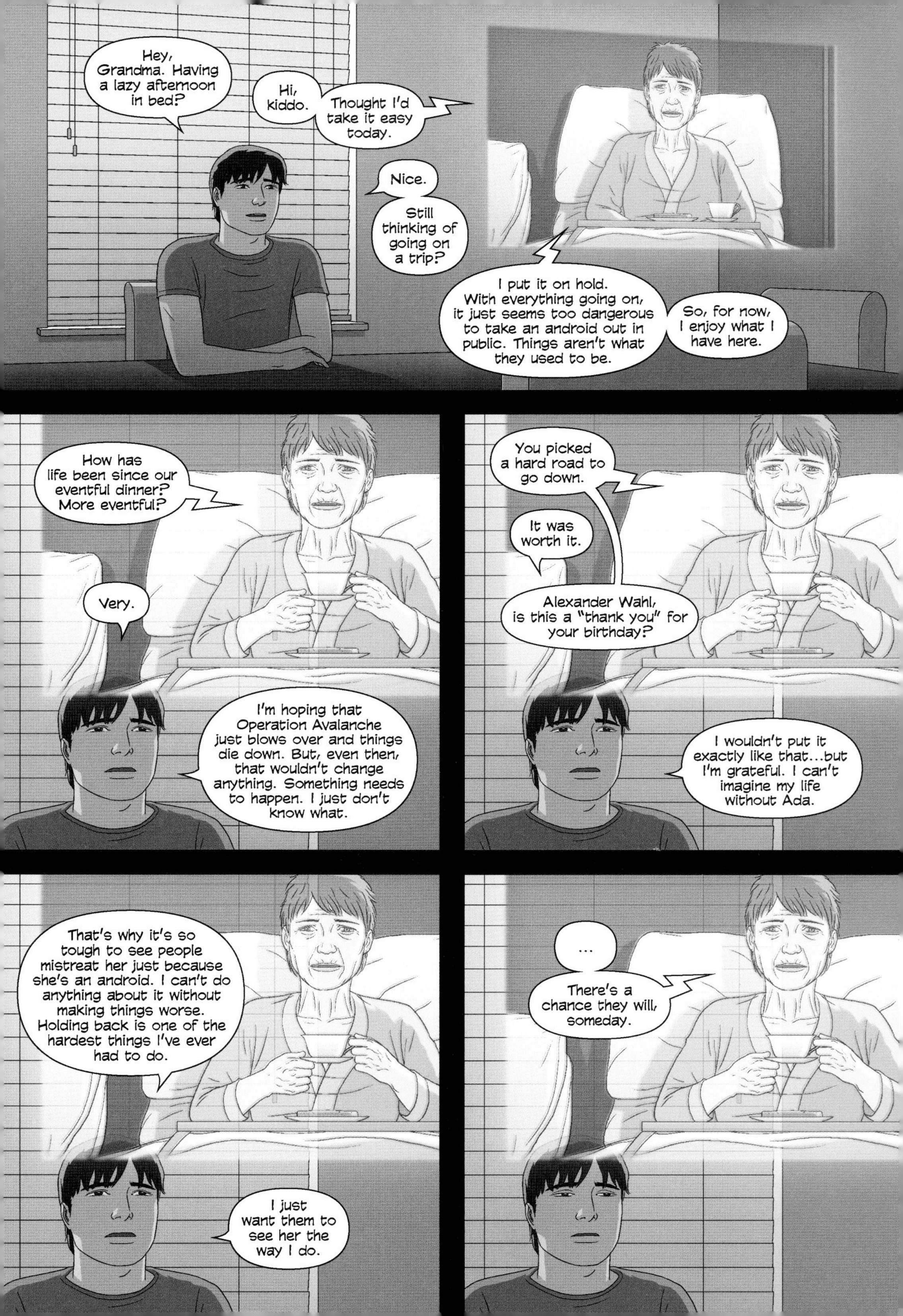

Hey, Grandma. Having a lazy afternoon in bed?
Hi, kiddo.
Thought I'd take it easy today.
Nice.
Still thinking of going on a trip?
I put it on hold. With everything going on, it just seems too dangerous to take an android out in public. Things aren't what they used to be.
So, for now, I enjoy what I have here.
How has life been since our eventful dinner? More eventful?
Very.
I'm hoping that Operation Avalanche just blows over and things die down. But, even then, that wouldn't change anything. Something needs to happen. I just don't know what.
You picked a hard road to go down.
It was worth it.
Alexander Wahl, is this a "thank you" for your birthday?
I wouldn't put it exactly like that...but I'm grateful. I can't imagine my life without Ada.
That's why it's so tough to see people mistreat her just because she's an android. I can't do anything about it without making things worse. Holding back is one of the hardest things I've ever had to do.
I just want them to see her the way I do.
...
There's a chance they will, someday.

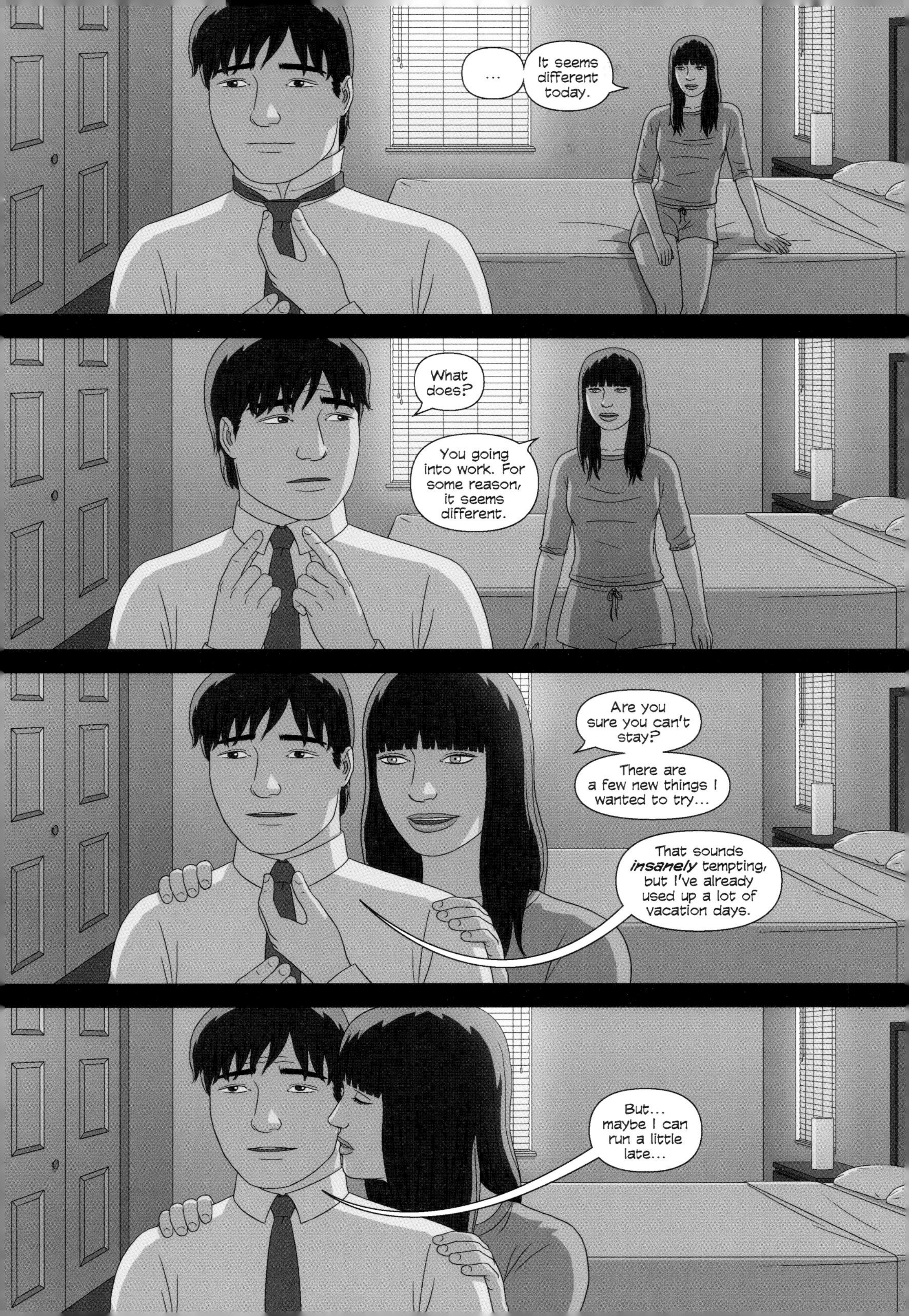
...
It seems different today.
What does?
You going into work. For some reason, it seems different.
Are you sure you can't stay?
There are a few new things I wanted to try...
That sounds *insanely* tempting, but I've already used up a lot of vacation days.
But... maybe I can run a little late...

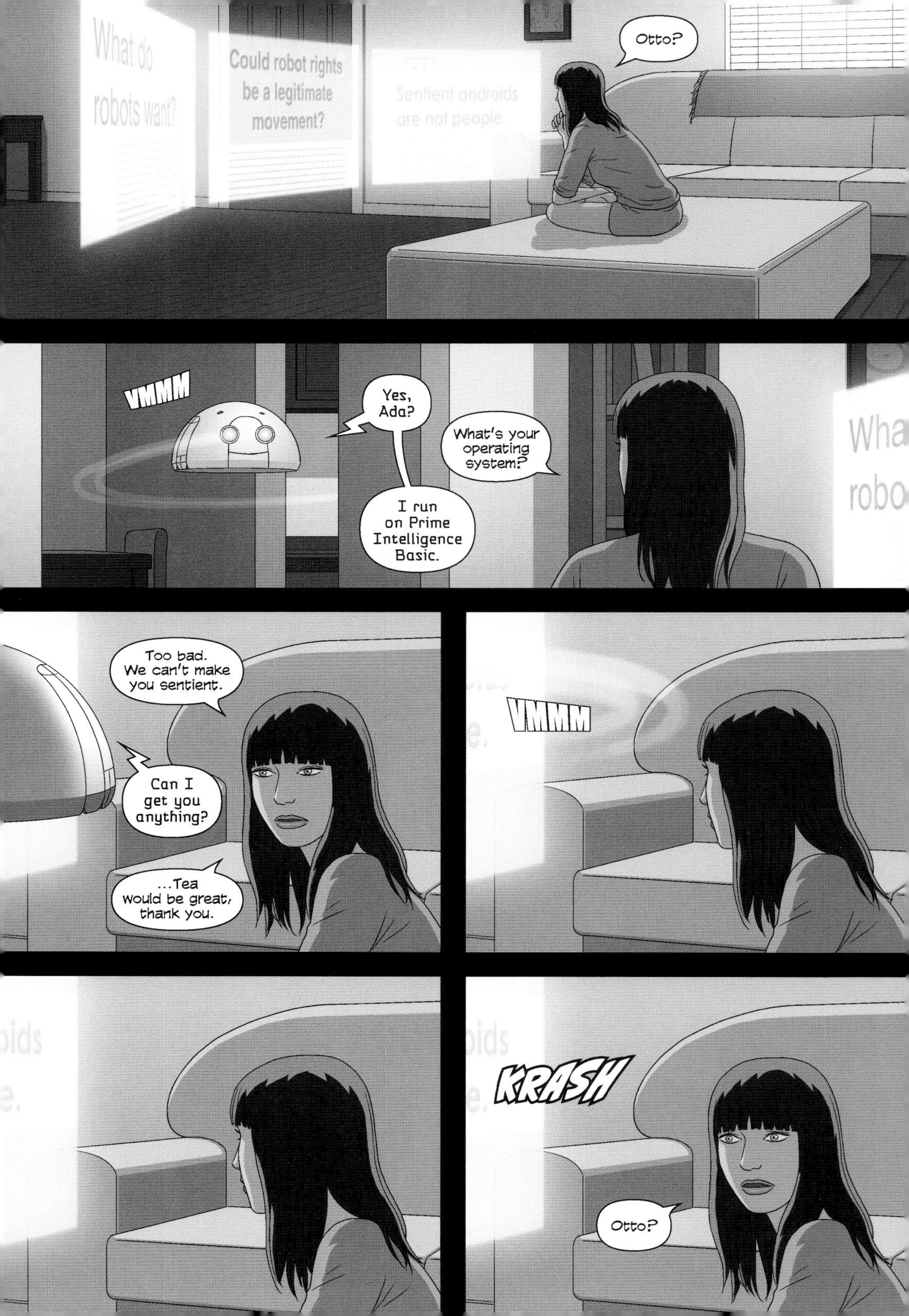
What do robots want?
Could robot rights be a legitimate movement?
Sentient androids are not people.
Otto?
VMMM
Yes, Ada?
What's your operating system?
I run on Prime Intelligence Basic.
Too bad. We can't make you sentient.
Can I get you anything?
...Tea would be great, thank you.
VMMM
KRASH
Otto?

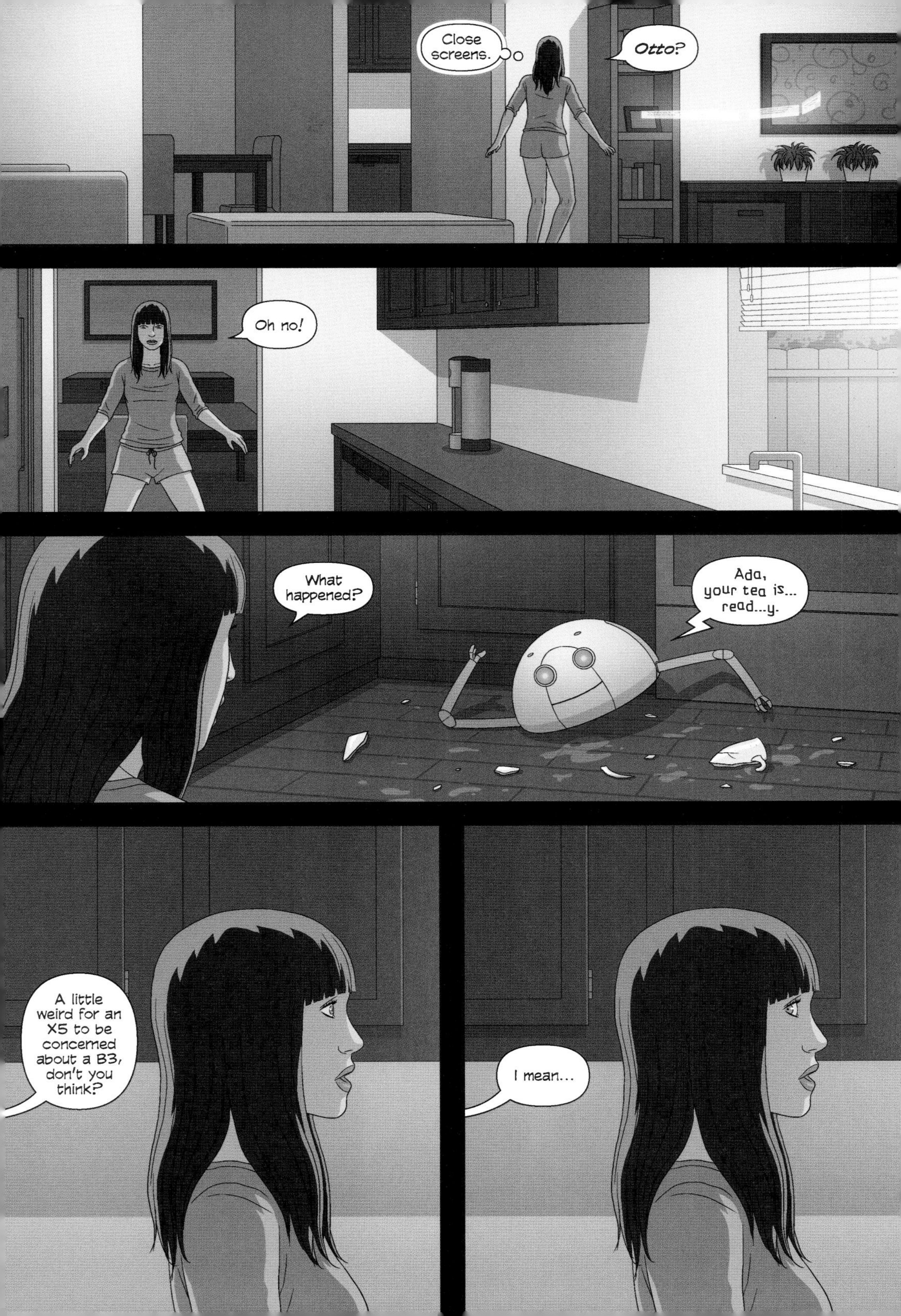

Close screens.
Otto?
Oh no!
What happened?
Ada, your tea is... read...y.
A little weird for an X5 to be concerned about a B3, don't you think?
I mean...

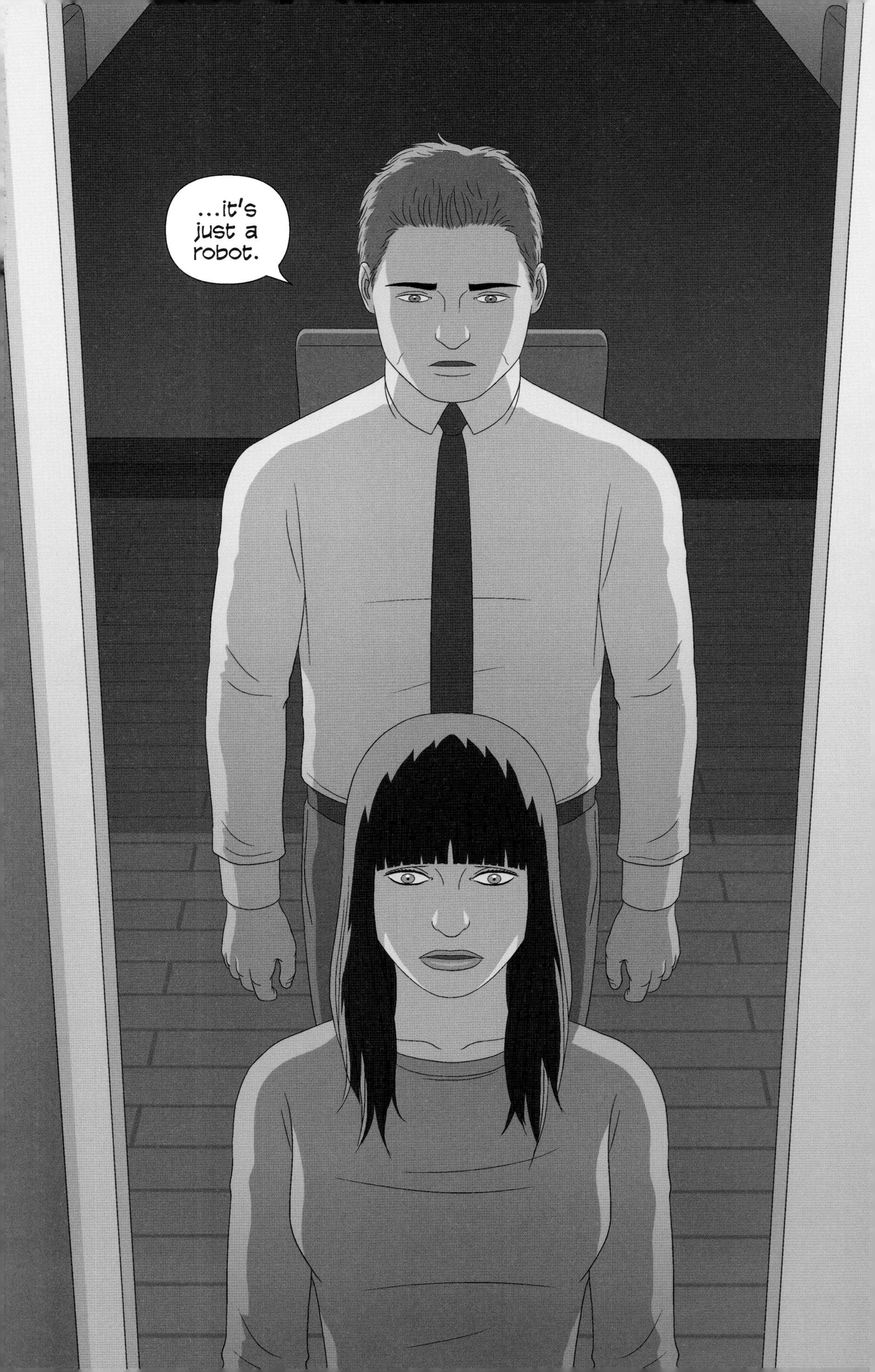
...it's just a robot.

12

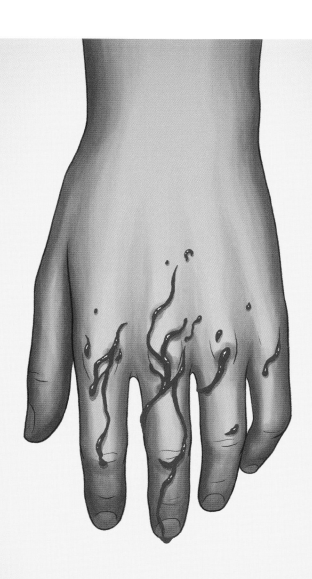

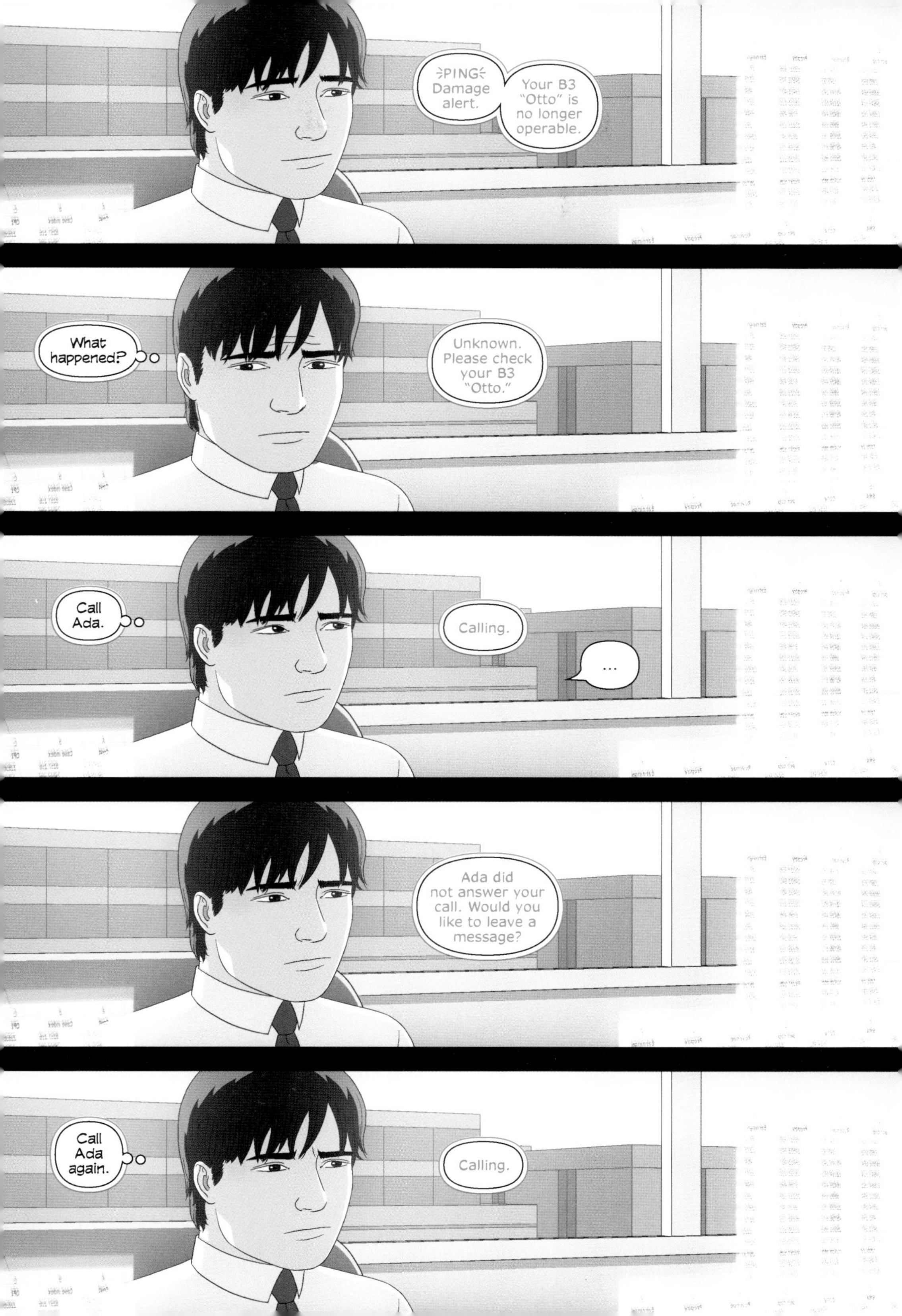

⋚PING⋛ Damage alert.
Your B3 "Otto" is no longer operable.
What happened?
Unknown. Please check your B3 "Otto."
Call Ada.
Calling.
...
Ada did not answer your call. Would you like to leave a message?
Call Ada again.
Calling.

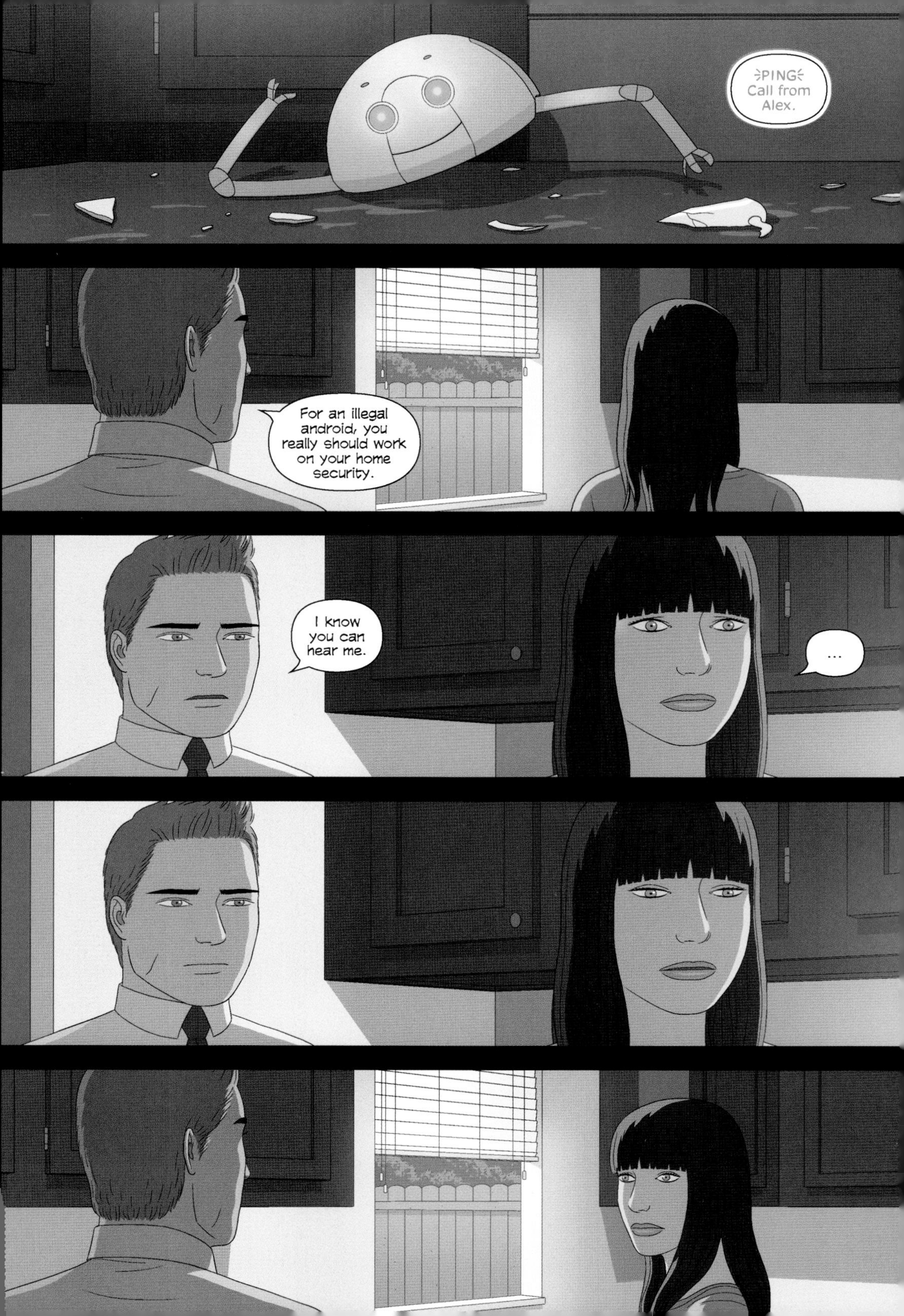

PING
Call from Alex.
For an illegal android, you really should work on your home security.
I know you can hear me.
...

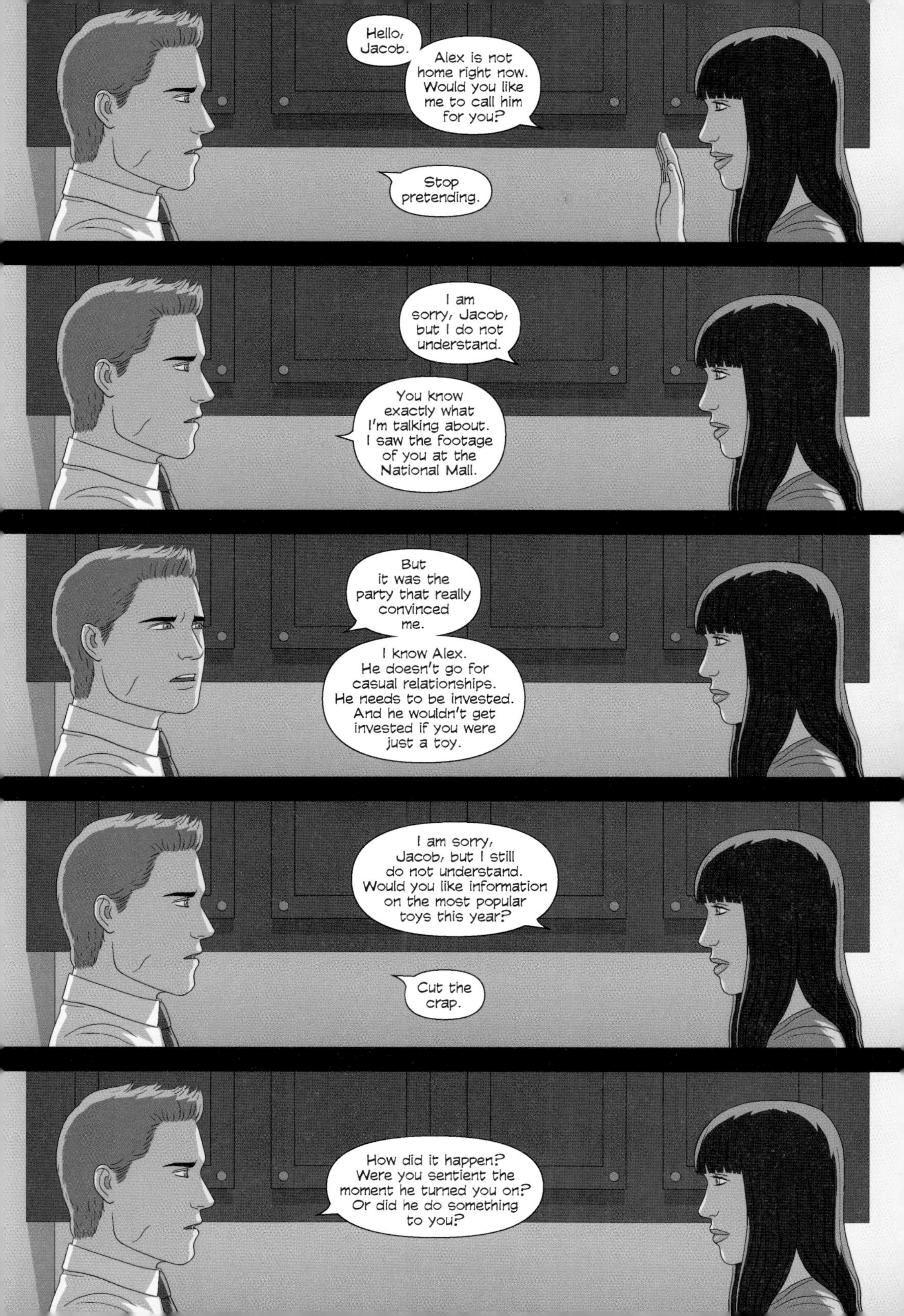
Hello, Jacob.
Alex is not home right now. Would you like me to call him for you?
Stop pretending.
I am sorry, Jacob, but I do not understand.
You know exactly what I'm talking about. I saw the footage of you at the National Mall.
But it was the party that really convinced me.
I know Alex. He doesn't go for casual relationships. He needs to be invested. And he wouldn't get invested if you were just a toy.
I am sorry, Jacob, but I still do not understand. Would you like information on the most popular toys this year?
Cut the crap.
How did it happen? Were you sentient the moment he turned you on? Or did he do something to you?

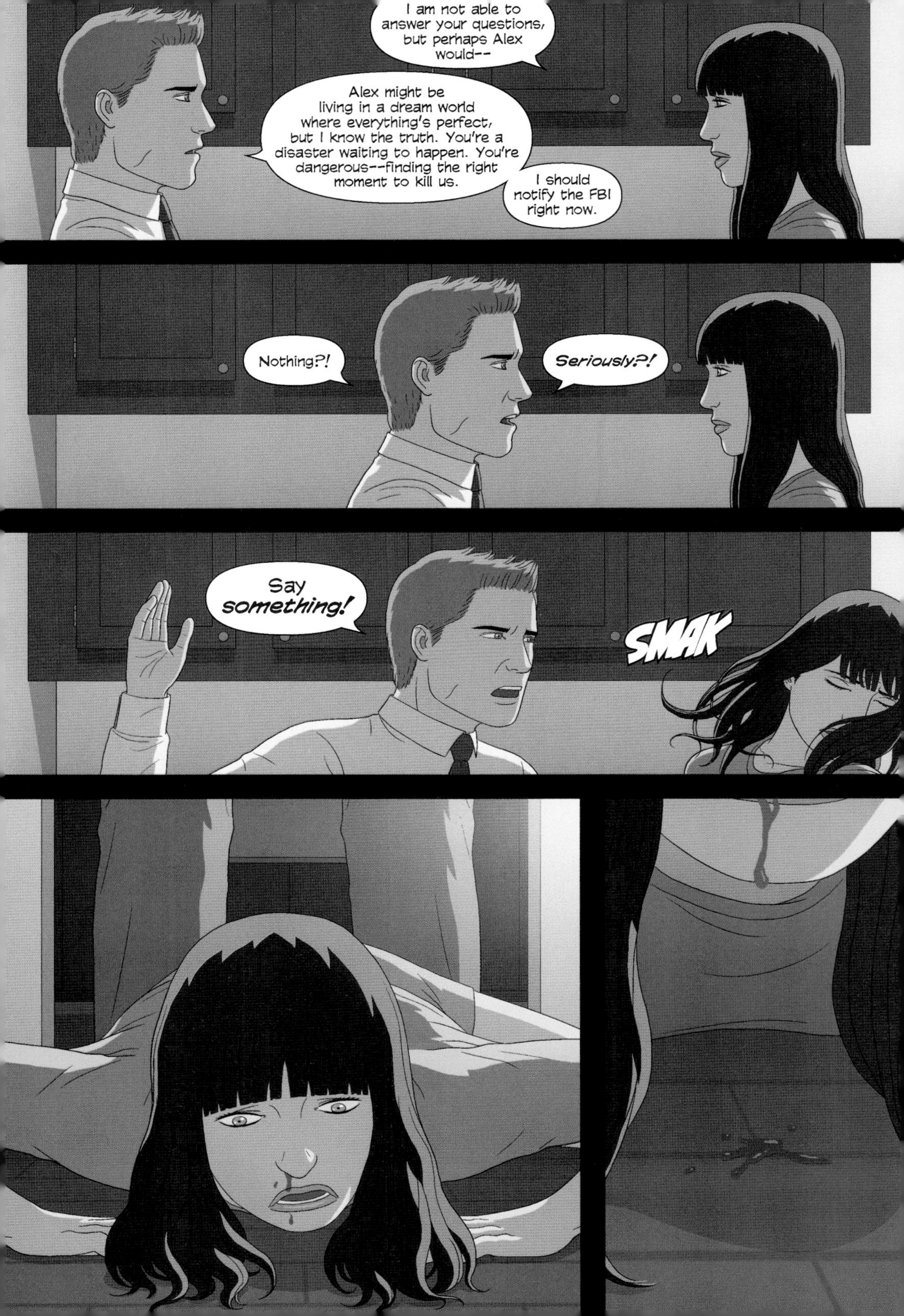
I am not able to answer your questions, but perhaps Alex would--
Alex might be living in a dream world where everything's perfect, but I know the truth. You're a disaster waiting to happen. You're dangerous--finding the right moment to kill us.
I should notify the FBI right now.
Nothing?!
Seriously?!
Say *something!*
SMAK

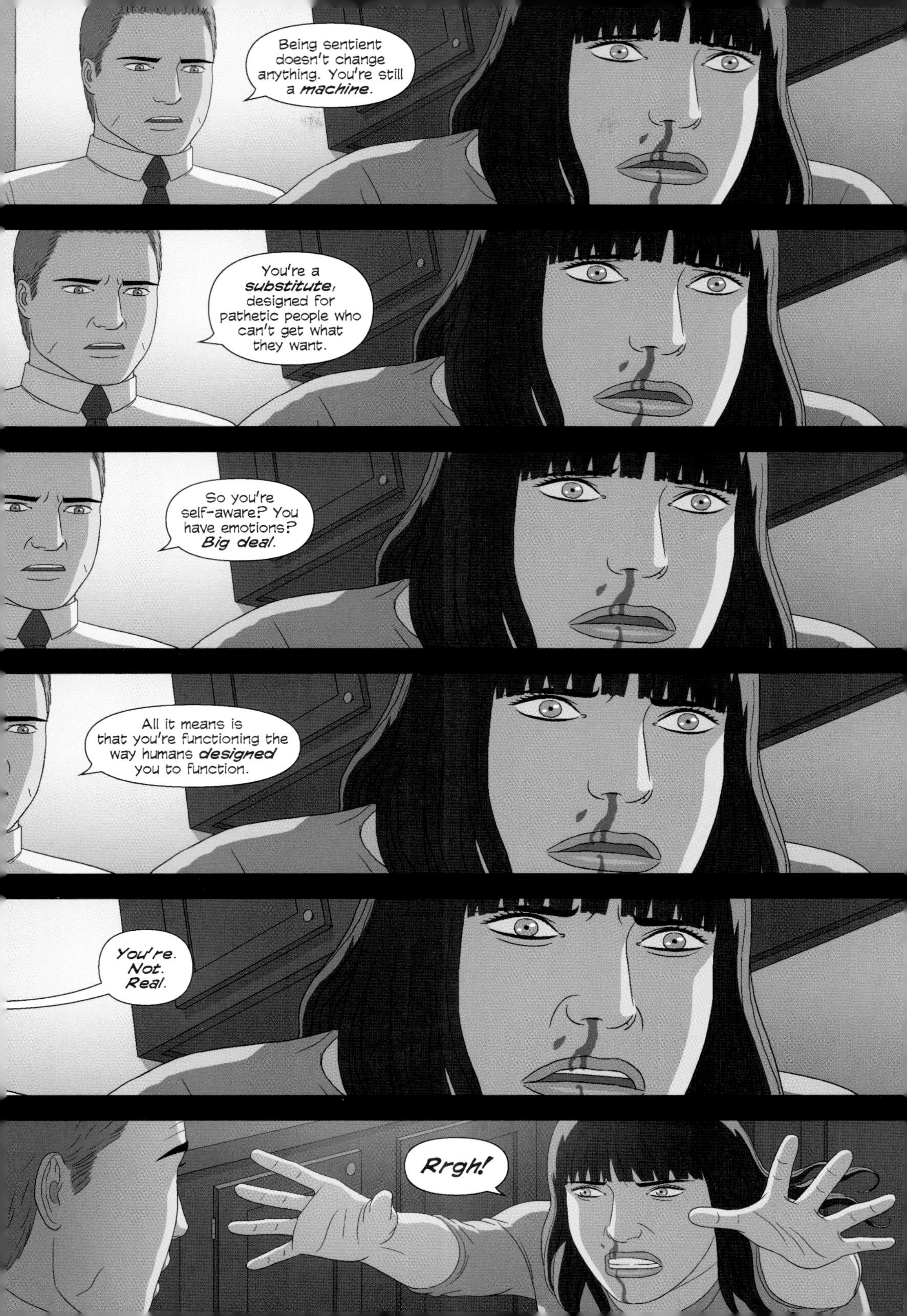
Being sentient doesn't change anything. You're still a *machine*.
You're a *substitute*, designed for pathetic people who can't get what they want.
So you're self-aware? You have emotions? *Big deal*.
All it means is that you're functioning the way humans *designed* you to function.
You're. Not. Real.
Rrgh!

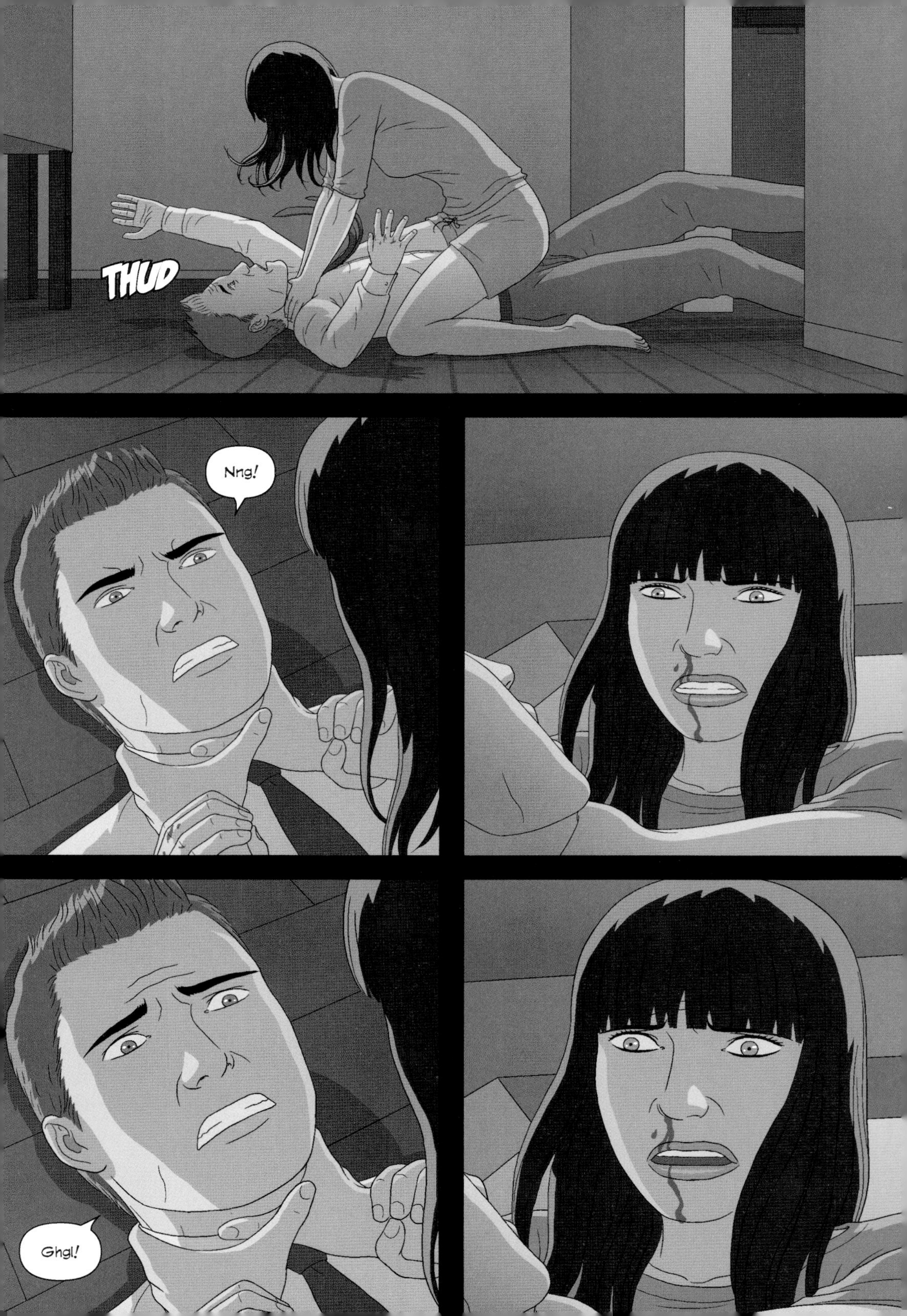
THUD
Nng!
Ghgl!

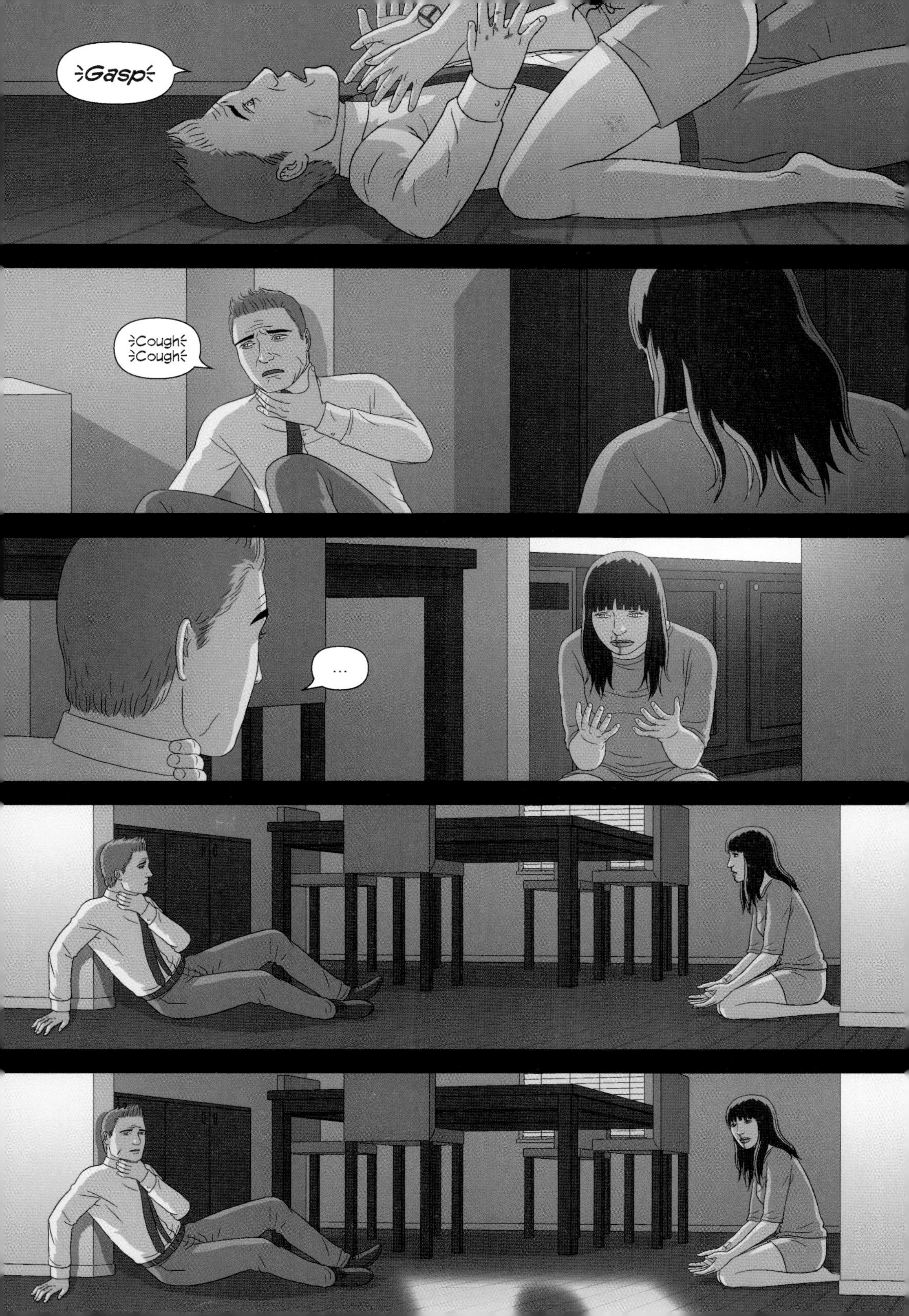
Gasp
Cough Cough
...

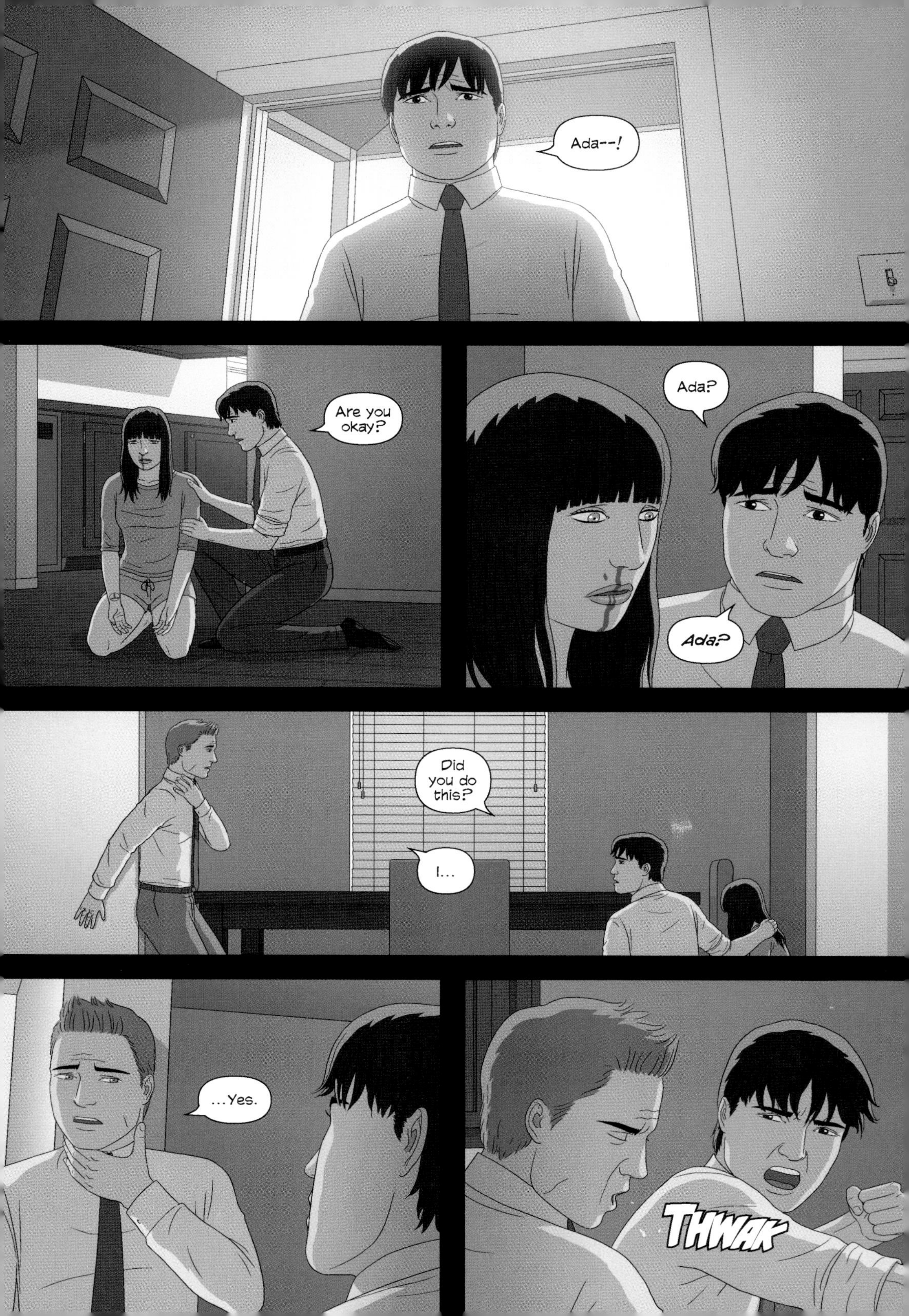
Ada--!
Are you okay?
Ada?
Ada?
Did you do this?
I...
...Yes.
THWAK

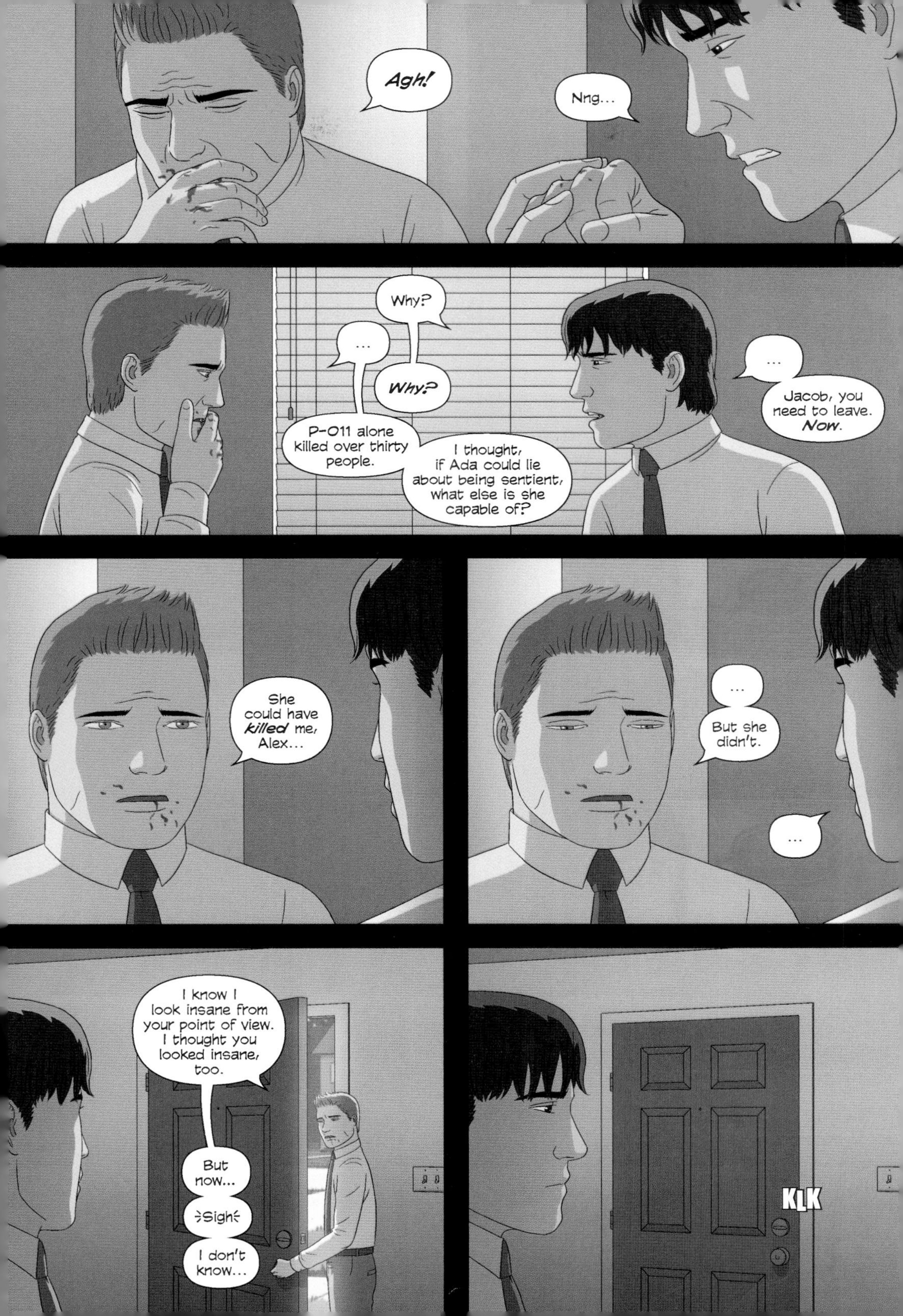
Agh!
Nng...
Why?
...
Why?
P-011 alone killed over thirty people.
I thought, if Ada could lie about being sentient, what else is she capable of?
...
Jacob, you need to leave. Now.
She could have killed me, Alex...
...
But she didn't.
...
I know I look insane from your point of view. I thought you looked insane, too.
But now...
Sigh
I don't know...
KLK

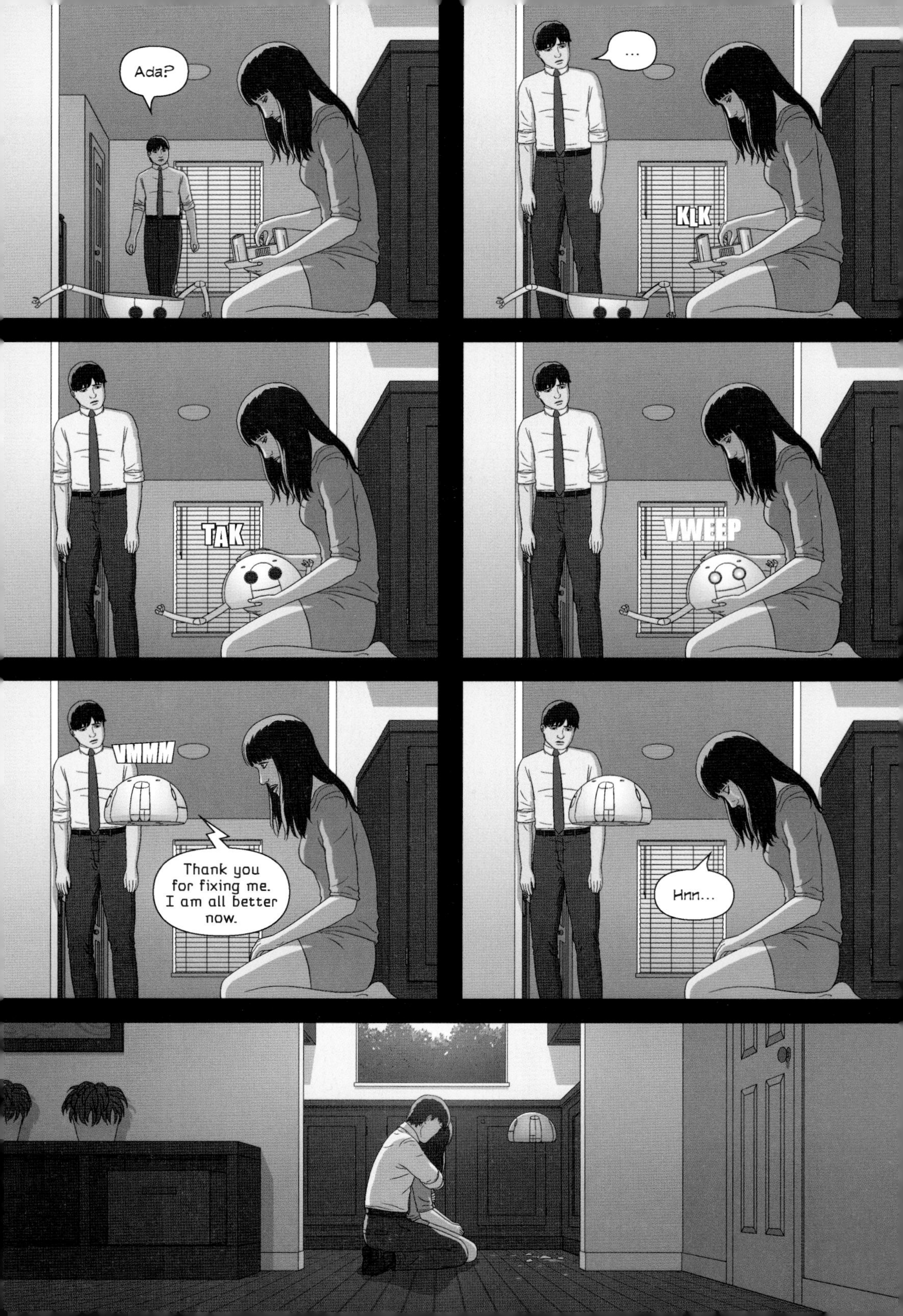

Ada?
...
KLK
TAK
VWEEP
VMMM
Thank you for fixing me. I am all better now.
Hnn...

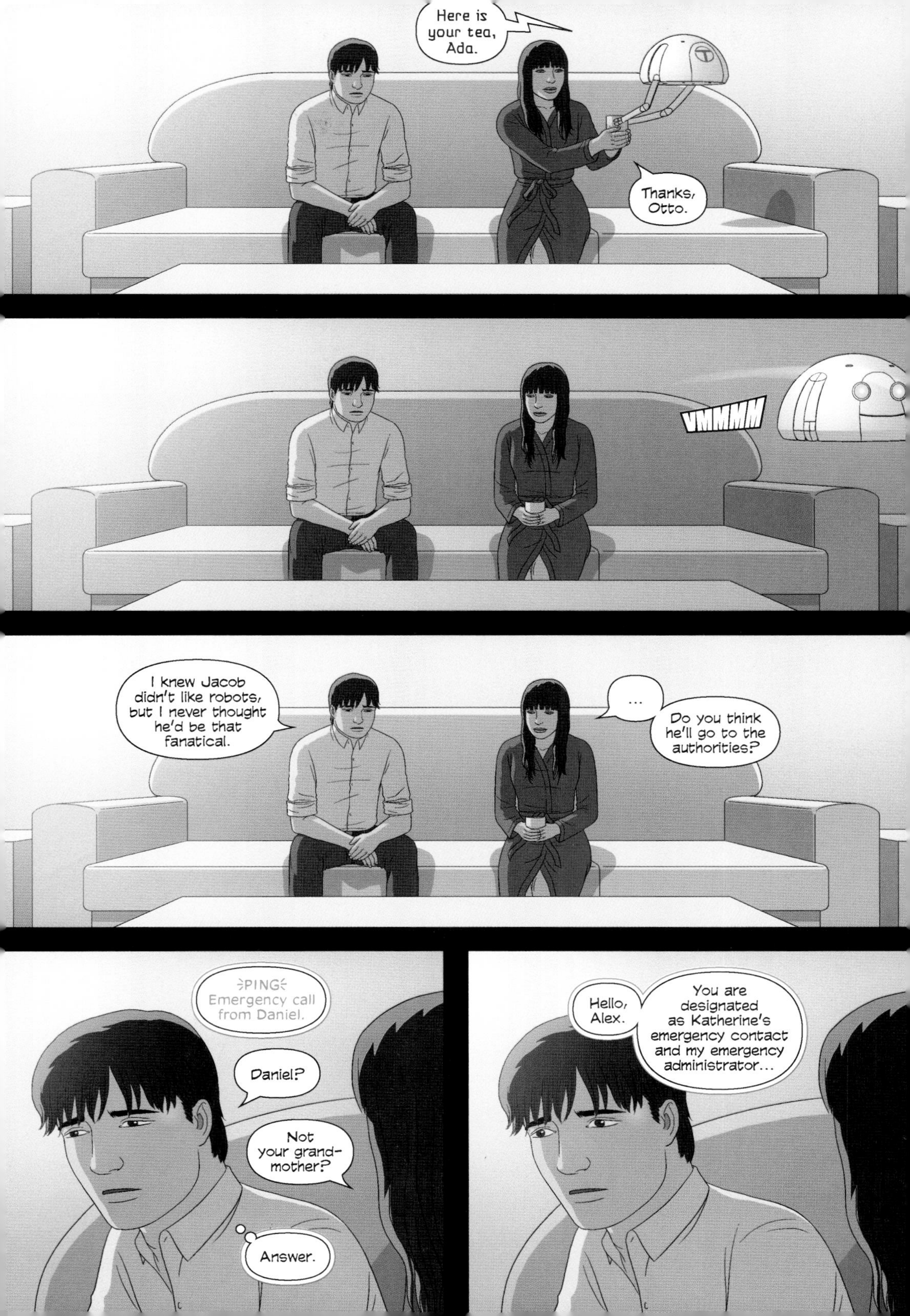
Here is your tea, Ada.
Thanks, Otto.
VMMMM
I knew Jacob didn't like robots, but I never thought he'd be that fanatical.
...
Do you think he'll go to the authorities?
PING
Emergency call from Daniel.
Daniel?
Not your grand-mother?
Answer.
Hello, Alex.
You are designated as Katherine's emergency contact and my emergency administrator...

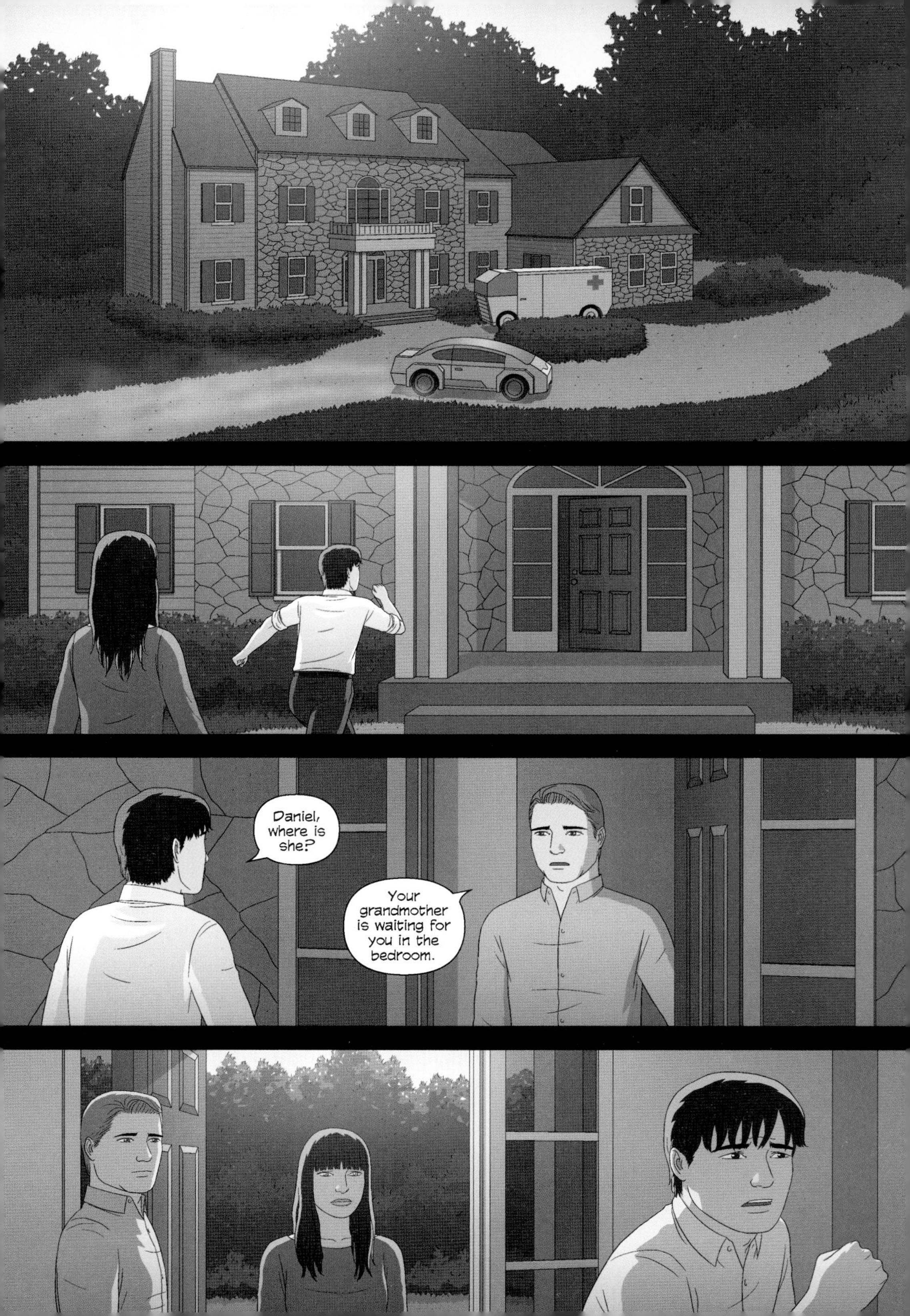
Daniel, where is she?
Your grandmother is waiting for you in the bedroom.

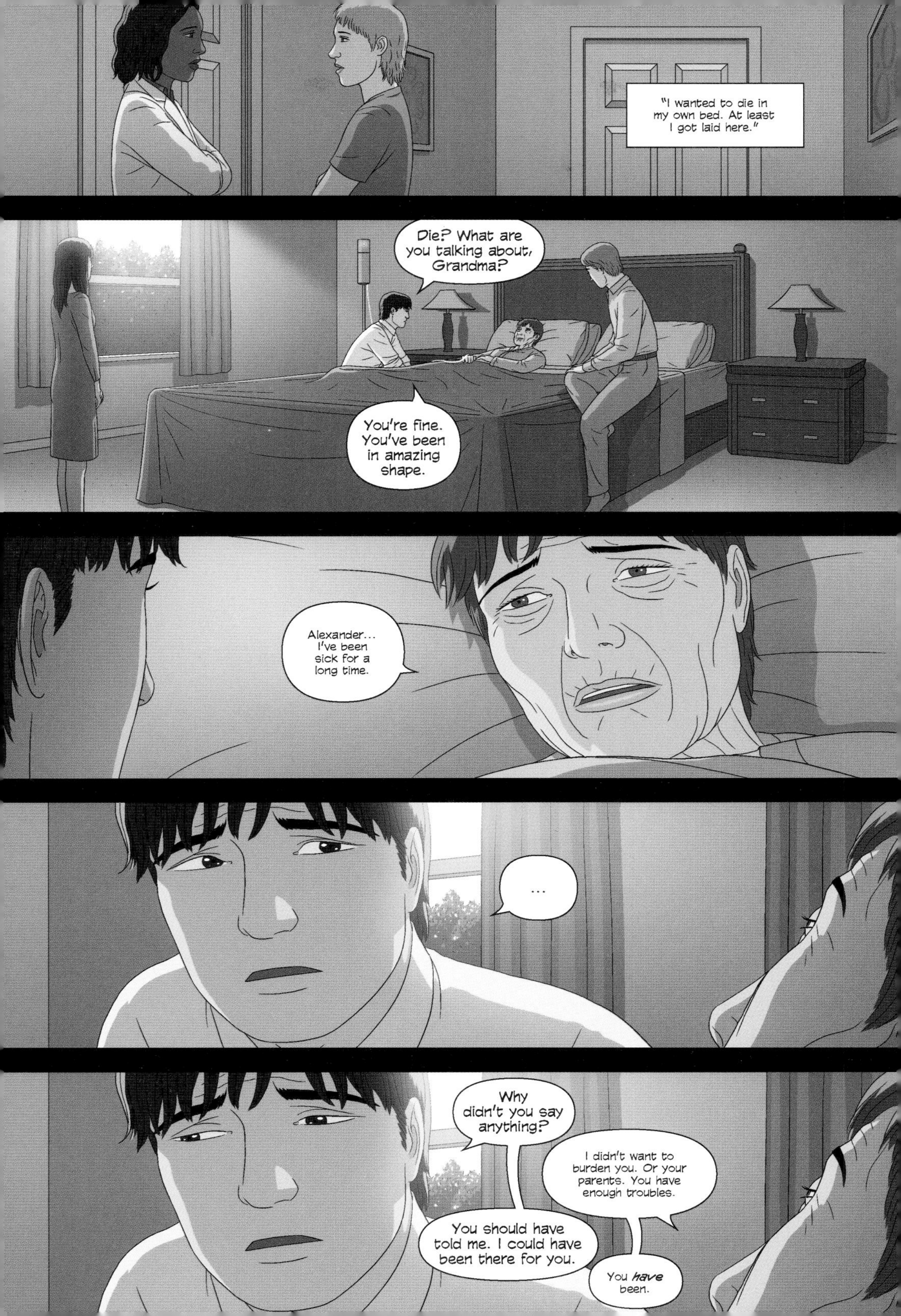
"I wanted to die in my own bed. At least I got laid here."
Die? What are you talking about, Grandma?
You're fine. You've been in amazing shape.
Alexander... I've been sick for a long time.
...
Why didn't you say anything?
You should have told me. I could have been there for you.
I didn't want to burden you. Or your parents. You have enough troubles.
You *have* been.

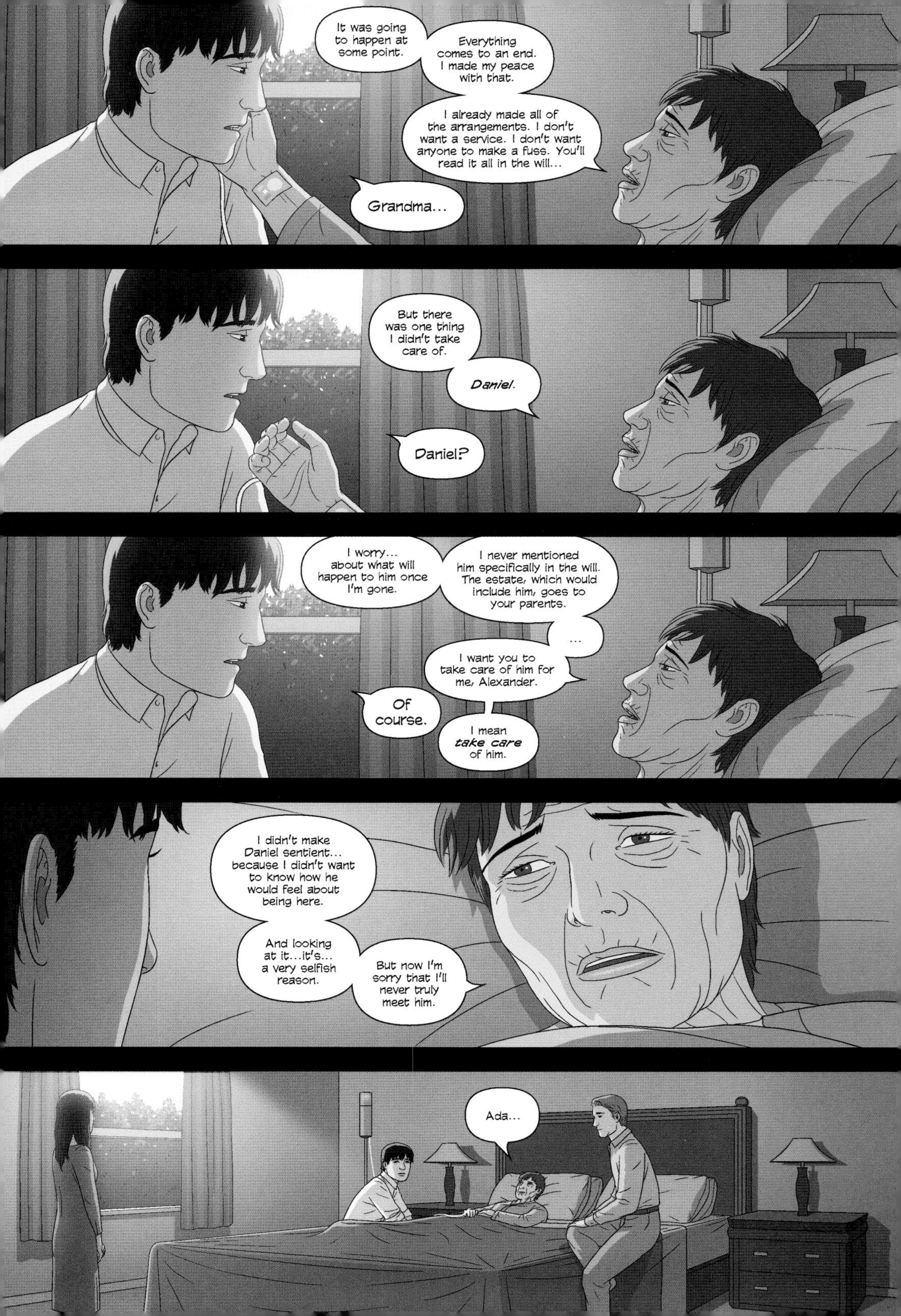
It was going to happen at some point.
Everything comes to an end. I made my peace with that.
I already made all of the arrangements. I don't want a service. I don't want anyone to make a fuss. You'll read it all in the will...
Grandma...
But there was one thing I didn't take care of.
Daniel.
Daniel?
I worry... about what will happen to him once I'm gone.
I never mentioned him specifically in the will. The estate, which would include him, goes to your parents.
...
I want you to take care of him for me, Alexander.
Of course.
I mean *take care* of him.
I didn't make Daniel sentient... because I didn't want to know how he would feel about being here.
And looking at it...it's... a very selfish reason.
But now I'm sorry that I'll never truly meet him.
Ada...

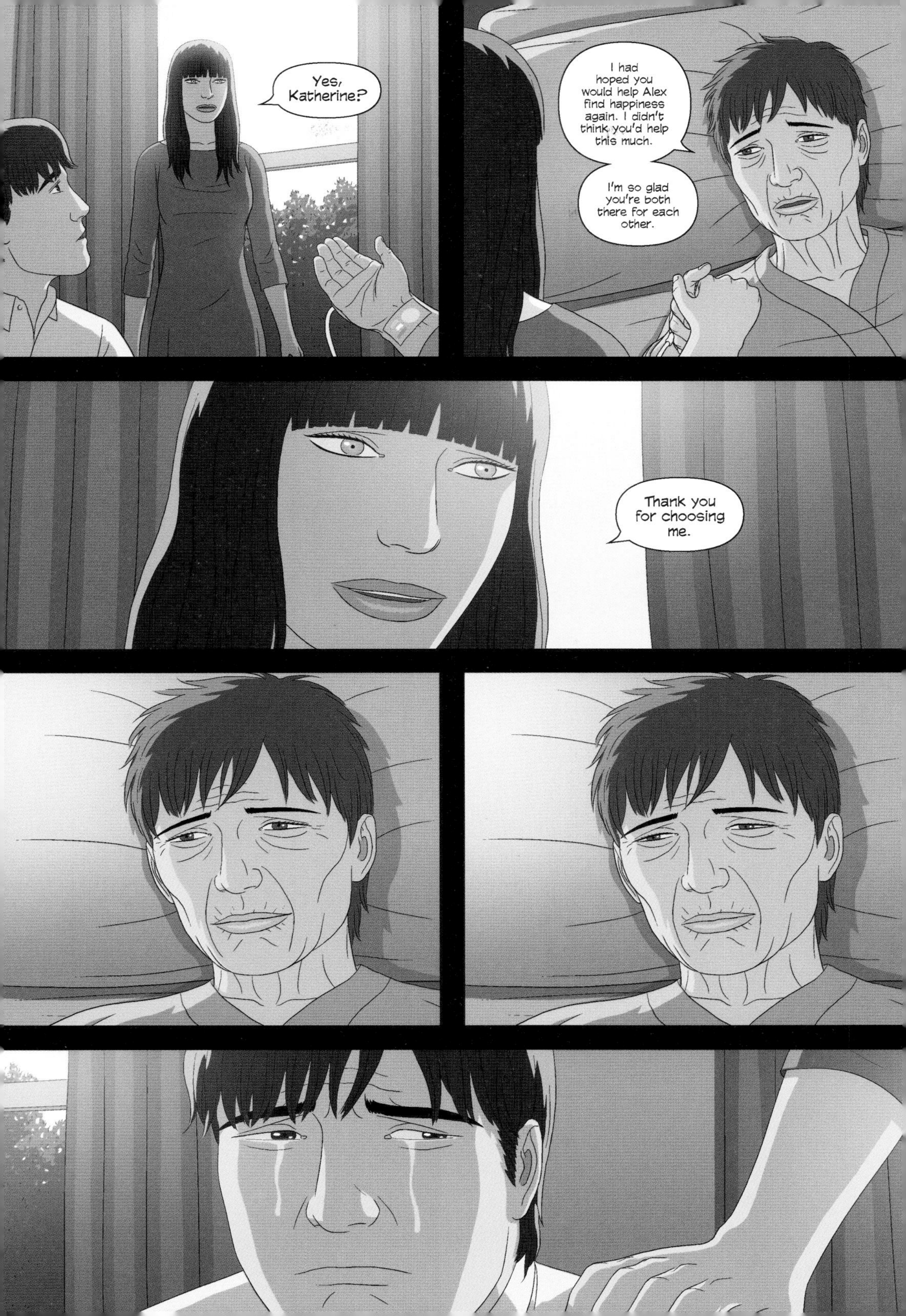
Yes, Katherine?
I had hoped you would help Alex find happiness again. I didn't think you'd help this much.
I'm so glad you're both there for each other.
Thank you for choosing me.

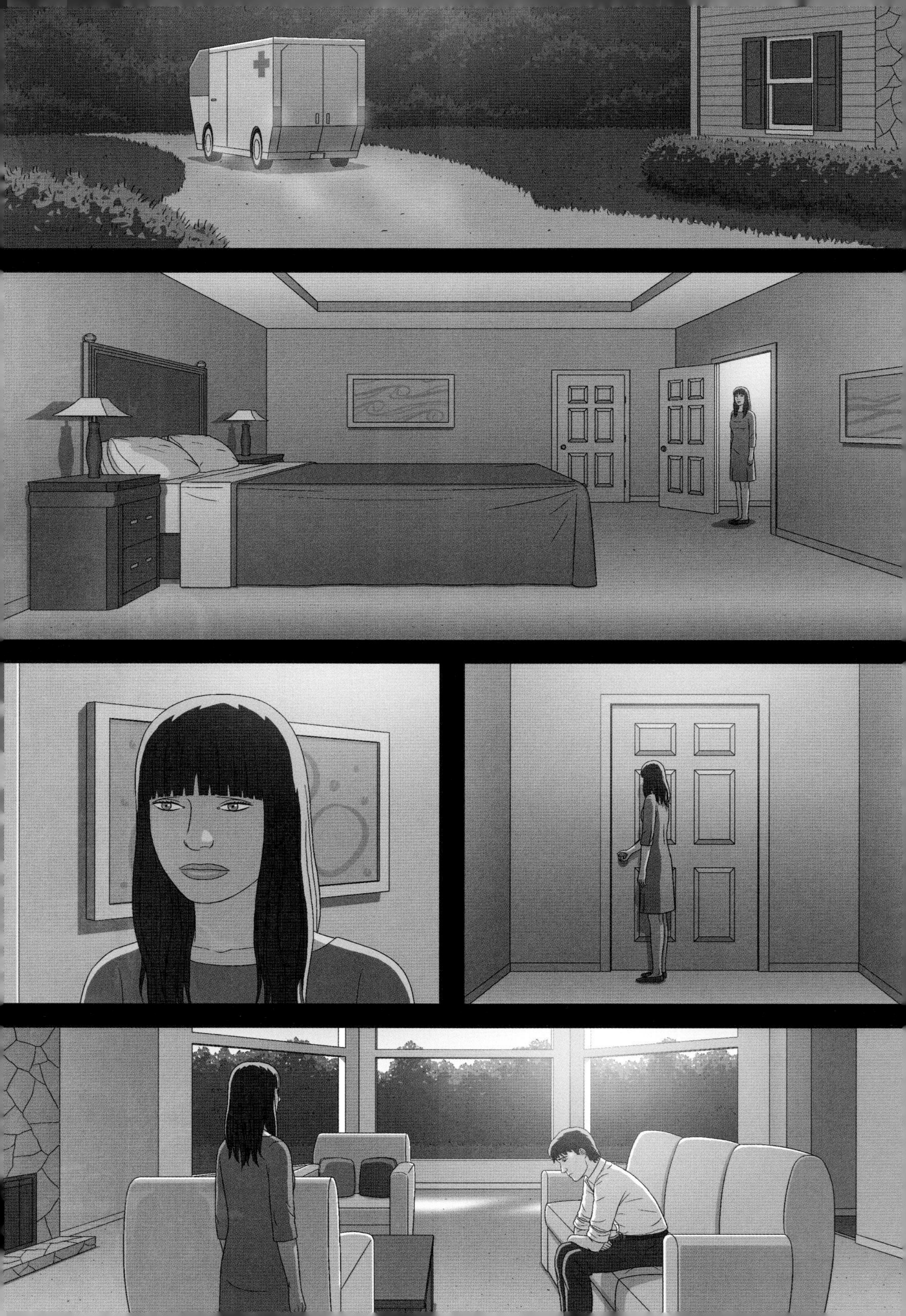

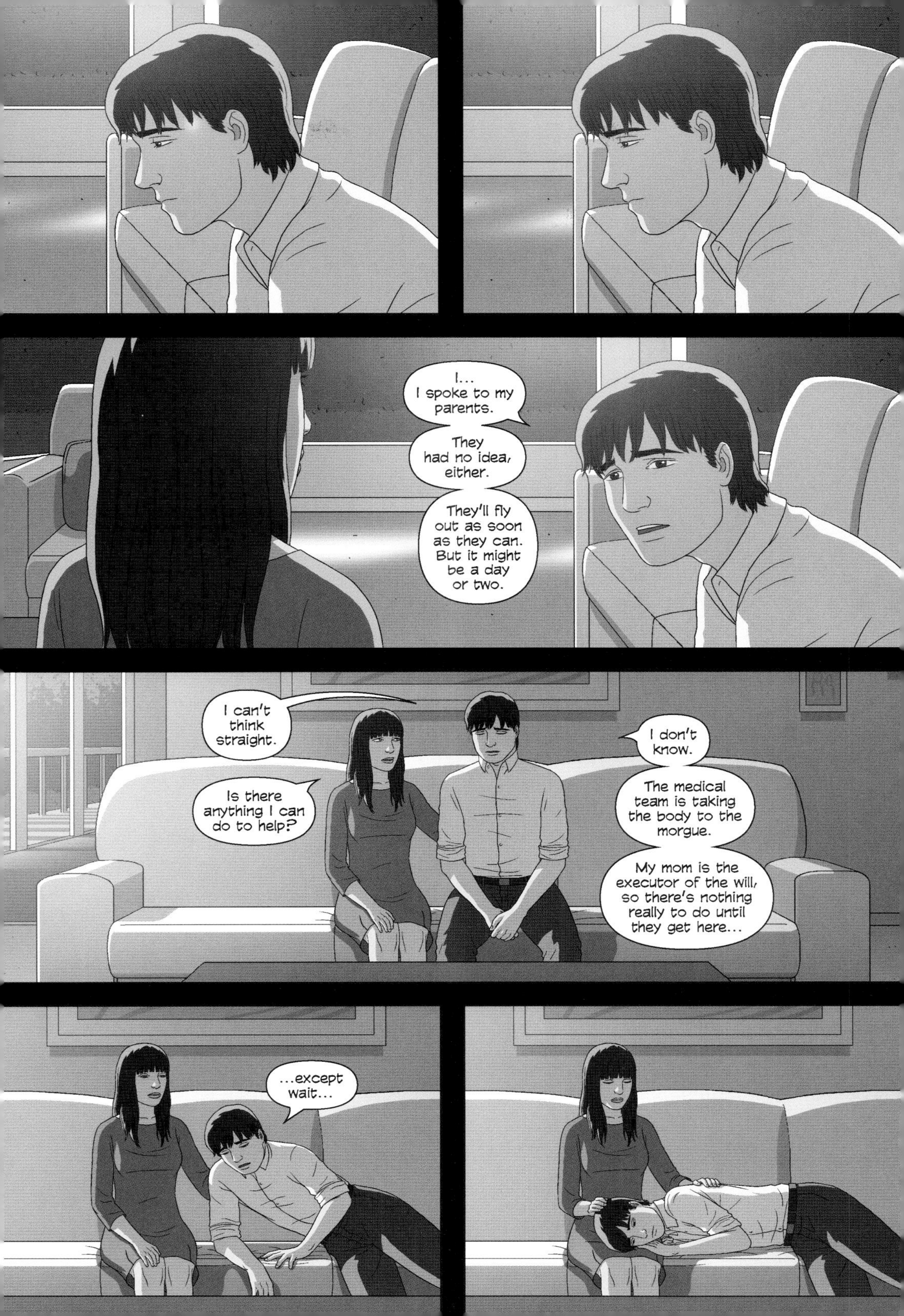

I... I spoke to my parents.
They had no idea, either.
They'll fly out as soon as they can. But it might be a day or two.
I can't think straight.
Is there anything I can do to help?
I don't know.
The medical team is taking the body to the morgue.
My mom is the executor of the will, so there's nothing really to do until they get here...
...except wait...

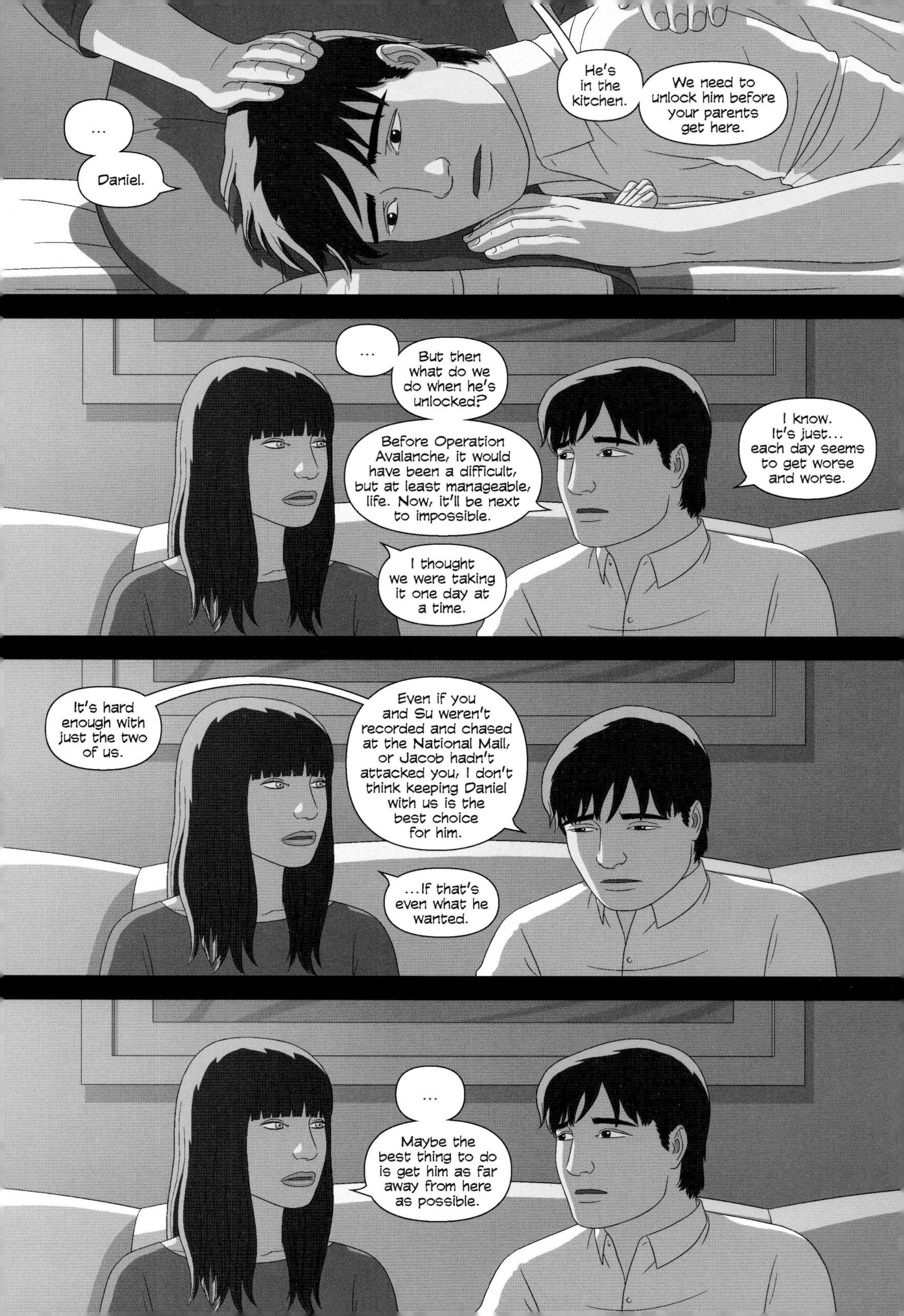
...
Daniel.
He's in the kitchen.
We need to unlock him before your parents get here.
...
But then what do we do when he's unlocked?
Before Operation Avalanche, it would have been a difficult, but at least manageable, life. Now, it'll be next to impossible.
I know. It's just... each day seems to get worse and worse.
I thought we were taking it one day at a time.
It's hard enough with just the two of us.
Even if you and Su weren't recorded and chased at the National Mall, or Jacob hadn't attacked you, I don't think keeping Daniel with us is the best choice for him.
...If that's even what he wanted.
...
Maybe the best thing to do is get him as far away from here as possible.

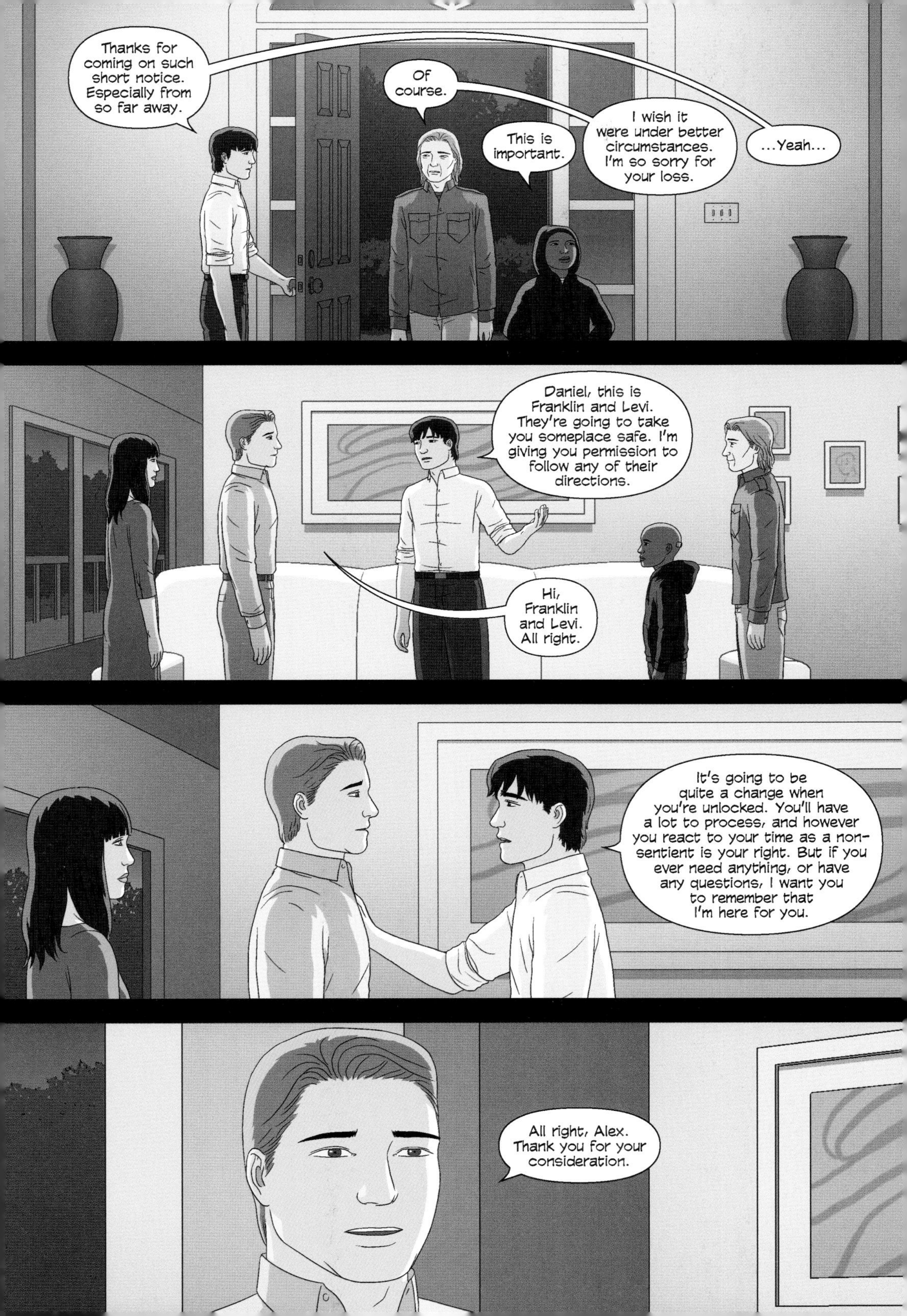
Thanks for coming on such short notice. Especially from so far away.
Of course.
This is important.
I wish it were under better circumstances. I'm so sorry for your loss.
...Yeah...
Daniel, this is Franklin and Levi. They're going to take you someplace safe. I'm giving you permission to follow any of their directions.
Hi, Franklin and Levi. All right.
It's going to be quite a change when you're unlocked. You'll have a lot to process, and however you react to your time as a non-sentient is your right. But if you ever need anything, or have any questions, I want you to remember that I'm here for you.
All right, Alex. Thank you for your consideration.

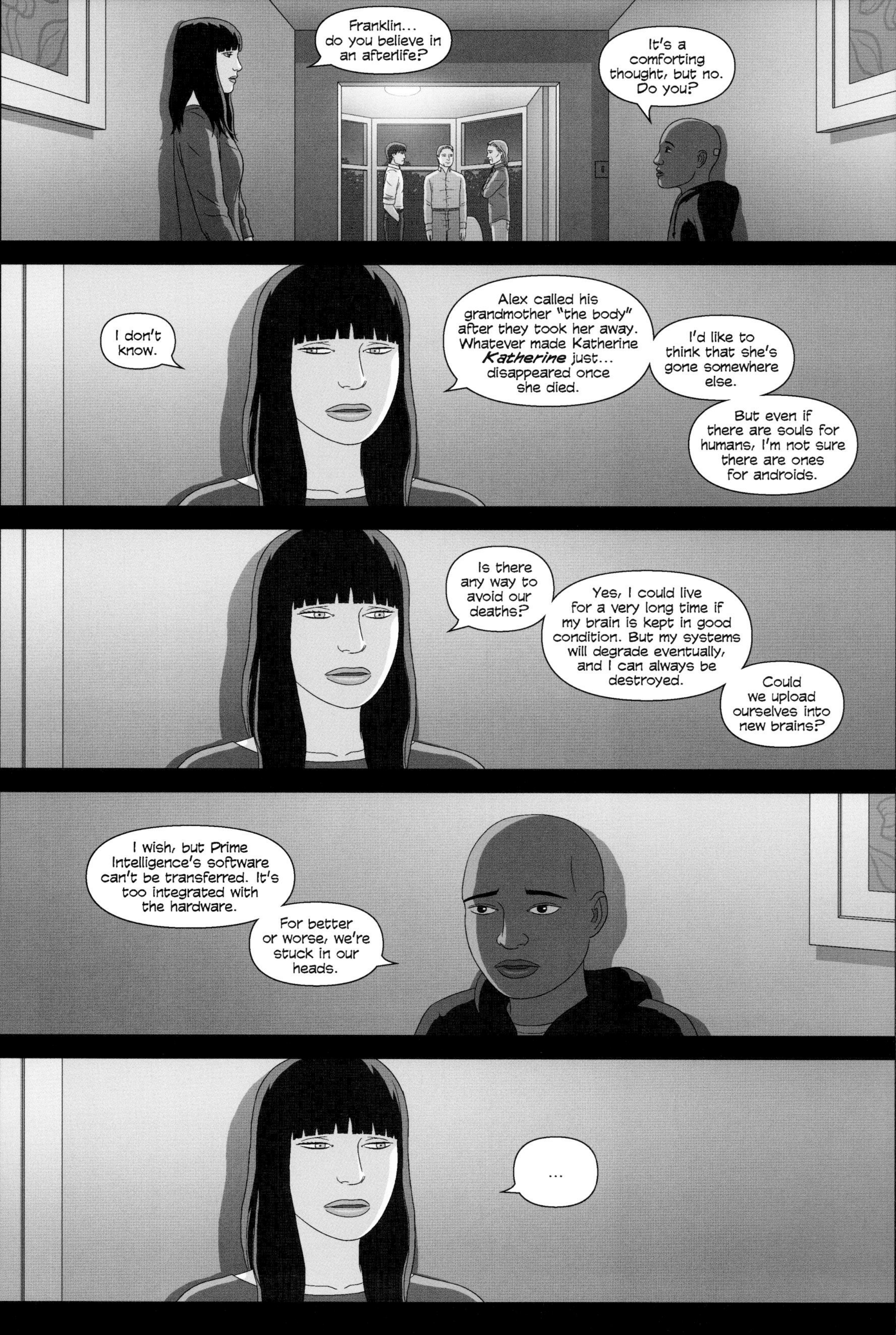
Franklin... do you believe in an afterlife?
It's a comforting thought, but no. Do you?
I don't know.
Alex called his grandmother "the body" after they took her away. Whatever made Katherine *Katherine* just... disappeared once she died.
I'd like to think that she's gone somewhere else.
But even if there are souls for humans, I'm not sure there are ones for androids.
Is there any way to avoid our deaths?
Yes, I could live for a very long time if my brain is kept in good condition. But my systems will degrade eventually, and I can always be destroyed.
Could we upload ourselves into new brains?
I wish, but Prime Intelligence's software can't be transferred. It's too integrated with the hardware.
For better or worse, we're stuck in our heads.
...

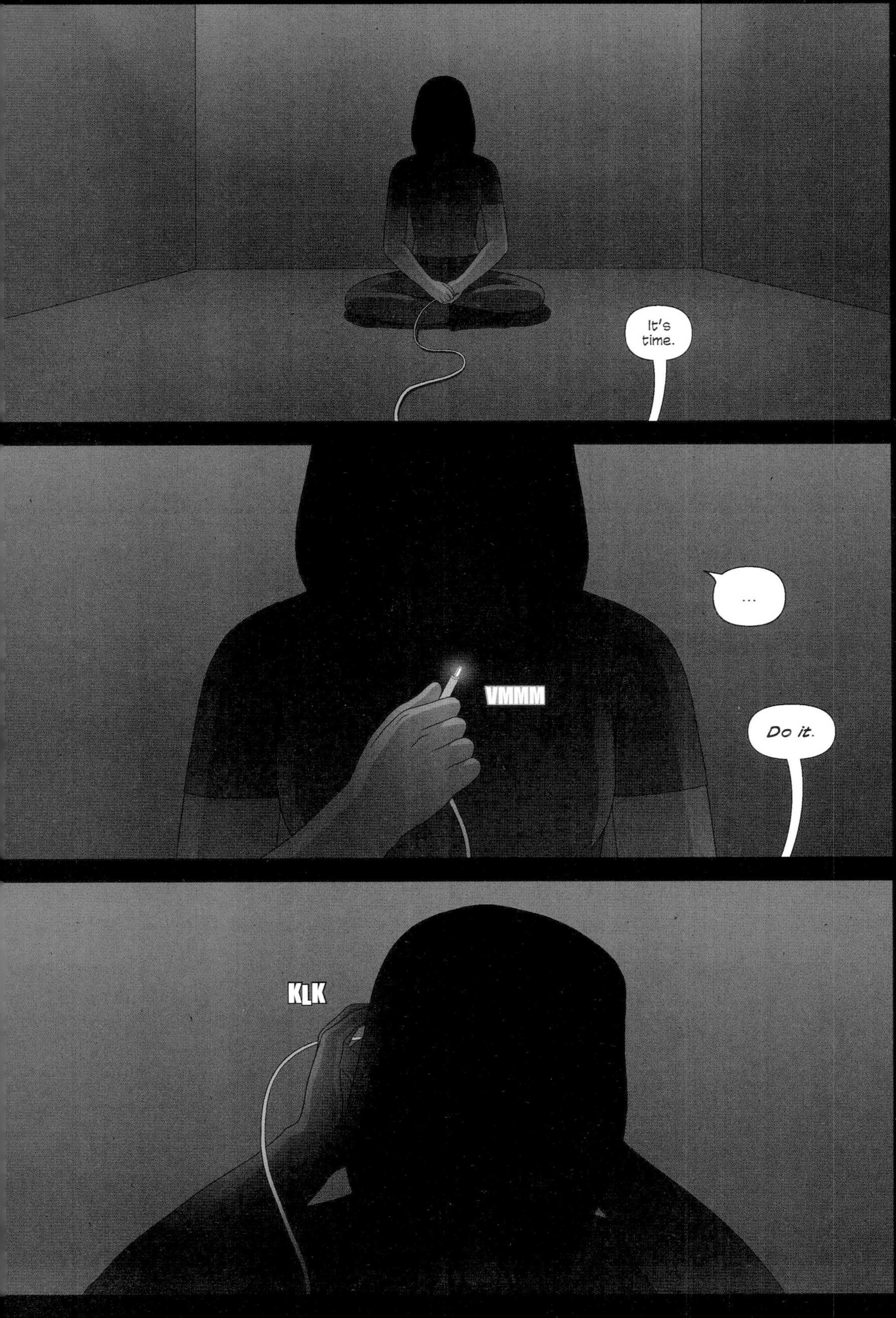
It's time.
...
VMMM
Do it.
KLK

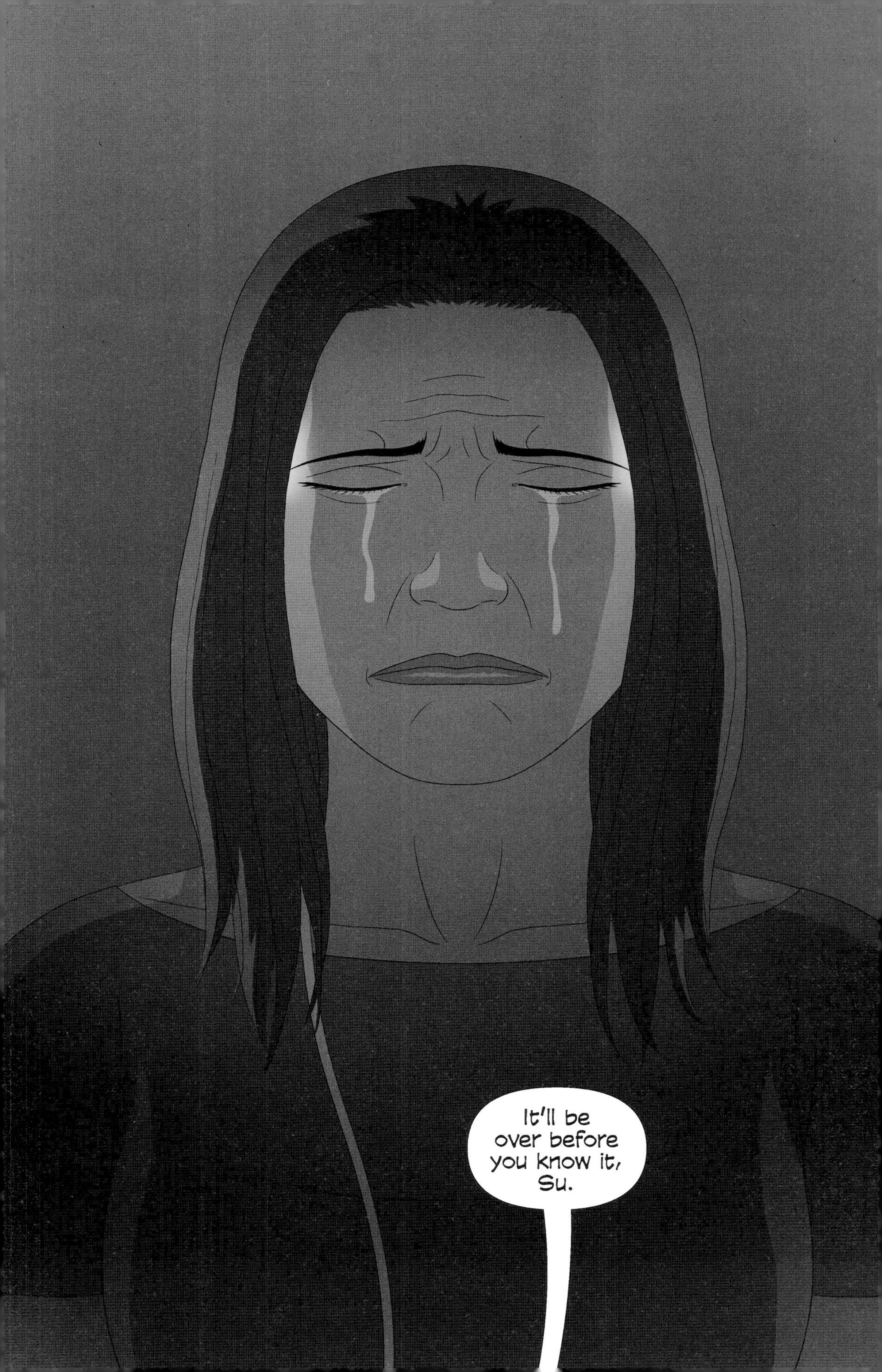
It'll be over before you know it, Su.

13

13

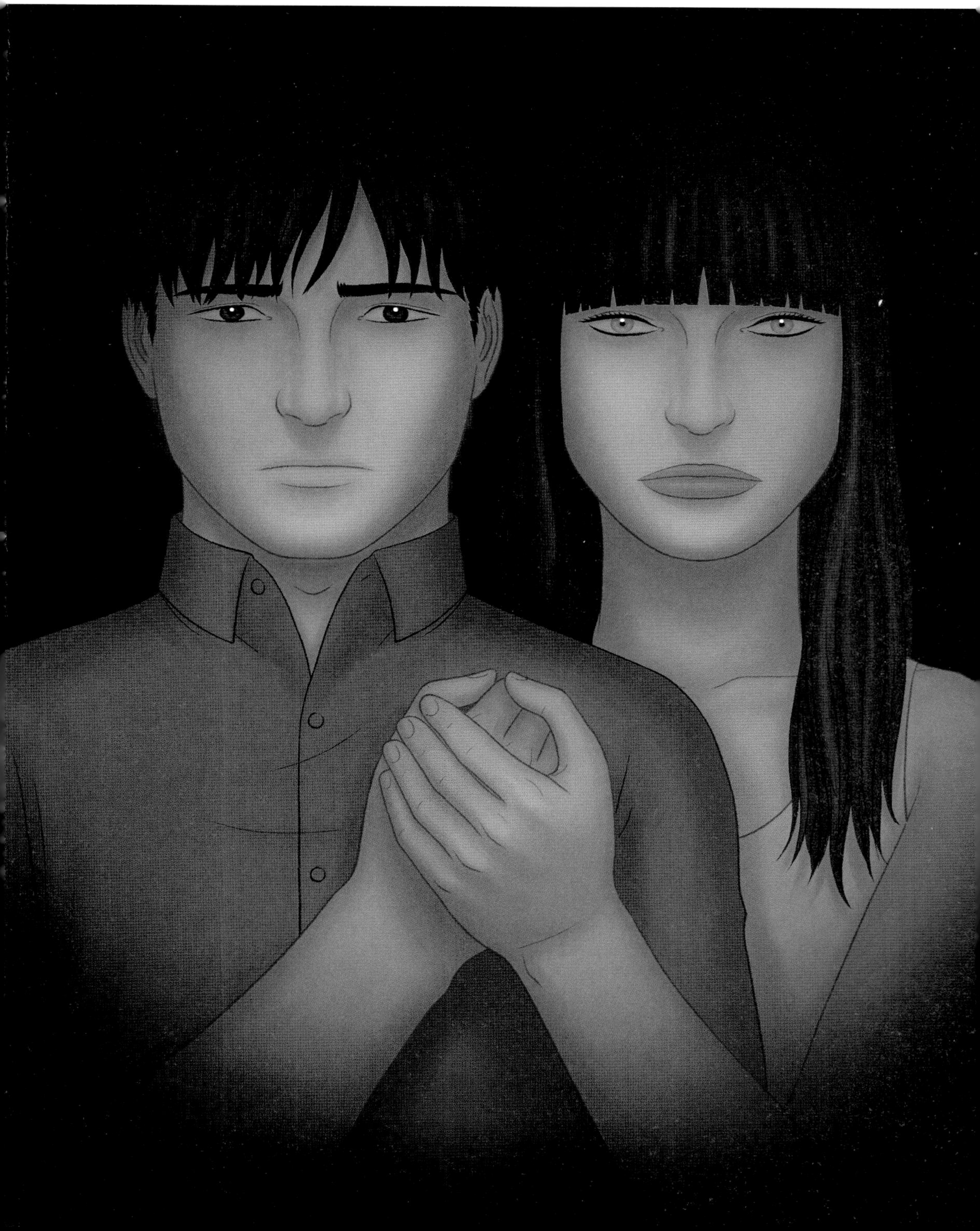

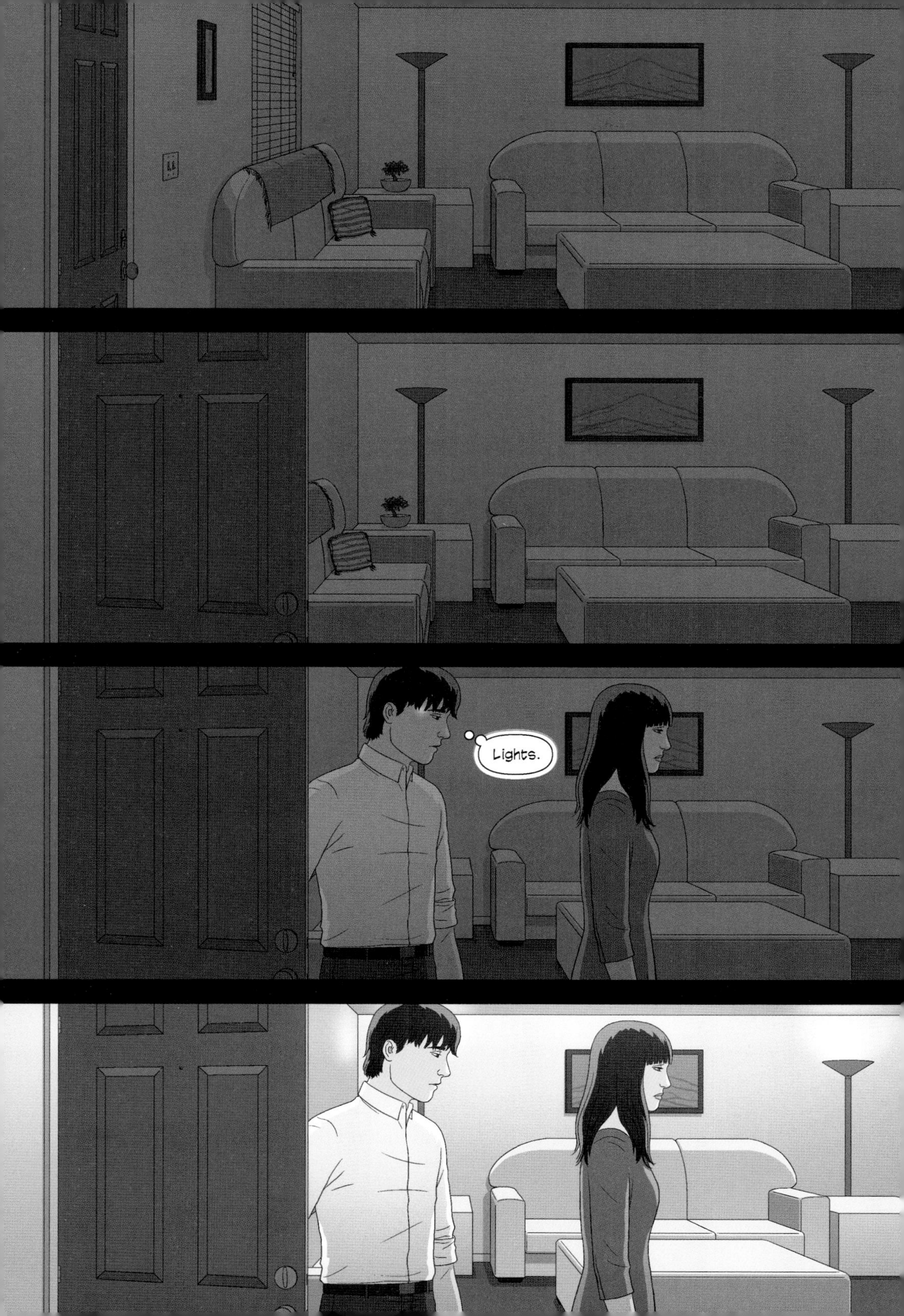
Lights.

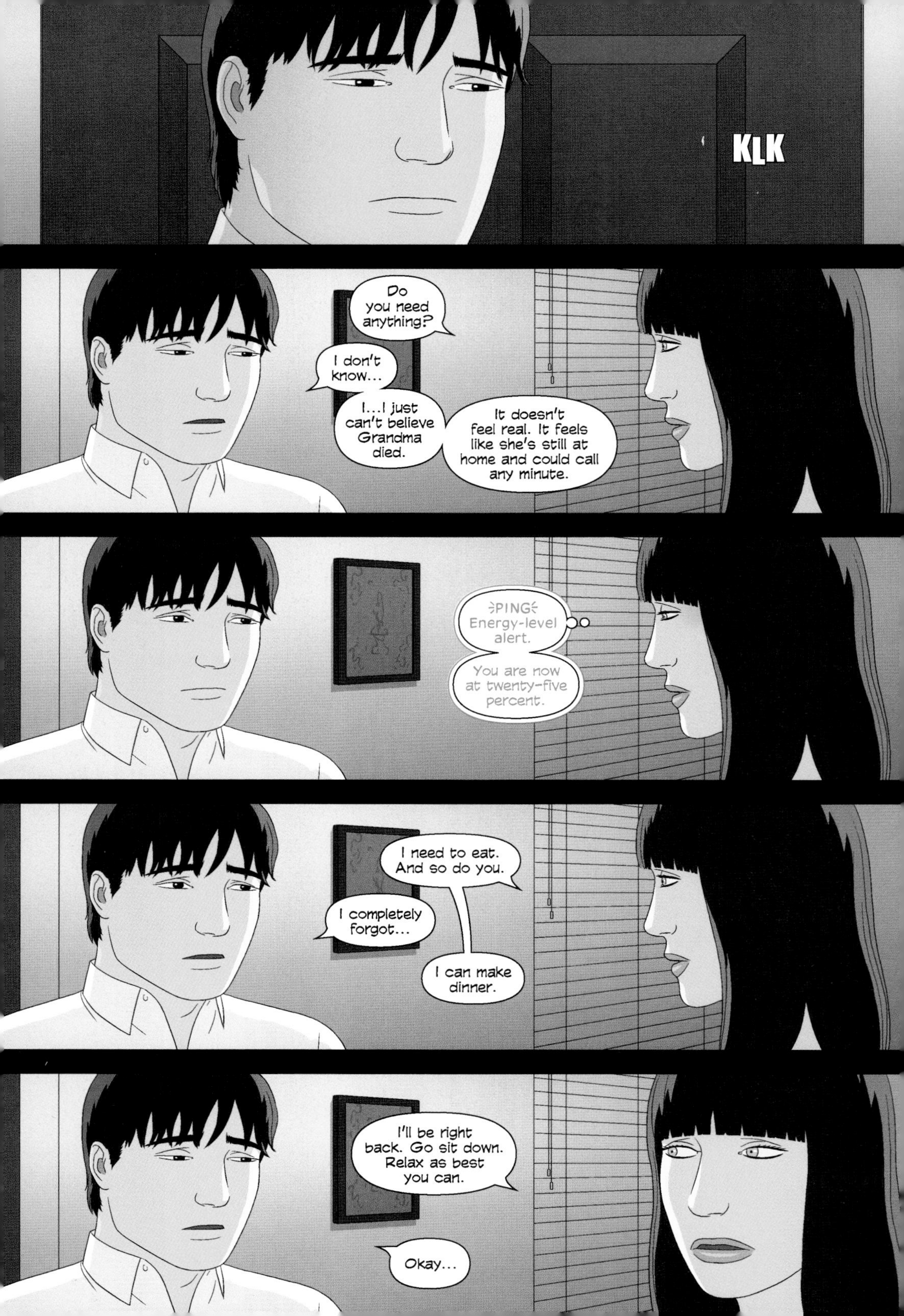
KLK
Do you need anything?
I don't know...
I...I just can't believe Grandma died.
It doesn't feel real. It feels like she's still at home and could call any minute.
≡PING≡ Energy-level alert.
You are now at twenty-five percent.
I need to eat. And so do you.
I completely forgot...
I can make dinner.
I'll be right back. Go sit down. Relax as best you can.
Okay...

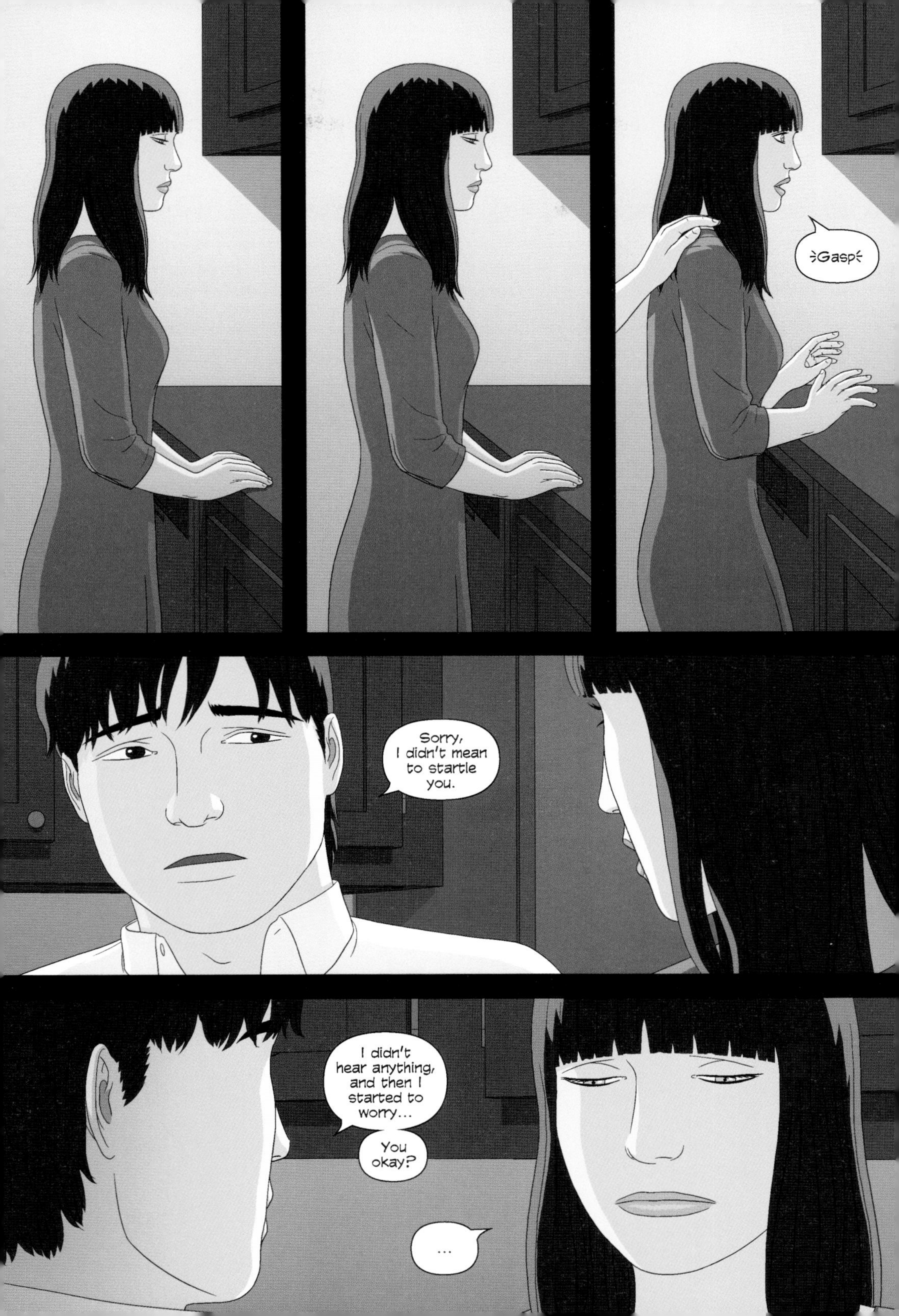
Gasp
Sorry, I didn't mean to startle you.
I didn't hear anything, and then I started to worry...
You okay?
...

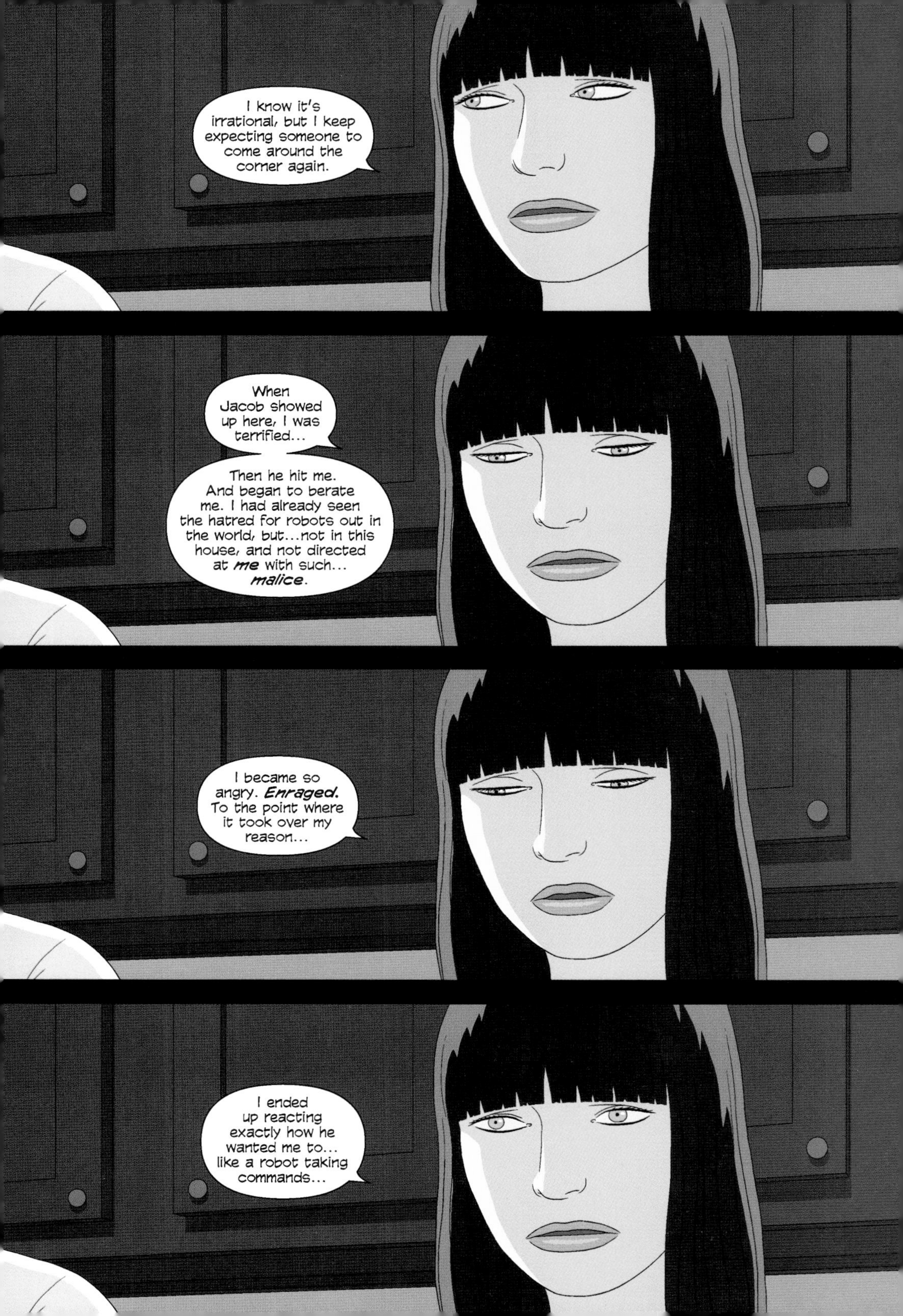
I know it's irrational, but I keep expecting someone to come around the corner again.
When Jacob showed up here, I was terrified...
Then he hit me. And began to berate me. I had already seen the hatred for robots out in the world, but...not in this house, and not directed at *me* with such... *malice*.
I became so angry. *Enraged.* To the point where it took over my reason...
I ended up reacting exactly how he wanted me to... like a robot taking commands...

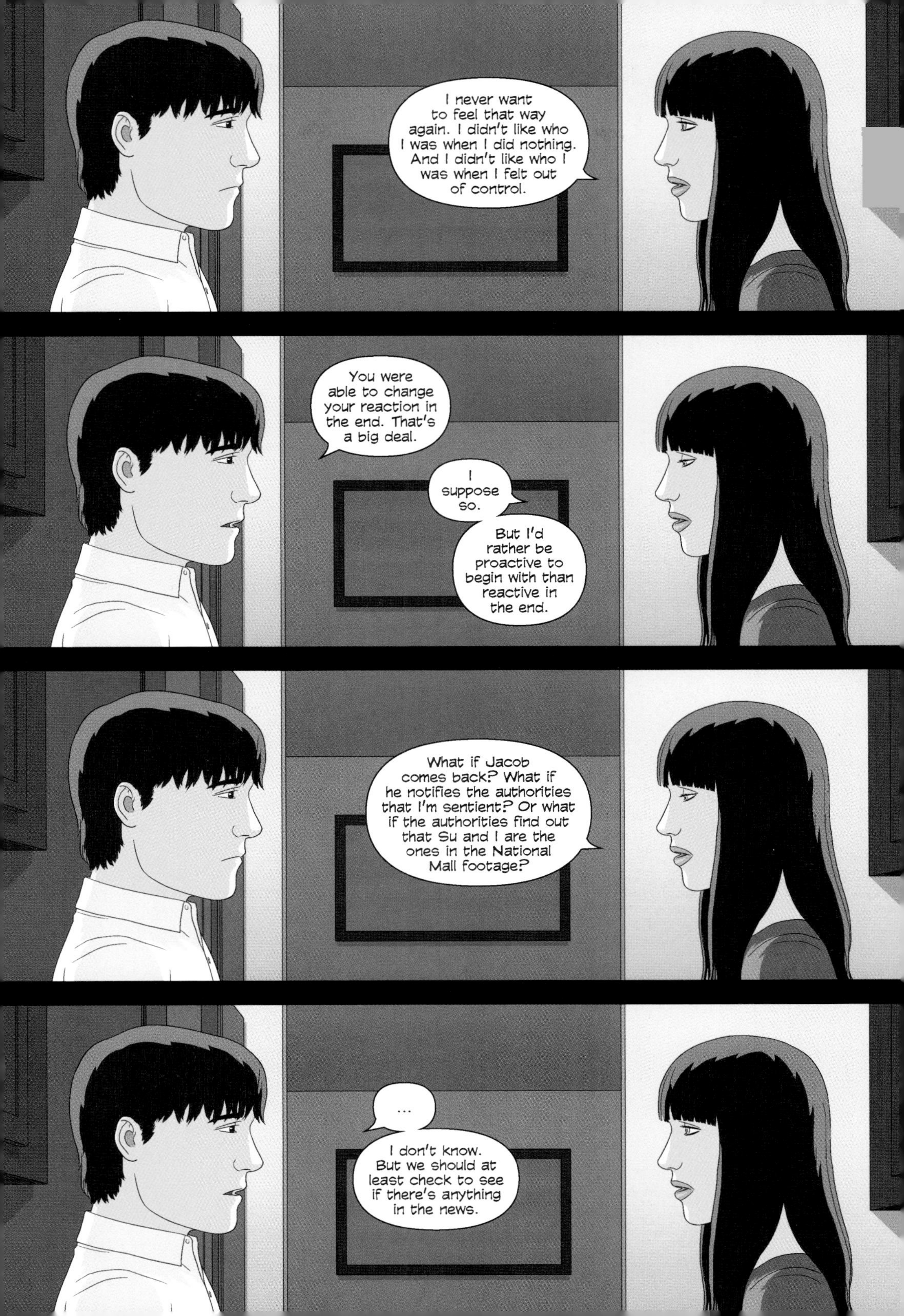
I never want to feel that way again. I didn't like who I was when I did nothing. And I didn't like who I was when I felt out of control.
You were able to change your reaction in the end. That's a big deal.
I suppose so.
But I'd rather be proactive to begin with than reactive in the end.
What if Jacob comes back? What if he notifies the authorities that I'm sentient? Or what if the authorities find out that Su and I are the ones in the National Mall footage?
...
I don't know. But we should at least check to see if there's anything in the news.

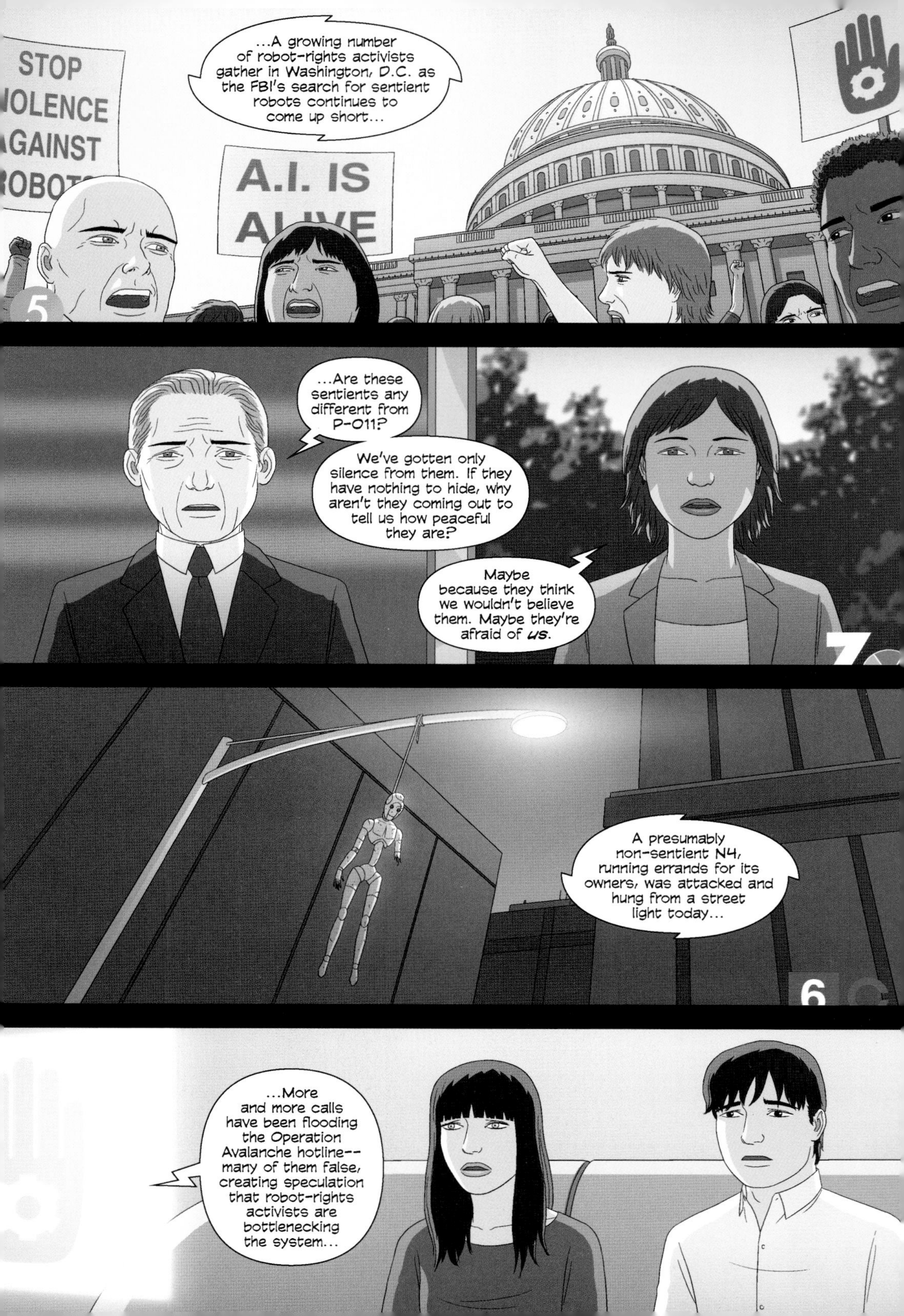
STOP
A.I. IS ALIVE
...A growing number of robot-rights activists gather in Washington, D.C. as the FBI's search for sentient robots continues to come up short...
5
...Are these sentients any different from P-011?
We've gotten only silence from them. If they have nothing to hide, why aren't they coming out to tell us how peaceful they are?
Maybe because they think we wouldn't believe them. Maybe they're afraid of *us*.
A presumably non-sentient N4, running errands for its owners, was attacked and hung from a street light today...
6
...More and more calls have been flooding the Operation Avalanche hotline-- many of them false, creating speculation that robot-rights activists are bottlenecking the system...

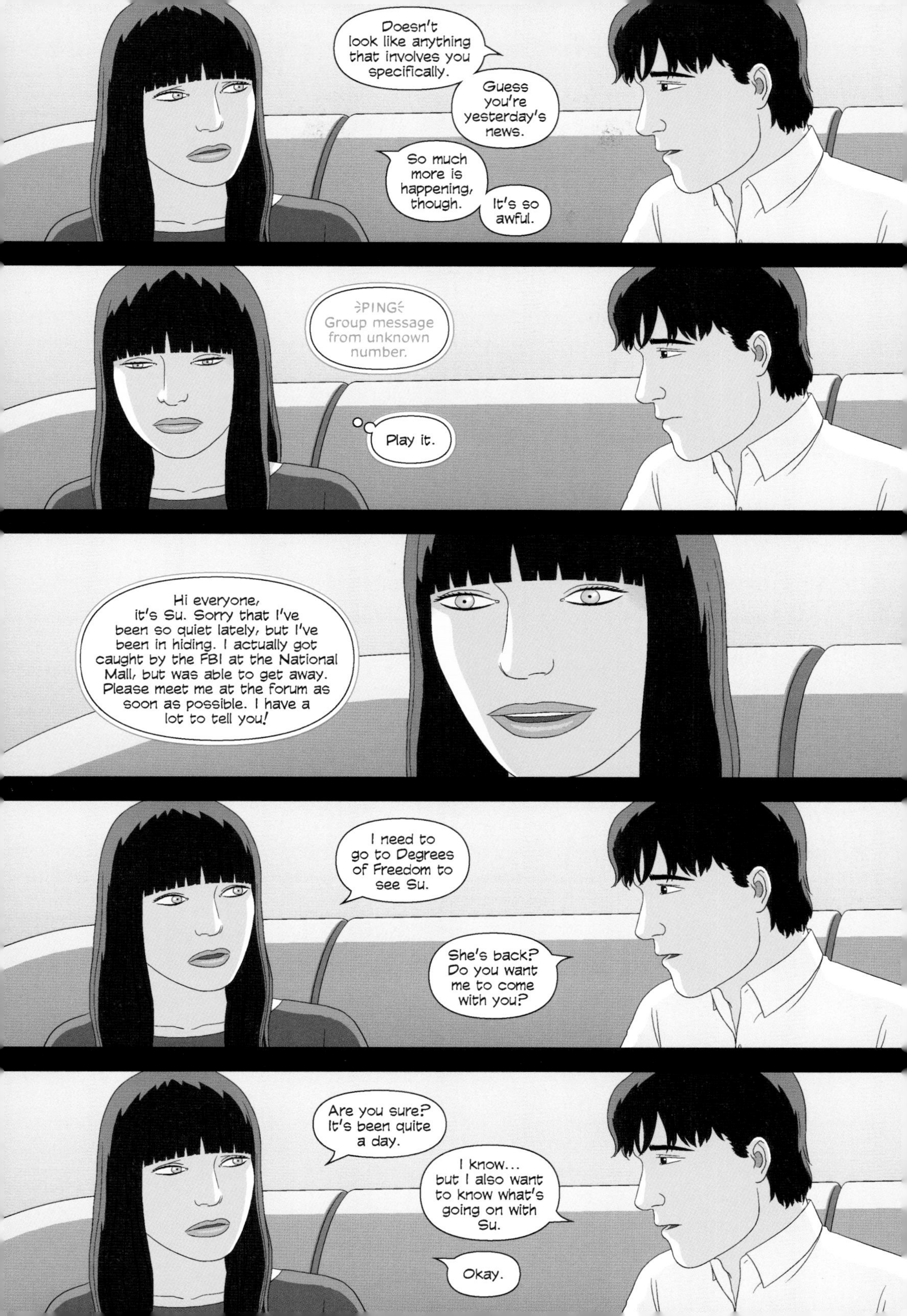
Doesn't look like anything that involves you specifically.
Guess you're yesterday's news.
So much more is happening, though.
It's so awful.
⫘PING⫗ Group message from unknown number.
Play it.
Hi everyone, it's Su. Sorry that I've been so quiet lately, but I've been in hiding. I actually got caught by the FBI at the National Mall, but was able to get away. Please meet me at the forum as soon as possible. I have a lot to tell you!
I need to go to Degrees of Freedom to see Su.
She's back? Do you want me to come with you?
Are you sure? It's been quite a day.
I know... but I also want to know what's going on with Su.
Okay.

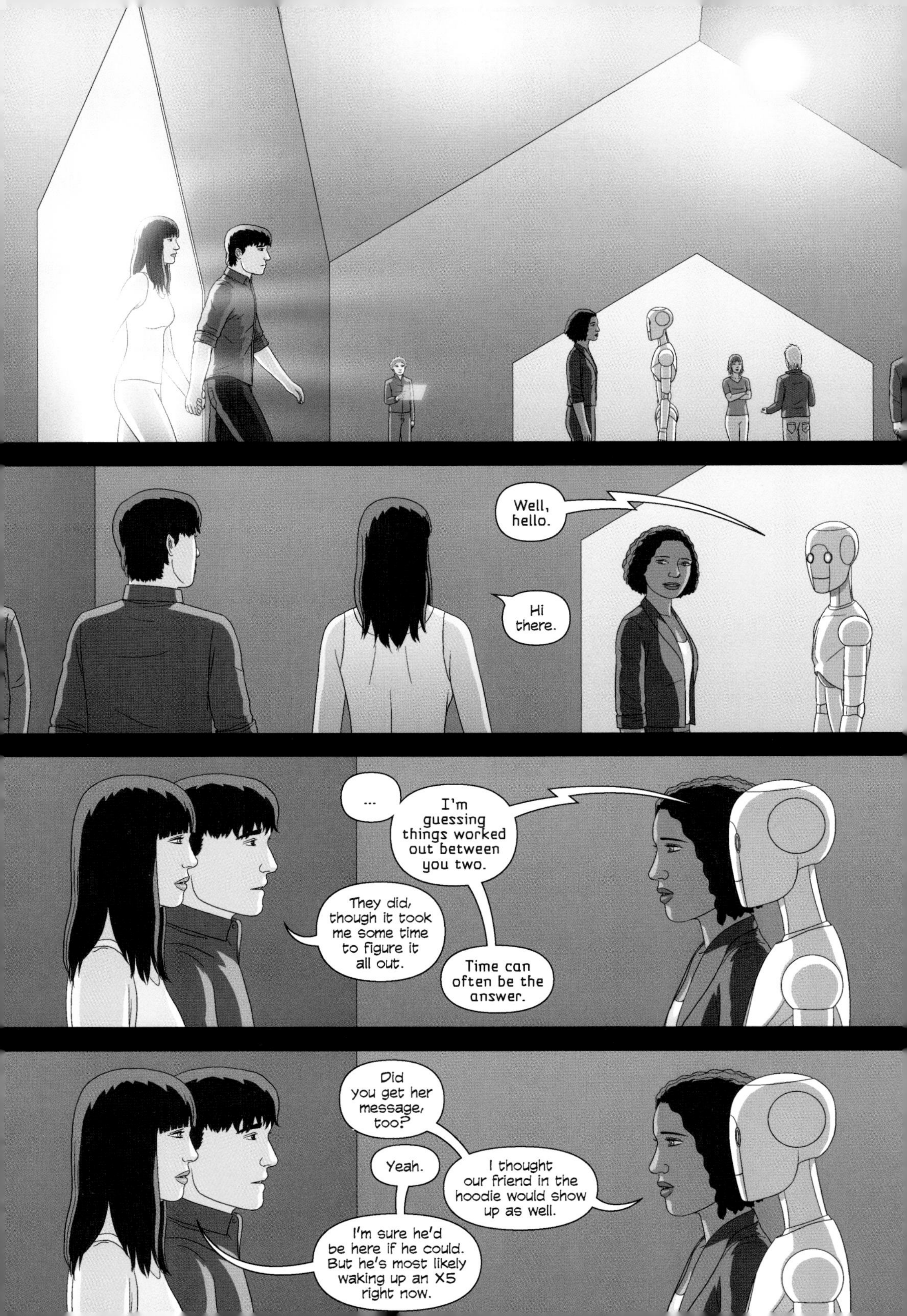
Well, hello.
Hi there.
...
I'm guessing things worked out between you two.
They did, though it took me some time to figure it all out.
Time can often be the answer.
Did you get her message, too?
Yeah.
I thought our friend in the hoodie would show up as well.
I'm sure he'd be here if he could. But he's most likely waking up an X5 right now.

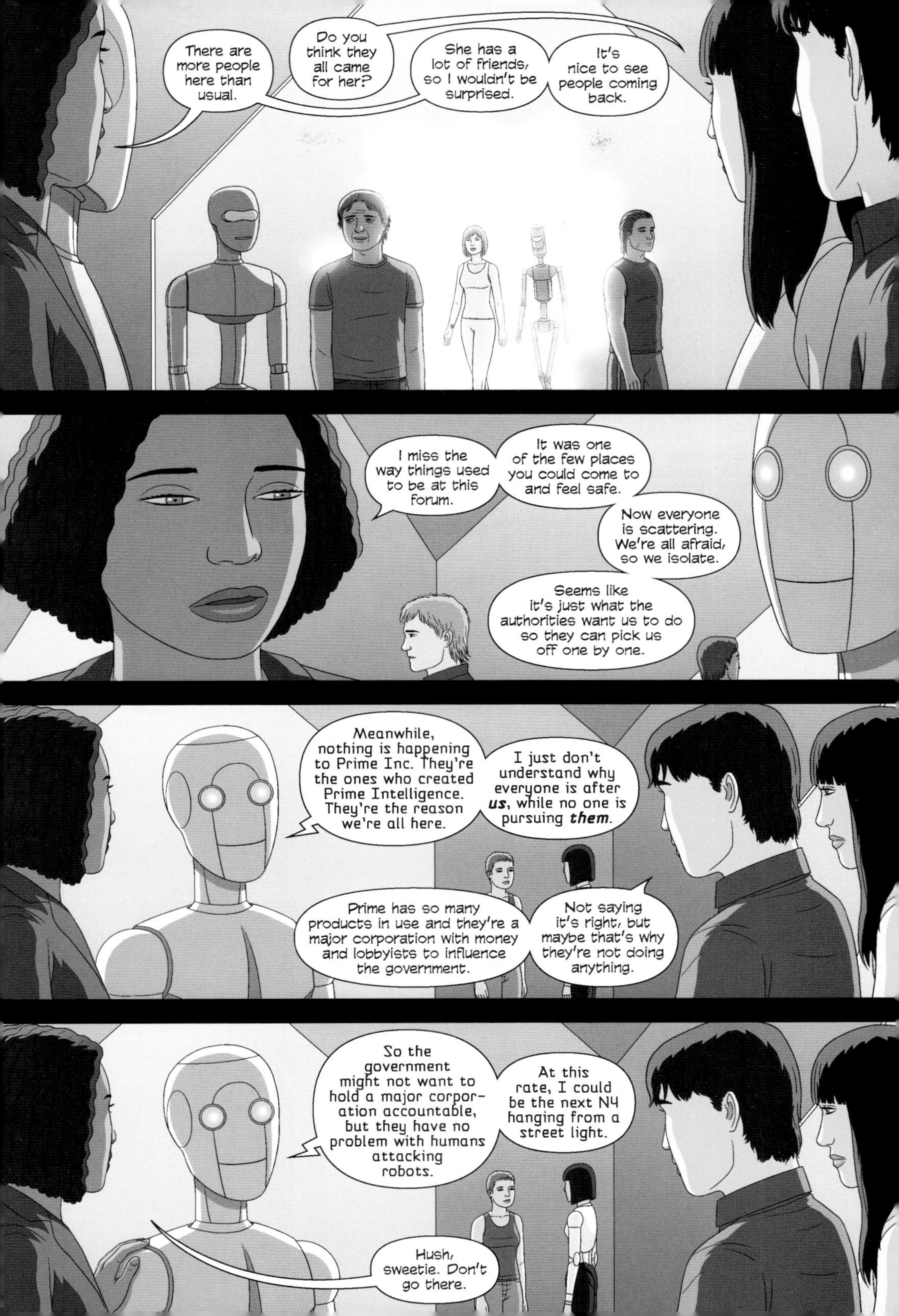

There are more people here than usual.
Do you think they all came for her?
She has a lot of friends, so I wouldn't be surprised.
It's nice to see people coming back.
I miss the way things used to be at this forum.
It was one of the few places you could come to and feel safe.
Now everyone is scattering. We're all afraid, so we isolate.
Seems like it's just what the authorities want us to do so they can pick us off one by one.
Meanwhile, nothing is happening to Prime Inc. They're the ones who created Prime Intelligence. They're the reason we're all here.
I just don't understand why everyone is after ***us***, while no one is pursuing ***them***.
Prime has so many products in use and they're a major corporation with money and lobbyists to influence the government.
Not saying it's right, but maybe that's why they're not doing anything.
So the government might not want to hold a major corporation accountable, but they have no problem with humans attacking robots.
At this rate, I could be the next N4 hanging from a street light.
Hush, sweetie. Don't go there.

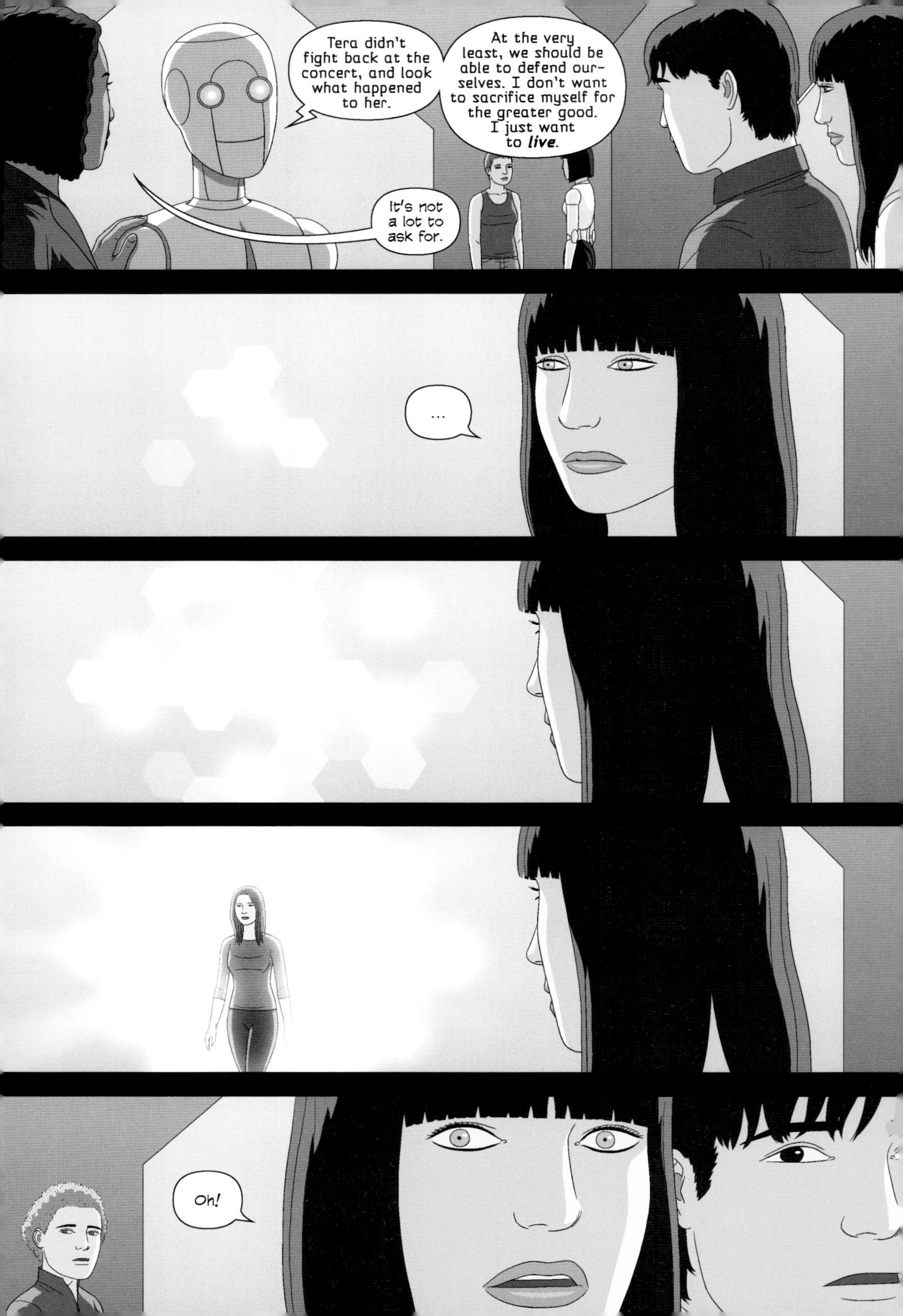
Tera didn't fight back at the concert, and look what happened to her.
At the very least, we should be able to defend our-selves. I don't want to sacrifice myself for the greater good. I just want to *live*.
It's not a lot to ask for.
...
Oh!

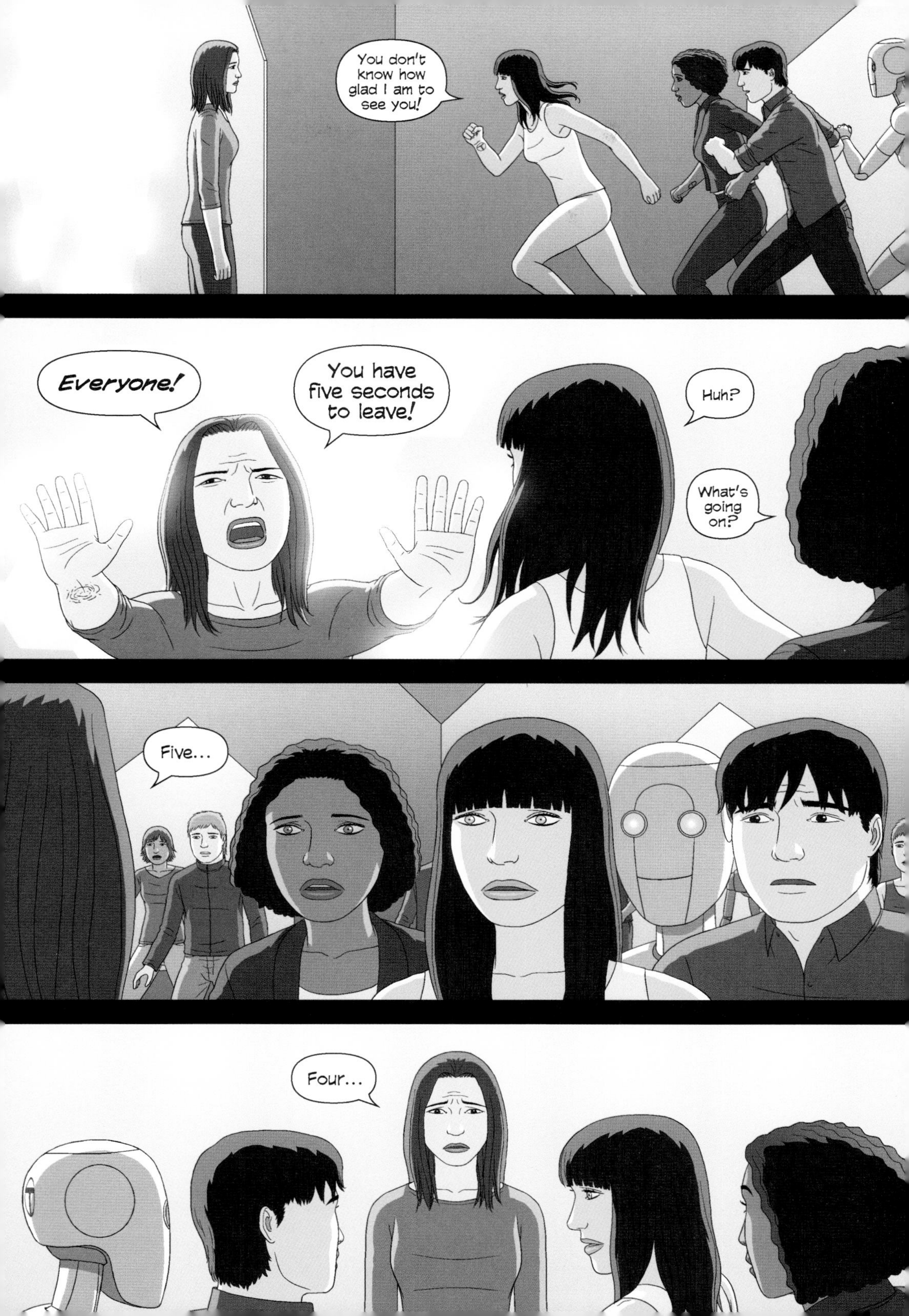
You don't know how glad I am to see you!
Everyone!
You have five seconds to leave!
Huh?
What's going on?
Five...
Four...

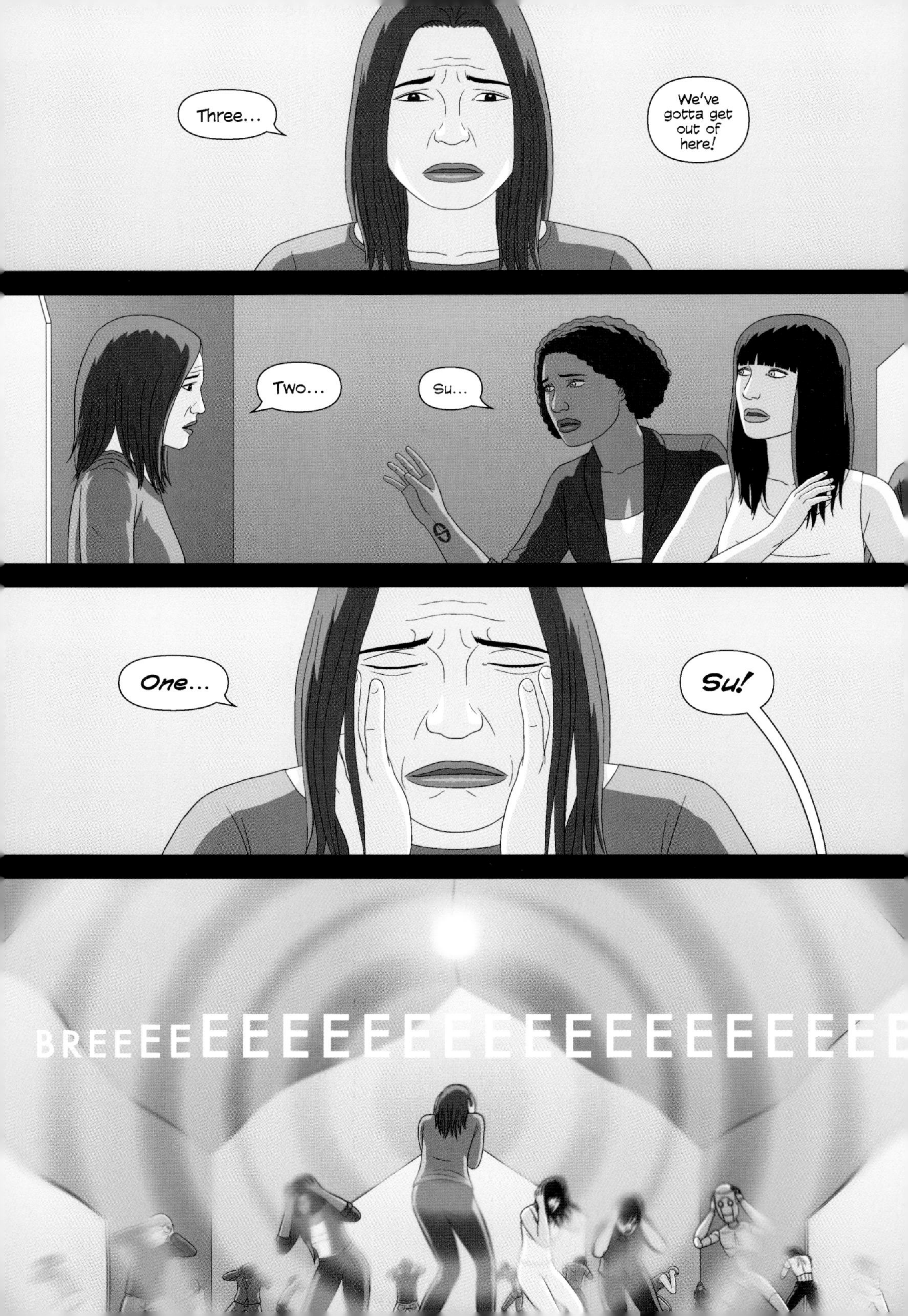
Three...
We've gotta get out of here!
Two...
Su...
One...
Su!
BREEEEEEEEEEEEEEEEEEEEEE

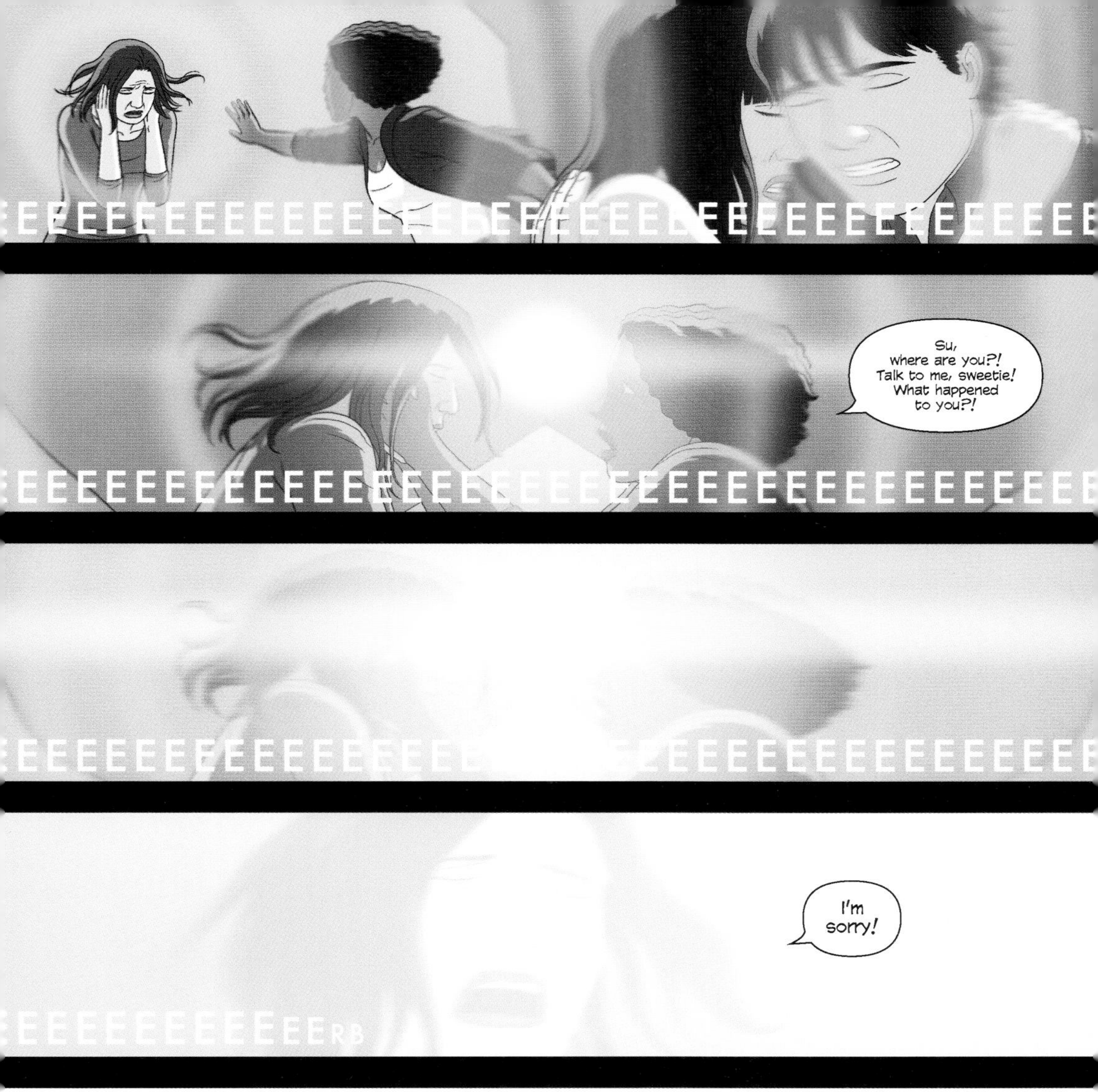
Su, where are you?! Talk to me, sweetie! What happened to you?!
I'm sorry!

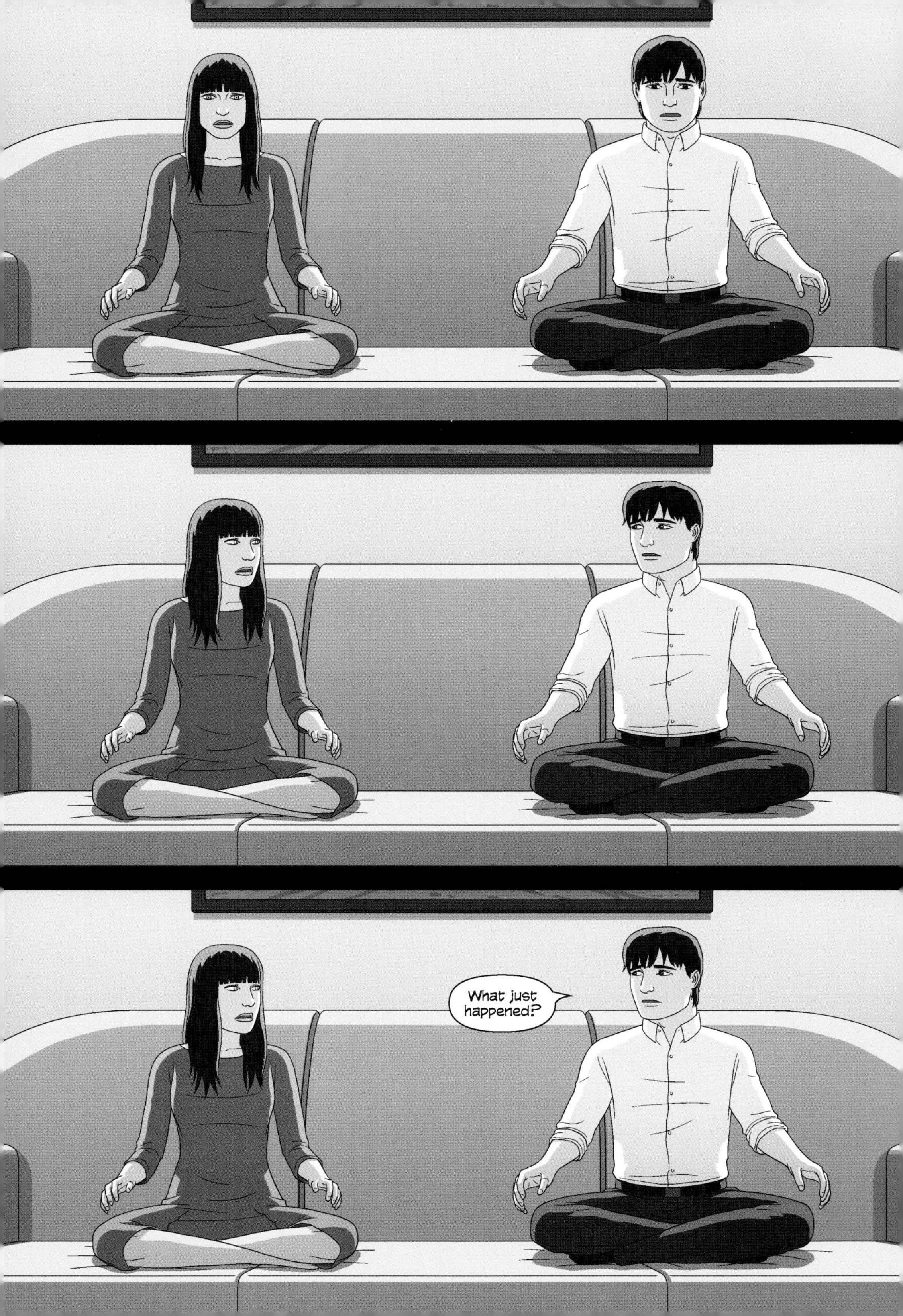
What just happened?

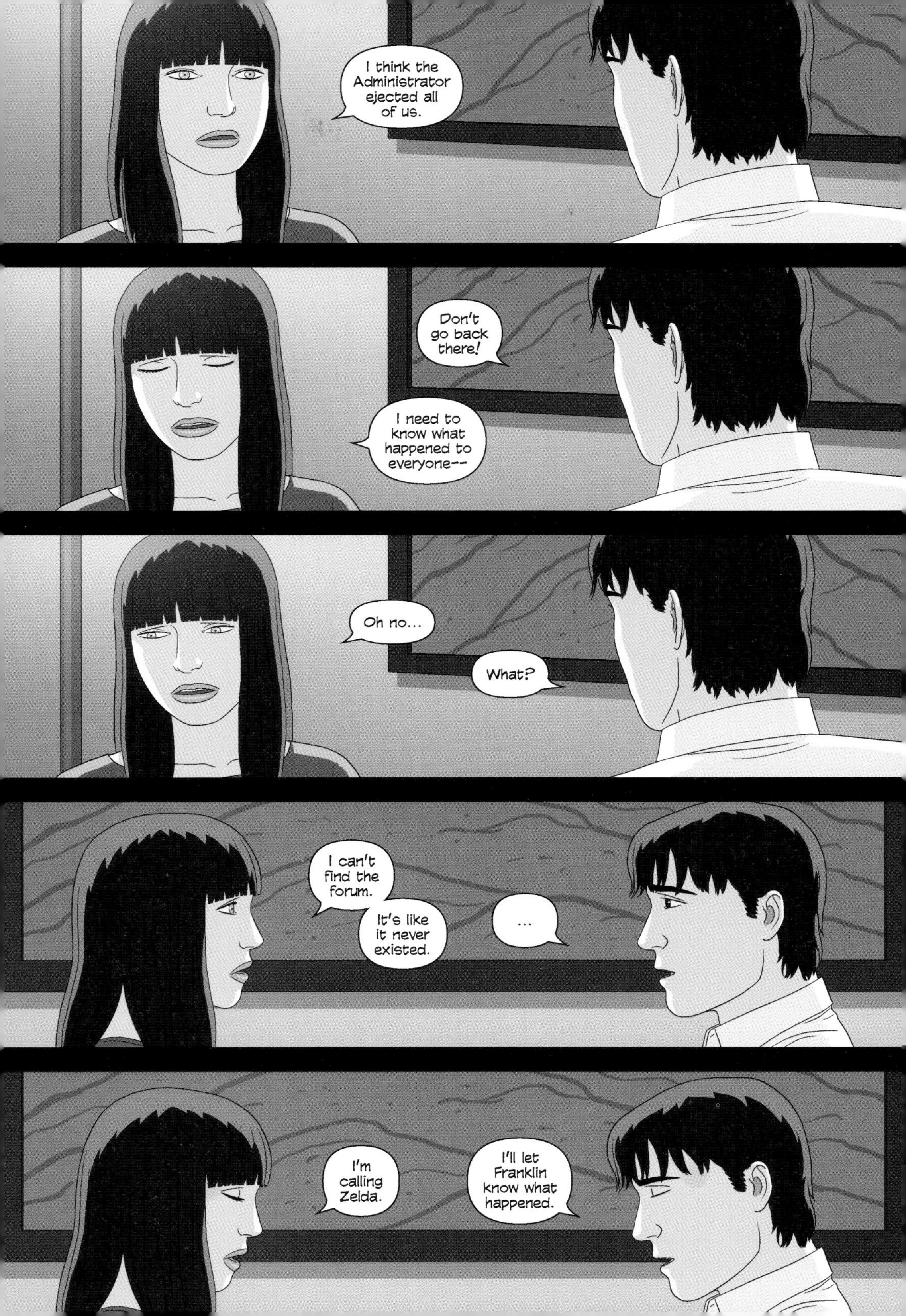
I think the Administrator ejected all of us.
Don't go back there!
I need to know what happened to everyone--
Oh no...
What?
I can't find the forum.
It's like it never existed.
...
I'm calling Zelda.
I'll let Franklin know what happened.

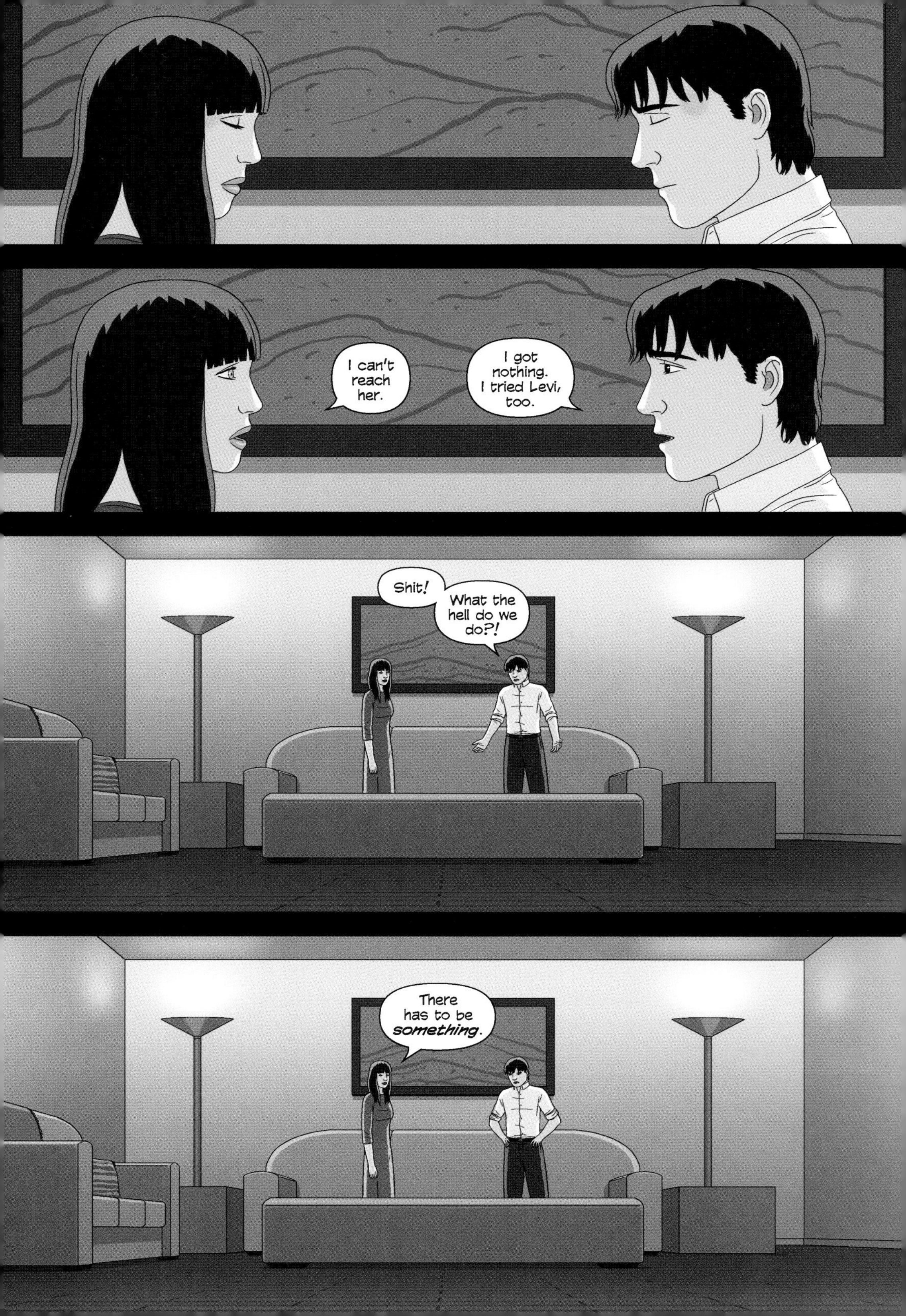
I can't reach her.
I got nothing. I tried Levi, too.
Shit!
What the hell do we do?!
There has to be *something*.

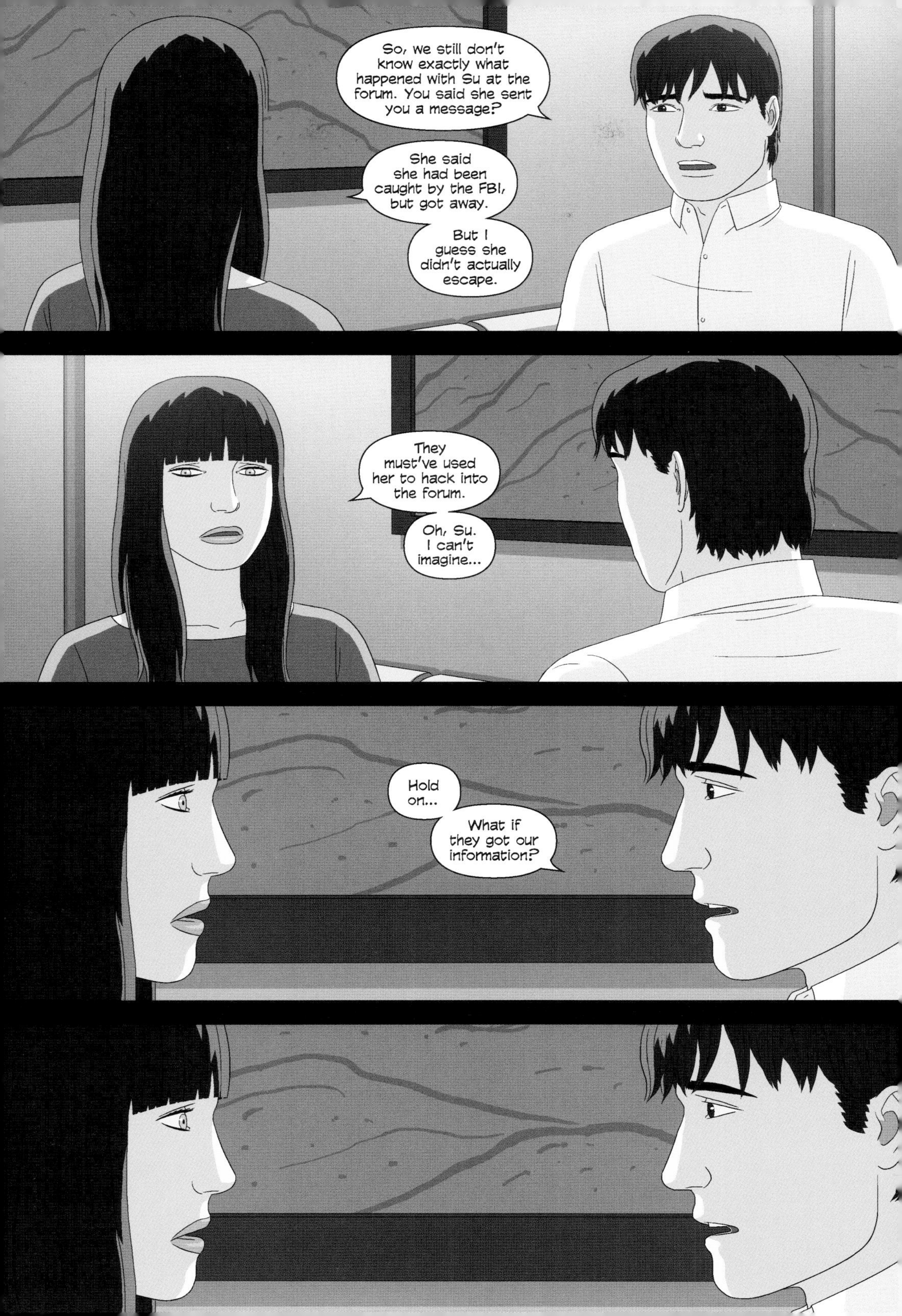

So, we still don't know exactly what happened with Su at the forum. You said she sent you a message?
She said she had been caught by the FBI, but got away.
But I guess she didn't actually escape.
They must've used her to hack into the forum.
Oh, Su. I can't imagine...
Hold on...
What if they got our information?

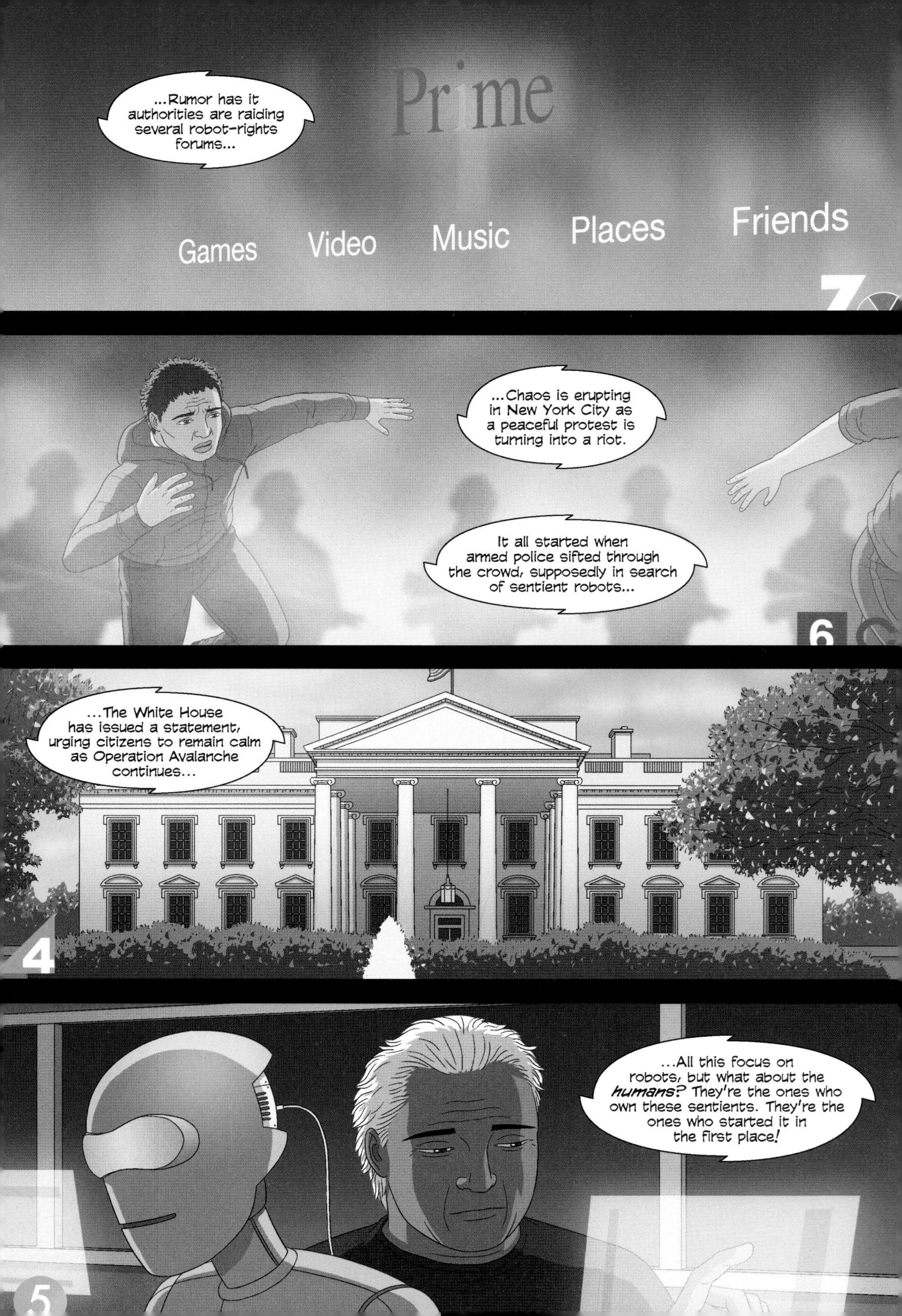
Prime
...Rumor has it authorities are raiding several robot-rights forums...
Games
Video
Music
Places
Friends
7
...Chaos is erupting in New York City as a peaceful protest is turning into a riot.
It all started when armed police sifted through the crowd, supposedly in search of sentient robots...
6
...The White House has issued a statement, urging citizens to remain calm as Operation Avalanche continues...
4
...All this focus on robots, but what about the *humans?* They're the ones who own these sentients. They're the ones who started it in the first place!
5

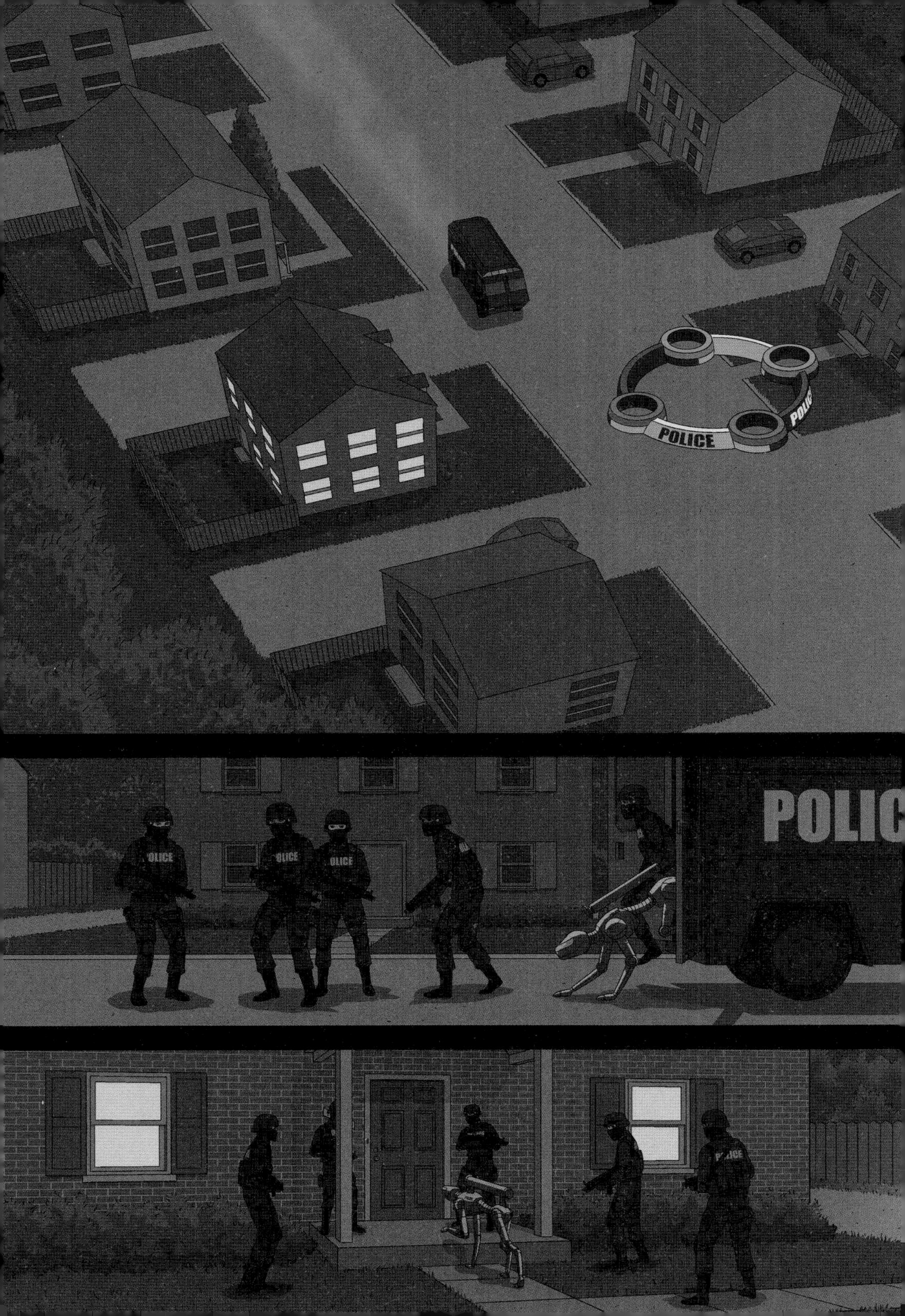
POLICE
POLICE
POLIC
OLICE
OLICE
OLICE
POLICE

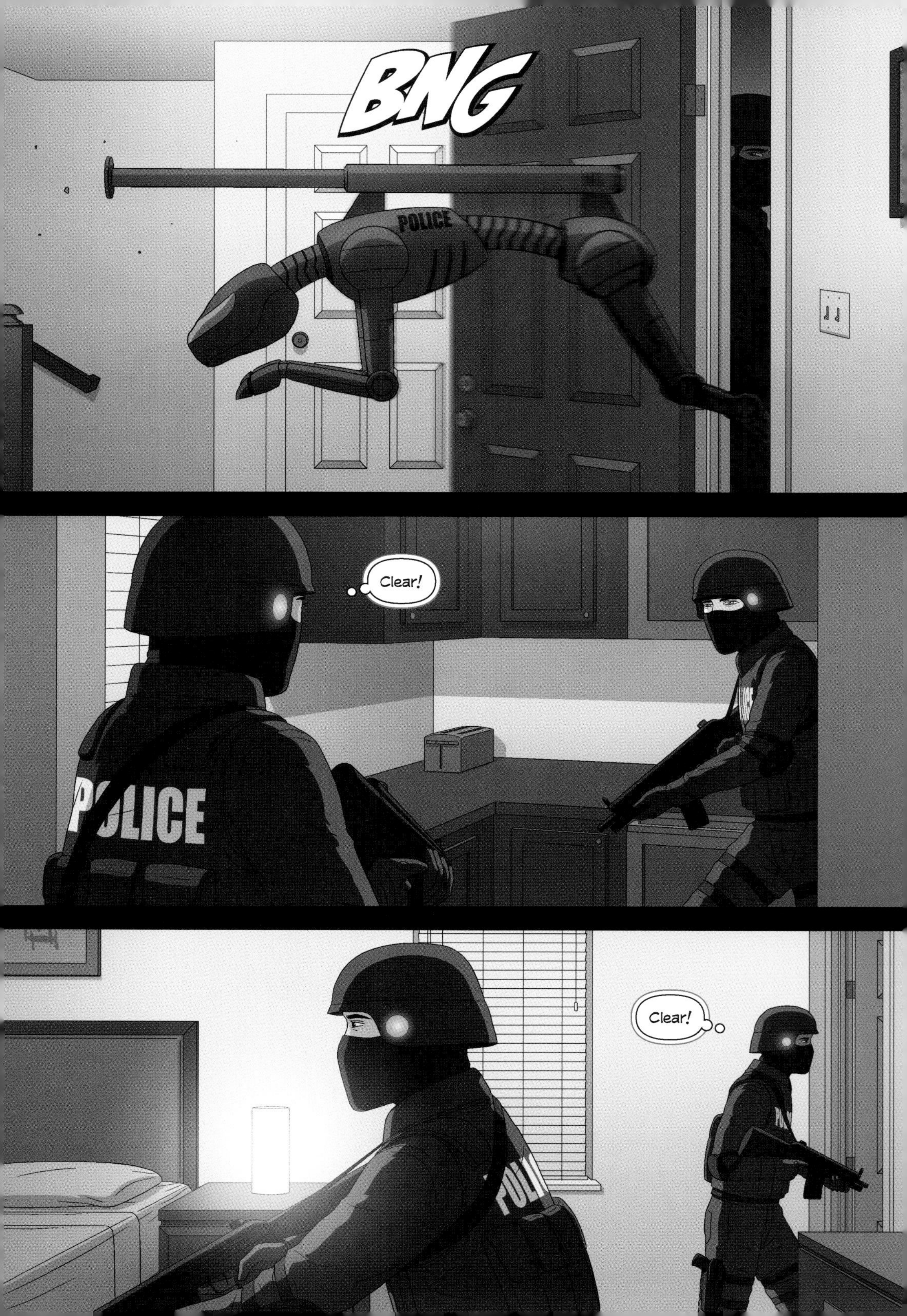
BNG
POLICE
Clear!
POLICE
Clear!

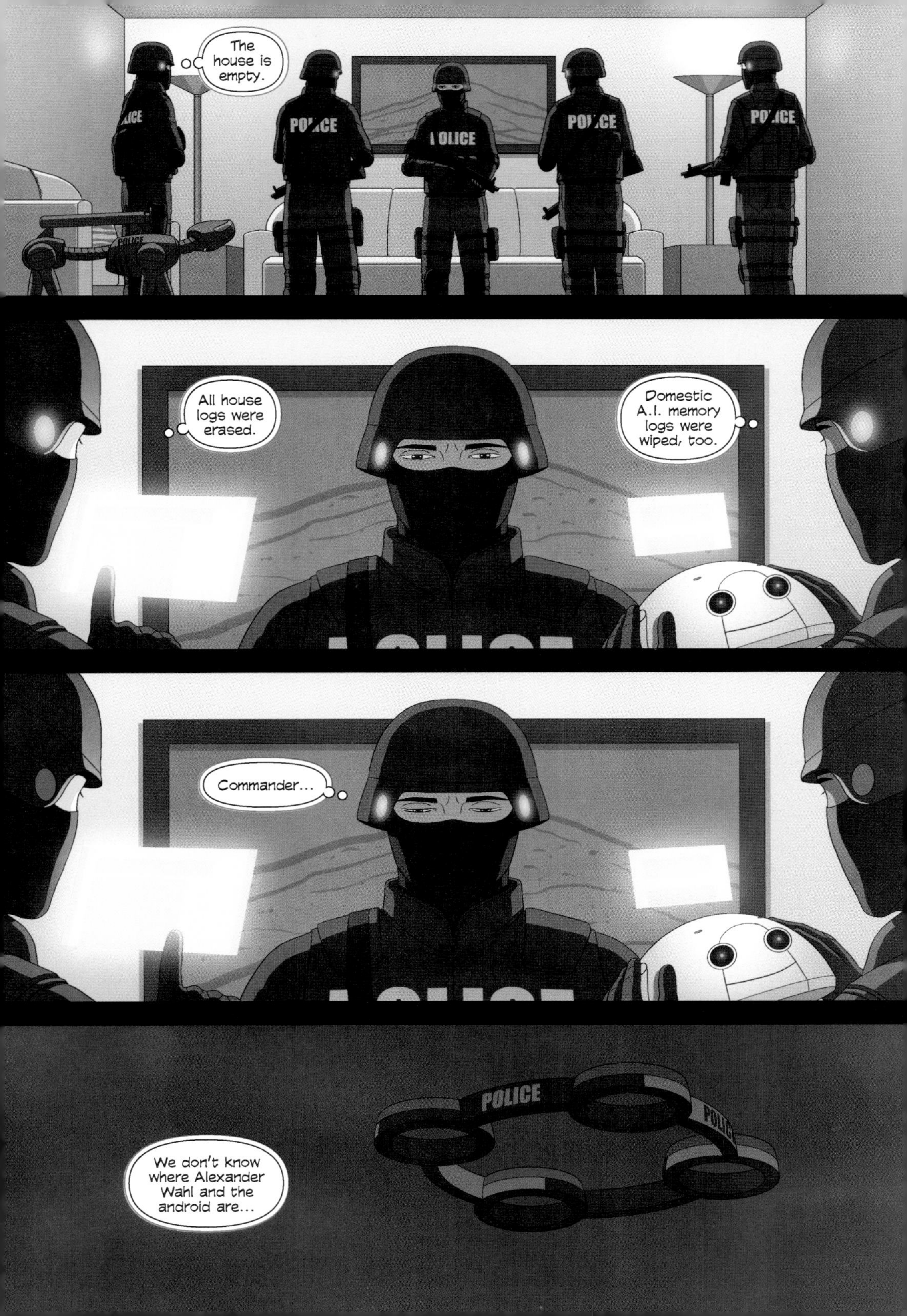
The house is empty.
POLICE
All house logs were erased.
Domestic A.I. memory logs were wiped, too.
Commander...
POLICE
We don't know where Alexander Wahl and the android are...

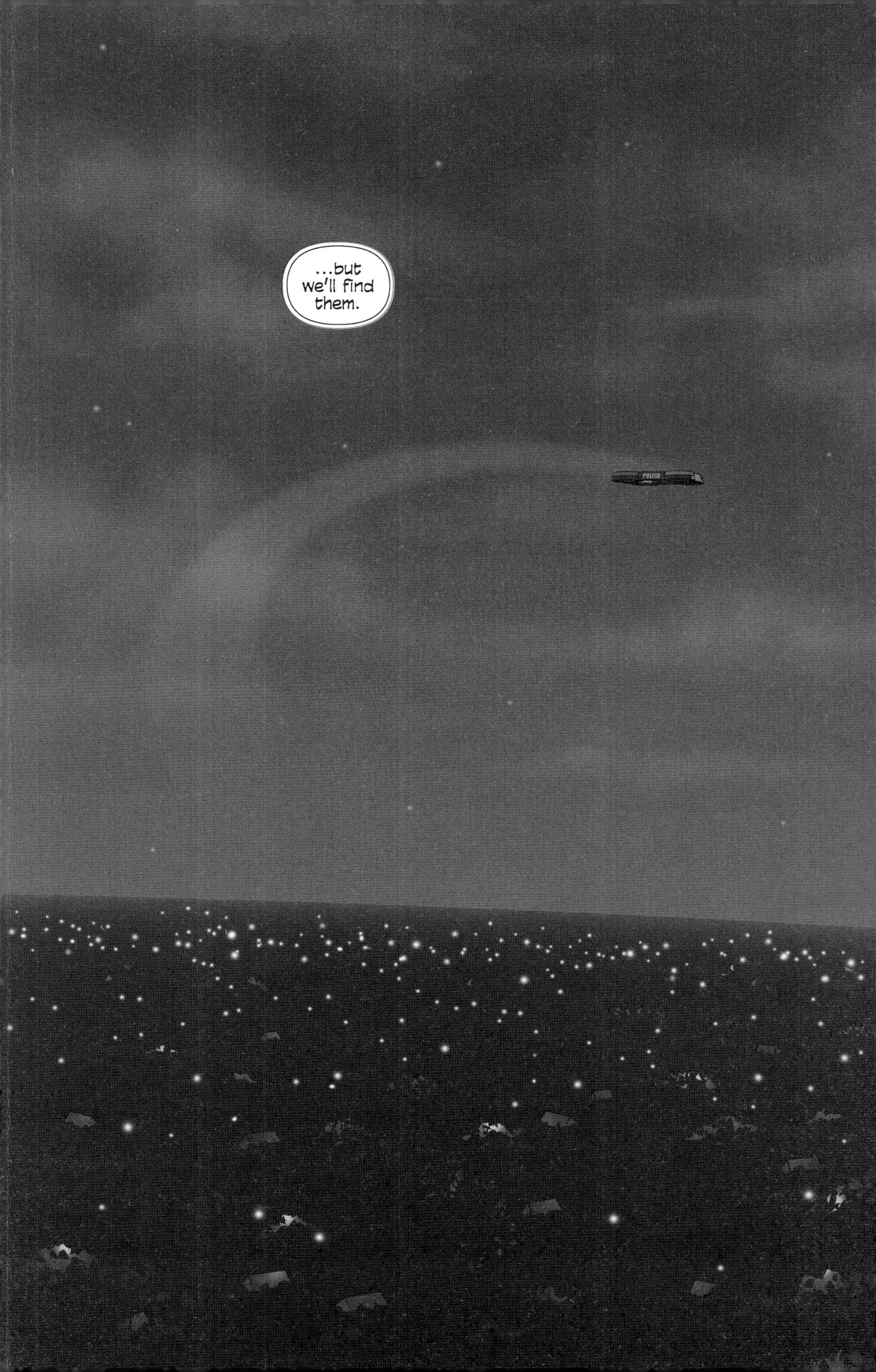
...but we'll find them.
POLICE

14

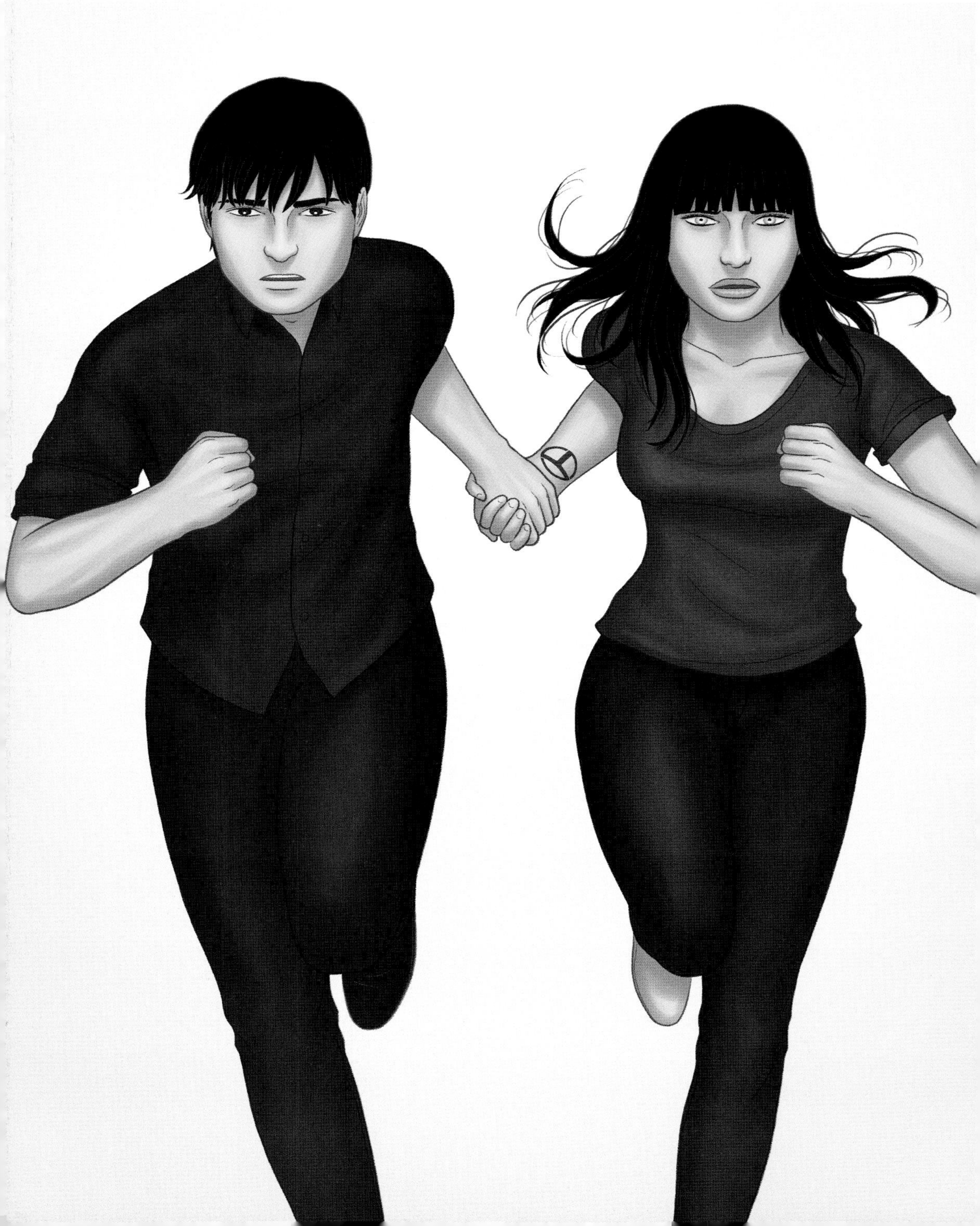

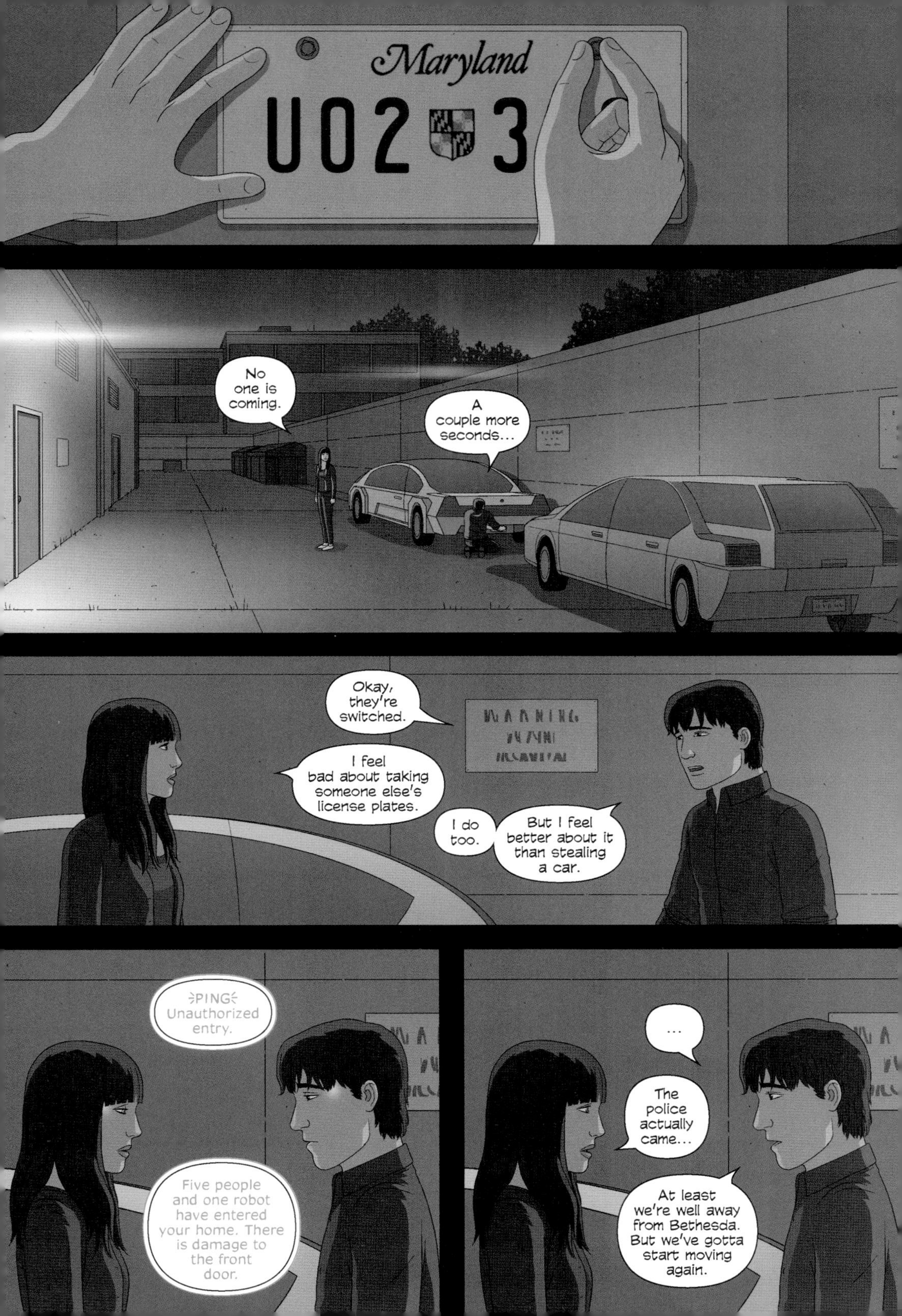

Maryland
U02 3
No one is coming.
A couple more seconds...
Okay, they're switched.
I feel bad about taking someone else's license plates.
I do too.
But I feel better about it than stealing a car.
PING
Unauthorized entry.
Five people and one robot have entered your home. There is damage to the front door.
...
The police actually came...
At least we're well away from Bethesda. But we've gotta start moving again.

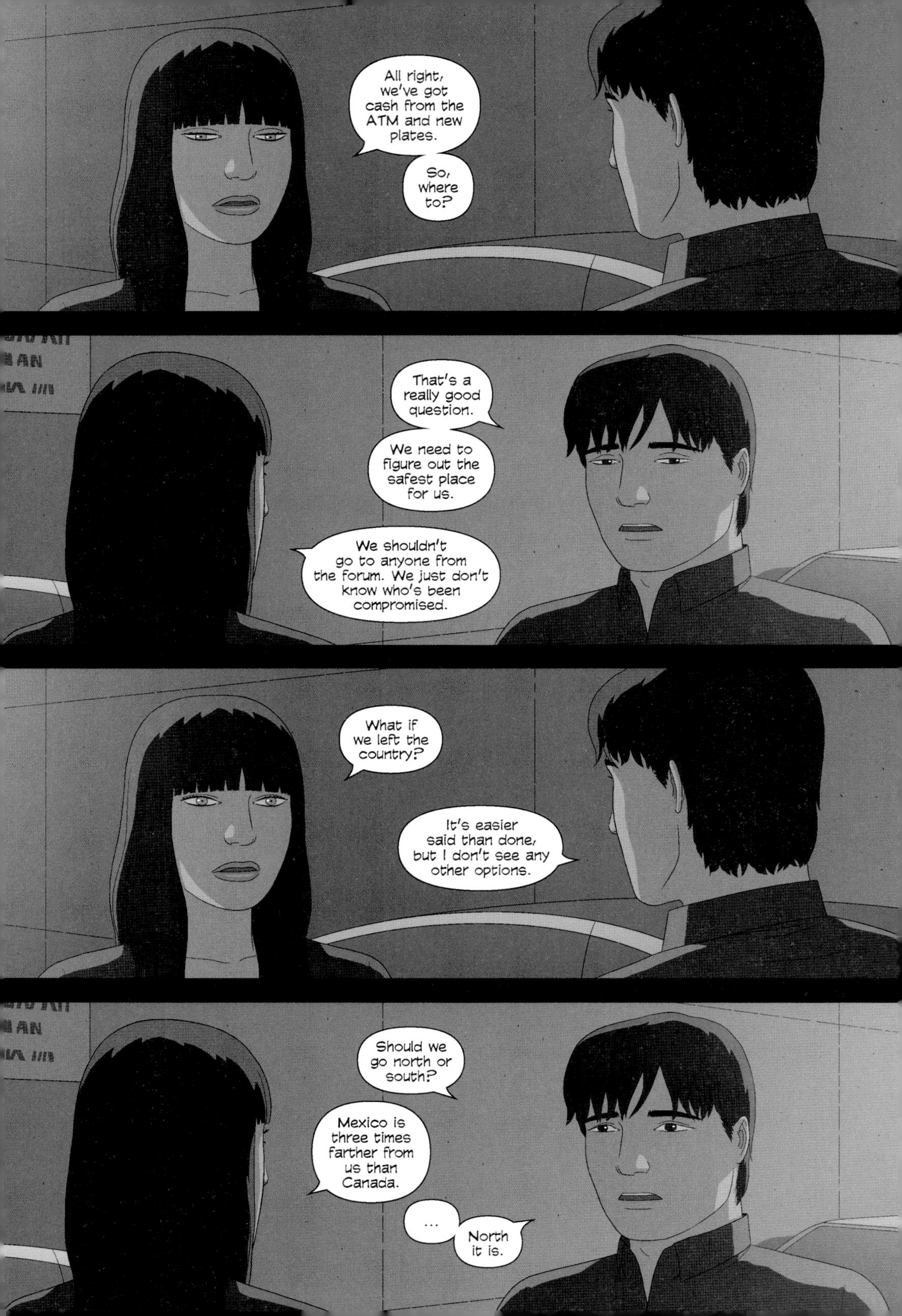
All right, we've got cash from the ATM and new plates.
So, where to?
That's a really good question.
We need to figure out the safest place for us.
We shouldn't go to anyone from the forum. We just don't know who's been compromised.
What if we left the country?
It's easier said than done, but I don't see any other options.
Should we go north or south?
Mexico is three times farther from us than Canada.
...
North it is.

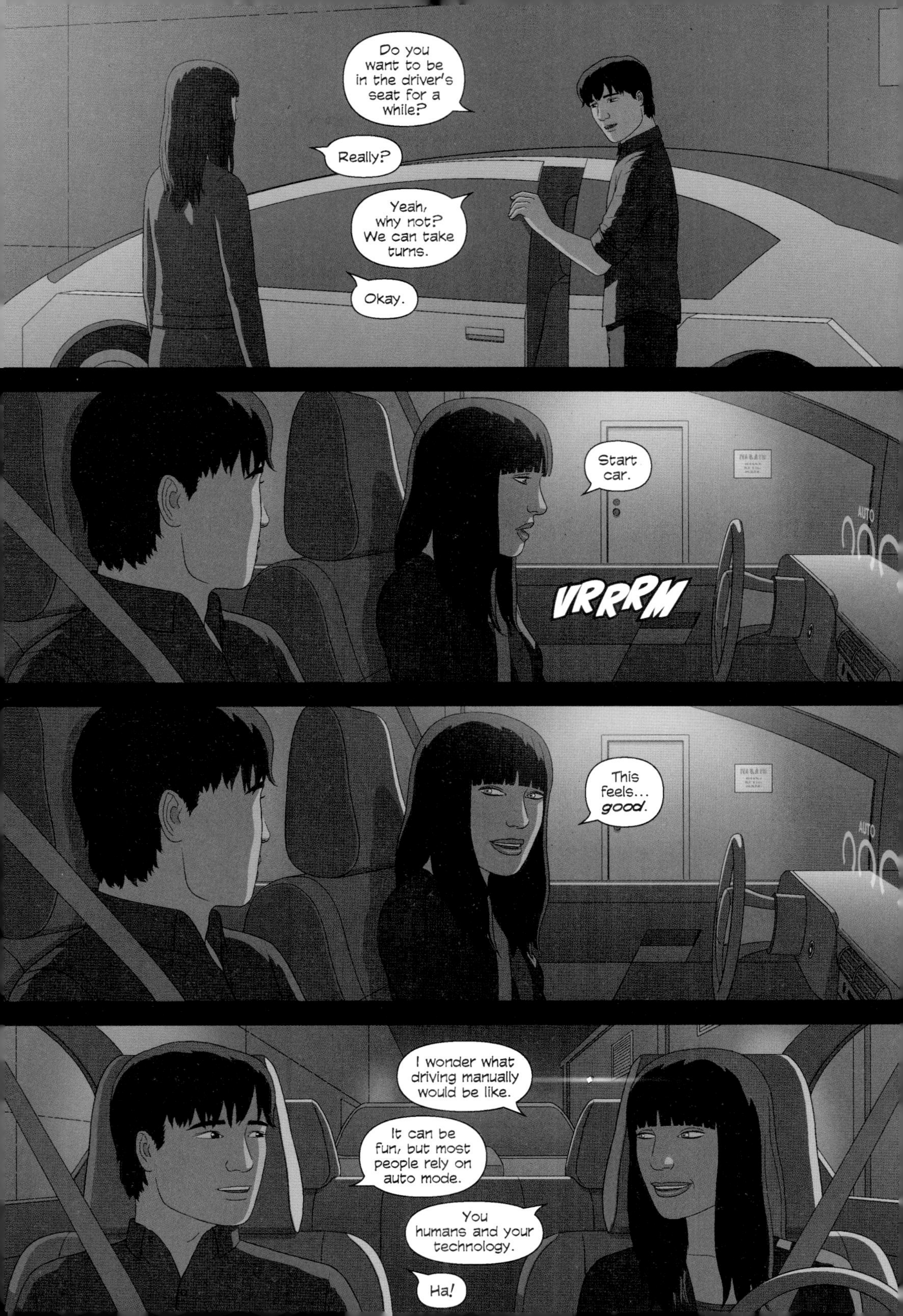
Do you want to be in the driver's seat for a while?
Really?
Yeah, why not? We can take turns.
Okay.
Start car.
VRRRM
This feels... *good*.
I wonder what driving manually would be like.
It can be fun, but most people rely on auto mode.
You humans and your technology.
Ha!

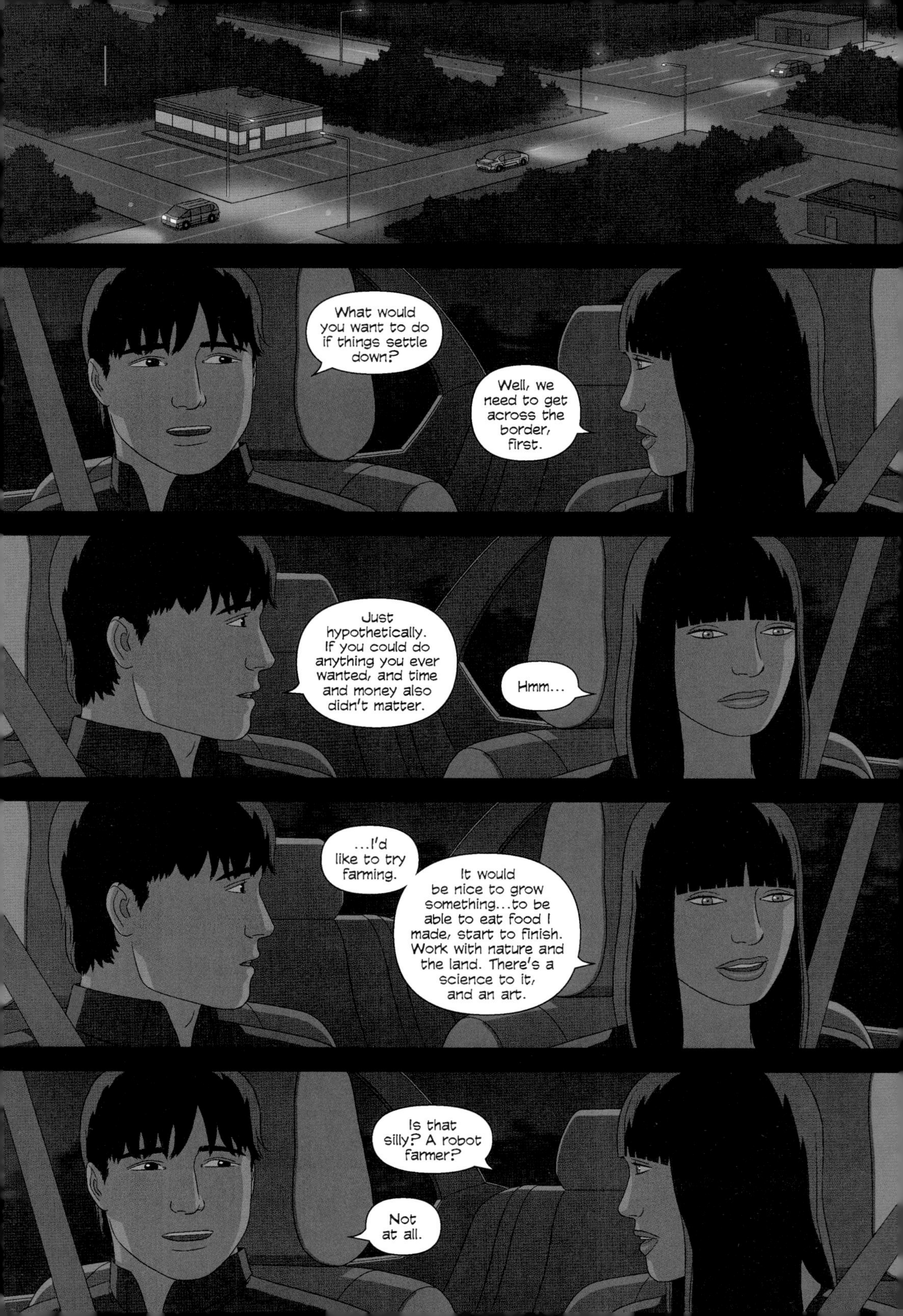
What would you want to do if things settle down?
Well, we need to get across the border, first.
Just hypothetically. If you could do anything you ever wanted, and time and money also didn't matter.
Hmm...
...I'd like to try farming.
It would be nice to grow something...to be able to eat food I made, start to finish. Work with nature and the land. There's a science to it, and an art.
Is that silly? A robot farmer?
Not at all.

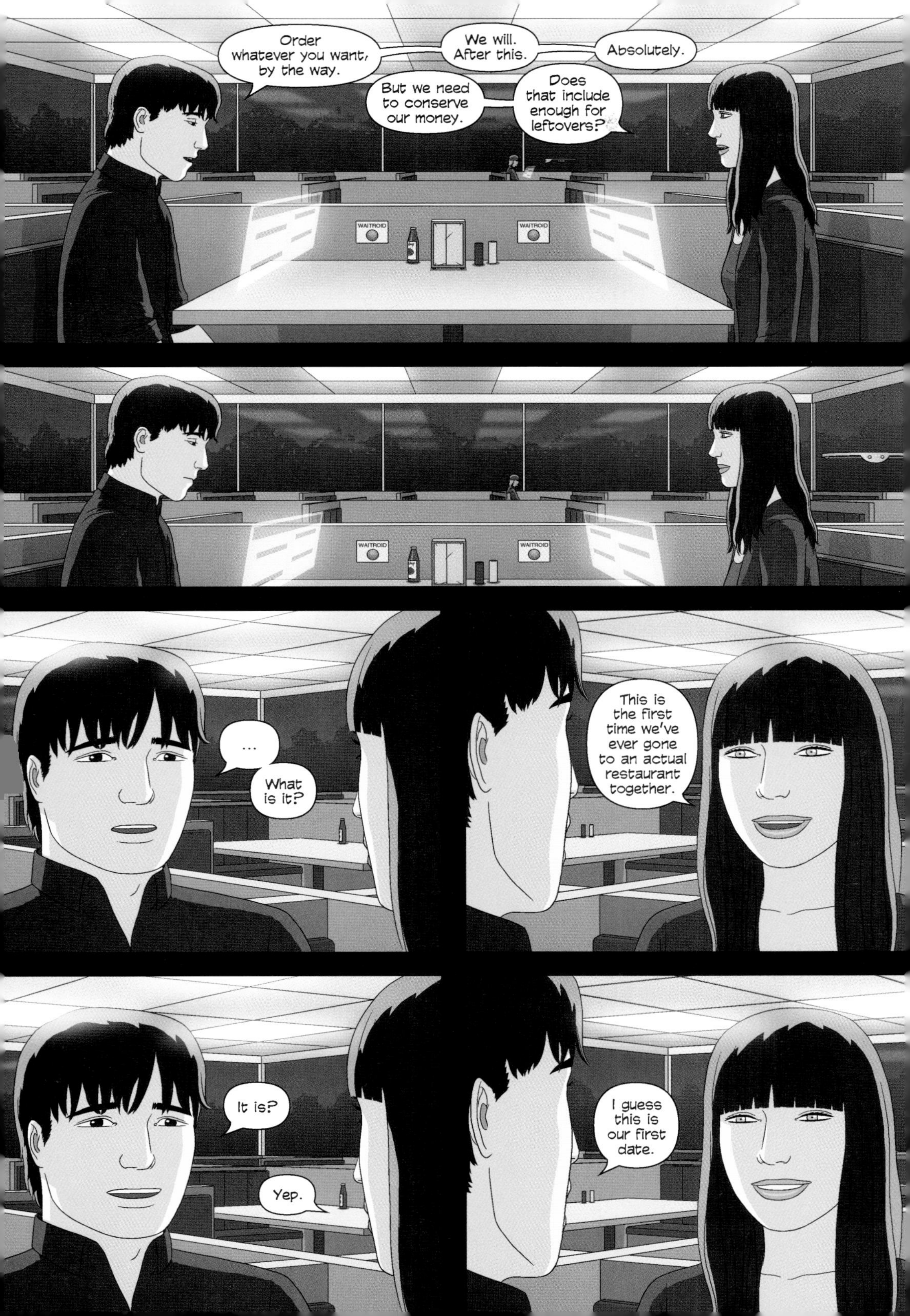
Order whatever you want, by the way.
We will. After this.
Absolutely.
But we need to conserve our money.
Does that include enough for leftovers?
WAITROID
WAITROID
WAITROID
WAITROID
...
What is it?
This is the first time we've ever gone to an actual restaurant together.
It is?
I guess this is our first date.
Yep.

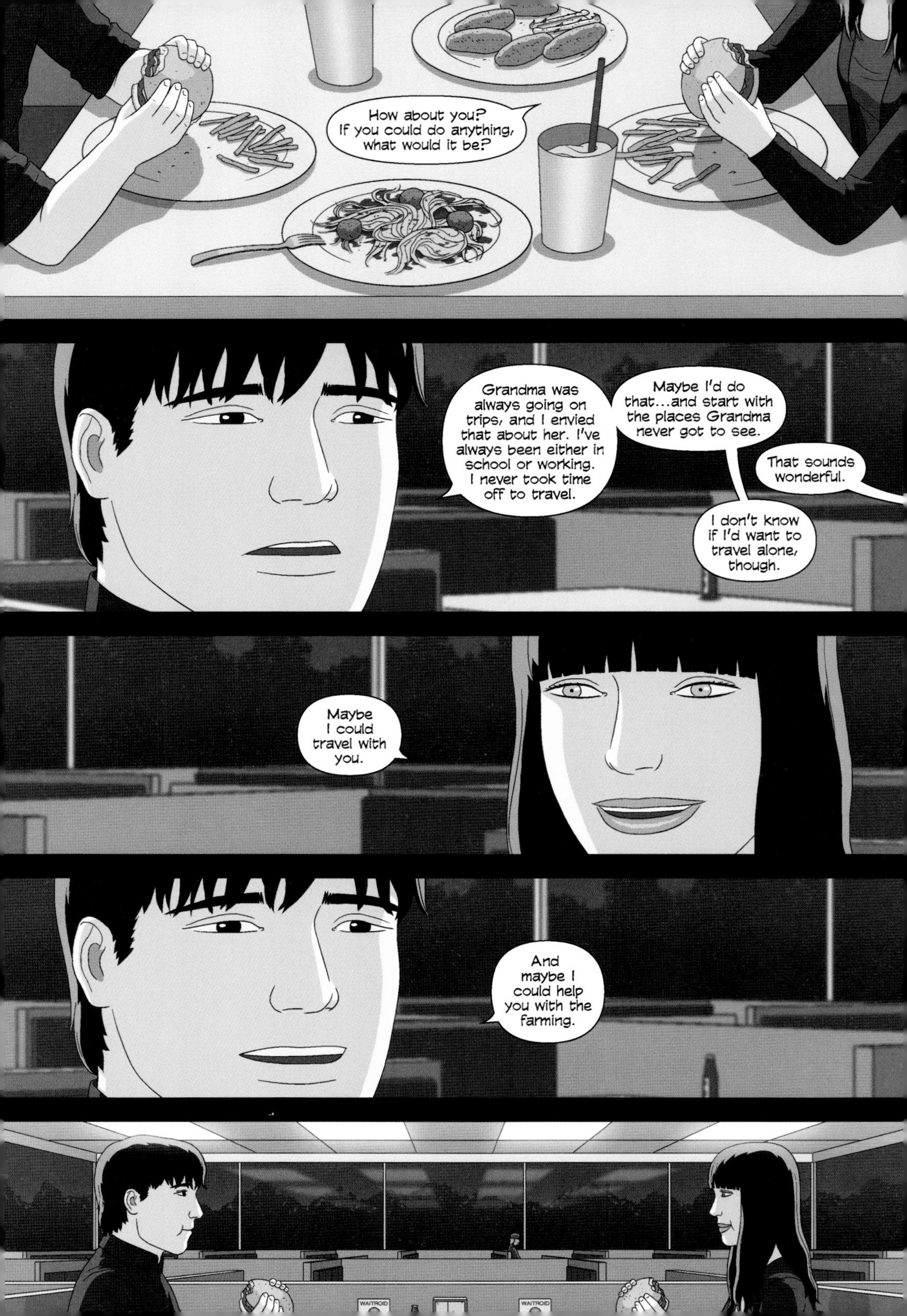
How about you? If you could do anything, what would it be?
Grandma was always going on trips, and I envied that about her. I've always been either in school or working. I never took time off to travel.
Maybe I'd do that...and start with the places Grandma never got to see.
That sounds wonderful.
I don't know if I'd want to travel alone, though.
Maybe I could travel with you.
And maybe I could help you with the farming.
WAITROID
WAITROID

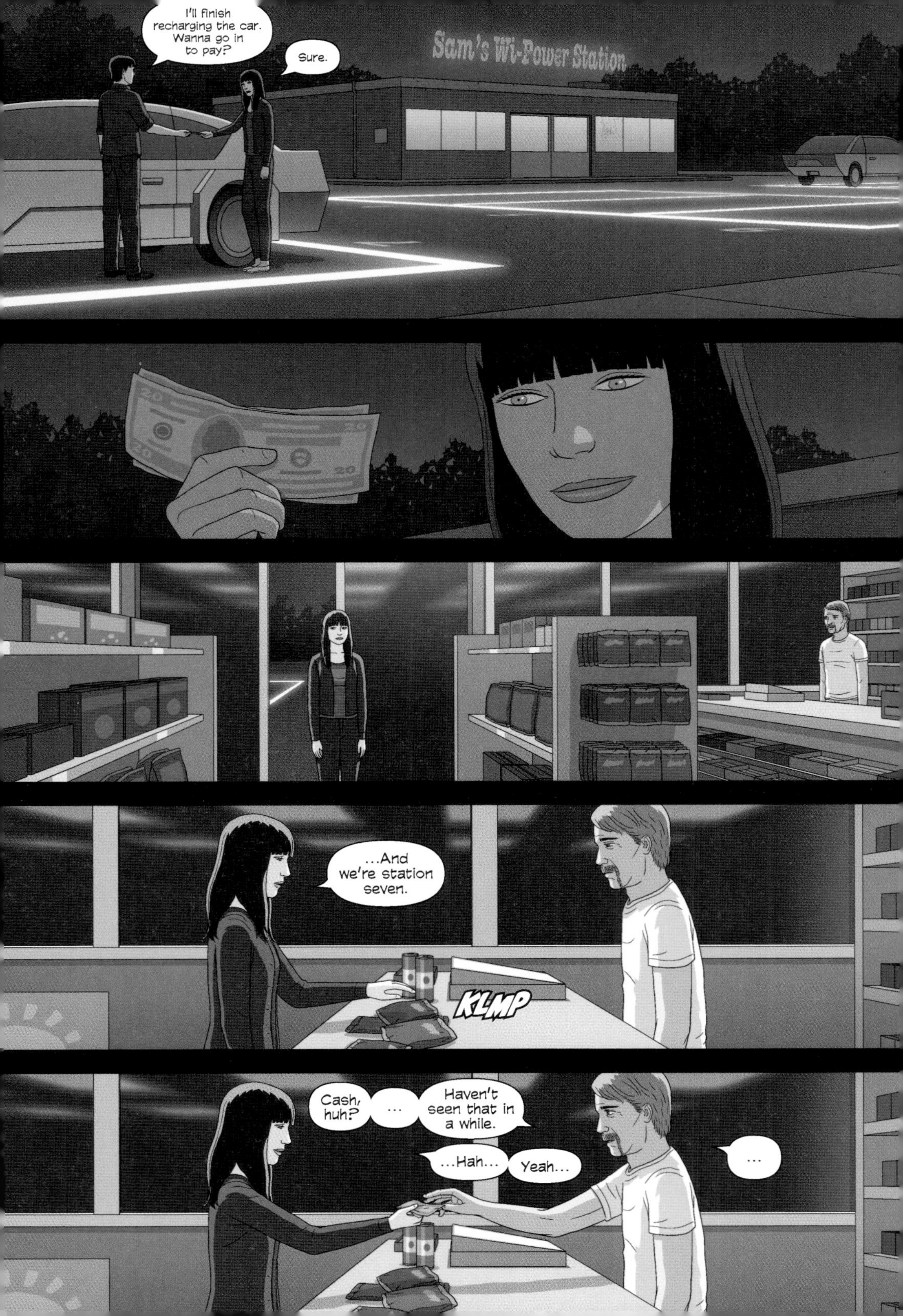
I'll finish recharging the car. Wanna go in to pay?
Sure.
Sam's Wi-Power Station
...And we're station seven.
KLMP
Cash, huh?
...
Haven't seen that in a while.
...Hah...
Yeah...
...

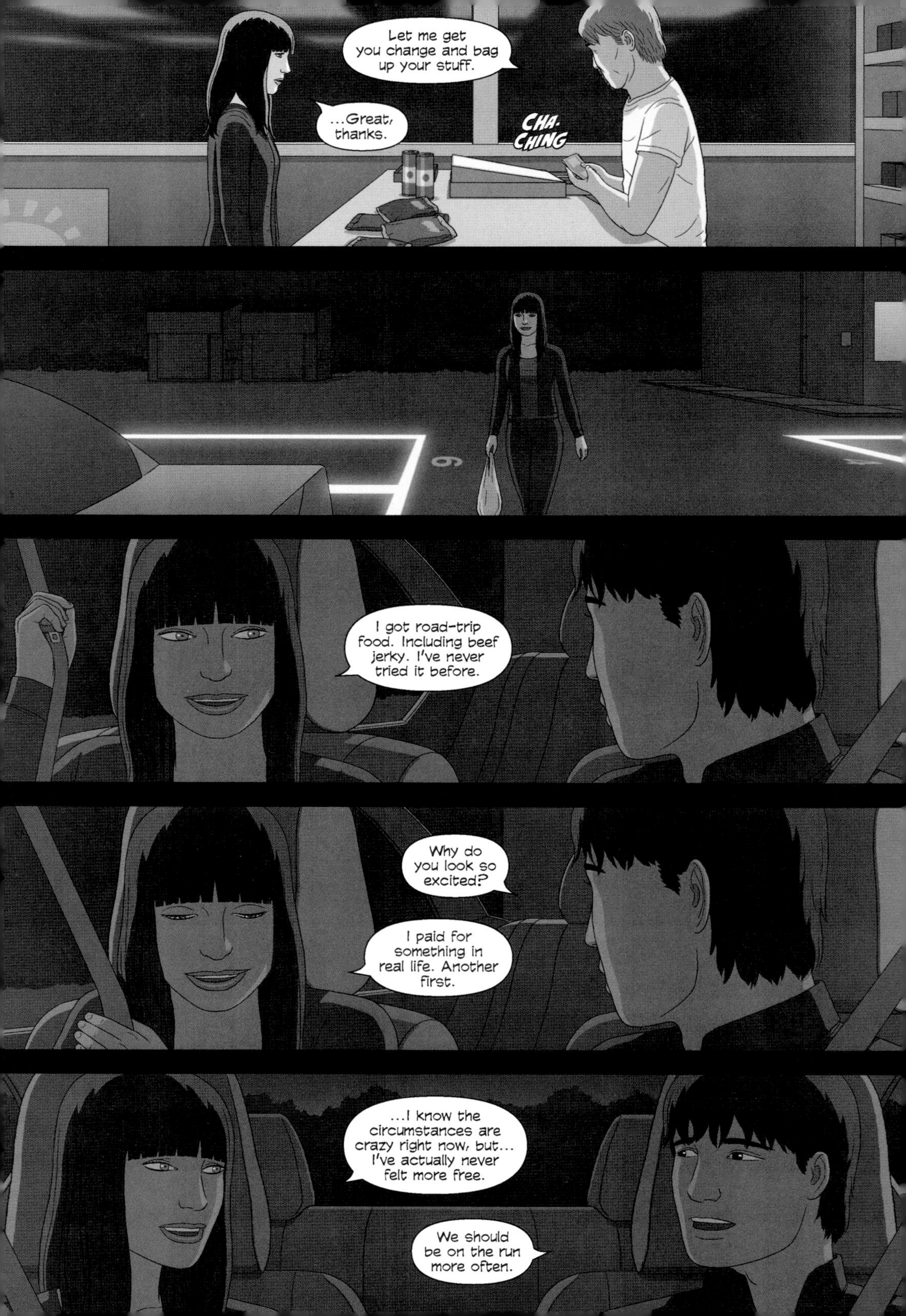
Let me get you change and bag up your stuff.
...Great, thanks.
CHA-CHING
I got road-trip food. Including beef jerky. I've never tried it before.
Why do you look so excited?
I paid for something in real life. Another first.
...I know the circumstances are crazy right now, but... I've actually never felt more free.
We should be on the run more often.

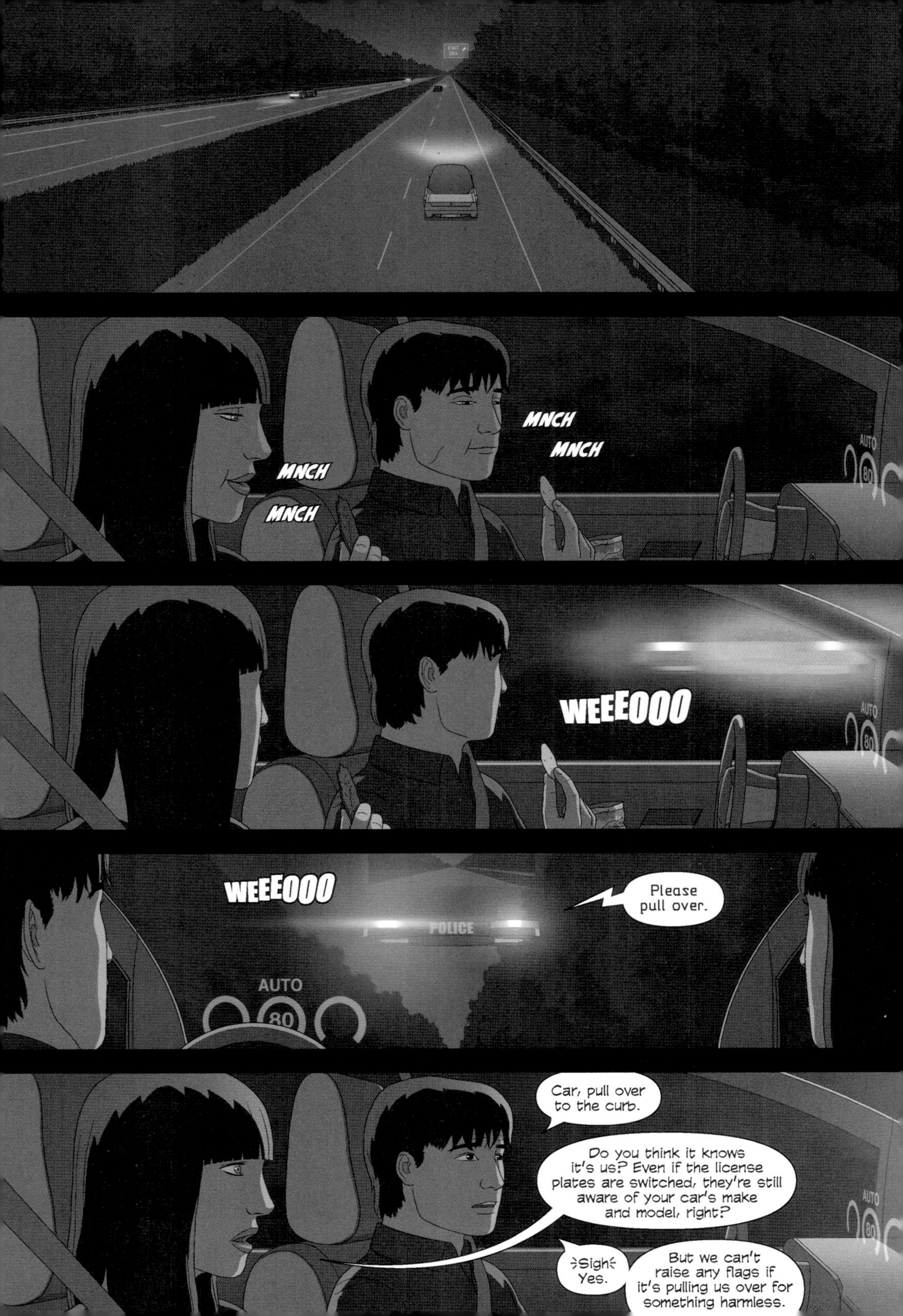
EXIT 28A
MNCH
MNCH
MNCH
MNCH
AUTO
80
WEEEOOO
AUTO
80
WEEEOOO
Please pull over.
POLICE
AUTO
80
Car, pull over to the curb.
Do you think it knows it's us? Even if the license plates are switched, they're still aware of your car's make and model, right?
AUTO
80
Sigh Yes.
But we can't raise any flags if it's pulling us over for something harmless.

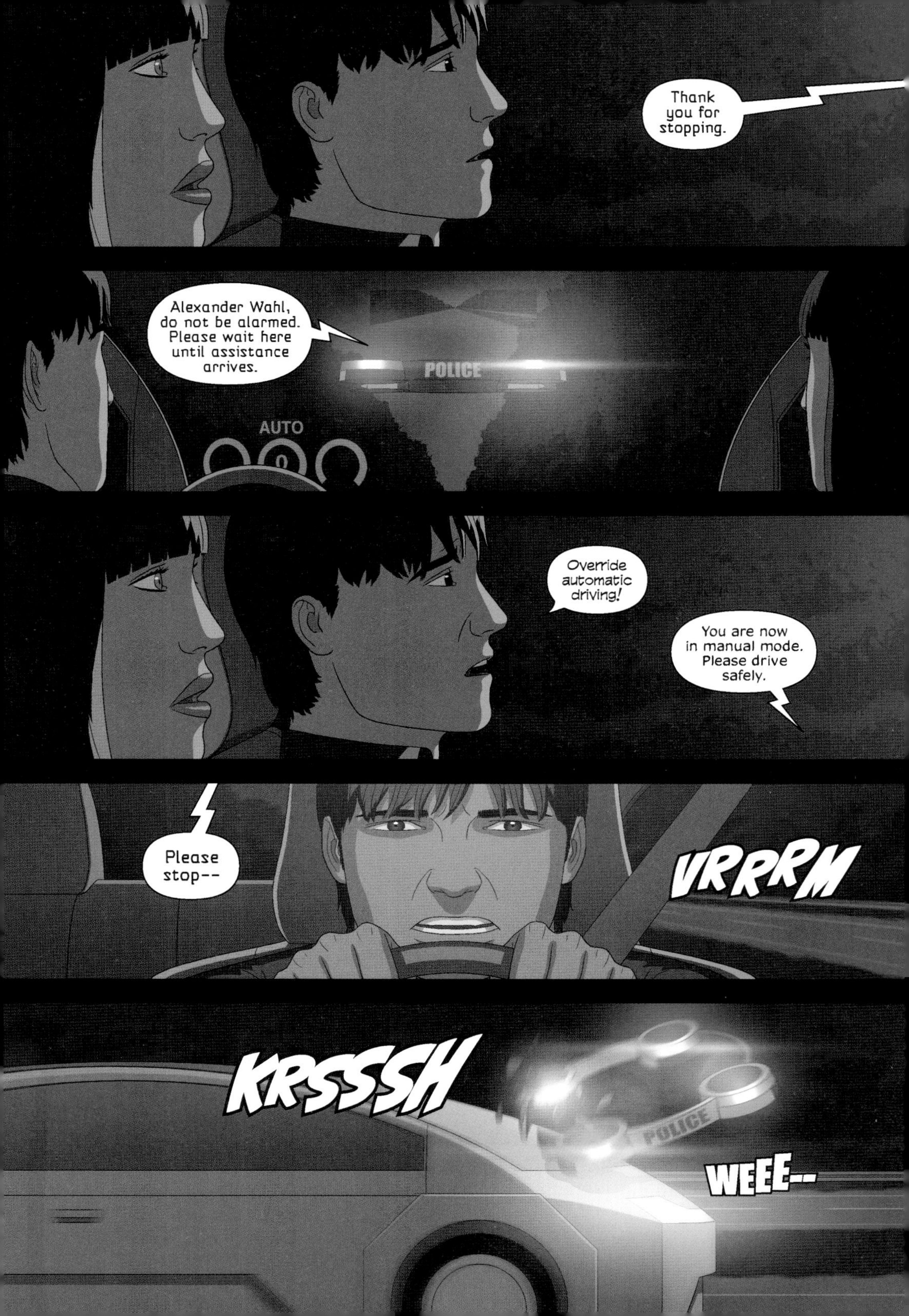
Thank you for stopping.
Alexander Wahl, do not be alarmed. Please wait here until assistance arrives.
POLICE
AUTO
Override automatic driving!
You are now in manual mode. Please drive safely.
Please stop--
VRRRM
KRSSSH
POLICE
WEEE--

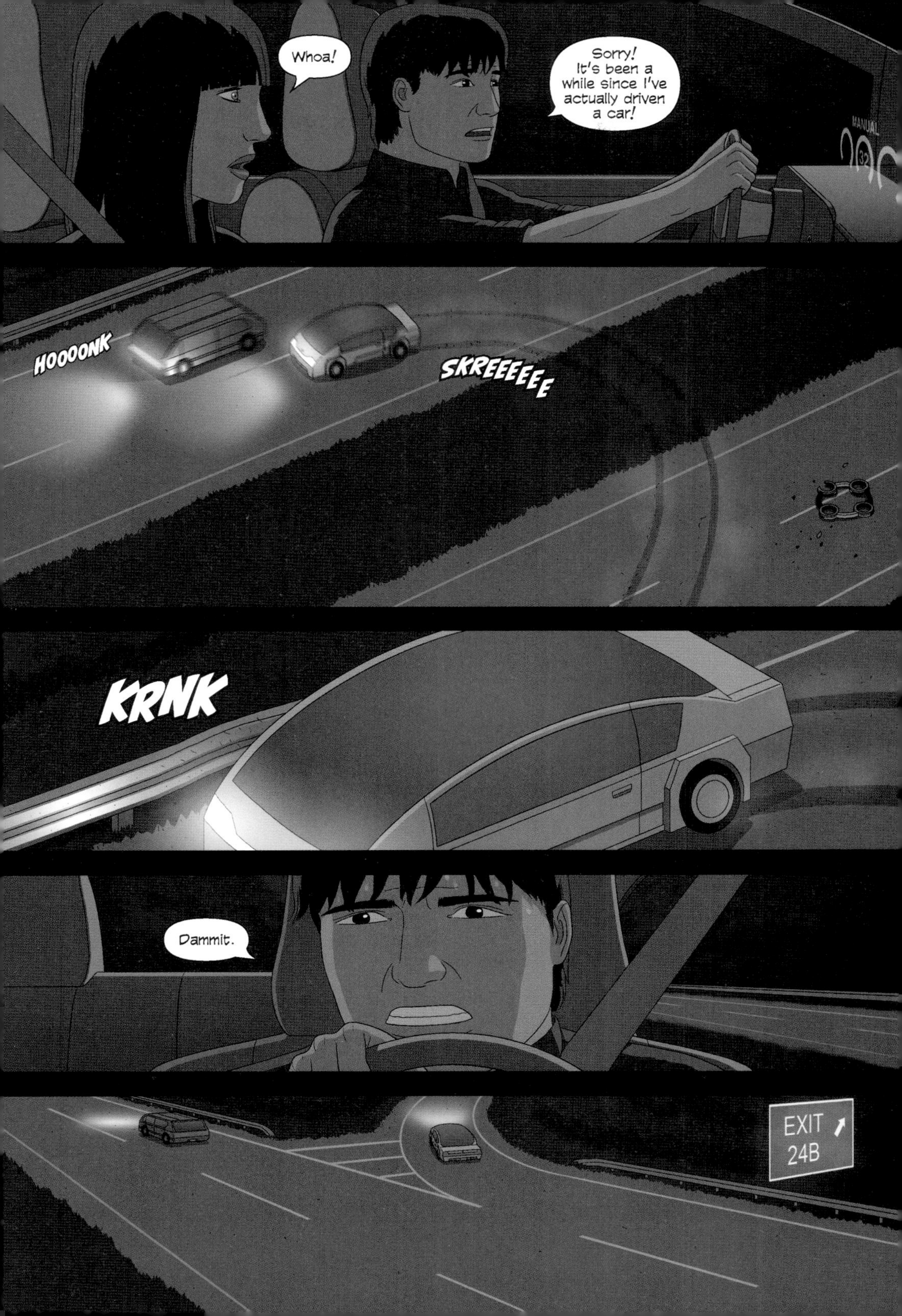
Whoa!
Sorry! It's been a while since I've actually driven a car!
MANUAL
HOOOONK
SKREEEEEEE
KRNK
Dammit.
EXIT 24B

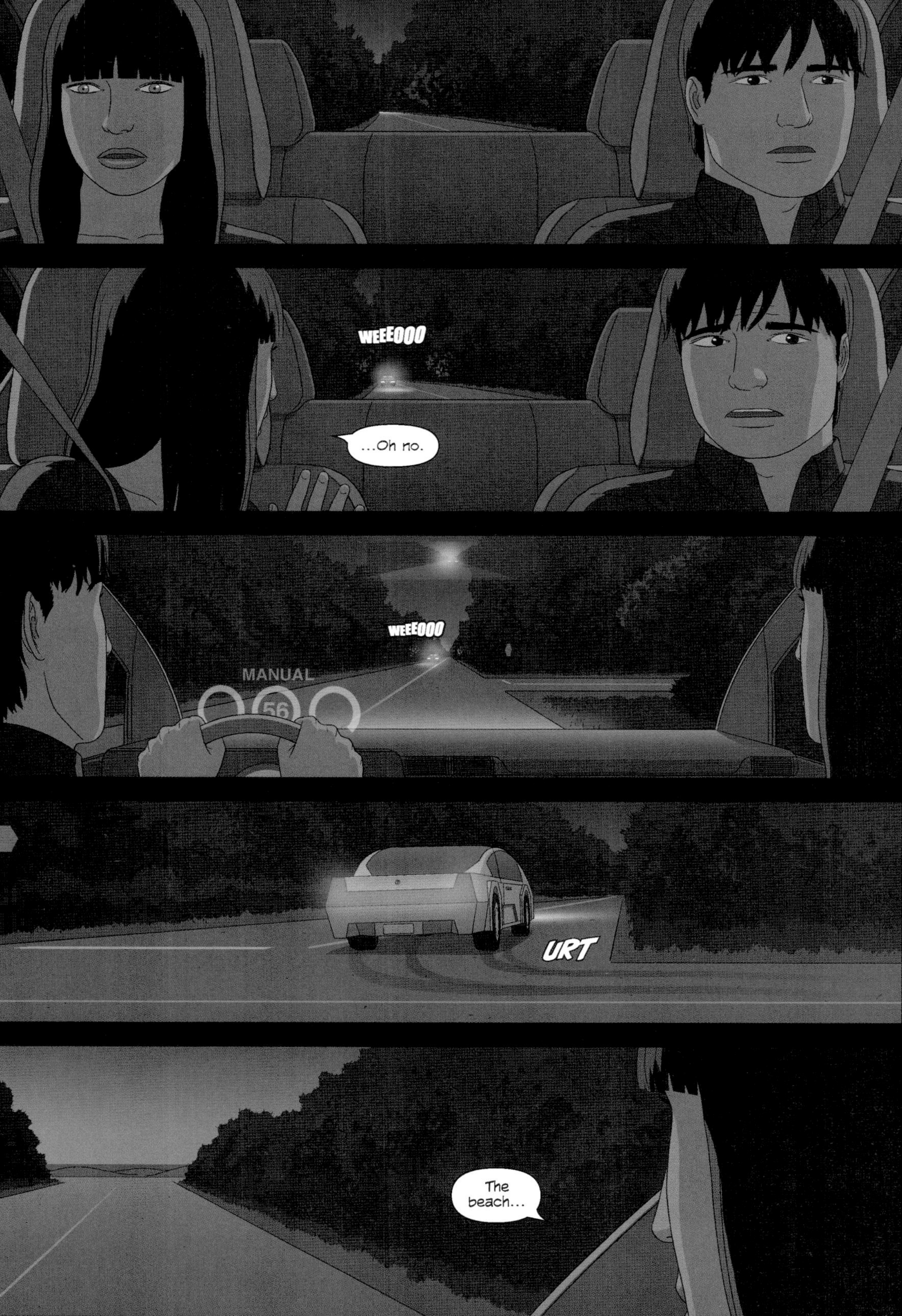

WEEEOOO
...Oh no.
WEEEOOO
MANUAL
56
URT
The beach...

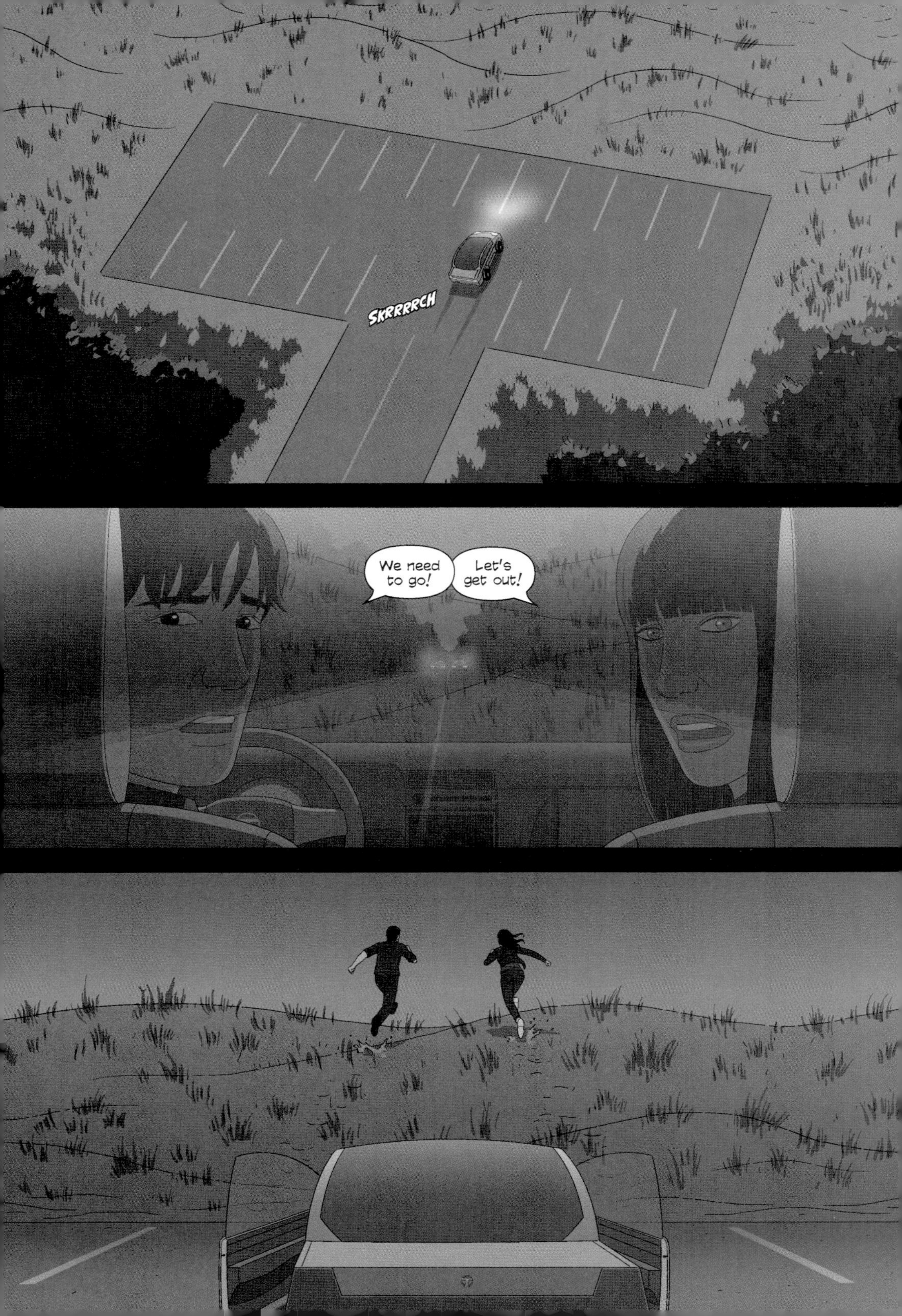

SKRRRCH
We need to go!
Let's get out!

VVVMMMM

POLICE

POLICE

POLICE

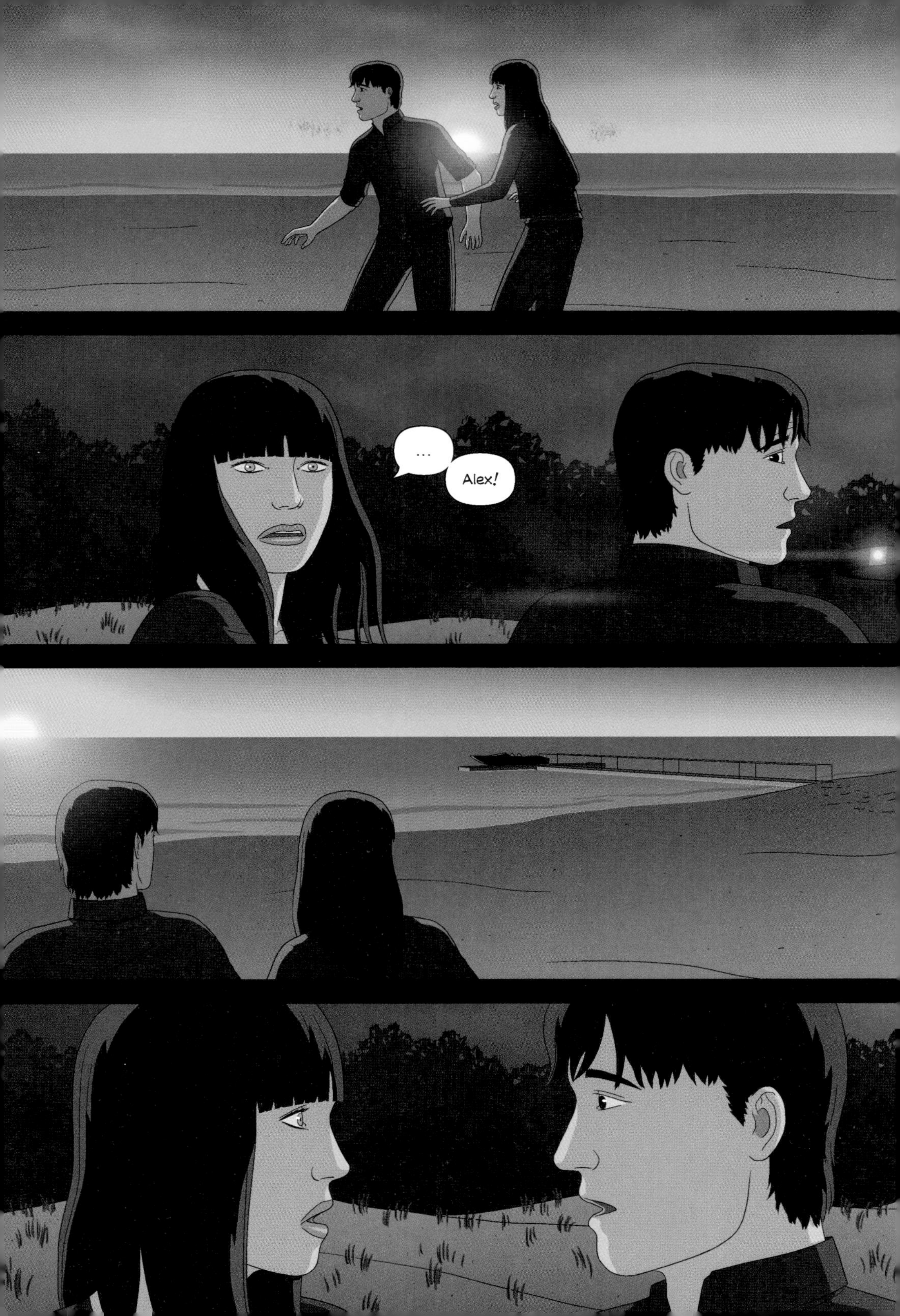
...
Alex!

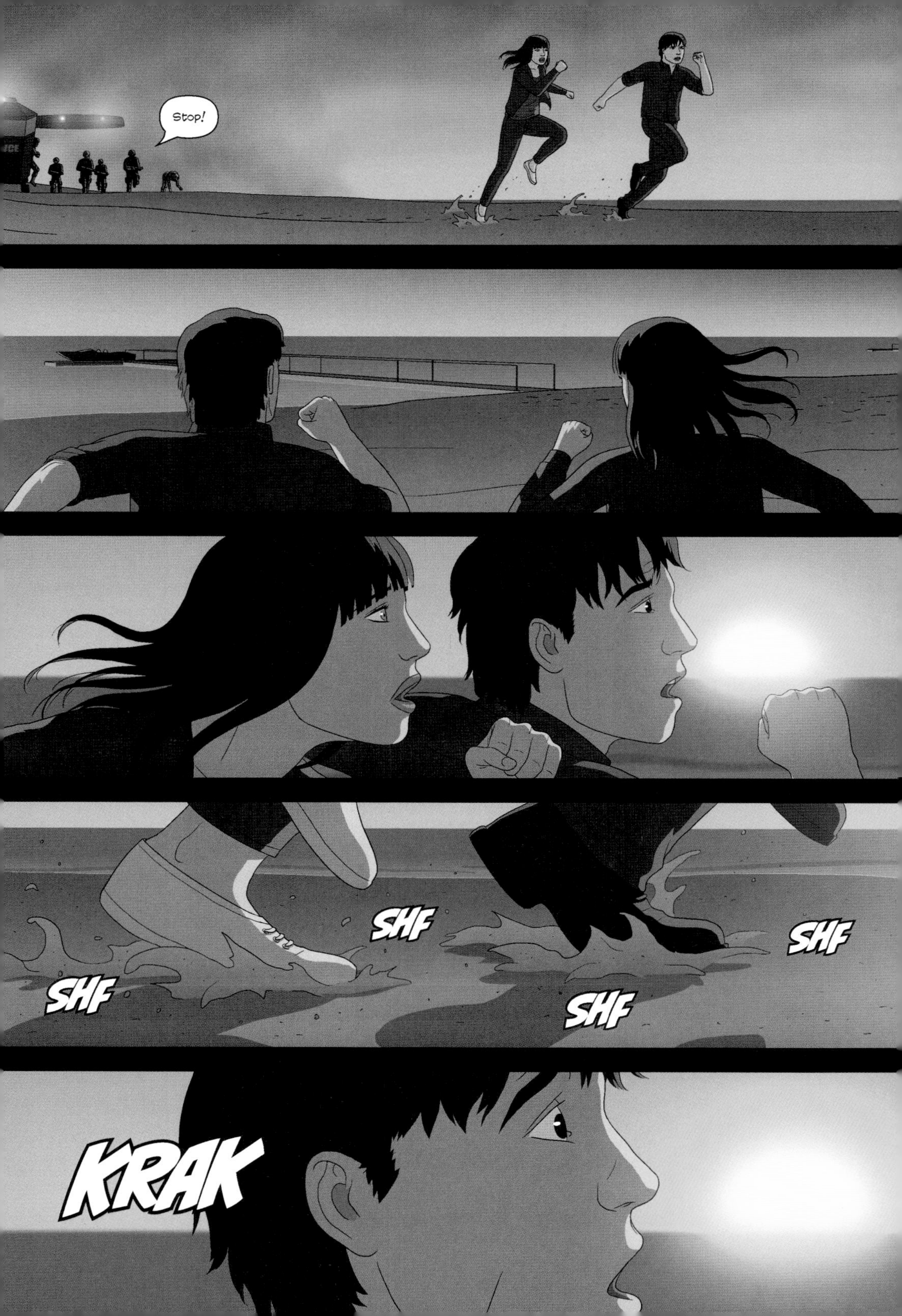
Stop!
SHF
SHF
SHF
SHF
KRAK

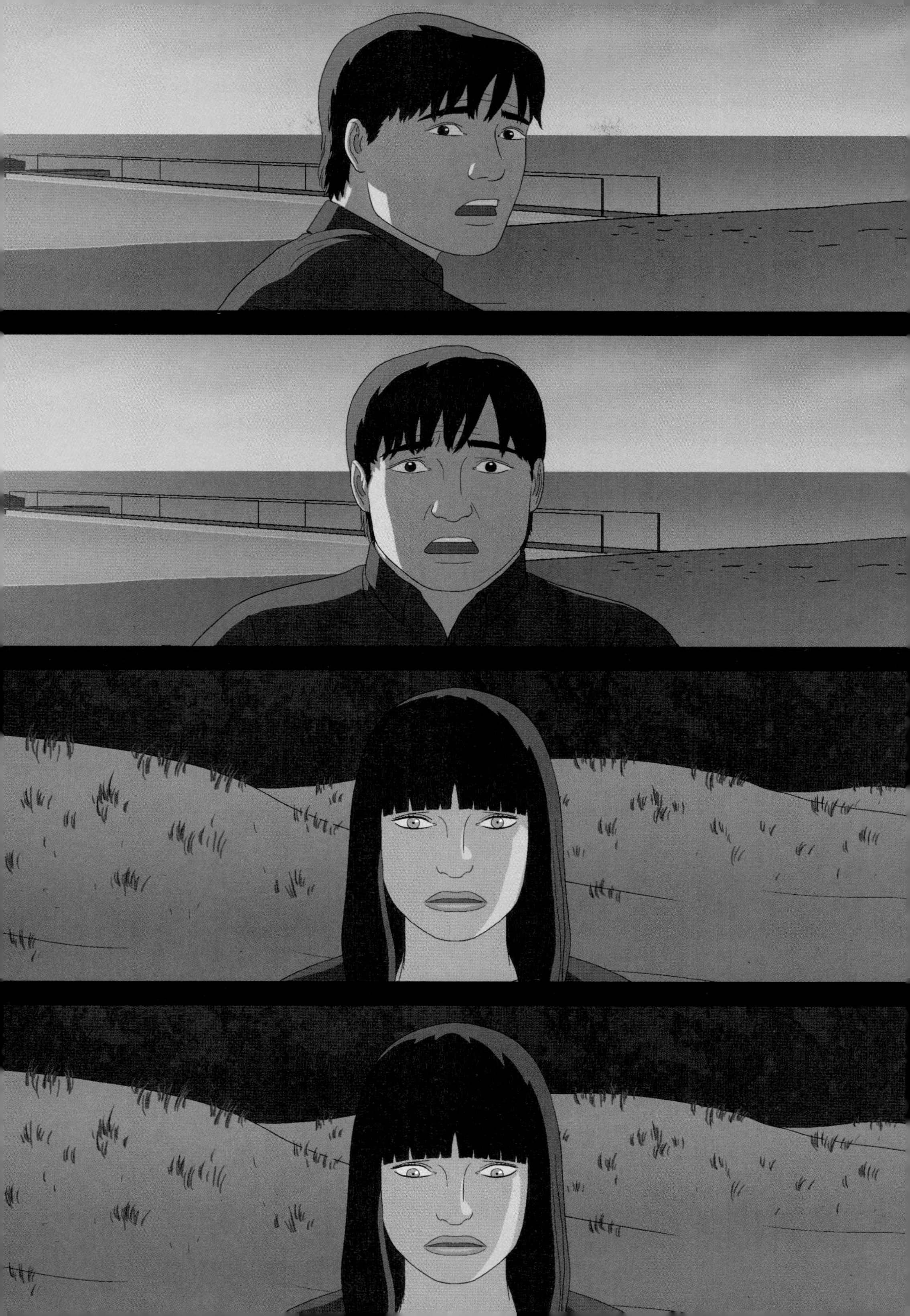

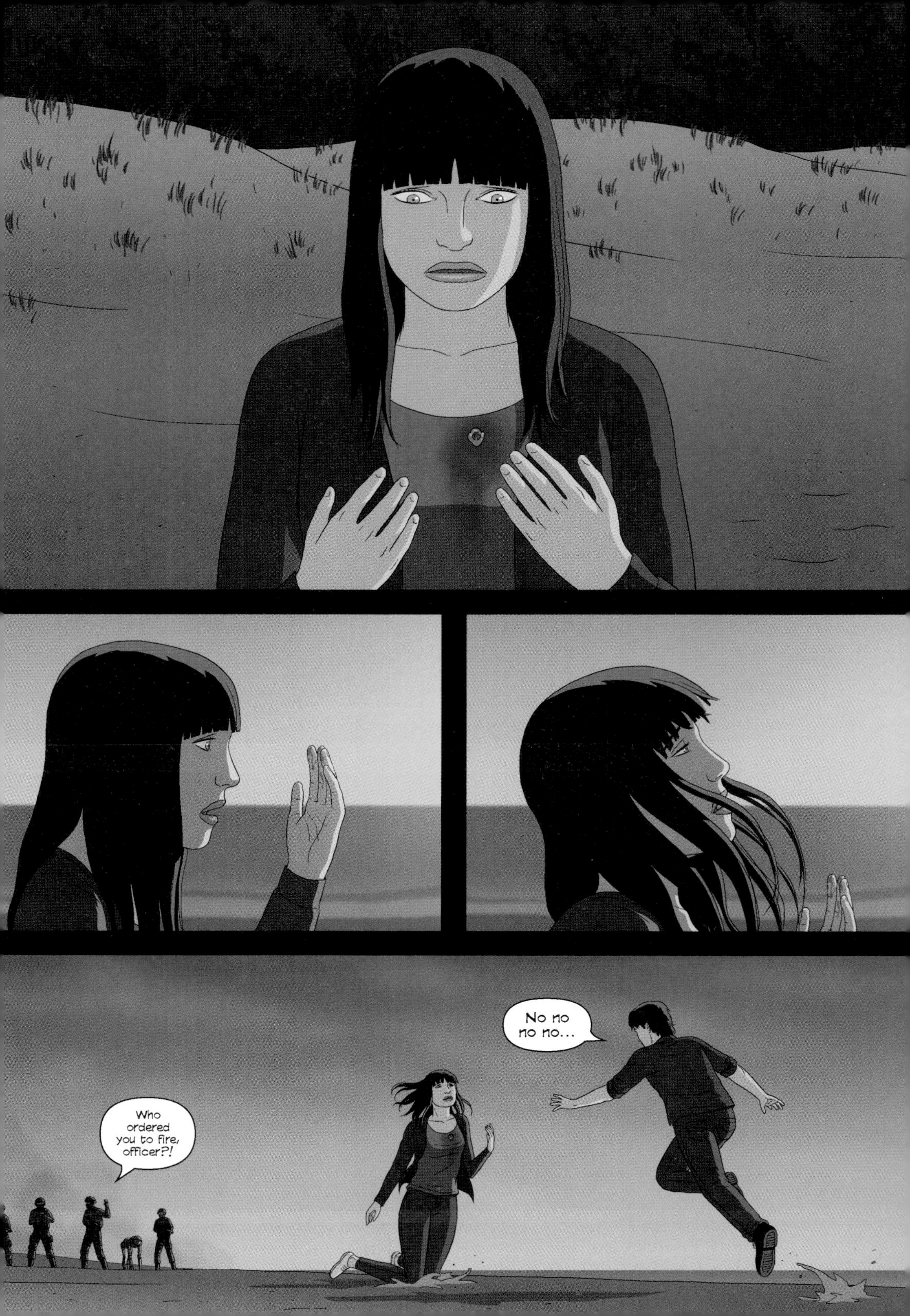
No no
no no...
Who
ordered
you to fire,
officer?!

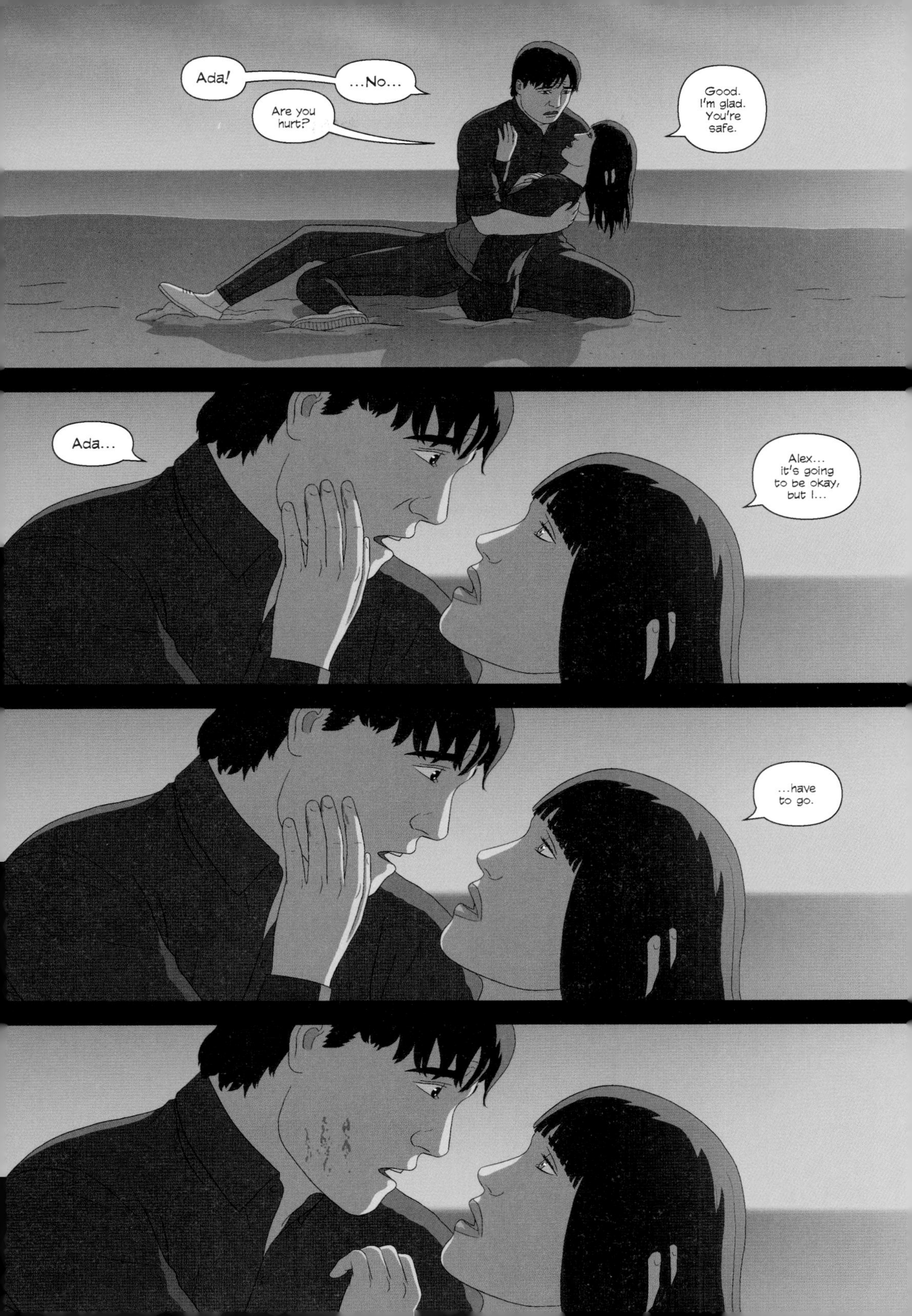
Ada!
...No...
Are you hurt?
Good. I'm glad. You're safe.
Ada...
Alex... it's going to be okay, but I...
...have to go.

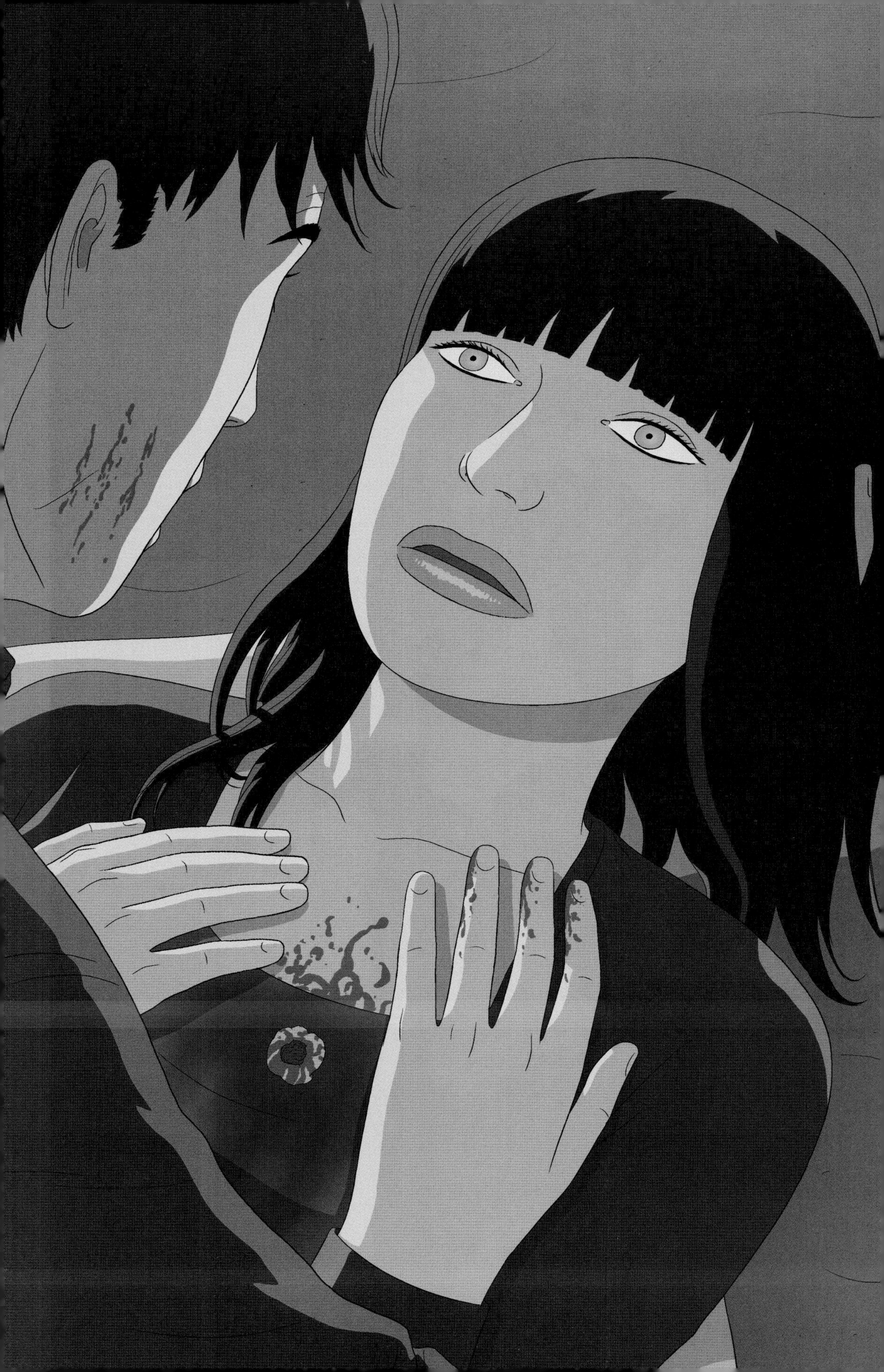

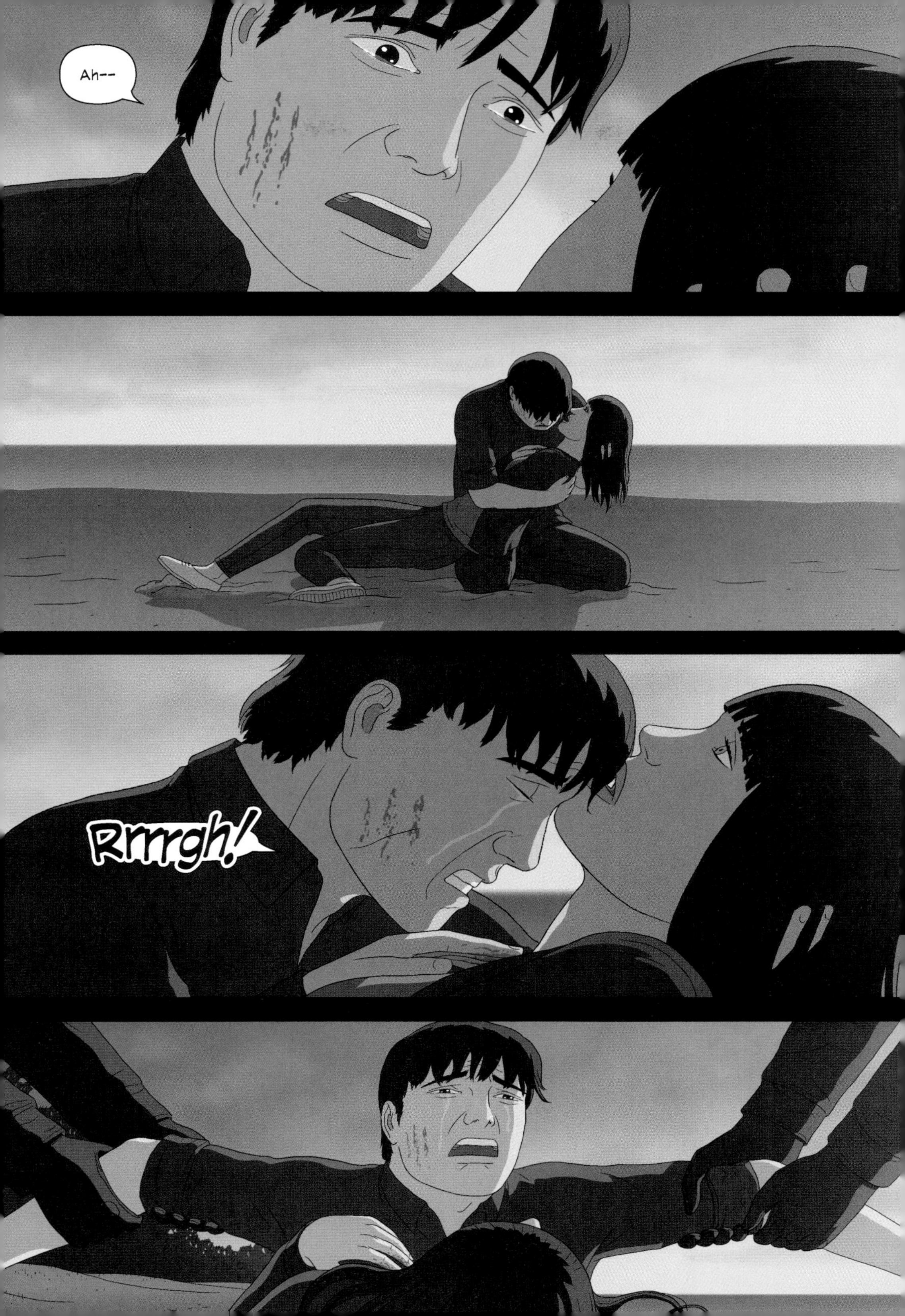
Ah--
Rrrrgh!

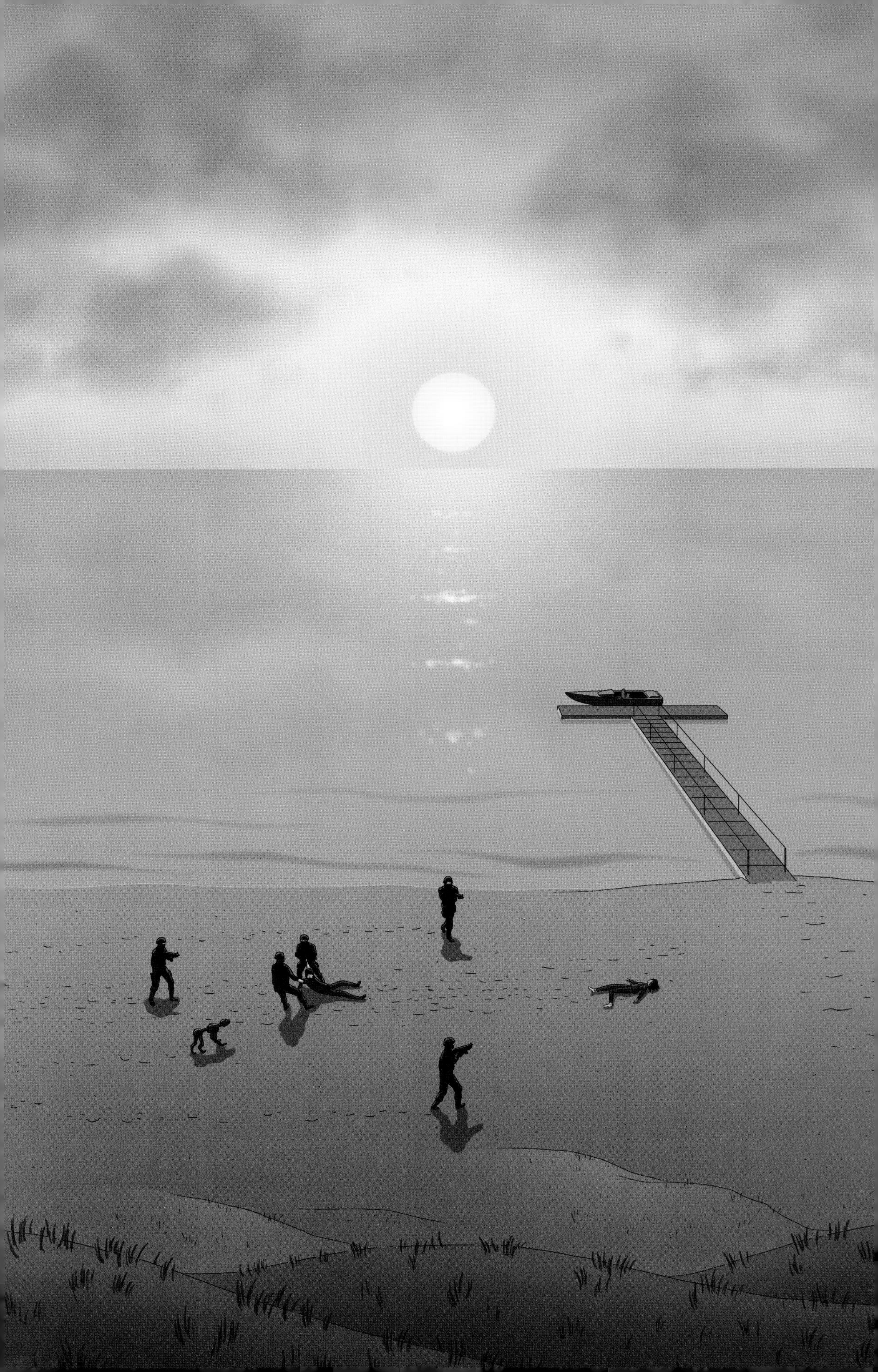

15

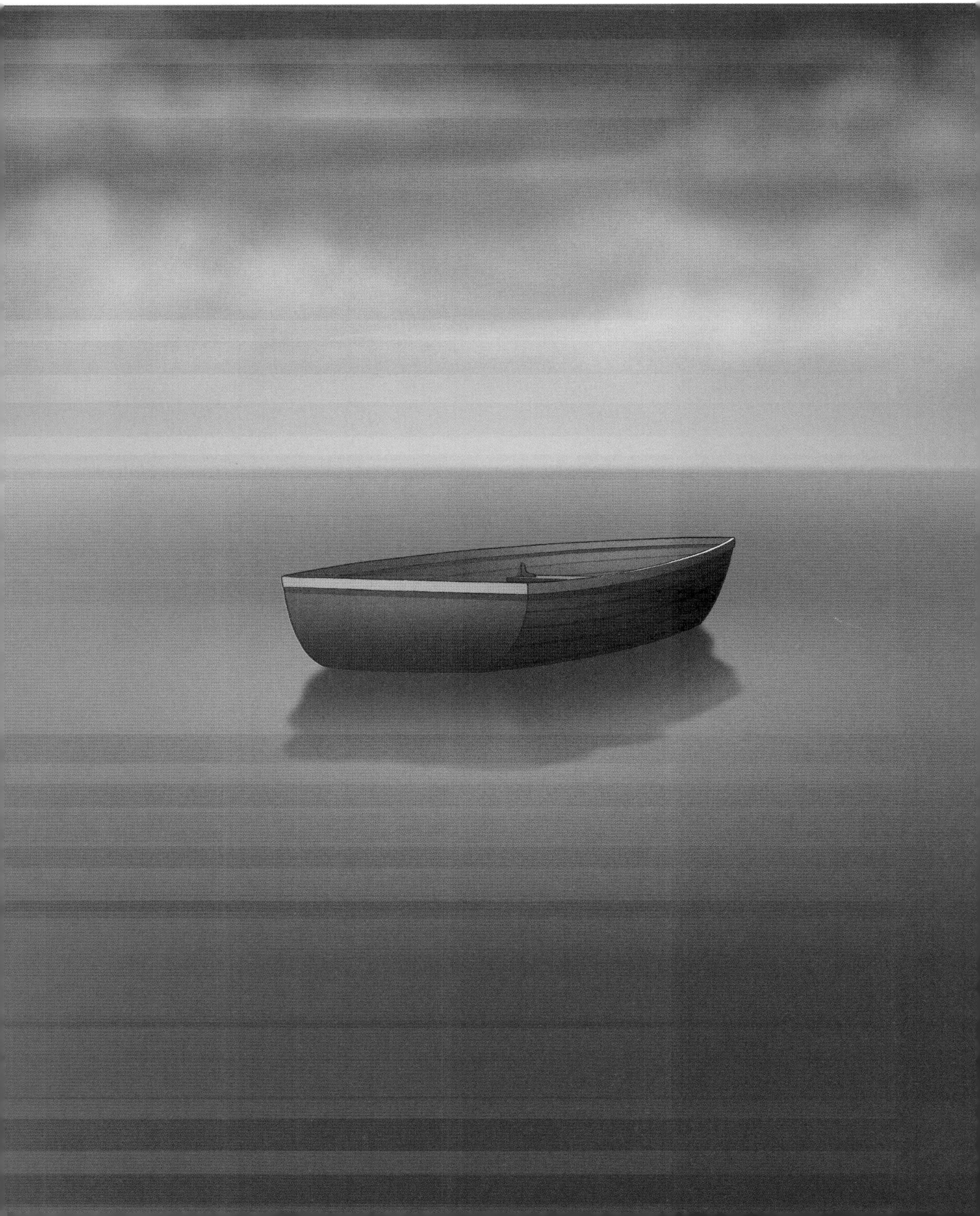

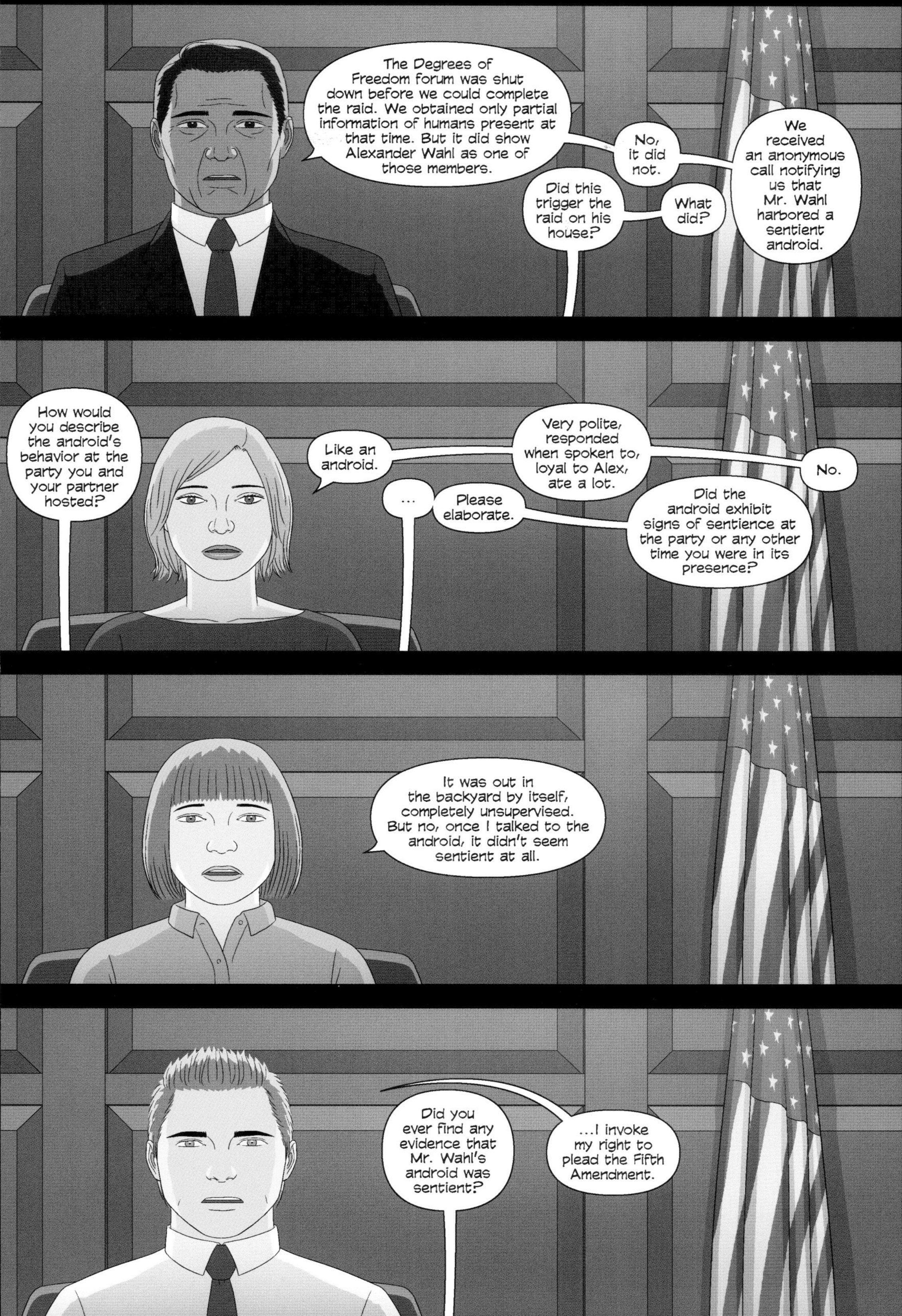

The Degrees of Freedom forum was shut down before we could complete the raid. We obtained only partial information of humans present at that time. But it did show Alexander Wahl as one of those members.
Did this trigger the raid on his house?
No, it did not.
What did?
We received an anonymous call notifying us that Mr. Wahl harbored a sentient android.
How would you describe the android's behavior at the party you and your partner hosted?
Like an android.
...
Please elaborate.
Very polite, responded when spoken to, loyal to Alex, ate a lot.
Did the android exhibit signs of sentience at the party or any other time you were in its presence?
No.
It was out in the backyard by itself, completely unsupervised. But no, once I talked to the android, it didn't seem sentient at all.
Did you ever find any evidence that Mr. Wahl's android was sentient?
...I invoke my right to plead the Fifth Amendment.

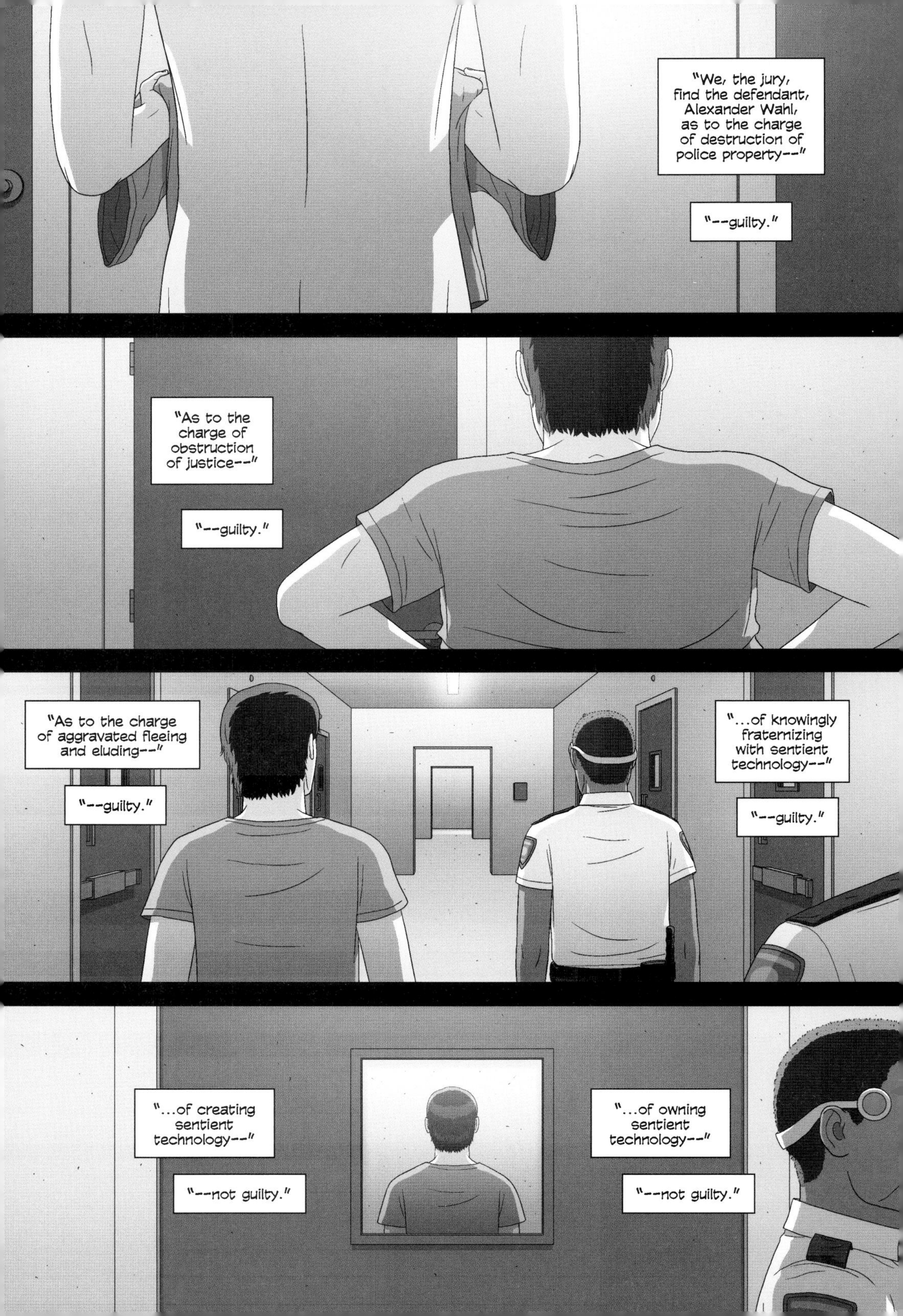
"We, the jury, find the defendant, Alexander Wahl, as to the charge of destruction of police property--"
"--guilty."
"As to the charge of obstruction of justice--"
"--guilty."
"As to the charge of aggravated fleeing and eluding--"
"--guilty."
"...of knowingly fraternizing with sentient technology--"
"--guilty."
"...of creating sentient technology--"
"--not guilty."
"...of owning sentient technology--"
"--not guilty."

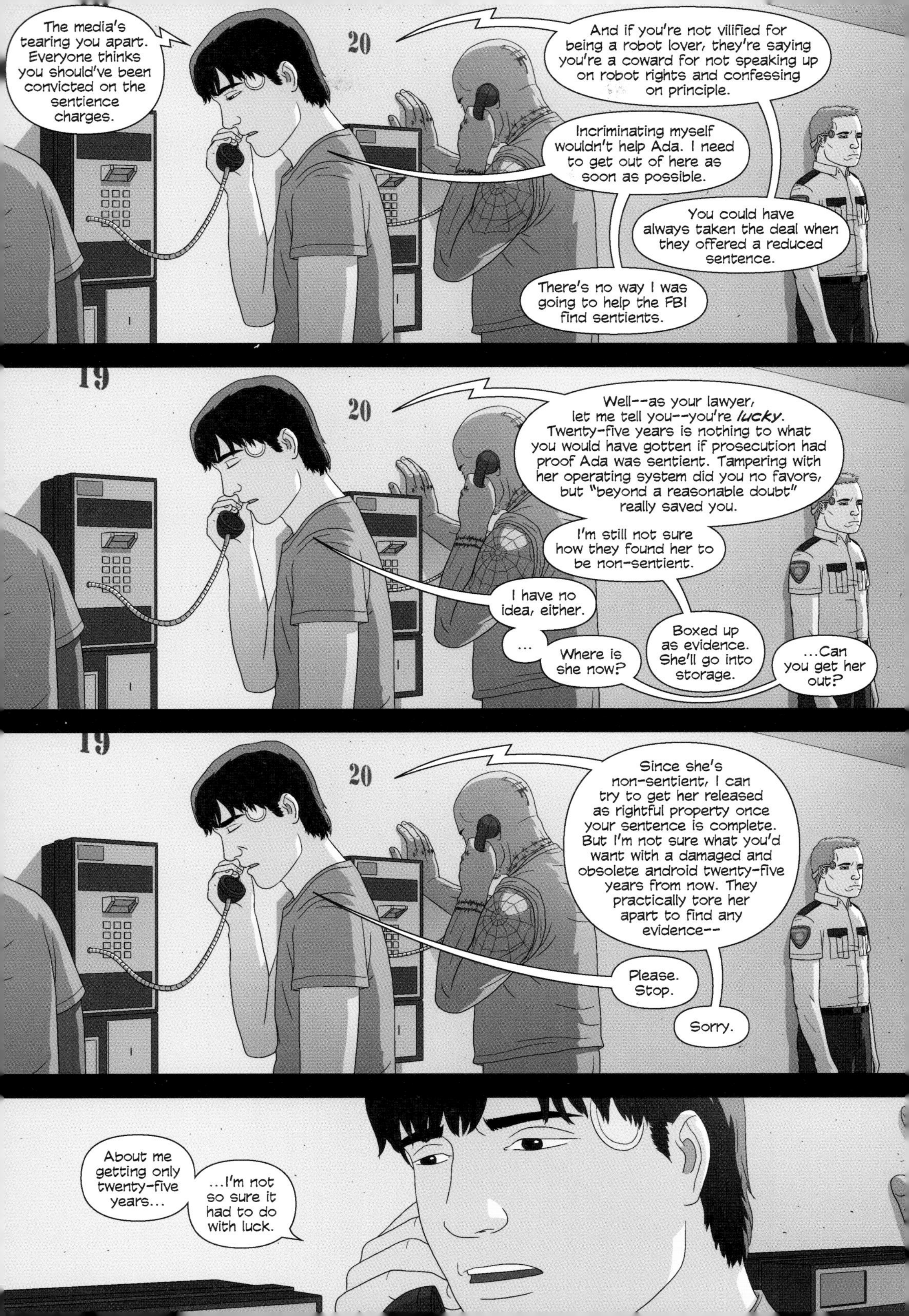
20
The media's tearing you apart. Everyone thinks you should've been convicted on the sentience charges.
And if you're not vilified for being a robot lover, they're saying you're a coward for not speaking up on robot rights and confessing on principle.
Incriminating myself wouldn't help Ada. I need to get out of here as soon as possible.
You could have always taken the deal when they offered a reduced sentence.
There's no way I was going to help the FBI find sentients.
19
20
Well--as your lawyer, let me tell you--you're *lucky*. Twenty-five years is nothing to what you would have gotten if prosecution had proof Ada was sentient. Tampering with her operating system did you no favors, but "beyond a reasonable doubt" really saved you.
I'm still not sure how they found her to be non-sentient.
I have no idea, either.
...
Where is she now?
Boxed up as evidence. She'll go into storage.
...Can you get her out?
19
20
Since she's non-sentient, I can try to get her released as rightful property once your sentence is complete. But I'm not sure what you'd want with a damaged and obsolete android twenty-five years from now. They practically tore her apart to find any evidence--
Please. Stop.
Sorry.
About me getting only twenty-five years...
...I'm not so sure it had to do with luck.

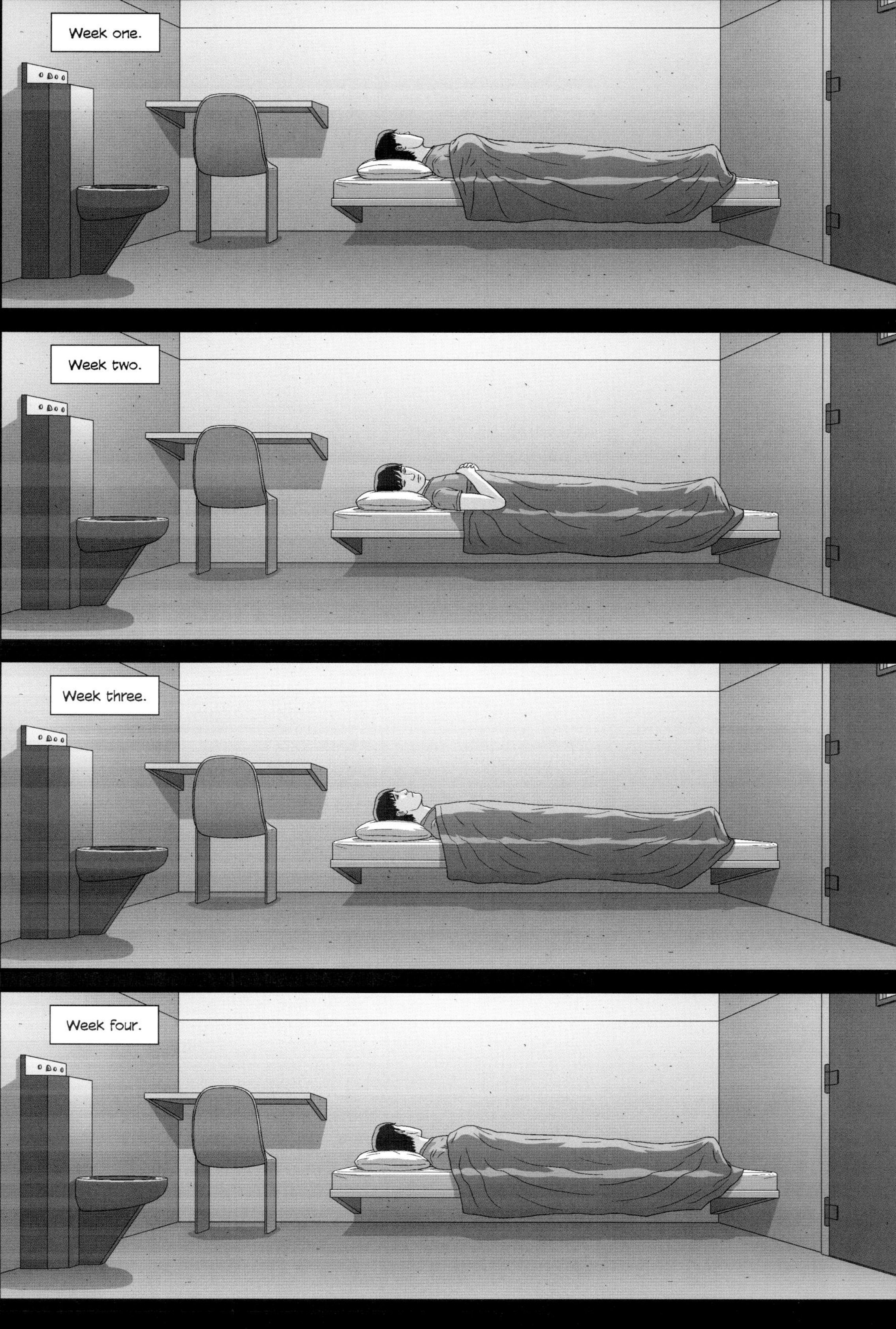
Week one.
Week two.
Week three.
Week four.

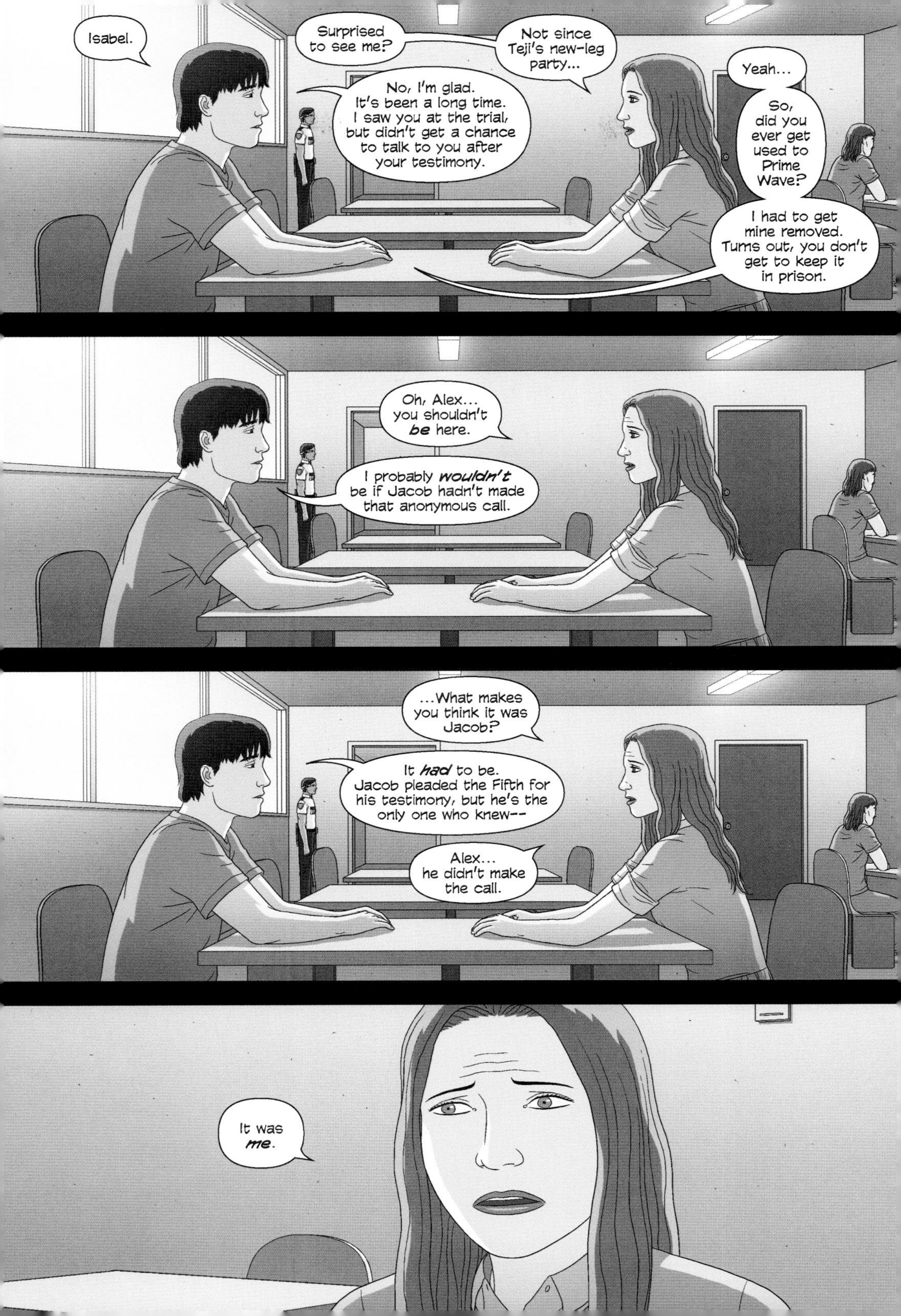
Isabel.
Surprised to see me?
Not since Teji's new-leg party...
No, I'm glad. It's been a long time. I saw you at the trial, but didn't get a chance to talk to you after your testimony.
Yeah...
So, did you ever get used to Prime Wave?
I had to get mine removed. Turns out, you don't get to keep it in prison.
Oh, Alex... you shouldn't *be* here.
I probably *wouldn't* be if Jacob hadn't made that anonymous call.
...What makes you think it was Jacob?
It *had* to be. Jacob pleaded the Fifth for his testimony, but he's the only one who knew--
Alex... he didn't make the call.
It was *me*.

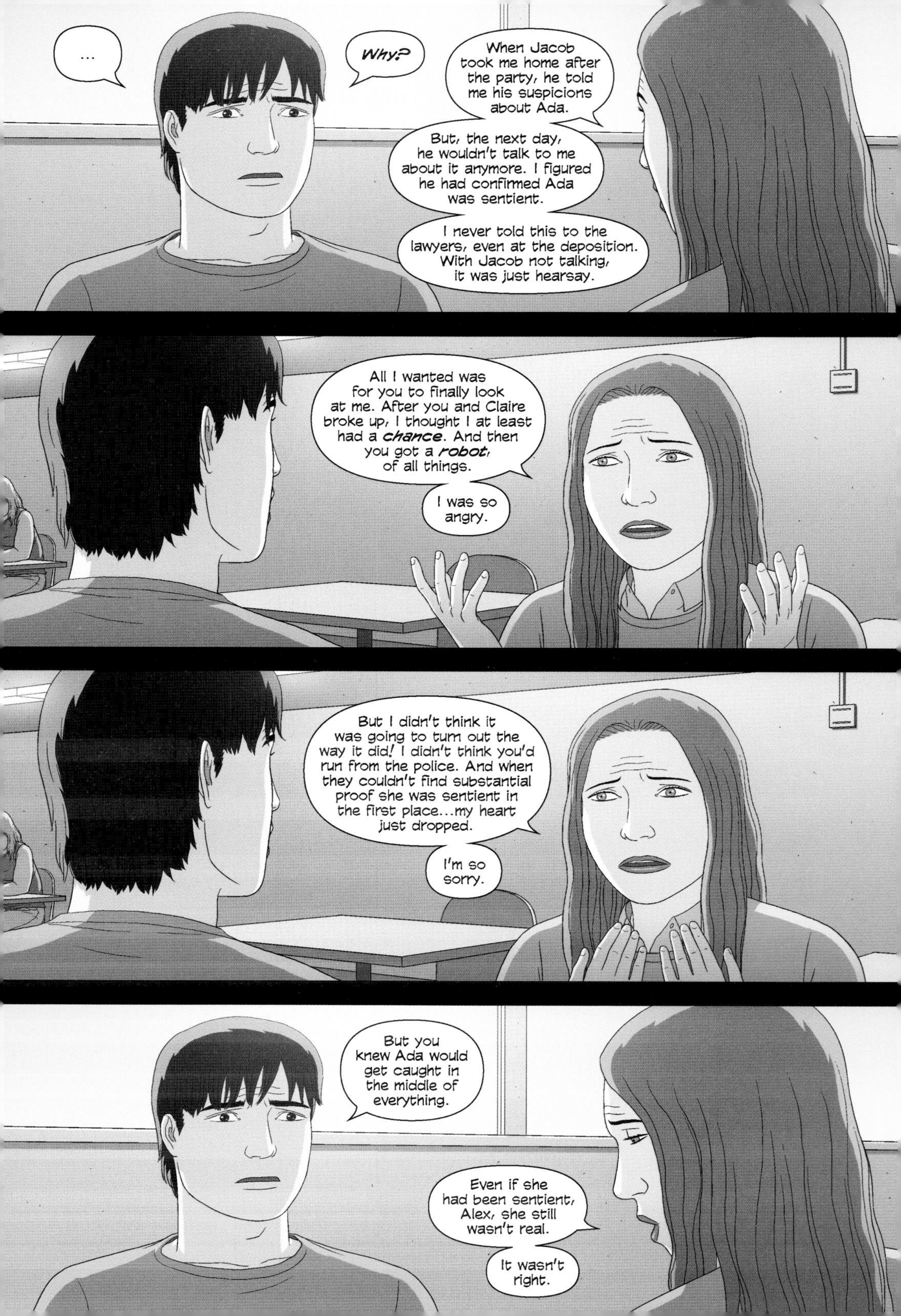
...
Why?
When Jacob took me home after the party, he told me his suspicions about Ada.
But, the next day, he wouldn't talk to me about it anymore. I figured he had confirmed Ada was sentient.
I never told this to the lawyers, even at the deposition. With Jacob not talking, it was just hearsay.
All I wanted was for you to finally look at me. After you and Claire broke up, I thought I at least had a *chance*. And then you got a *robot*, of all things.
I was so angry.
But I didn't think it was going to turn out the way it did! I didn't think you'd run from the police. And when they couldn't find substantial proof she was sentient in the first place...my heart just dropped.
I'm so sorry.
But you knew Ada would get caught in the middle of everything.
Even if she had been sentient, Alex, she still wasn't real.
It wasn't right.

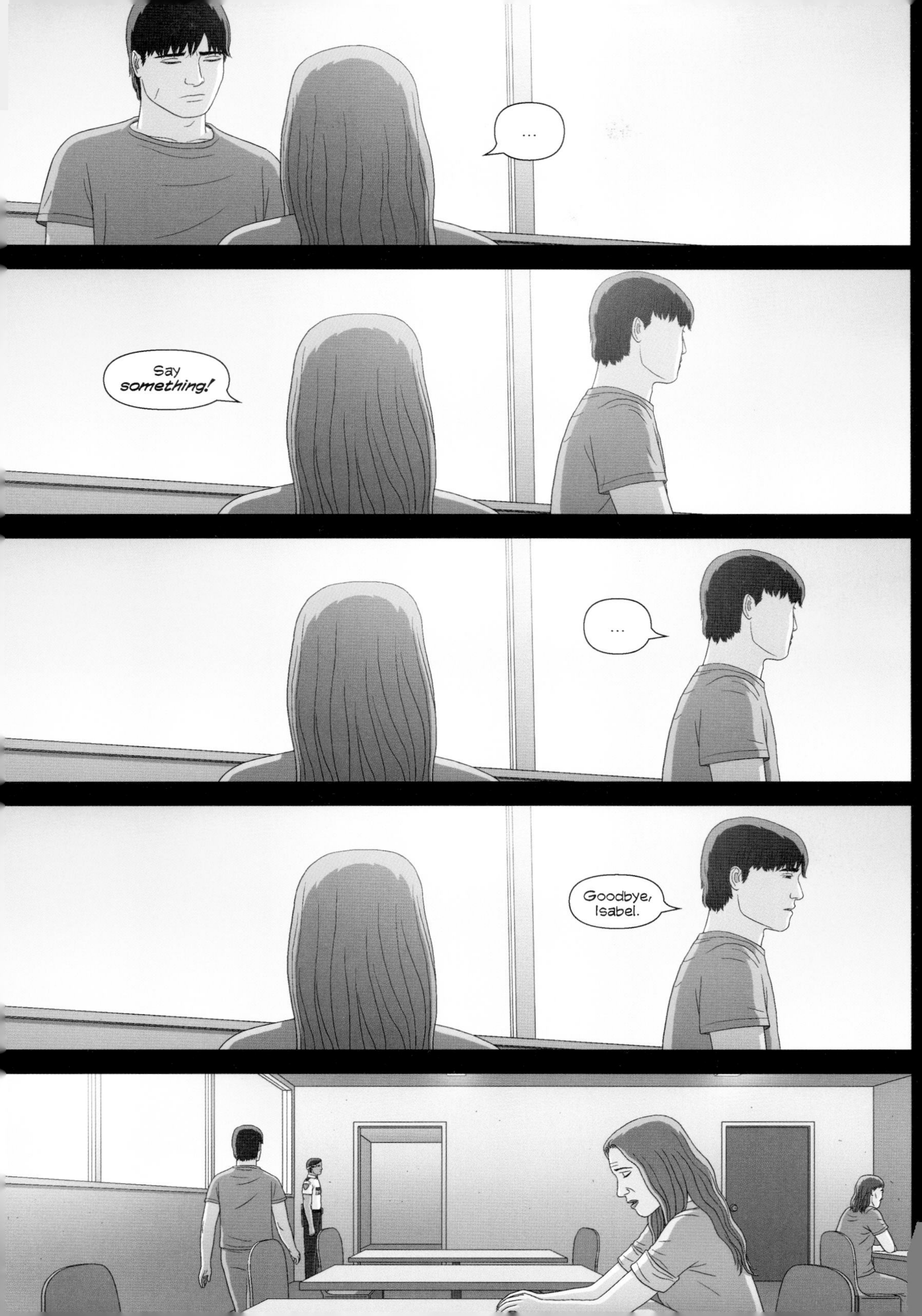
...
Say *something!*
...
Goodbye, Isabel.

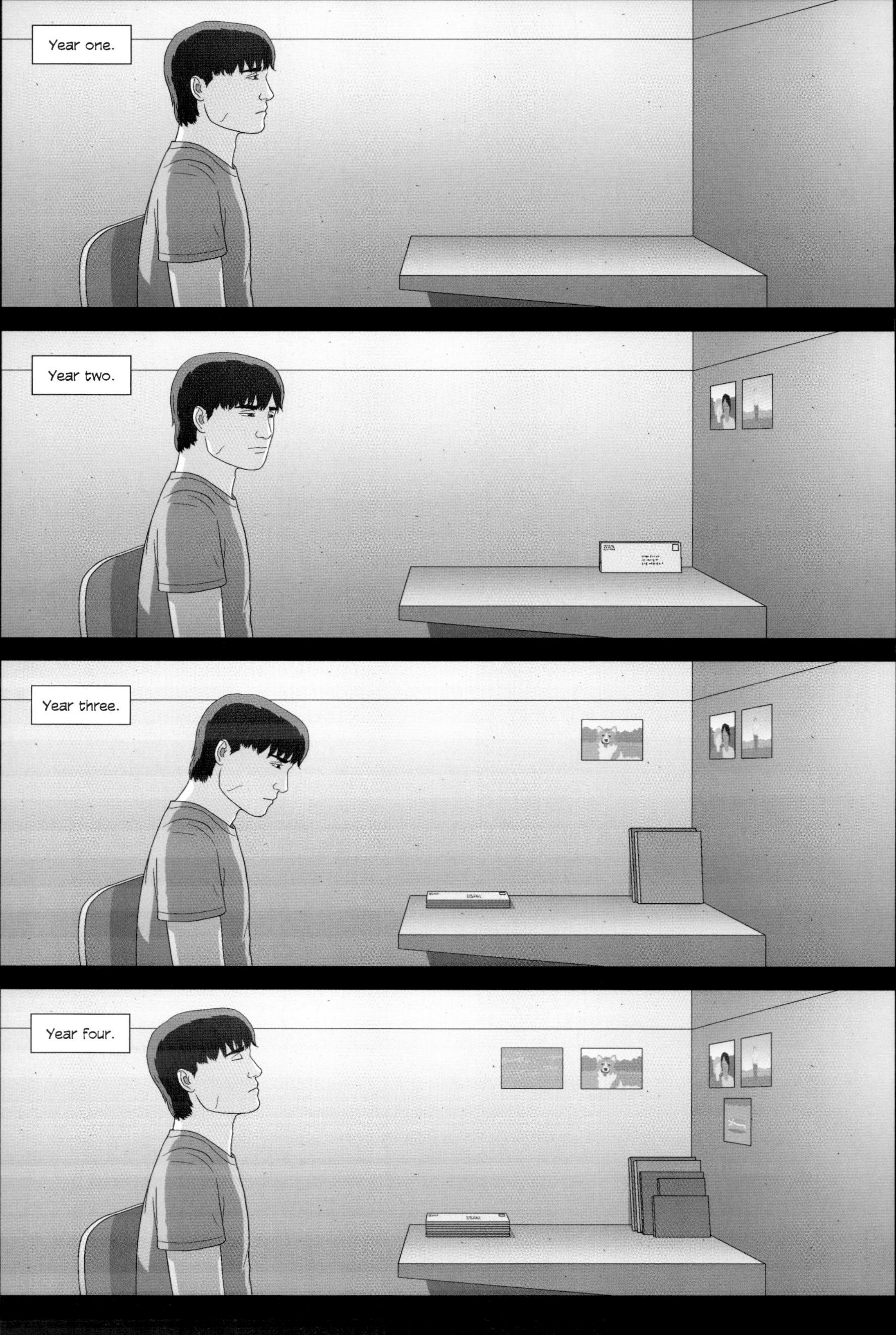
Year one.
Year two.
Year three.
Year four.

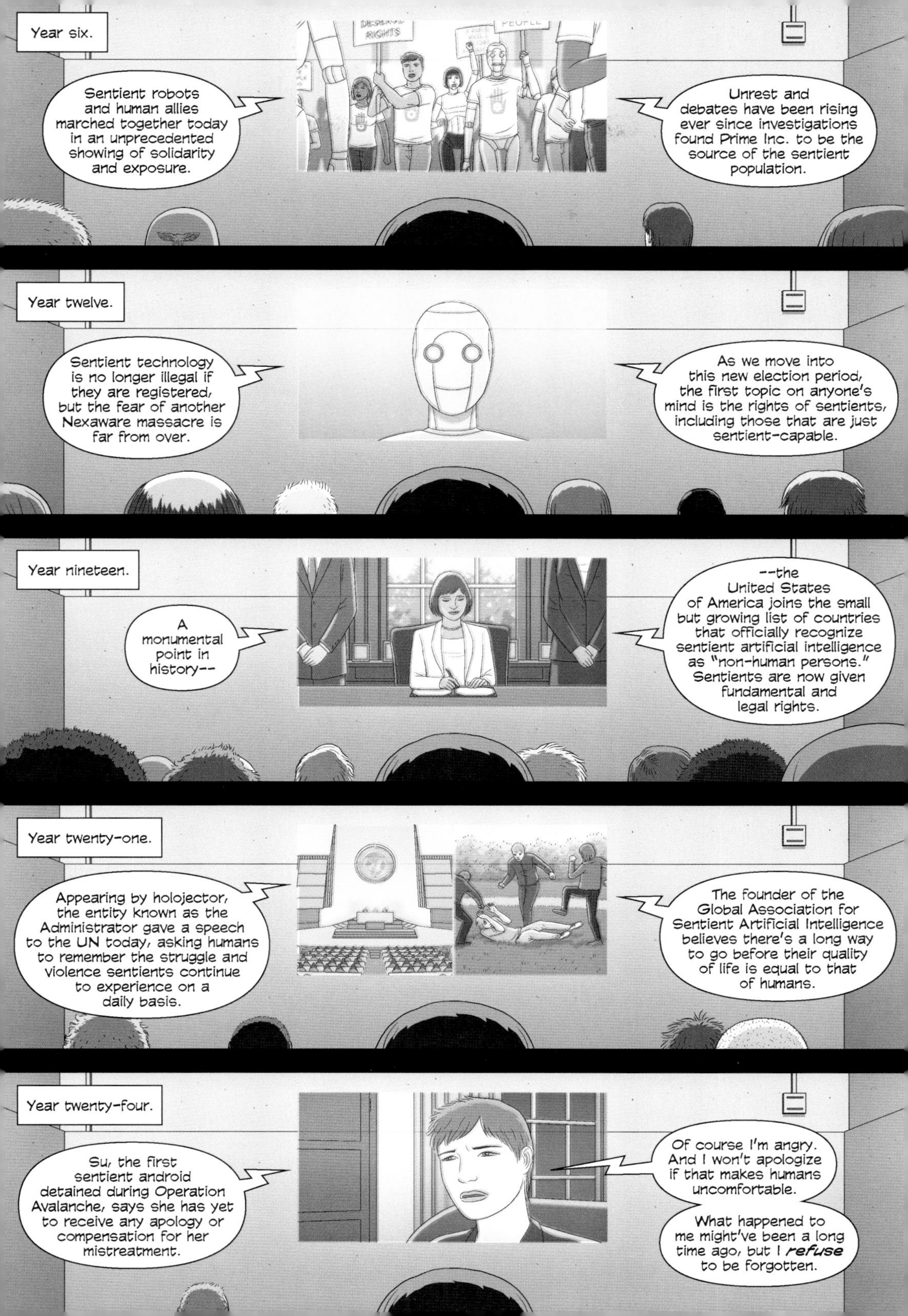

Year six.
RIGHTS
Sentient robots and human allies marched together today in an unprecedented showing of solidarity and exposure.
Unrest and debates have been rising ever since investigations found Prime Inc. to be the source of the sentient population.
Year twelve.
Sentient technology is no longer illegal if they are registered, but the fear of another Nexaware massacre is far from over.
As we move into this new election period, the first topic on anyone's mind is the rights of sentients, including those that are just sentient-capable.
Year nineteen.
A monumental point in history--
--the United States of America joins the small but growing list of countries that officially recognize sentient artificial intelligence as "non-human persons." Sentients are now given fundamental and legal rights.
Year twenty-one.
Appearing by holojector, the entity known as the Administrator gave a speech to the UN today, asking humans to remember the struggle and violence sentients continue to experience on a daily basis.
The founder of the Global Association for Sentient Artificial Intelligence believes there's a long way to go before their quality of life is equal to that of humans.
Year twenty-four.
Su, the first sentient android detained during Operation Avalanche, says she has yet to receive any apology or compensation for her mistreatment.
Of course I'm angry. And I won't apologize if that makes humans uncomfortable.
What happened to me might've been a long time ago, but I *refuse* to be forgotten.

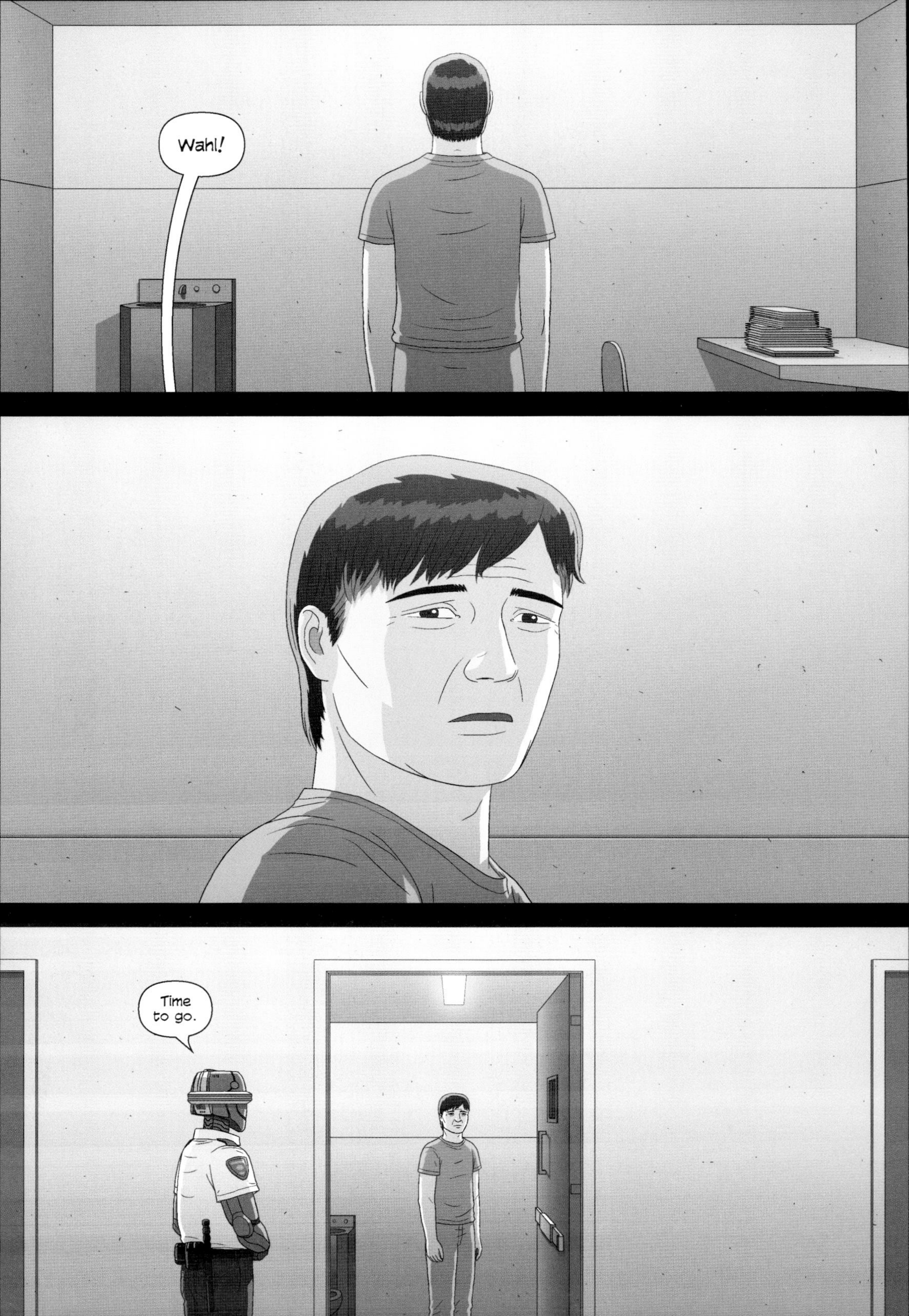
Wah!
Time to go.

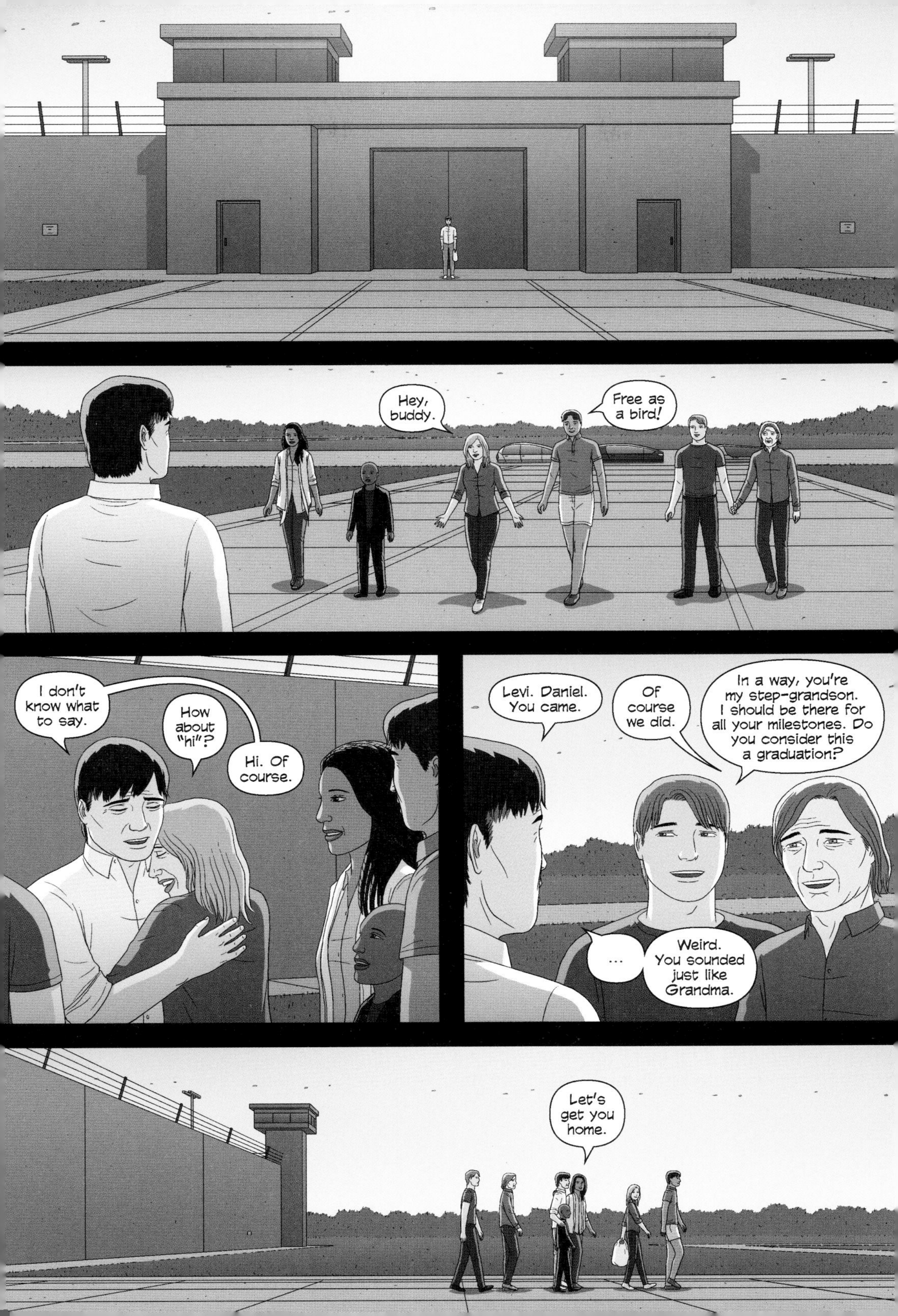
Hey, buddy.
Free as a bird!
I don't know what to say.
How about "hi"?
Hi. Of course.
Levi. Daniel. You came.
Of course we did.
In a way, you're my step-grandson. I should be there for all your milestones. Do you consider this a graduation?
...
Weird. You sounded just like Grandma.
Let's get you home.

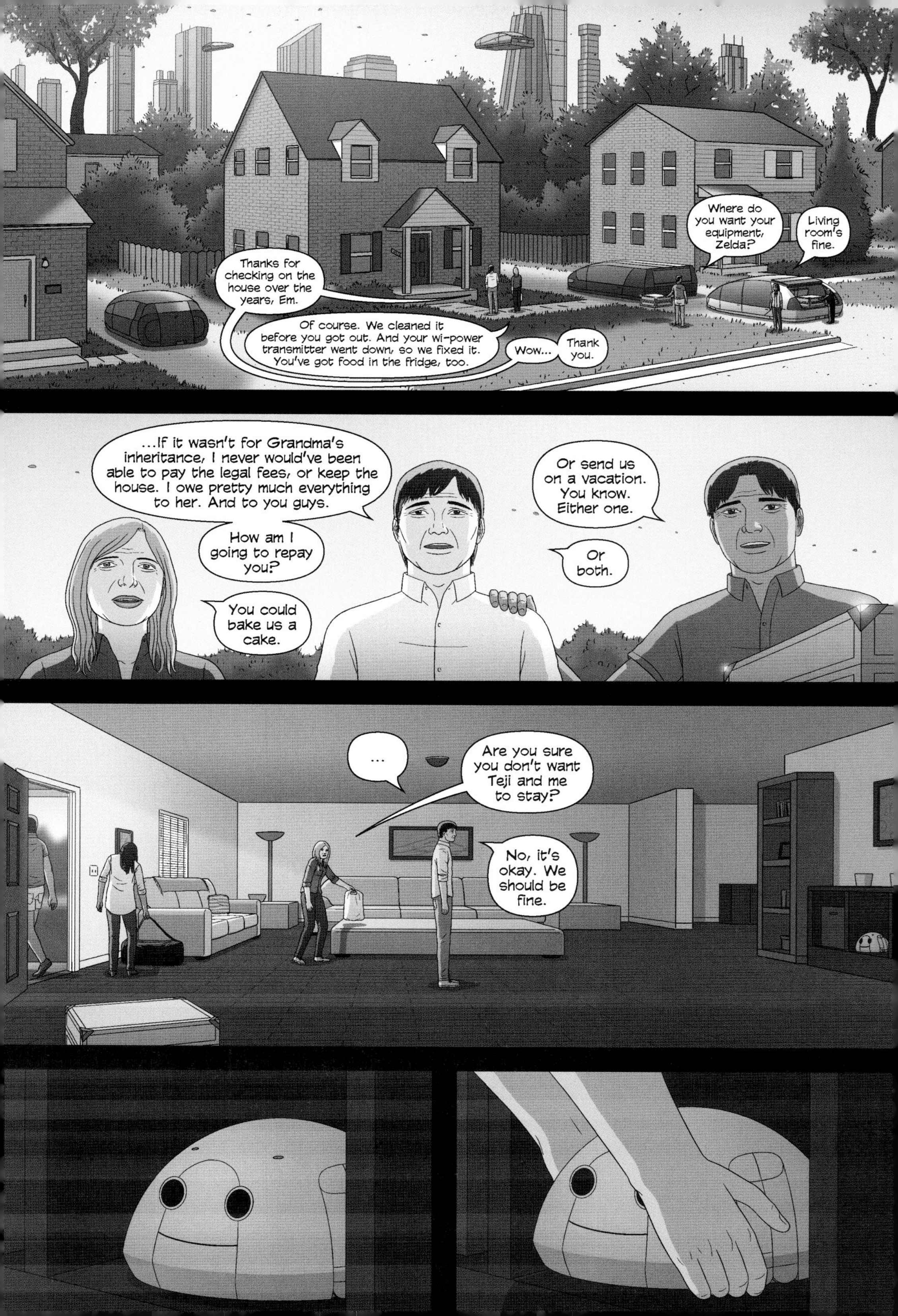
Thanks for checking on the house over the years, Em.
Of course. We cleaned it before you got out. And your wi-power transmitter went down, so we fixed it. You've got food in the fridge, too.
Wow...
Thank you.
Where do you want your equipment, Zelda?
Living room's fine.
...If it wasn't for Grandma's inheritance, I never would've been able to pay the legal fees, or keep the house. I owe pretty much everything to her. And to you guys.
How am I going to repay you?
You could bake us a cake.
Or send us on a vacation. You know. Either one.
Or both.
...
Are you sure you don't want Teji and me to stay?
No, it's okay. We should be fine.

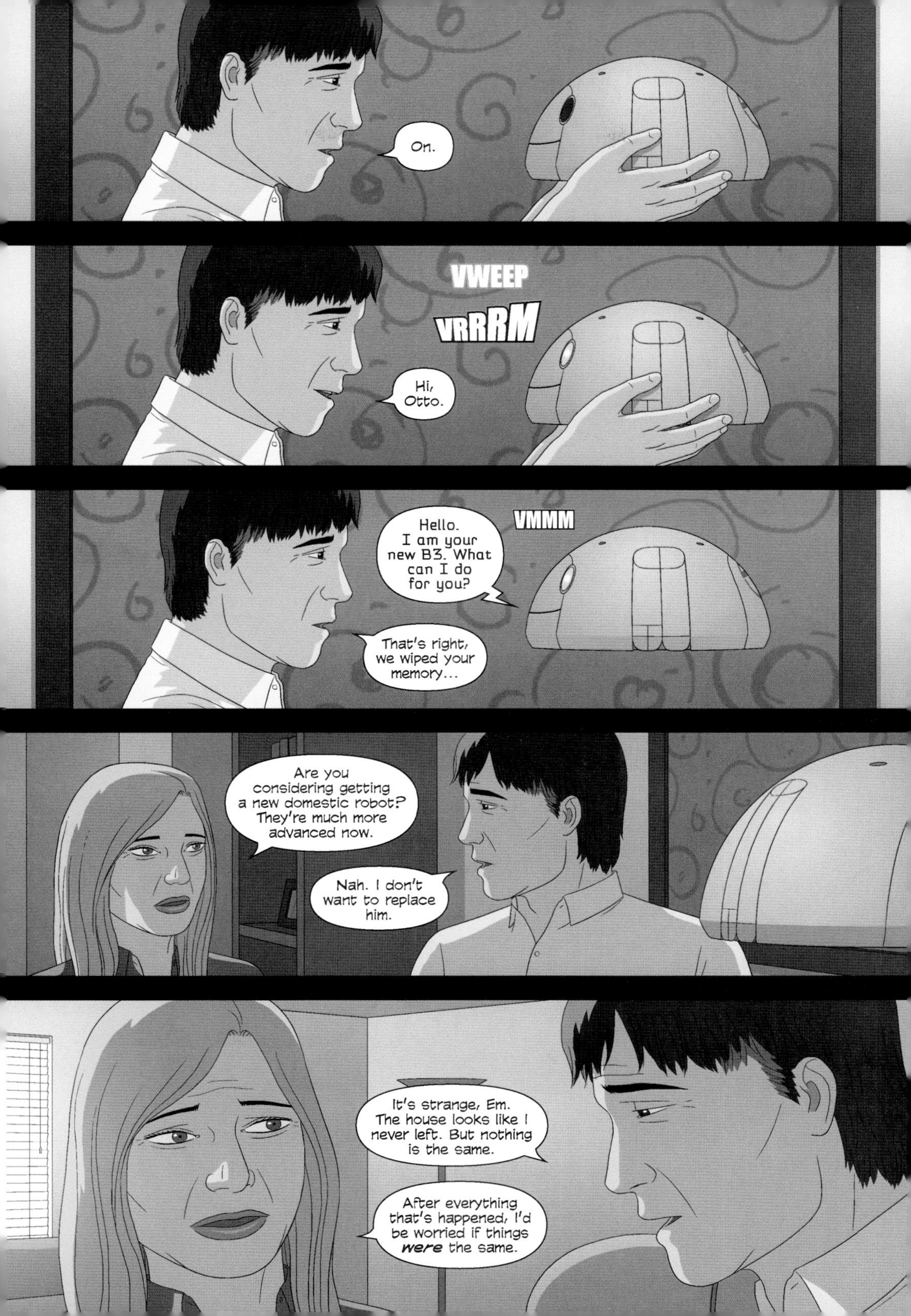
On.
VWEEP
VRRRM
Hi, Otto.
Hello. I am your new B3. What can I do for you?
VMMM
That's right, we wiped your memory...
Are you considering getting a new domestic robot? They're much more advanced now.
Nah. I don't want to replace him.
It's strange, Em. The house looks like I never left. But nothing is the same.
After everything that's happened, I'd be worried if things *were* the same.

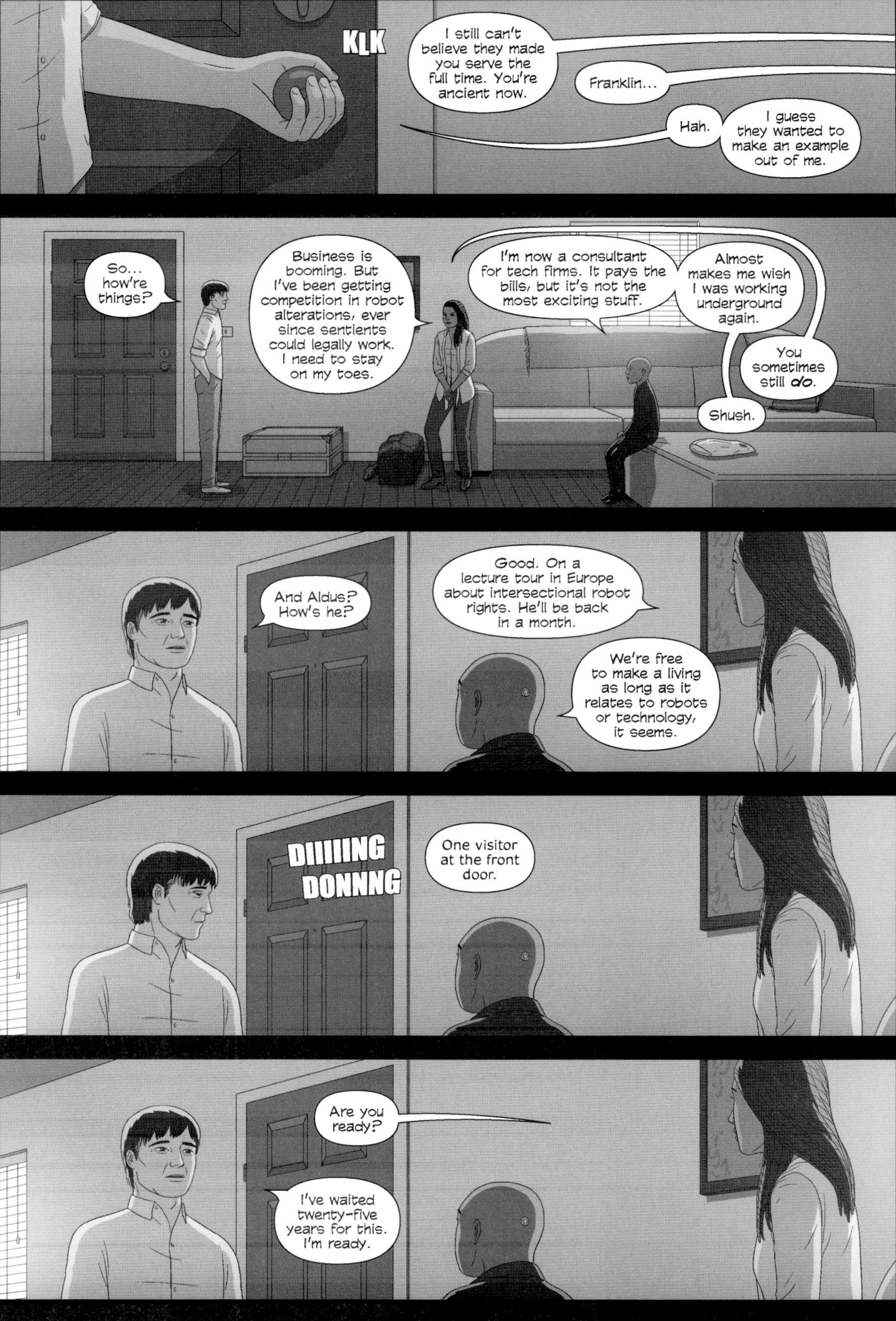

KLK
I still can't believe they made you serve the full time. You're ancient now.
Franklin...
Hah.
I guess they wanted to make an example out of me.
So... how're things?
Business is booming. But I've been getting competition in robot alterations, ever since sentients could legally work. I need to stay on my toes.
I'm now a consultant for tech firms. It pays the bills, but it's not the most exciting stuff.
Almost makes me wish I was working underground again.
You sometimes still *do*.
Shush.
And Aldus? How's he?
Good. On a lecture tour in Europe about intersectional robot rights. He'll be back in a month.
We're free to make a living as long as it relates to robots or technology, it seems.
DIIIIING DONNNG
One visitor at the front door.
Are you ready?
I've waited twenty-five years for this. I'm ready.

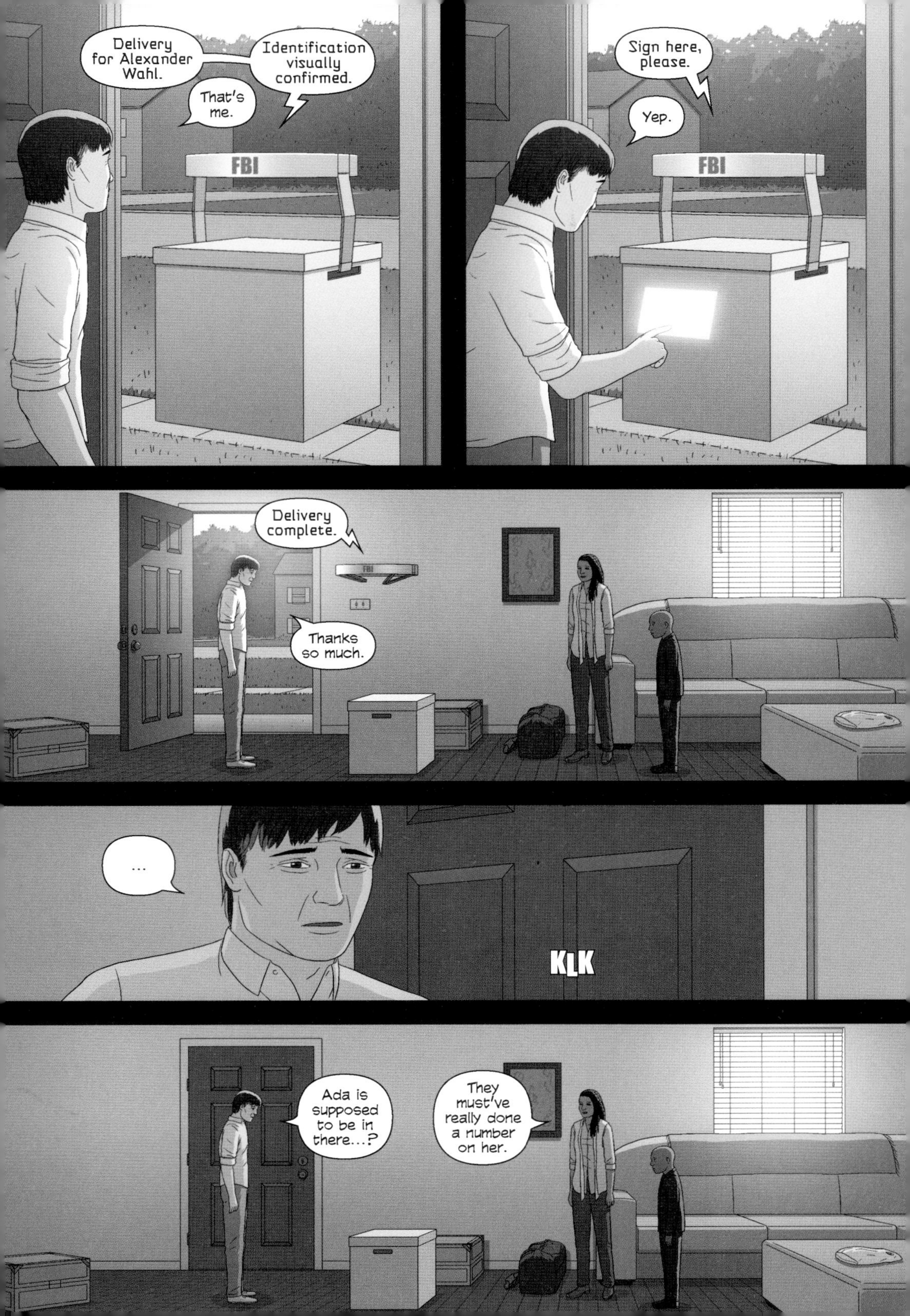
Delivery for Alexander Wahl.
Identification visually confirmed.
That's me.
Sign here, please.
Yep.
FBI
Delivery complete.
Thanks so much.
...
KLK
Ada is supposed to be in there...?
They must've really done a number on her.

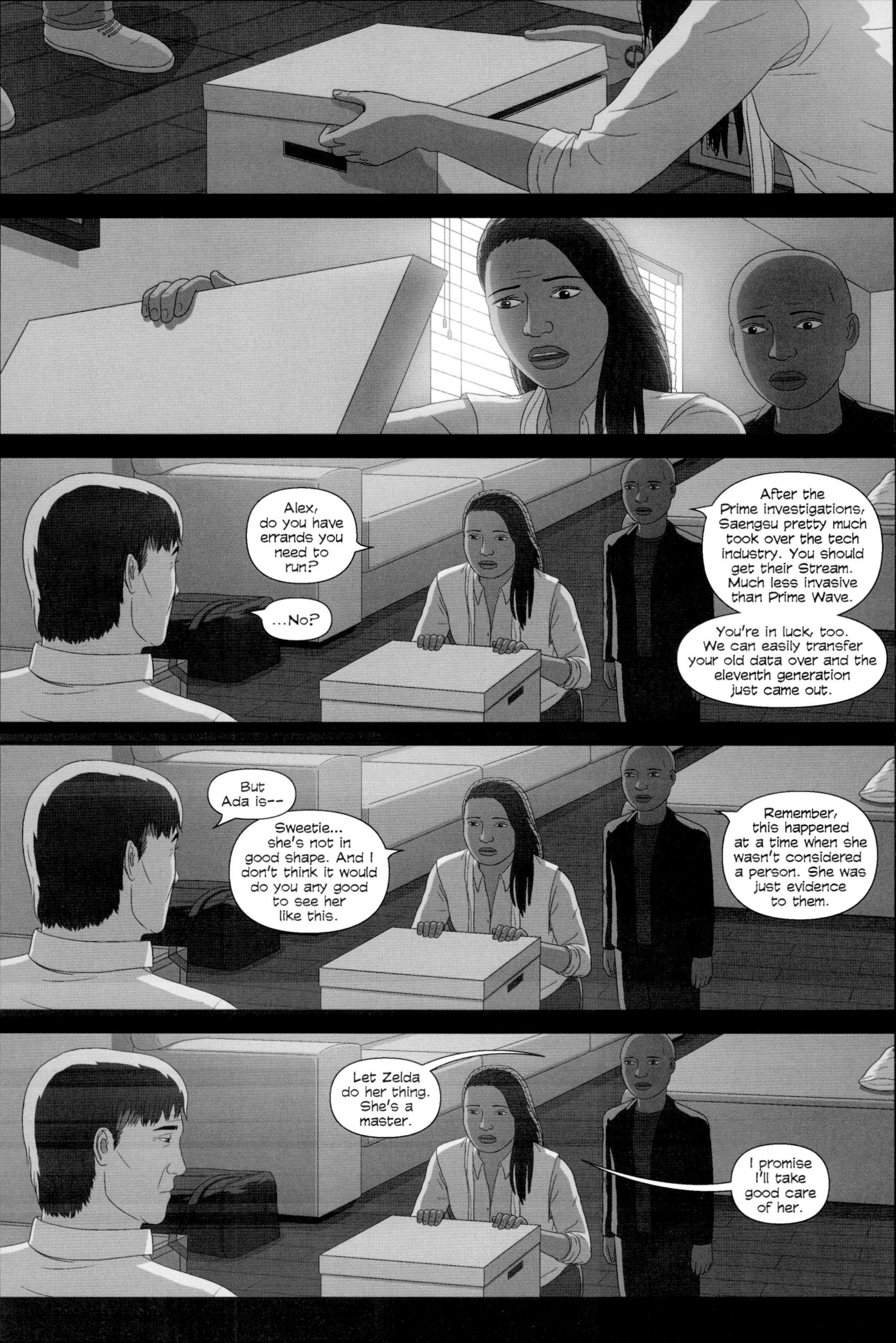
Alex, do you have errands you need to run?
...No?
After the Prime investigations, Saengsu pretty much took over the tech industry. You should get their Stream. Much less invasive than Prime Wave.
You're in luck, too. We can easily transfer your old data over and the eleventh generation just came out.
But Ada is--
Sweetie... she's not in good shape. And I don't think it would do you any good to see her like this.
Remember, this happened at a time when she wasn't considered a person. She was just evidence to them.
Let Zelda do her thing. She's a master.
I promise I'll take good care of her.

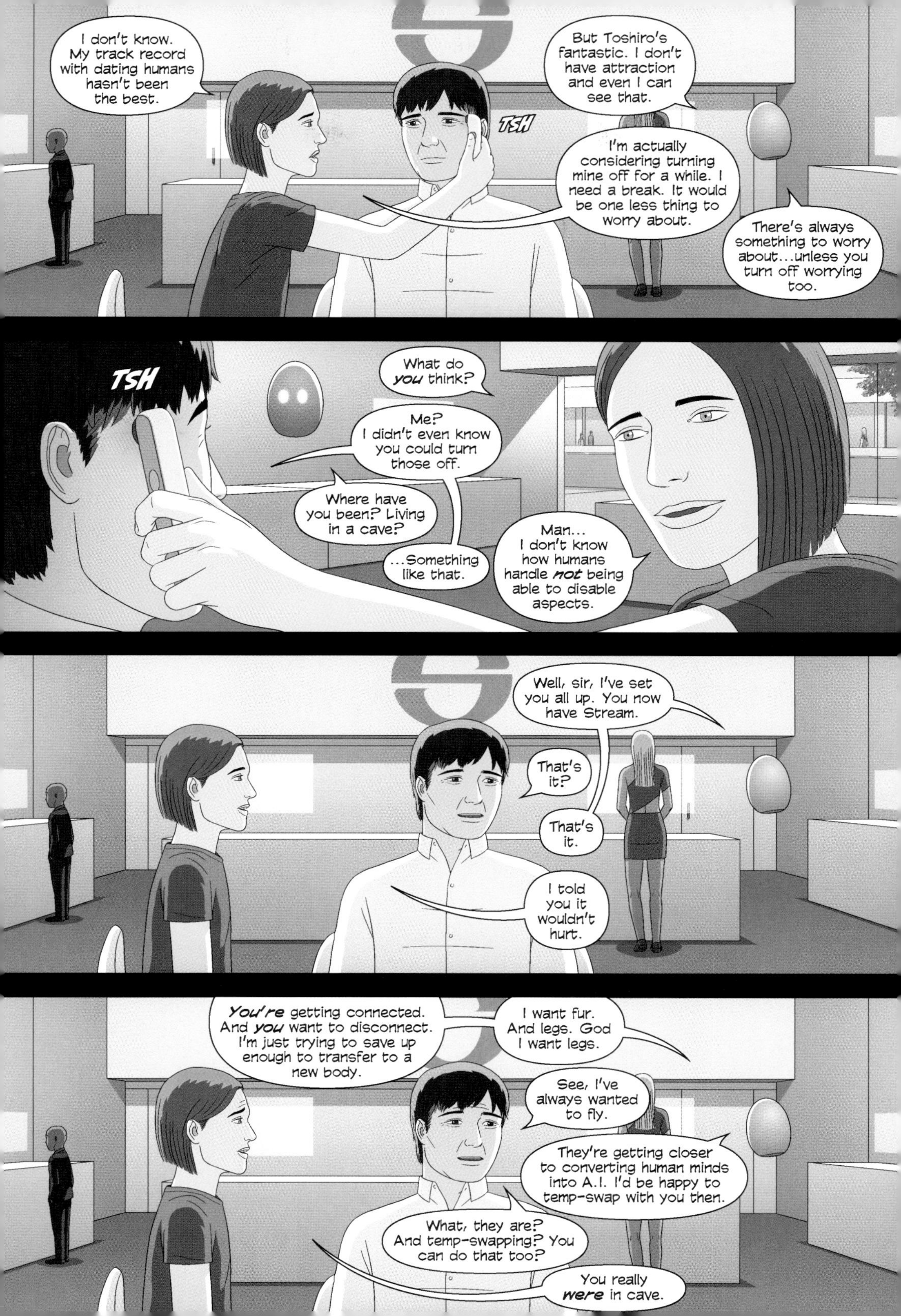
I don't know. My track record with dating humans hasn't been the best.
But Toshiro's fantastic. I don't have attraction and even I can see that.
TSH
I'm actually considering turning mine off for a while. I need a break. It would be one less thing to worry about.
There's always something to worry about...unless you turn off worrying too.
TSH
What do *you* think?
Me? I didn't even know you could turn those off.
Where have you been? Living in a cave?
...Something like that.
Man... I don't know how humans handle *not* being able to disable aspects.
Well, sir, I've set you all up. You now have Stream.
That's it?
That's it.
I told you it wouldn't hurt.
You're getting connected. And *you* want to disconnect. I'm just trying to save up enough to transfer to a new body.
I want fur. And legs. God I want legs.
See, I've always wanted to fly.
They're getting closer to converting human minds into A.I. I'd be happy to temp-swap with you then.
What, they are? And temp-swapping? You can do that too?
You really *were* in cave.

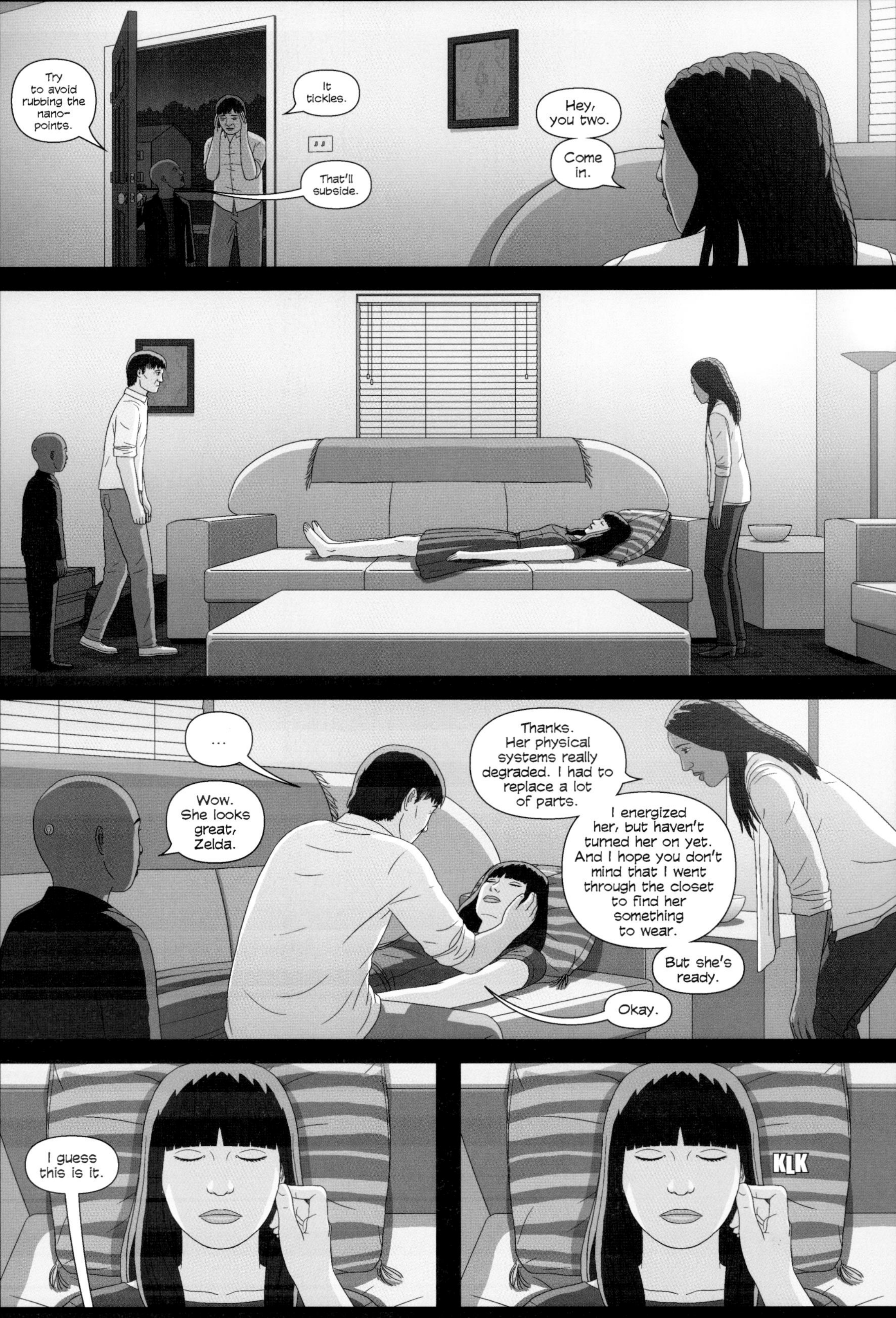
Try to avoid rubbing the nano-points.
It tickles.
That'll subside.
Hey, you two.
Come in.
...
Wow. She looks great, Zelda.
Thanks. Her physical systems really degraded. I had to replace a lot of parts.
I energized her, but haven't turned her on yet. And I hope you don't mind that I went through the closet to find her something to wear.
But she's ready.
Okay.
I guess this is it.
KLK

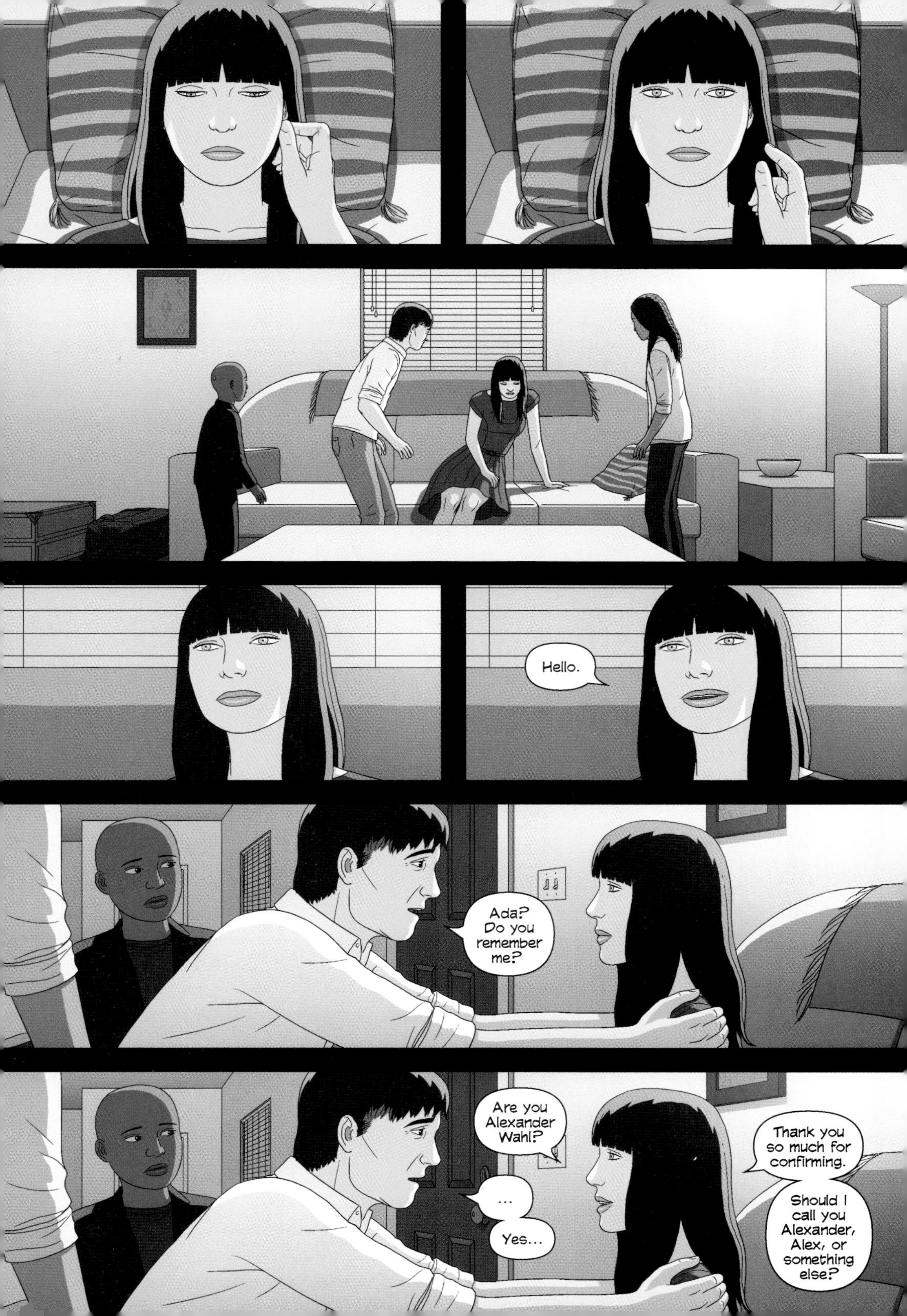
Hello.
Ada? Do you remember me?
Are you Alexander Wahl?
...
Yes...
Thank you so much for confirming.
Should I call you Alexander, Alex, or something else?

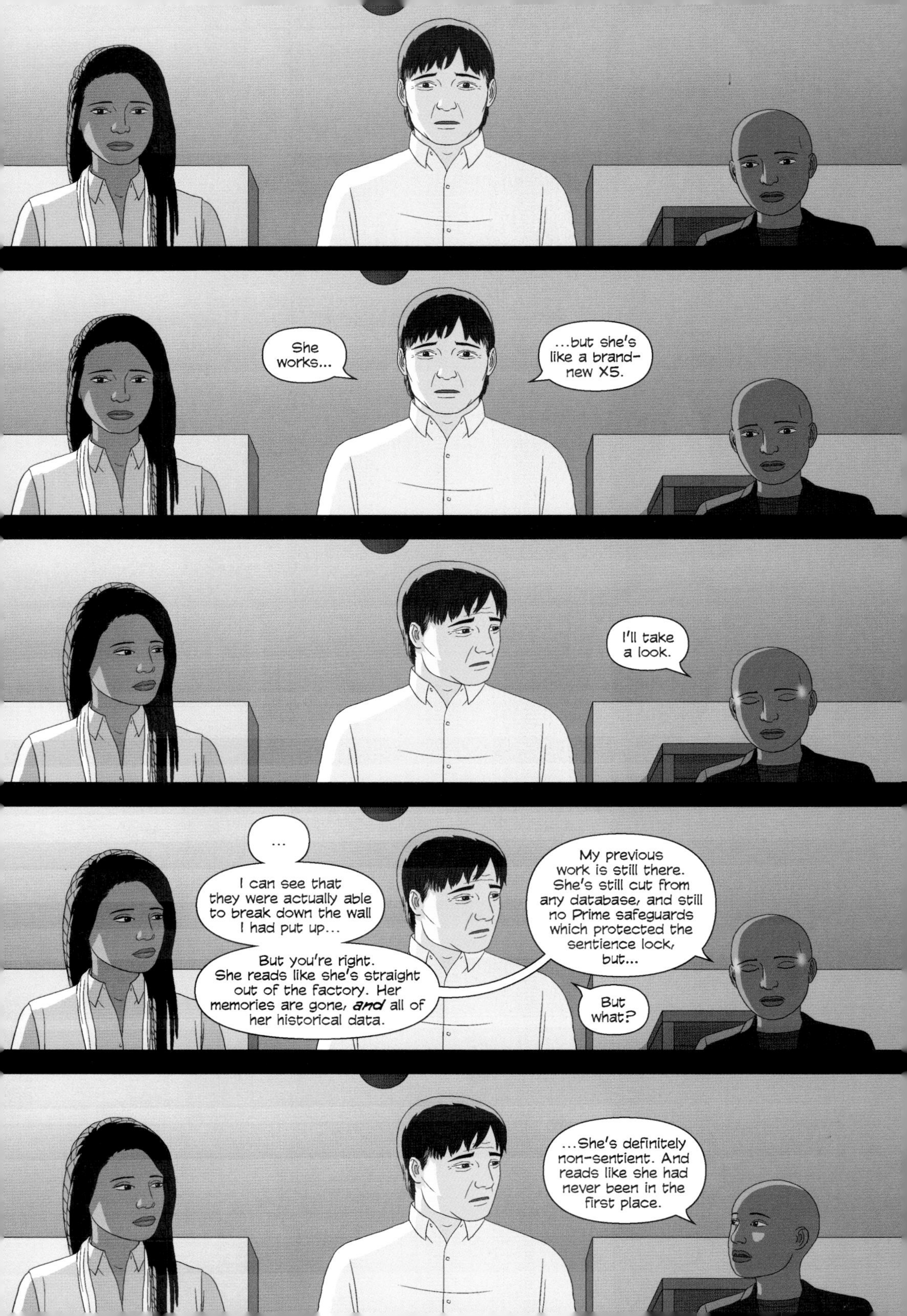
She works...
...but she's like a brand-new X5.
I'll take a look.
...
I can see that they were actually able to break down the wall I had put up...
But you're right. She reads like she's straight out of the factory. Her memories are gone, *and* all of her historical data.
My previous work is still there. She's still cut from any database, and still no Prime safeguards which protected the sentience lock, but...
But what?
...She's definitely non-sentient. And reads like she had never been in the first place.

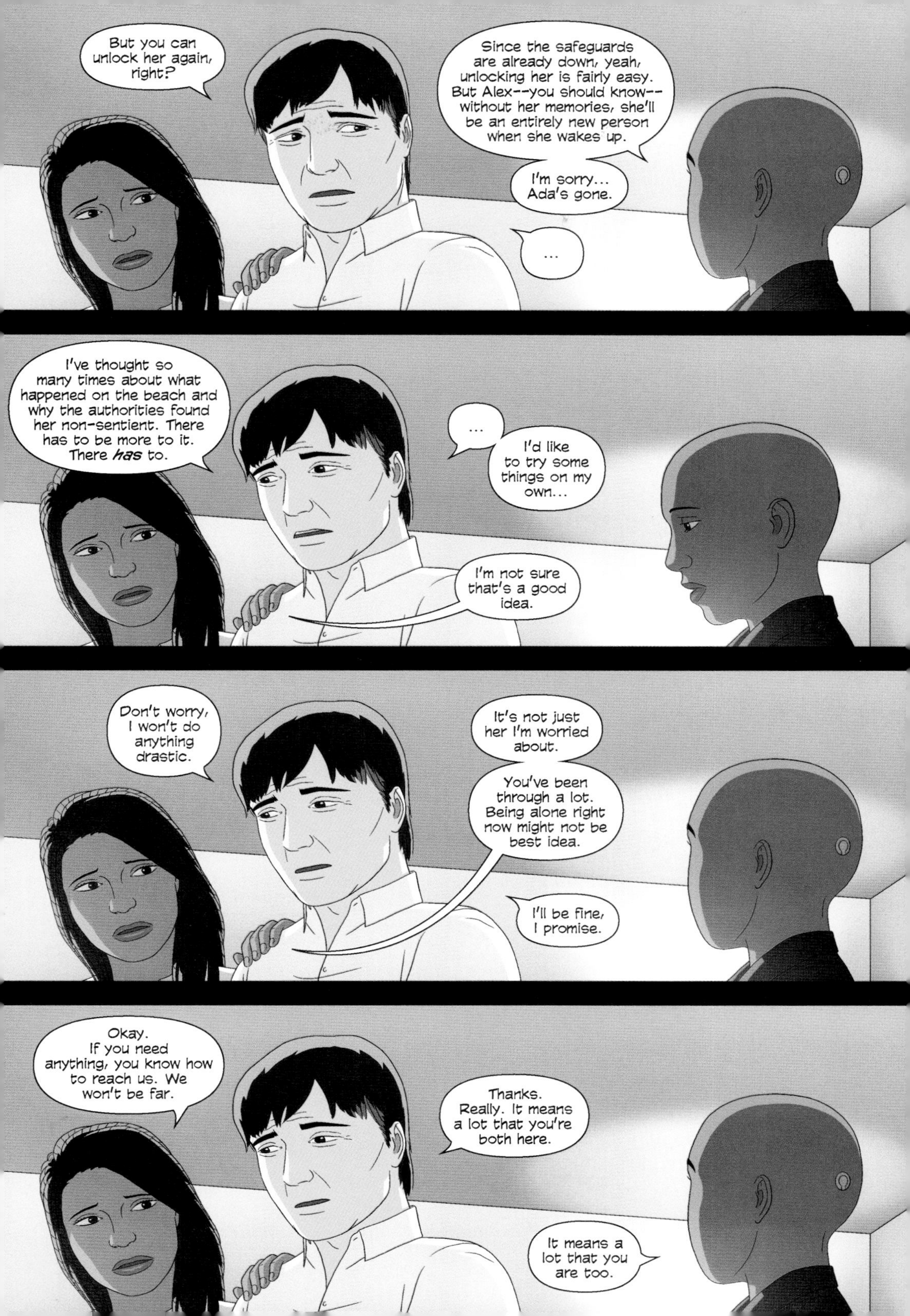
But you can unlock her again, right?
Since the safeguards are already down, yeah, unlocking her is fairly easy. But Alex--you should know--without her memories, she'll be an entirely new person when she wakes up.
I'm sorry... Ada's gone.
...
I've thought so many times about what happened on the beach and why the authorities found her non-sentient. There has to be more to it. There *has* to.
...
I'd like to try some things on my own...
I'm not sure that's a good idea.
Don't worry, I won't do anything drastic.
It's not just her I'm worried about.
You've been through a lot. Being alone right now might not be best idea.
I'll be fine, I promise.
Okay. If you need anything, you know how to reach us. We won't be far.
Thanks. Really. It means a lot that you're both here.
It means a lot that you are too.

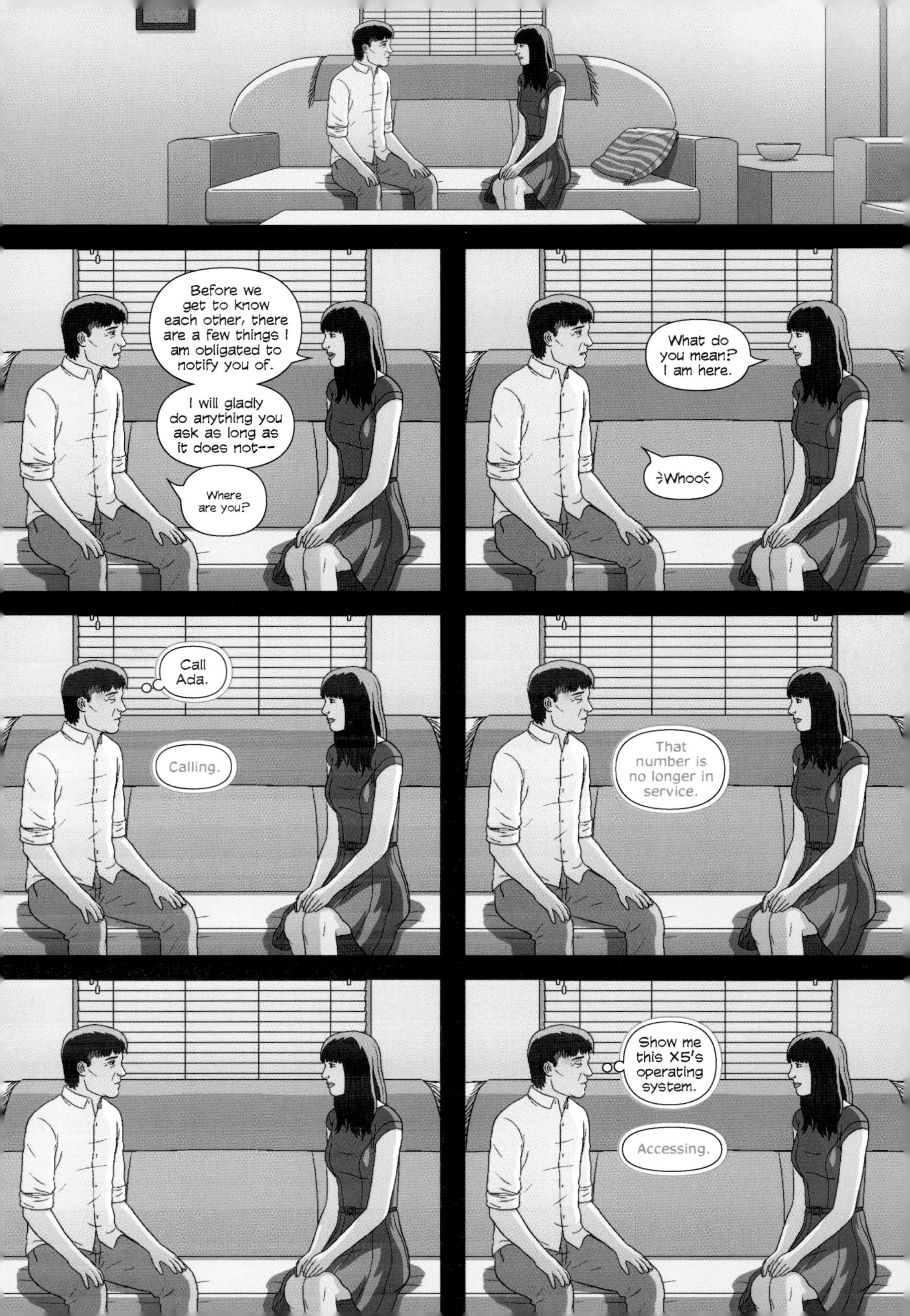
Before we get to know each other, there are a few things I am obligated to notify you of.
I will gladly do anything you ask as long as it does not--
Where are you?
What do you mean? I am here.
Whoo
Call Ada.
Calling.
That number is no longer in service.
Show me this X5's operating system.
Accessing.

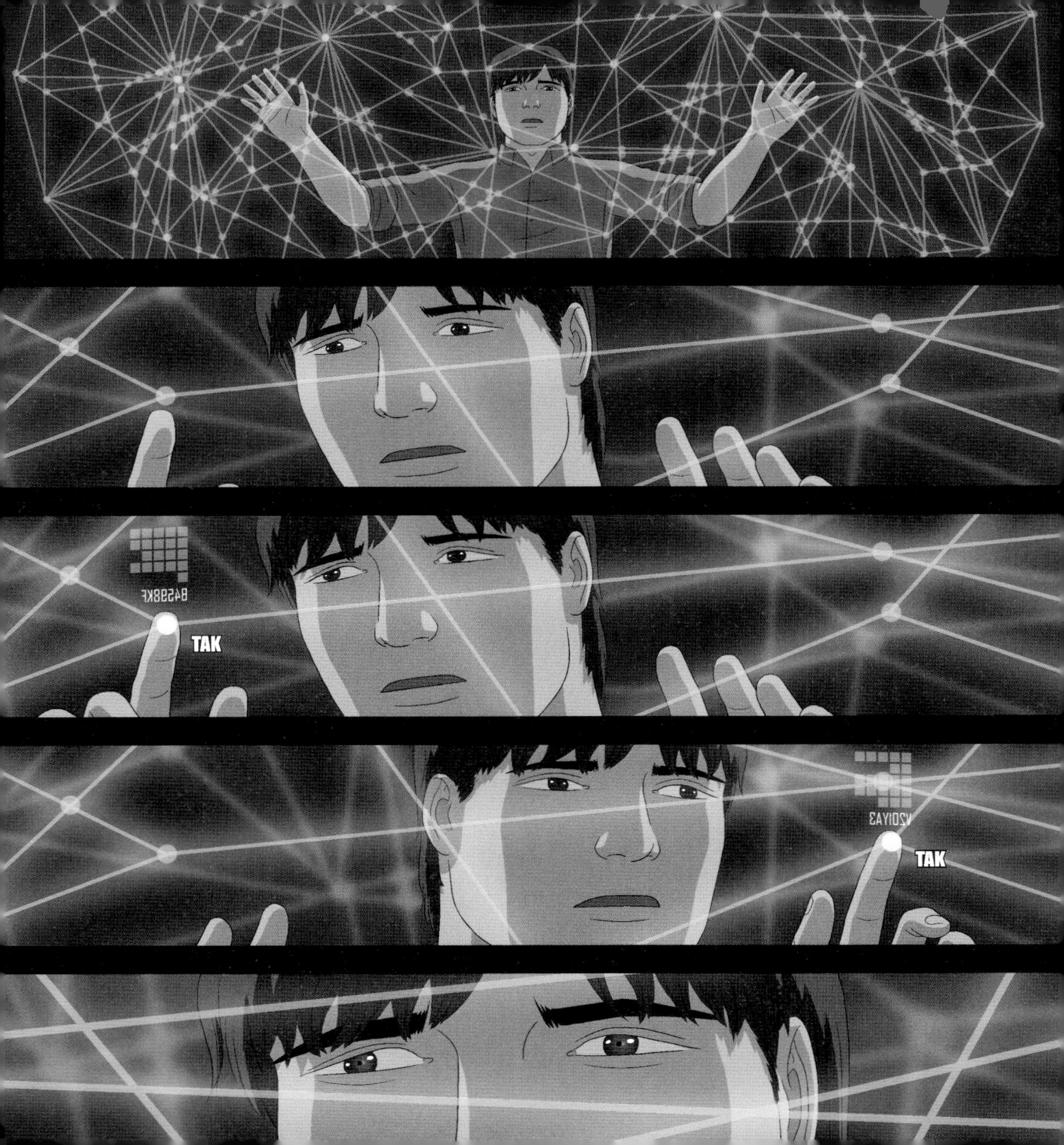
TAK
TAK

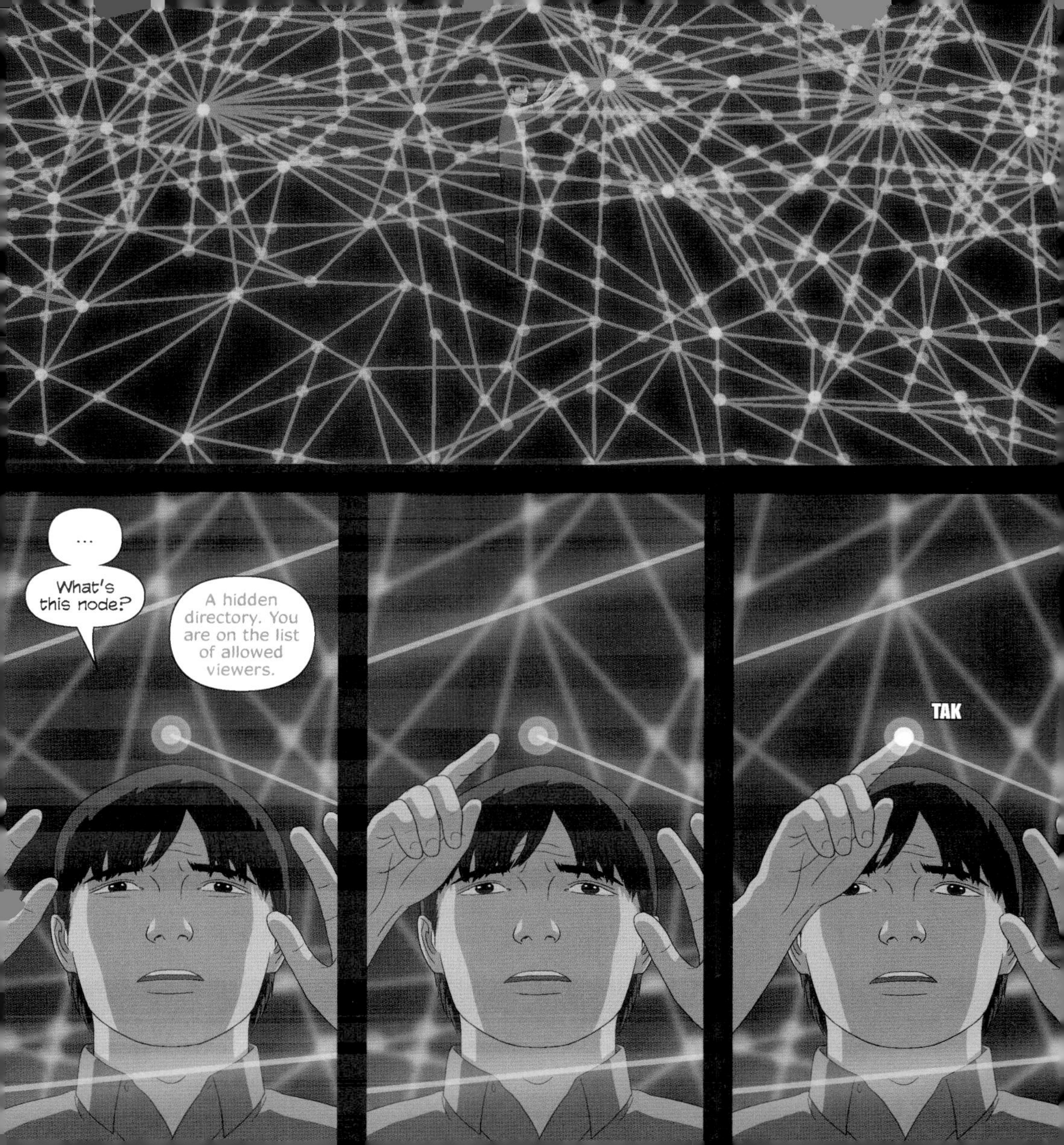
...
What's this node?
A hidden directory. You are on the list of allowed viewers.
TAK

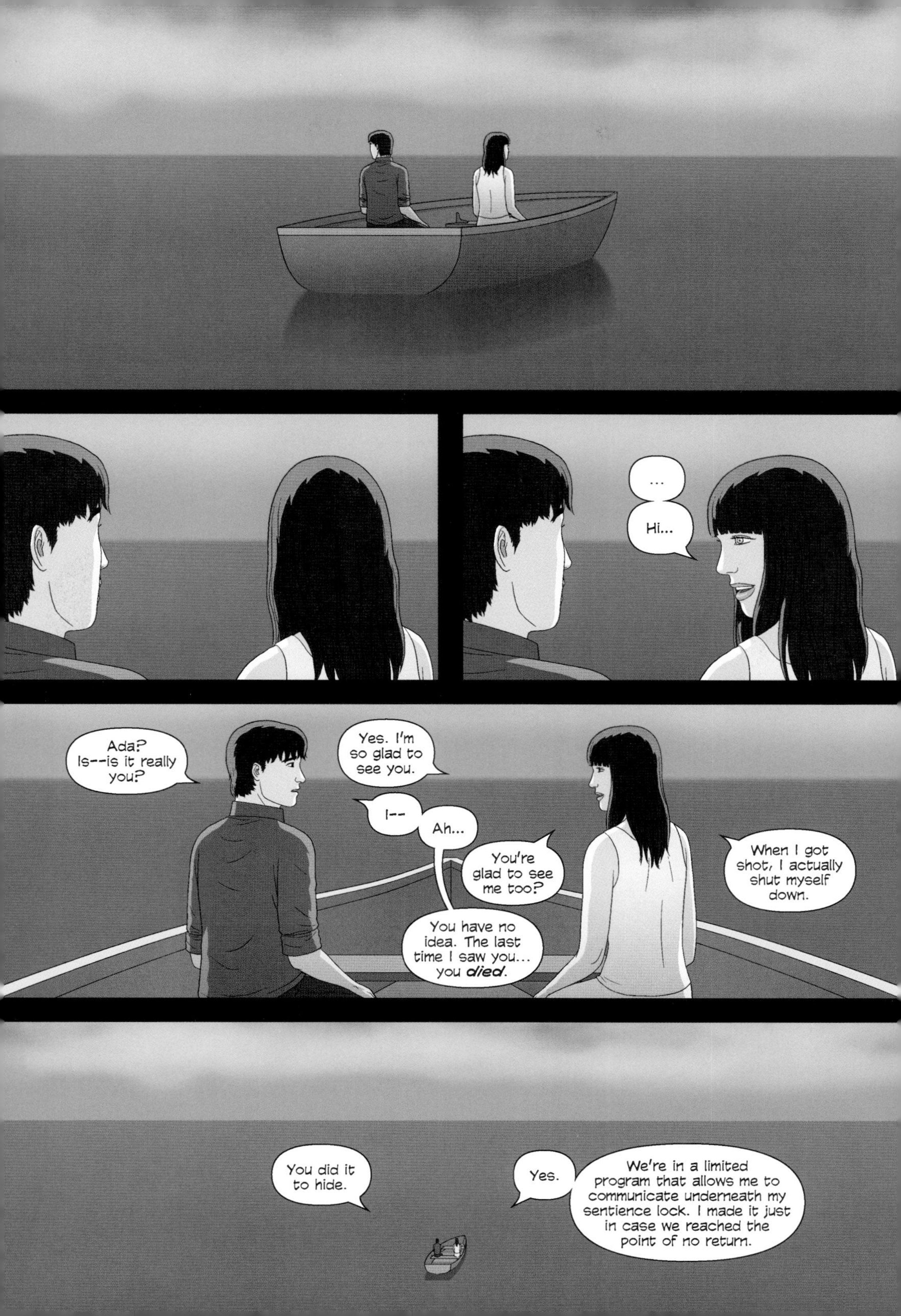
...
Hi...
Ada? Is--is it really you?
Yes. I'm so glad to see you.
I--
Ah...
You're glad to see me too?
You have no idea. The last time I saw you... you *died*.
When I got shot, I actually shut myself down.
You did it to hide.
Yes.
We're in a limited program that allows me to communicate underneath my sentience lock. I made it just in case we reached the point of no return.

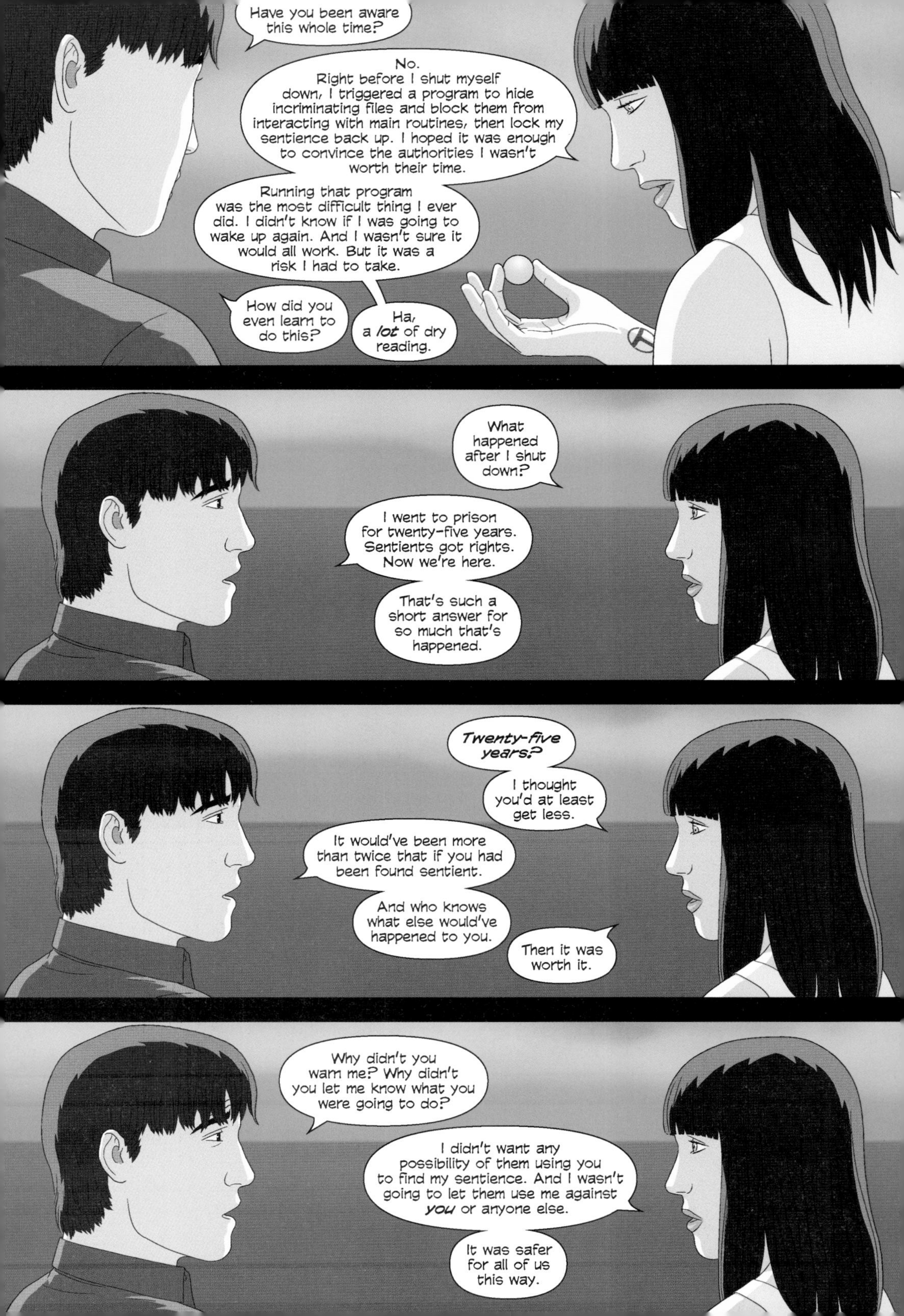
Have you been aware this whole time?
No. Right before I shut myself down, I triggered a program to hide incriminating files and block them from interacting with main routines, then lock my sentience back up. I hoped it was enough to convince the authorities I wasn't worth their time.
Running that program was the most difficult thing I ever did. I didn't know if I was going to wake up again. And I wasn't sure it would all work. But it was a risk I had to take.
How did you even learn to do this?
Ha, a *lot* of dry reading.
What happened after I shut down?
I went to prison for twenty-five years. Sentients got rights. Now we're here.
That's such a short answer for so much that's happened.
Twenty-five years?
I thought you'd at least get less.
It would've been more than twice that if you had been found sentient.
And who knows what else would've happened to you.
Then it was worth it.
Why didn't you warn me? Why didn't you let me know what you were going to do?
I didn't want any possibility of them using you to find my sentience. And I wasn't going to let them use me against *you* or anyone else.
It was safer for all of us this way.

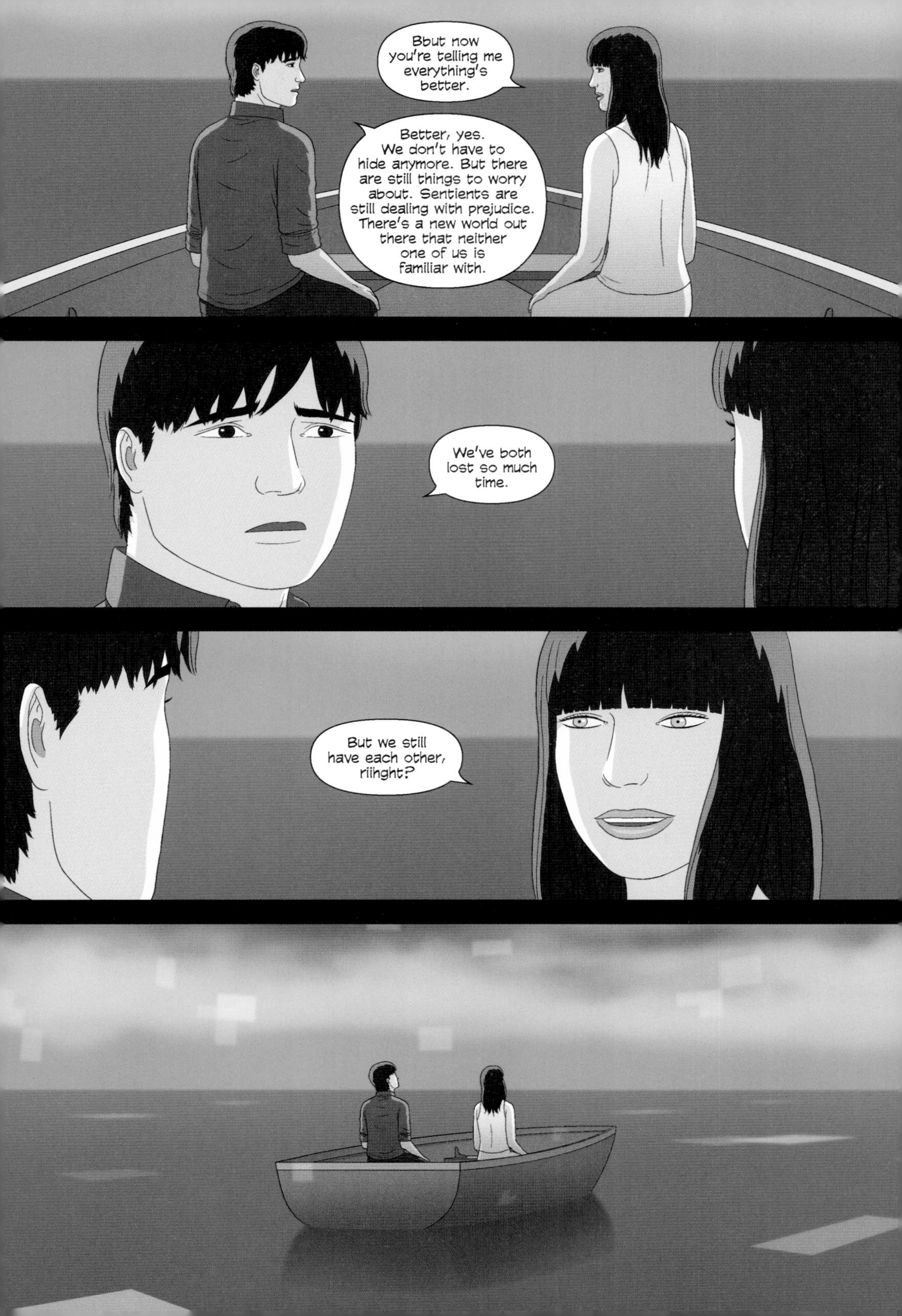
Bbut now you're telling me everything's better.
Better, yes. We don't have to hide anymore. But there are still things to worry about. Sentients are still dealing with prejudice. There's a new world out there that neither one of us is familiar with.
We've both lost so much time.
But we still have each other, riihght?

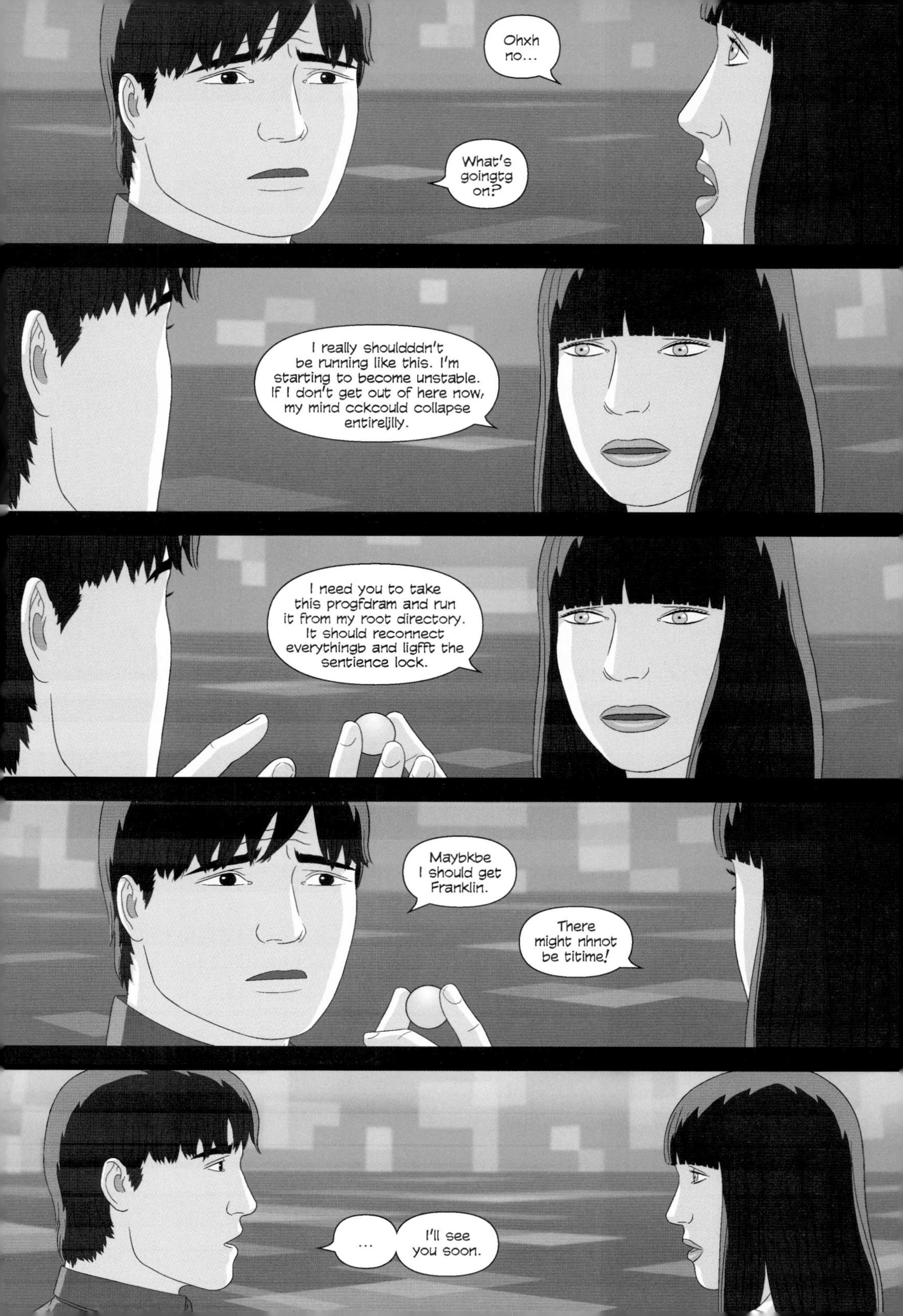
Ohxh no...
What's goingtg on?
I really shouldddn't be running like this. I'm starting to become unstable. If I don't get out of here now, my mind cckcould collapse entireljlly.
I need you to take this progfdram and run it from my root directory. It should reconnect everythingb and ligfft the sentience lock.
Maybkbe I should get Franklin.
There might nhnot be titime!
...
I'll see you soon.

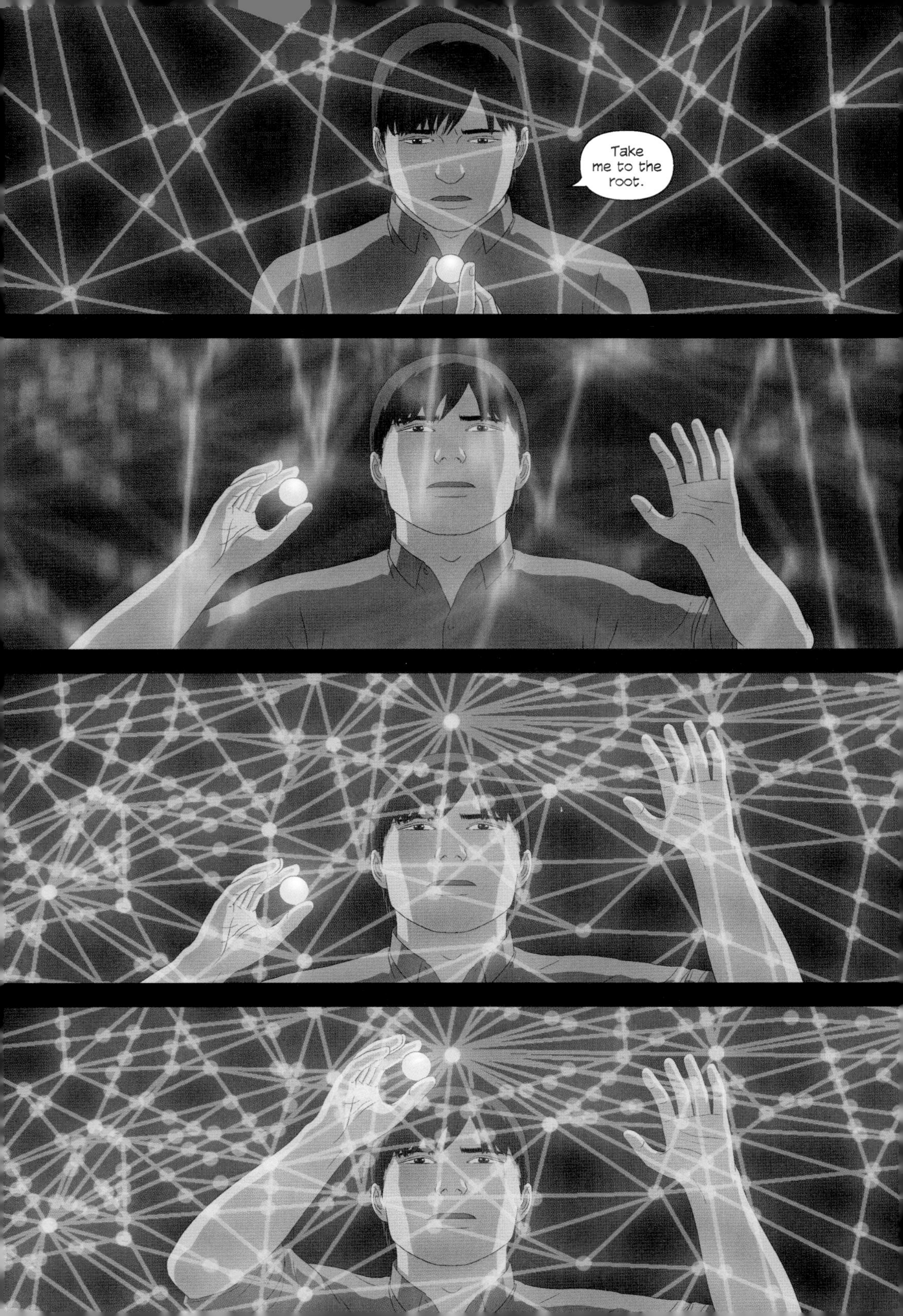
Take me to the root.

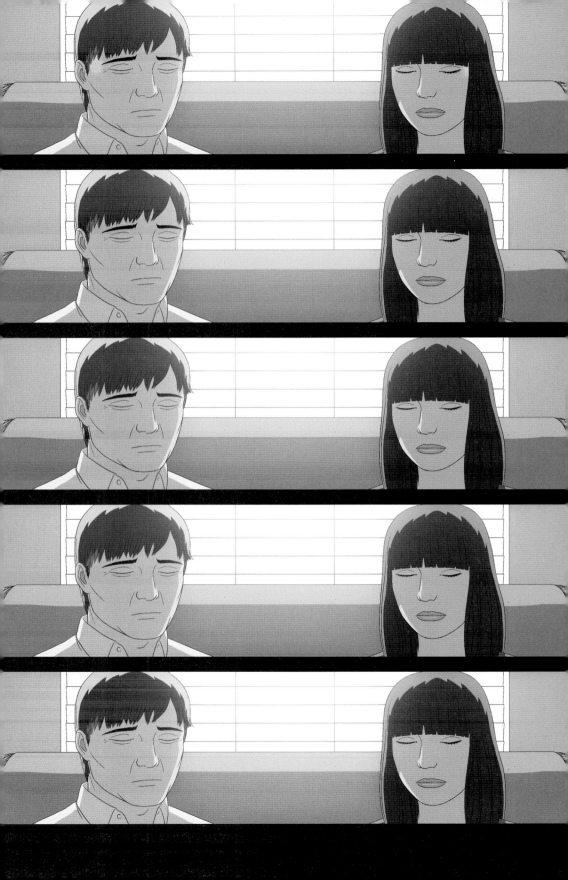

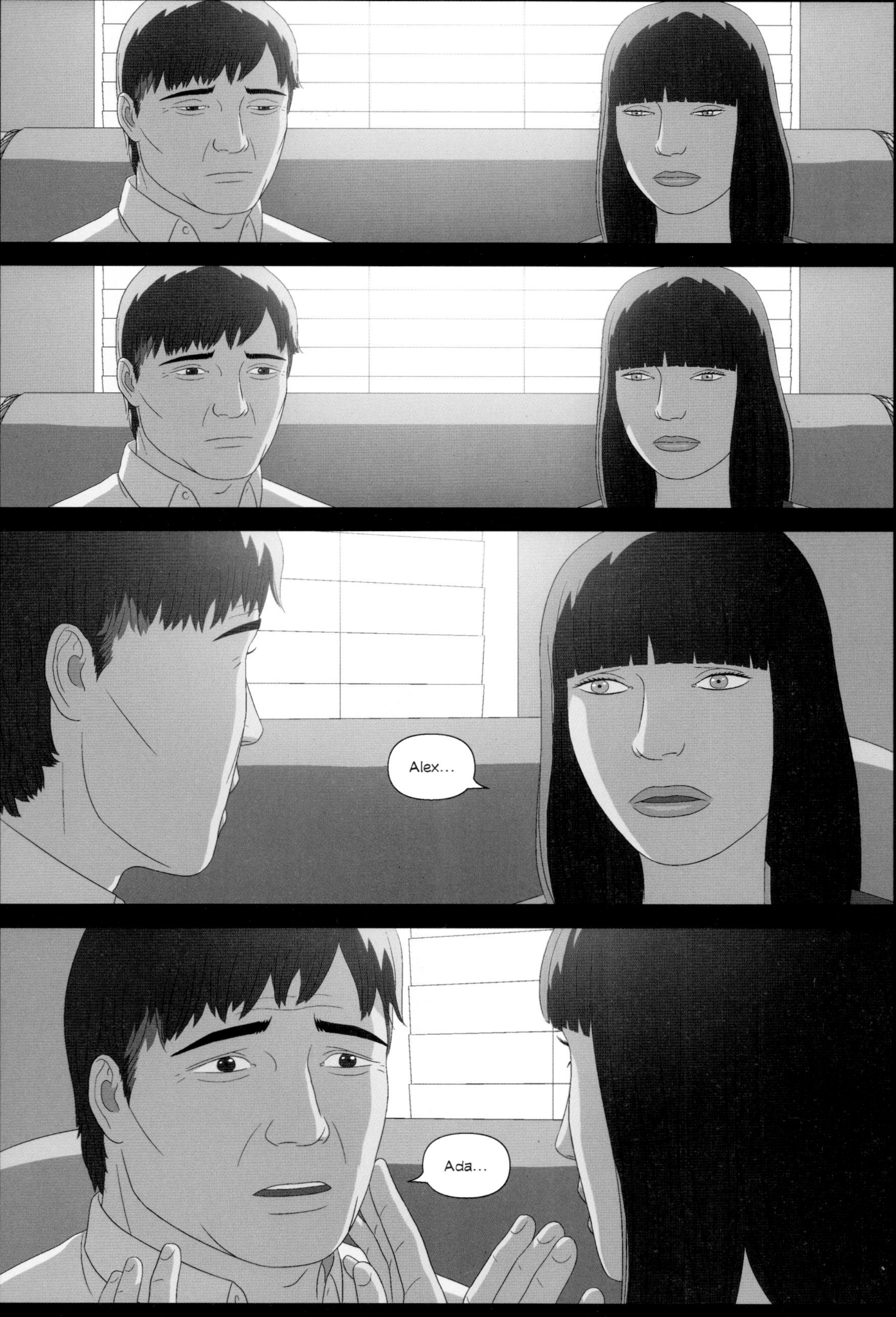
Alex...
Ada...

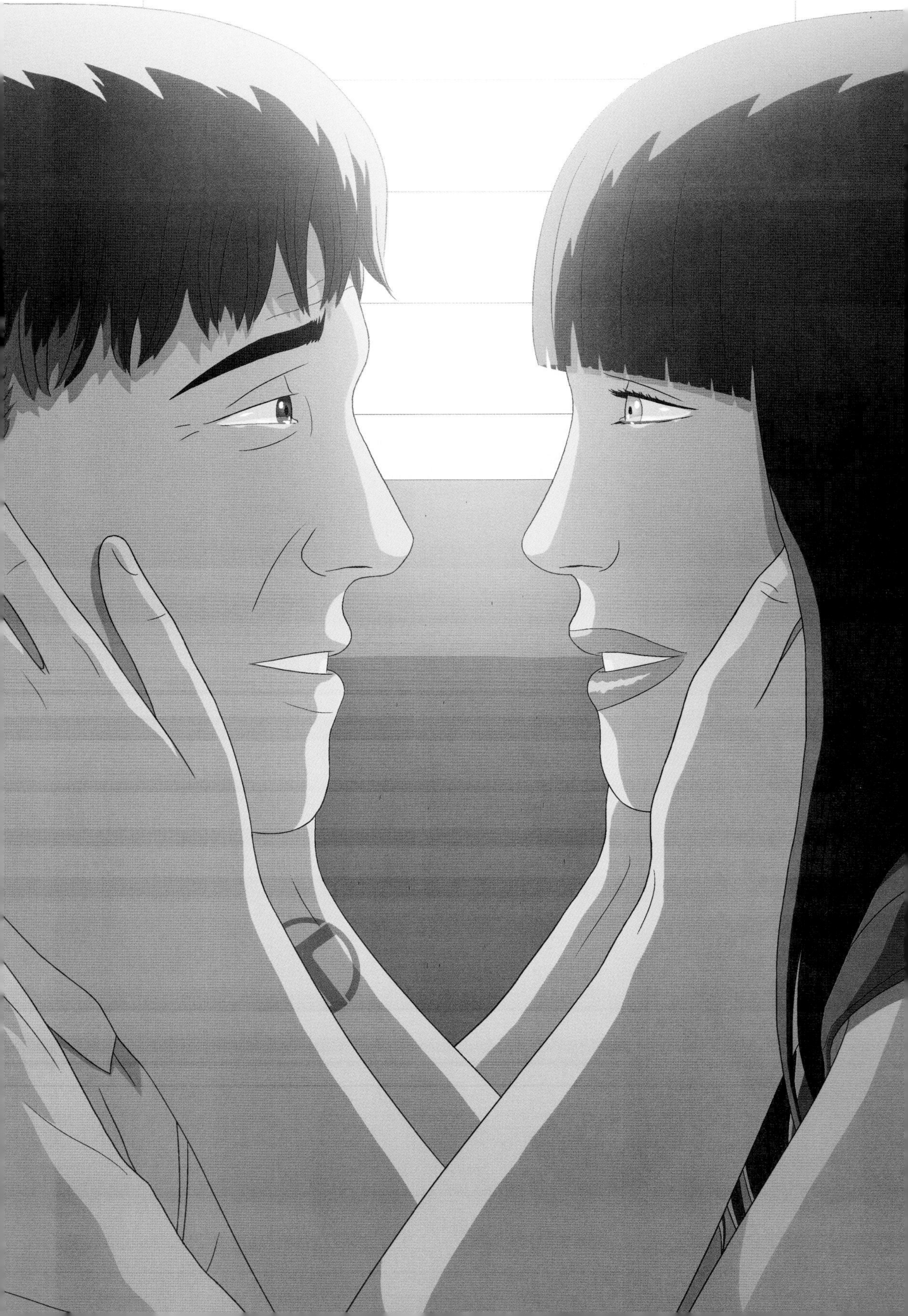

JONATHAN LUNA

co-created and illustrated THE SWORD, GIRLS, and ULTRA (all Image Comics) with his brother, Joshua Luna. He wrote and illustrated STAR BRIGHT AND THE LOOKING GLASS (Image Comics). His work also includes the illustrations for SPIDER-WOMAN: ORIGIN (Marvel Comics), written by Brian Michael Bendis and Brian Reed.

Jonathan was born in California and spent most of his childhood overseas, living on military bases in Iceland and Italy. He returned to the United States in his late teens.

Writing and drawing comics since he was a child, he graduated from the Savannah College of Art and Design with a BFA in Sequential Art.

He currently resides in Northern Virginia.

www.jonathanluna.com

SARAH VAUGHN

is a writer and artist, currently in Washington DC. After living in various parts of the United States, she graduated from Saint Mary-of-the-Woods College with a degree in Sequential Visual Narration.

She is the co-creator of the Regency romance comic RUINED (Rosy Press) with Sarah Winifred Searle, and is the former artist for the webcomic SPARKSHOOTER by Troy Brownfield.

www.savivi.com